WITCH OF THE SHADOW WOOD

WITCH OF THE SHADOW WOOD

A Novel

TORI ANNE MARTIN

Published in the United States by Alcove Press, an imprint of The Quick Brown Fox & Company LLC.

Alcove Press and its logo are trademarks of The Quick Brown Fox & Company LLC.

Library of Congress Catalog-in-Publication data available upon request.

ISBN (hardcover): 979-8-89242-465-3
ISBN (paperback): 979-8-89242-466-0
ISBN (ebook): 979-8-89242-467-7

Cover design by Olivia Hintz

Printed in the United States.

www.alcovepress.com

Alcove Press
34 West 27th St., 10th Floor
New York, NY 10001

First Edition: March 2026

The authorized representative in the EU for product safety and compliance is eucomply OÜPärnu mnt 139b-14, 11317 Tallinn, Estonia, hello@eucompliancepartner.com, +33757690241

10 9 8 7 6 5 4 3 2 1

To the woods witches and the bog witches, the witches by the moors and the witches at the seaside, the urban and suburban witches, and to all those who push against the chaos to create a better, more equitable, and more just world.

"Go to the woods and see"—Dar Williams

Author's Note

Thank you for picking up *Witch of the Shadow Wood*. This fairytale fantasy contains a lot of cozy elements, such as a quirky cottage, walks through the woods, foraging for mushrooms, baking pies, and drinking tea. It also contains some topics that are decidedly not cozy: child abandonment, allusions to abortion, off-page death of a parental figure, fires (off page) and burn injuries, light gore and horror elements, allusions to sexual assault, and mild violence. Please protect yourself and only read when you're in the right mindset for these topics.

PART I

THE WITCH IN THE WOODS

Chapter One

Fifteen Years Before the Wedding

Even during the early afternoon, the forest was as dark and forbidding as Greta had always imagined it to be. She tried to wiggle her fingers about in her father's hand, but his grip on her was too tight. It should have been comforting the way he held onto her—strong and sturdy, protective—but all she felt was winded as her short legs struggled to keep up with his long ones.

Well, that, and afraid—although she should not have been afraid because her papa was holding her left hand and Hans was on her other side. Hans couldn't match their father's height or strength yet, but Papa always said to just wait, that he was getting there. Occasionally, Papa praised the way Hans could swing an ax and chop wood, unlike her, who couldn't even lift the ax.

"If your mother or grandmother were still alive, they'd probably find a use for you," he would say, "but all you do is eat our food and grow out of your shoes too quickly."

There was never any praise for Greta.

Remembering this made Greta wiggle her fingers harder, but that merely caused her father to grip her more tightly, and now her fingers were feeling as pinched as her toes. Maybe he thought she would run away, but where would she run? They'd entered the Shadow Wood, and Greta knew better than to do that alone. Even with her father and Hans, the Shadow Wood was terrifying. They were the witch's woods.

Be a good girl, be a good boy.
Do your chores just as you should.
Be a good girl, be a good boy.
Naughty children are prey
For the witch in the wood.

The rhyme rang through Greta's head, discordant against the constant thud-thud of three pairs of boots along the dirt path. She'd played the witch game with the children down the street just yesterday. You passed the leather ball (or a stick or a stone if no one could find a ball) around in a circle, and whoever was left holding it when the chanting stopped had to drop the object and run for the safety wall while the person playing the witch chased you. If you didn't make it to the wall before they caught you, you became the new witch. The game was fun enough, though Greta hated being the witch because she was slow.

But everyone knew the Shadow Wood's witch was not a game. The witch was real.

She'll feast on your bones.
She'll drink all your blood.
She's coming for you—
The horrible, terrible
The witch in the wood!

Things everyone in Swiftdok knew: The witch could fly. The witch had horns and cavorted with evil spirts. The witch used her large nose to sniff out bad children, and she stole their blood for her magic. You could only find the witch in the woods if she let you.

Things Greta did not know: Why her father would want to find the witch. It seemed like a bad idea, but if her papa thought it was a good one, then maybe some of the other things Greta knew were wrong. Maybe she shouldn't be afraid.

The overhead canopy was lush and heavy, the summer foliage competing for the sun with the pines and firs that kept it green year-round. Greta knew the names of the trees because her father cut them for people, but she didn't know how to identify one tree from another. When he was in a good mood, her papa taught Hans a little. But his good moods had grown less frequent over the last winter, and unlike the leaves on the trees, they hadn't returned with the lengthening days.

Still, Hans got to learn *something*. Greta didn't think she'd be so useless if someone taught her things, too.

Pressed between her father and her brother, she buried this ungrateful thought deep in her gut. If the witch didn't steal the good children's blood, she needed to be good and grateful. And typically she was. She fetched water even when she was so tired she could barely walk, and she let Hans scrape the bottom of the porridge pot without complaint even when her stomach whined for more.

Well, that was to say, she didn't spill much water when it was her turn to fetch it, and she didn't complain much about being hungry. There was that incident two nights ago when Papa had yelled at her because she'd reached for another slice of bread, and he said Hans needed it because he was a growing boy, and Hans had broken it in two and given her half when Papa's back was turned. Did that count as being naughty?

Greta didn't like that question, so she concentrated on her feet. The path was soft with fragrant pine needles crushed beneath the thin soles of her shoes (already too small again). She listened to the leaves rustling overhead and the skitter of unseen feet in the brush. She watched the path become narrower and narrower the deeper they trod. Her father said nothing about this, but her brother's brow wrinkled the longer they walked, and at one point he started to speak, but a blistering glance from Papa sealed his lips. Rather than risk his wrath, Hans took Greta's other hand. His grip was lighter than their father's and so more comforting.

Unfortunately, that comfort did nothing to ease the weariness in her legs. Greta was worried she would stumble when the path ahead vanished altogether. Only then did she notice the forest had grown quieter, too. The air was heavier, hazier, like a fog was rolling in all around them.

Her father muttered something too low to hear, and Hans squeezed her fingers. With his free hand, Greta watched him discreetly drop another white pebble on the ground when their father's gaze was turned away. He'd been dropping them periodically during the walk. They had stuffed his pockets full that morning.

"Why did you steal the chicken feed?" she'd asked Hans when she caught him sneaking out of their neighbor's tiny coop with a purloined handful.

Hans had shushed her and dragged her away before answering, but that was how she'd learned they were going into the forest. Hans had overheard Papa talking about it to the neighbor.

"People who go into the forest don't always come out," Hans had told her. He hadn't needed to say why, nor who was least likely to reemerge. Greta knew it was the witch's doing. And it was children who disappeared. "We can use the feed to leave a path so we'll find the way home if we get lost."

"Papa will get us home," Greta had countered, not because she didn't have doubts but because she needed it to be true.

Hans had flinched and looked at his shoes. "Probably, yes. But it's better to be safe. Just don't tell him. He won't like it if he knows."

Greta didn't question that. Their father would be angry if he thought that she and Hans didn't trust he could protect them.

Chicken feed, however, struck her as a poor substance for marking a trail. What if chickens ate it, and it disappeared?

"Don't be stupid. There are no chickens in the forest," Hans had said when she mentioned this. But his face expressed doubt, so Greta had picked up one of the many white pebbles that lined the road and offered it to him instead.

"Nothing will eat these." She'd thought for a moment her brother would argue, but he tossed the feed onto the ground and began collecting pebbles with her.

As Greta glanced over her shoulder, she took some pride in her idea. Nothing was eating the pebbles, and they stood out against the dirt brown path. Maybe she could be useful after all, even if no one taught her anything.

"Does this mean we go home?" Hans asked. He sounded hopeful, and Greta realized that although he did a better job of acting brave than she did, he must be scared as well.

A bird took flight in the silence that followed, and Greta jumped with the sudden flutter of wings. Even Hans looked shaken.

Still, their father didn't speak. Then a single leaf drifted onto the path. The mist dissipated and the forest lightened. More path spread out ahead.

Greta swallowed and bit her lip to keep silent as her father tugged her along again.

They didn't have far to go. Soon after, the path ended abruptly in a clearing illuminated by bright sunshine, and there, in the center of the golden light, was the most spectacular cottage Greta could imagine.

The roof was tiled with cinnamon rolls and fried breads, and scalloped in thick white frosting. Peppermint sticks outlined the windows and doors, and the walls were covered in tarts and pastries of every fruit and flavor, donuts and snow balls, sugared almonds and jellied orange peels that all swirled together in beautiful designs like lace. It reminded Greta of the fanciful gingerbread homes she saw displayed in bakery windows around the winter solstice, only more fantastic. Not an inch didn't make her mouth water.

But even as she longed to touch those treats, to see if they were real, the house swam in and out of Greta's view, rippling like a reflection in the water. The delectable sweets melted away. In front of her stood a normal structure made of stones and wood, neither tall nor short, nor entirely house-like at all. Rather it was a home that had been carved straight out of the landscape, a happy coincidence of boulders and logs and plants that had sprouted a door and windows and a roof. A tall, fat chimney sent smoke trailing into the sky.

Greta blinked, mourning the loss of the house of sweets, but the second image remained.

It was not without its own charms. Not only did flowering shrubs hug the arched doorway, other blossoms cascaded down the sides of the cottage like curtains—tiny blooms in yellows and blues and pinks that added to the illusion that the cottage was simply a natural outgrowth of the woods. A path ran from the doorway past a well and into a walled-off area to the left. Tall plants and stubby trees rose above the stones, heavy with bounties that Greta mostly didn't recognize.

With so much wonder to absorb, she almost forgot where she was and why. Then the cottage door opened, and Greta's attention snapped back into her body with a single jolt of her heart.

Hans's grip on her right hand tightened, but her father dropped her left entirely.

Greta swallowed and tried to look brave and good and completely invisible. Every instinct had her feet itching to hide her behind her father's body, but she held still. Held her breath.

A woman emerged from the cottage, but this time, while Greta's vision played no tricks on her, she could not entirely tell what she was seeing. The woman's face was lightly wrinkled, but her skin sported none of the spots and marks that covered the older men and women in town. Her eyes were as gray as the hair braided down her back, but neither cruel nor kind. Her dress was neither fancy nor tattered, and it took a moment for Greta to realize it was no dress at all but a long tunic over a pair of heavy stockings, much like a man might wear. Only the bright green scarf she had tied around her waist, a scarf that almost appeared to be made of leaves, gave the impression of a flowing skirt.

The witch—she had to be the witch—also did not appear to have an overly large nose or any discernable horns, which was a small relief, and despite her cane, she strode forward with a spriteliness that belied its need. But perhaps the cane was not meant for walking. It looked like it would hurt if someone smacked you on the backside with it.

"Well," she said, stopping several feet away. "What is this?"

Greta's father stood up straighter. "My name is Garulf." He barked out the words the way he did when the town tax collector came to their house, and Greta thought that was odd. "I'm a woodcutter from Swiftdok."

"I said what is this, not who."

"I'd like to make a trade." He stepped forward and glanced at Greta.

She didn't pause to wonder why he looked her way or what he had to trade because, at that moment, there was a commotion from the left, and two chickens flapped their way to land ungainly upon the garden wall. At least, Greta thought they were chickens. They were chicken-like, except one had feathers of the brightest blue, as stunning as a lady's gown, tucked among the white. The other was a mix of brown and purple, similar in shade to the flowering bushes by the cottage. Greta gasped.

The witch turned her attention from Garulf to Greta. Her expression didn't soften, but there was something appraising about it, and Greta hoped the witch wasn't contemplating how much blood she contained.

"Pretty, aren't they?" said the witch at last. "Go on, there are others in the garden to see, and the raspberries are ripe. You two can have a look and a bite while your father tells me about his trade."

She should have said no, but the chickens descended back into the garden, and Greta, stupidly, impulsively, forgot that she should be afraid of the witch, that the witch might try to lure her away to steal her blood. The chickens were too fascinating to resist—and, if she were being honest—so was the possibility of raspberries. The house made of pastries and candy had whipped up her appetite as surely as the aroma from a warm oven.

The garden fence opened on its own as she approached, and neither her father nor her brother called out to stop her from entering. If they weren't concerned, it seemed safe to assume that she had no reason to be either.

"Tell me about your trade," she heard the witch say. But whatever her father responded, Greta wasn't listening. Once she passed through the gate and her attention was diverted by all the splendor before her, their voices dimmed as though they existed in another world entirely. She was barely aware that her brother had paused at the entry and wasn't continuing to follow her.

Like the cottage, the garden was nothing she had ever seen before. There were plants in every shape and color and size, varieties completely unlike those spindly weeds that grew around their house or the colorful flowers that filled window boxes in the nicer part of town. Here, there were plants with thick broad leaves and others with ones as delicate as the finest lace. Some were as short as her knees, and others were trees covered in fruit that Greta thought she should have seen beyond the garden walls but could not recall having done so.

Some of the smaller plants were heavy with fruits and vegetables as well, in yellows and greens and reds. Many were unfamiliar, but a few she knew—beans, peas, gooseberries, and finally the raspberries. The blue chicken had led her to the latter as she followed the bird through the overgrown paths. There were several bushes, each heads taller than she was. Each dazzling with hundreds of bright red berries, the biggest, juiciest looking raspberries Greta had ever seen. They hung from the vines like jewels.

She reached out—the witch had invited her to eat some—but her hand froze before it could pluck the first berry. Was this a test? The witch hadn't handed her any portion of berries, and at home, taking food in front of her without expressly being given her allotment was a way to get her hand slapped. To be naughty.

Greta's stomach growled, and for the first time that day, she acknowledged how hollow it felt, how hungry she was. Surely, one berry was okay. They'd been offered to her.

The fruit was heavy, so heavy in her hand—practically the size of her thumb. Greta popped it into her mouth before she could think twice, and sweet juice burst over her tongue, more flavorful than anything she'd eaten for as long as she could remember. It left behind a trail of sticky redness on her palm, and she licked the juice up, trying not to notice the dirt on her skin that she licked up with it.

Her gut felt a little less empty after she swallowed, though hardly full, and her mouth craved more. She didn't remember picking another, but the raspberry landed in her hand. Quickly, she ate that one as well, though her heart beat faster as she wondered if she should have.

Same with a third and fourth.

She ate so quickly that the fear didn't catch up to her until her stomach truly began to feel content—a strange and foreign sensation, but one that was hard to enjoy, despite the delicious flavors lingering in her mouth, when she began to fear what it meant. A single berry was one thing. Two, perhaps, was acceptable when the plants were laden with so many. But Greta wasn't sure how many she'd eaten.

She wet her sweet-tart lips and scurried away from the plant before temptation bettered her again.

Around her feet, the chickens pecked contentedly at the ground. They paid her no mind as she searched among them for the pretty blue one that had led her to the raspberries. She didn't see it, but a purple feather caught her eye, lying in the middle of a path. Delighted, she picked it up and marveled at the color. Chickens, in her limited experience, were only supposed to be white or brown, so this feather must be magic.

Greta poked it into her braid. It didn't want to stay without much finagling, and her hair started to come undone. Eventually, she made the feather stick, although it might have been raspberry juice gluing it in place.

As she neared the garden gate again, snippets of her father's conversation with the witch floated by her ears. Hans didn't appear to have moved the entire time. Instead, he seemed to be listening intently, and he pressed a finger to his lips, silently warning her to be quiet.

"We all know what you need," her father was saying. "I'm making it easy."

The witch cackled. "Men always think they know what a woman needs."

"You don't want a trade then?"

In the pause that ensued, Greta crept closer to the garden wall.

"I didn't say that." The witch's voice took on a darker, more serious tone. "But it's presumptuous. If you know what I need, then you know I can take it on my own. But this is far worse than that, and I hope *you* know *it*. I will grant you one wish for your trade."

"One?" Her father sounded indignant. "For all I'm giving up?"

"It doesn't seem to me like you consider all you're giving up much of a sacrifice," the witch snapped. "Besides, don't be greedy." Here, Greta rubbed her sticky hands on her dress, her gut tightening with renewed worry. "A wish is the most potent of magic, but you get no more than one. A man who overreaches loses his balance and will fall to his doom one day. Take it or leave it."

"Fine. It's a deal."

Had her father really traded with the witch then? Greta temporarily forgot to worry about the raspberries as curiosity about what a wish looked like overcame her. She peeked her head around the garden gate for a better view.

The witch was reaching into a small purse that she wore around her neck, and she pulled out an object no larger than the raspberries had been. Even in the high sunlight it glowed a mysterious white, as though she held the moon between her fingers.

She offered it to Greta's father. "Use it only when the moon is full and tell no one what you did. If you do, the magic will fail. Understood?"

"Yes." Her father's hand closed around the wish, hungrily, hiding it from Greta's view as soon as the witch placed it on his palm. "I'll go now."

At those words, Hans charged through the gate, and Greta after him, her tangled hair flying behind her. She was grateful to the witch, and knew she ought to thank her for the berries, but she was so relieved that her papa's business was done. That they would get to go home. She would be safe.

Her father's cheeks twitched as she paused, panting, before him, but the witch let out a sharp laugh. "You're a wild little thing, aren't you? Part chicken now?"

Greta patted her hair, searching for where the feather had ended up in her mad dash. "Thank you for the raspberries."

"Wild, but with good manners. I can tell you enjoyed them." The witch snorted. "They're all over your face and hands. We'll have to wash you up."

That didn't make sense, so Greta ignored it, which was easy to do because Hans unexpectedly knelt down and whispered in her ear. "Stay close to me."

Confusion thrummed in Greta's blood, and with every heart beat, it inched closer to another emotion. One she didn't want to acknowledge but that wouldn't be denied. The fear she'd felt in the garden nipped at her insides like the raspberries had grown teeth in her stomach.

When Hans stood, her father was already heading down the path toward home, and her brother—his mouth was thin with determination. He took a step toward their father.

So did Greta. "Wait, Papa!"

He turned, slowly, an unsettling expression on his face. "Greta, you need to stay," he said. And then, speaking over her shoulder. "Tell them."

A hand landed on Greta's shoulder. "You will stay with me, child."

The witch's voice was not cruel, but it was the *witch's* voice. Fear sharpened into panic, dizzying and choking. Greta pulled away, and suddenly Hans had her hand again. He yanked her toward him and took off, running like his life depended on it, dragging her with him.

Greta stumbled, unable to match his longer strides, and Hans's hand slipped from her grasp. She picked herself up in a heartbeat, barely noticing the pain in her haste to escape.

"Greta, come on!" Several steps ahead, her brother turned, and his face was white and sweaty with fear. He waved an arm behind him as he sprinted, urging her along, but he didn't slow down or reach for her a second time. Somehow, their father was already vanishing in the distance, and Hans was caught in the middle, unsure what to do. "Hurry!"

"Hans, wait! Papa, wait!" Her lungs burned as she ran, and her shouting slowed her down.

Hans's steps faltered for a moment, and Greta had hope she might catch up, but then he was off again, yelling at her to move faster (sounding so much like their father), and she could see why. The forest path was fading before her eyes as though it had never existed at all. The trees and shrubs closed in on where there had once been a road of dirt, swallowing the trail of pebbles.

No, no. No. This couldn't be happening. She was going home, too. She didn't want to stay. She needed to leave, to be safe. Where had her father gone? Why wasn't Hans waiting for her?

"Greta!" She could hear her brother somewhere through the trees, calling her name repeatedly in a panicky pitch, but she could no longer see him ahead. "Where are you? Run faster!"

Greta screamed after him and kept running through the wooded maze, running where the path had been—where the path *should have* been—until the underbrush tangled her ankles and tripped her. The dappled sunlight made it hard to see through her tears as she climbed to her feet.

Hans's voice grew fainter as the forest grew thicker around her. Darker. Over and over Greta yelled for her family, and finally the trees parted and . . .

She was back in the clearing. The cottage was in front of her, the garden on her right now. It was as though she'd run in a circle, but that made no sense.

And neither her brother nor her father were anywhere in sight.

Greta shrieked in frustration and took off through the trees again. She was so turned around; she didn't know which direction led toward home anymore. The forest was moving, blocking and corralling her, trapping her in a cage with bars made of tree trunks and branches made of spears to keep her pressed within them. Even the birdsong had gone quiet.

No matter how long or hard she searched, not a single white pebble revealed itself to guide the way. Her nose ran and her lungs ached, and thorns poked through her stockings. Branches snagged her hair. And yet she never got far. The path never returned. Every time Greta thought she discovered an opening through the woods, it was always the cottage that eventually appeared in the distance.

Only the cottage. Always the cottage. She couldn't escape it. She couldn't *escape.*

Greta screamed for Hans and received no answer. His voice was now as lost as she was. She couldn't recall how long it had been since she'd last heard him yelling for her.

Fear drove her a little farther until her legs gave out and defeat won, and she collapsed to her knees near a bush sprouting cheerful pink flowers. She crawled beneath its bark-like branches and cried until her eyes ran dry and burned like ashes.

The witch wouldn't let her leave, and there was nowhere to go anyway. There was no more home. Now she knew what her father had traded for his wish, and that was worse than the fear. That hurt more than the rawest of bloodied knees or a thousand thorns clawing at her skin.

Greta shrieked with all the rage and betrayal a five-year-old body contained, a scream that tore her lungs from her throat and carved scars into her heart. Then exhausted, she crumpled into a ball in the dirt.

Chapter Two

Fifteen Years Before the Wedding, Continued

Greta had no memory of crying herself to sleep, but the next thing she knew, she was waking up in a world that was distinctly wrong. The blankets around her were soft and warm, and the air smelled fragrant with flowers and something else—sweet and unfamiliar. The sensations were almost enough to lull her back to sleep, almost enough to overpower the awful certainty in the back of her mind that this much comfort could not be trusted.

Her eyes were raw and heavy when she opened them, and she gasped. The last, peaceful tendrils of unconsciousness slipped away like the blanket when she sat up and glanced around. The shutters on the room's single window had been cracked to let in light. It was scant but enough for her to see by, and there was so much to see.

Aside from the bed—a large bed, bigger than her father's and covered not just in finer blankets but softer pillows, as well—there was a lone chair and an ornately carved trunk. The wall behind the bed was covered in a tapestry that appeared to be made of flower petals that swooped and swirled in shades of light to the darkest pink. When Greta tentatively touched them, they felt like petals, too.

The room was roundish, and opposite the bed was a bigger hearth than any Greta had ever beheld. Its enormous chimney climbed high into a tall ceiling, and there were no doors or walls on either side of it, only curtains that had been pushed aside, offering hints of another room beyond. If she'd cared to, she could have run in circles around the hearth.

Greta rubbed her fingers over the pillow's silky embroidered fabric. The design showed a solitary brown owl on a tree branch, and the pillow yielded gently against her chest as she pressed it to herself, neither lumpy nor scratchy like the thing she'd made do with at home. It smelled of lavender as she crushed it.

Home. The terrible sense of wrongness in the back of her mind finally made sense as yesterday's memories rose to the surface and sucked the breath right out of her. She had run, but somehow she'd ended up in the witch's house. In her bed.

It seemed a strange place to put a prisoner, but what did Greta know? She wasn't a witch.

Greta's lip trembled, but she remembered Hans's parting words. "Stay close to me."

She'd tried, yet he hadn't stayed close to *her*. Had he escaped? Had he made it home? Or was he in the other room, also a strangely kept prisoner?

There was no sign of the witch at the moment, and only one way to answer these questions. Perhaps she could try to escape again. Yesterday's attempts hadn't gone well, but maybe if the witch wasn't watching and couldn't thwart her with magic, she could find the pebbles . . .

The witch must have removed her shoes while she slept, but they sat at the foot of the bed, and Greta squished her feet into them, wincing. Quietly as she could, she peeked around the other side of the central chimney.

This side of the cottage was larger still. Two chairs, each decorated with more fine pillows, faced the hearth, and a large table, simple but clean, took up much of the room. It was covered in pots and pitchers and jars, as were the shelves built into the white-washed walls. The shelves held stacks of books too, thicker ones than the book the priest carried at the chapel. Greta hadn't realized the world contained enough words to fill so many. Herbs and flowers hung from the tall ceiling, and more light seeped in through long, unshuttered windows. The room looked cozy, and with a definitive shortage of blood and bones and all the horrible things the witch was said to collect.

Since there was still no sign of her brother nor the witch herself, Greta crept in deeper. The coals on this side of the hearth were lit, and the scent of food emanated from an oven so large she could have crawled into it. Greta's stomach growled, and she ignored it. Yesterday, she'd wanted to be good, and she had failed. She wouldn't make the same mistake with the raspberries again. If she got out of here, she would ignore the garden and its promise of food, and just run.

It was harder to ignore the lure of the strange items on the table, though. One bowl was filled with blue liquid the color of the afternoon sky. Another jar contained spheres in a rainbow of colors. Their glow reminded her of the wish the witch had given her father. Were these magic spheres then? If she took one when she escaped, could she use it to find the path—

Home. Find the path home. The thought's final word strangled her with its meaning, closing her throat. She had no home anymore. Nowhere to go if she escaped. She'd been traded away.

Tears threatened, and her hands curled into fists. She wanted to leave. It wasn't fair.

The cottage door swung open, and Greta backed up into the curtained doorway.

"Awake at last, I see." The witch's hair was wrapped today in a black scarf, and she carried a basket that she set on the table. "Good."

Greta glanced around, her hopes of escape withering as her heart beat faster. Could she dash past the witch? Yesterday, she'd seemed to move so fast; Greta wasn't sure.

It didn't matter, for the witch seemed able to read her thoughts. "Calm yourself, child. Let me show you something."

Curiosity and fear kept Greta's feet rooted to the meticulously swept wood floor as the witch pulled one of her many jars off a shelf. "Here, take a look."

When Greta didn't move, the witch sighed and brought the jar to her. Greta shrank back farther, but there was nowhere left to go.

The witch unstopped the jar and held it closer, and Greta was unable to stop herself from peering inside. Color swirled within the glass—more reds than anything else, but also blues and purples. Some was so dark it might have been black. It was more magic, clearly, but something about it felt familiar. In a strange, unfriendly place, the substance in the jar was like finding her favorite socks or the doll her grandmother had made her years ago, before she died. A bit of familiarity.

"These are your emotions," the witch said, putting the stopper back. "All your rage, all your fear—it's full of power. I captured it for you as you ran around and screamed like a panicked chicken, and I'll store it here for you. So, you see, your misery isn't gone. You can have it back anytime. If you want to hold onto it now, you can. All I ask is that you leave it bottled for the moment so we can have a calm, reasonable talk. Can we do that if I give this to you?"

Up close, the witch's skin was neither as unblemished nor as fair as Greta recalled it appearing, but lightly brown and slightly wrinkled. Tucked among the silvery gray of her hair were a few strands that remained even darker than Greta's own. She looked older than she had in Greta's memory, yet stronger for it and less frightening. The creases around her eyes lent them a kindness that Greta was afraid to trust.

The witch offered Greta the jar, and she took it, instinctively. There had to be some trick here, but she didn't know what it was. All she did know is that whatever was in that jar felt like it belonged to her. She wanted to hold it, and more—she wanted to understand what the witch was talking about, but she barely knew what to ask.

Greta clutched the jar to her chest. It was faintly warm in her hands, and it gave her the courage to speak. "Are you going to steal all my blood?"

The witch rolled her eyes. "I hope we are going to do a good many things together, but your blood will always belong to you."

"What are we going to do?" Eat her? Some people whispered that the witch had a pet monster, and after she took your blood, she would feed your remains to it. Greta had seen no signs of a monster yet, but she hadn't gotten very far today. And as she'd already noted, she could easily fit in the witch's oven.

"First, we are going to feed you," the witch said. She opened the oven and removed a small pan from within. "You're nothing but skin and bones. Sit."

Although the smell of food grew stronger, Greta hesitated. "Where's Hans?"

The witch slid something out of the pan onto a trestle, and she patted the seat in front of it. "Back home with your father, I imagine. Whether the man will be pleased to see him is another story, and not my problem, though I'd have liked to help him if he gave me the chance. Both of you need to put some flesh on your skeletons, and with a father like that . . . Bah. But your brother was less valuable than you, so I couldn't bear to keep him here when he was determined to leave."

A weird sensation settled in Greta's chest. Hans had made it home, but without her. She thought she should be happy about that, but then she remembered how he'd sounded like their father as he yelled at her to hurry. The way he hadn't waited, as though his patience for her shortcomings could only go so far—farther than their father's, but not far enough to risk himself for her sake.

She didn't feel capable of happiness, and her lip quivered, and she clutched the jar more tightly.

"Put the jar down," the witch said, not unkindly. "I told you—it's yours. But there's nothing worse than cold eggs when they're supposed to be hot, and goodness knows, you need better food than whatever scraps your father was feeding you. Come on."

Greta inched forward, urged on by her stomach and the increasing certainty that she was not going to be able to escape, but she didn't sit.

The witch's face lit up, and she moved the basket closer to the eggs. Then she backed away, as though Greta were a feral animal she was trying to lure into a trap. "I have more raspberries for you since you seemed to like them so much."

Greta's stomach commanded her to move. She was already in the trap, it insisted, so she might as well eat.

Unable to resist this logic, she set the magical jar down in the spot the witch had cleared and reached for a raspberry. It was just as delicious as yesterday's had been, but the witch pointed to the eggs, and Greta feared angering her, so she took a bite of those next.

The eggs were surprisingly as good as the raspberries, rich and sweet with butter. Although Greta was still barely keeping her fear at bay, her stomach had never been so happy. She gobbled down the eggs and wiped her hands on the wet cloth the witch gave her before reaching for more raspberries.

The witch did not scold her for helping herself. In fact, she moved the basket closer so Greta could reach more easily.

Sitting across from her, the witch took a berry for herself. "Now, two out of the three of our initial problems are solved—you're not running away, and you're fed. There's still the issue of your bath to contend with, and how I'm going to fix that bird's nest of hair on your head, but all in good time. Let's proceed. We should be properly introduced. My name is Yali, although if you like, you may call me Nana."

The oddness of this information made Greta pause chewing her berry, and not just because the name was unusual. Of course the witch had a name. Everyone had a name. But to hear her say it, to learn it, felt like Greta had achieved something impossible. A bit of magic herself. Just as importantly, did it signify anything that Yali had shared her name? A witch who was merely going to steal her blood for magic or feed her to a monster might offer her food so she had plenty of blood to give, but the witch had no reason to give her name away.

"I'm Greta," she said, but it sounded like a question. "Am I really going to live here?"

For the first time, the witch's lips cracked into a smile, and the terror of the woods—Yali, Nana—didn't seem so scary at all.

"Child, I think you will not only live here, you will thrive here," Yali said. She rested a gnarled finger against the jar filled with Greta's emotions and tapped it. "I know you are still sad and angry and scared, and you should be. But when those feelings become overwhelming, I want you to scream or cry or do whatever you need to let them out, and then add them to this jar. There is power in our emotions, and you have earned that power in a way lucky children never do. You don't know how to use it yet, but one day you will, and one day your grief and rage may be useful to you. Do you understand?"

Greta started to nod, but that was a lie. And no matter how kindly Yali seemed at the moment, lying to a witch had to be a bad idea. "I don't know how."

"No, not yet. But that is what I'm going to teach you."

"But I'm not a witch."

"No?" Yali raised an eyebrow. "What did my house look like the first time you saw it?"

Greta had no trouble recalling the house of sweets. She thought she might dream of it for the rest of her life, and she recounted what she remembered, including how the house had changed into something else.

Yali nodded. "And what color were the chickens you saw?"

That came back to her just as easily. Blue and purple chickens were also difficult to forget.

Yali poured the contents of a pitcher into two clay cups and slid one toward Greta. After she took a sip from her own cup, Greta tried hers. It was only water, but it tasted sweet and clean, and it made her realize how thirsty she was. She gulped it all down while Yali spoke.

"My chickens are not ordinary chickens, but only one with magic in her blood could see them for what they truly look like on her own. And my home? Again, only those with magic will see it how it is. The first image you saw—that was how you wished to see it, a child's fancy. But your eyes couldn't deny you the truth for long, and you broke the spell without even knowing what you did." Yali refilled Greta's cup. "You have strong magic in you, and you will make a great witch if you choose to be one."

Greta wasn't quite sure what to think of this. Being a witch was better than having a witch take her blood, but the witch was bad. So everyone said. Yet, so far, Yali didn't seem particularly awful or cruel. Greta had heard stories of the witch stealing children away from their families, but in those stories, it was never so she could teach those children how to do magic.

And the witch had not stolen Greta. Her father had traded her away.

That memory curdled the raspberries in her belly and soured her blood, so Greta pushed it aside. The important matter was this: Greta really wanted to learn how to do magic, just as long as she didn't have to take anyone's blood for it.

"I can be a witch? Without hurting people?"

Yali said nothing for a moment as she folded her hands around her water cup, and Greta couldn't tell whether she found the question funny or tiring. Yali was much harder to read than her father. But then, her father had always found her tiring, which made it easy.

"I won't say a witch never hurts anyone," Yali said at last, "but if she does, I can promise you that person did something to deserve it. Will that satisfy you?"

Greta chewed on her lip. There were definitely times when hurting people was necessary to protect yourself. Hans had taught her that when the miller's daughter had pushed Greta down and taken her hair ribbon. *Next time,* Hans had told her, *you get up and you push her back, and you retake what she stole.* There never had been a next time, but that had sounded fair. As did what Yali proposed.

"All right," Greta said, and Yali did seem to think something about *that* was funny. "I want to be a witch."

"I'm glad you're taking the decision seriously. This is why I agreed to the trade with your father. Just as the carpenter and the blacksmith need an apprentice, so does a witch." Yali picked up the jar of emotions and stuck it back on the shelf, and Greta didn't feel the need to stop her. Her yearning to hold the jar had passed. She had, at some point in the last several minutes, come to trust that it would still be there for her. Just as promised.

Greta started to reach for another raspberry, but for once, her stomach signaled her to stop. She was pleasantly full. And like with the magical jar, she had no fear of the raspberries being gone away forever. This was not home, where if she didn't eat her share gratefully and quickly, it would be taken. Her future had become more strange and uncertain than she'd ever have dreamed, but rather than finding that scary, she was hopeful.

Yali looked her over and nodded. "On to the bath next, I think. But first, you need a new name. Greta is a fine name for an ordinary girl, but you must leave that ordinary girl behind. From now on, you are an apprentice witch, and your name will be Miria."

Chapter Three

One Month Before the Wedding

The young witch perched on a rowan branch at the edge of the cemetery. To the north, a flock of blackbirds coasted on an air current, lazily following the river toward the white-capped mountains that separated the port town of Swiftdok from Waere's capital. Miria had never been to the capital, but she imagined it was much like the town behind her—two- and three-story buildings of cheerfully painted wood and plaster beneath the monotonous dusky orange of their clay-tiled roofs. Only the capital, she assumed, would be grander and filthier.

Mostly grander, she hoped. Since that was where her heart was kept.

Miria longed to join the birds on their journey, but she had never flown that far, didn't know if she could, and was fairly certain that regardless, it wouldn't be wise to try. So instead, she watched the feathery storm glide silently across the mottled gray sky, beautiful in its freedom. And, given the news she'd received this morning, perhaps ominous as well.

The feeling settled in her gut like a warning, but no. Miria shook off the idea that the birds were a portent before it could take hold. She had already received her ill news, and besides, omens weren't nearly as common as most people believed. Her nana had taught her to never waste her time searching for them or to put much stock in any she found.

Not that such instruction had ever stopped Miria from wishing for signs. Maybe it was a weakness in her, but she longed to believe, deep in her heart, that there were unseen forces pushing everyone toward fates both well-earned and justly deserved. If the number of robins on a tree branch at the equinox or the color of the dawn sky on your birthday were sent to foretell a greater truth, then why could there not also be a guiding hand giving everyone a rightful shove?

According to her nana, that was another foolish notion. To be a witch was to *be* the one who shoved. Which was why, even now, when pushing and shoving felt like an impossible endeavor, Miria had left her woods in an attempt to change fate. She was too stubborn not to.

Stubbornness would only get her so far, though. Witches were mortal and not at all omnipotent. If they were, no tiny casket would be waiting to return its inhabitant to the earth below her. No sounds of women's tears would be drowning out the birdsong. No freshly turned dirt would be filling the air with the rich scent of decay.

Unable to avert her gaze any longer, Miria glanced toward the funeral below, sorry for the gathered crowds' pain and for her mission causing her to intrude on it. It was a small group who had assembled, as possibly befit a small casket, consisting mainly of women and a few older children. No doubt it was whoever could be spared from their daily tasks to support a grieving family, and no more.

Confident that she was hidden from view and that no one was looking in her direction in the first place, Miria landed gently on the grass and returned to her natural form. Wings became arms; talons turned to feet. Wild black curls replaced snowy white feathers. It would have been simpler to walk into town, but sometimes flying—seeing the world from so far above—helped put her emotions into perspective.

But not today. The sparrow carrying Adaline's letter from the capitol had arrived while Miria was making her morning tea, and she had scarcely thought of anything else since. Adaline's normally pretty handwriting had been shaky, the ink blotchy with either barely suppressed grief or rage or, knowing Adaline, some combination of both.

I'm to be married to the Overseer's son at midsummer. Do you know anything of him? I met him only once that year. Can you—

Adaline had let the sentence go unfinished, probably not wanting to ask for help. Either all those lessons being stuffed into Adaline's head about what it was to be a lady—sweet, biddable, *unimposing*—were getting through to her or she simply thought the situation was too hopeless to even bother.

Or, she despised needing help. That was also possible with Adaline. She was as stubborn and uncontainable as Miria, or she had been the last time they'd seen each other. But that was nearly two years ago. It was hard to tell what effect her family's admonishments were having on her behavior without constantly spying, and Miria wouldn't do that, no matter how strong the temptation.

Ultimately, the reason for Adaline's reticence was meaningless. Miria was a witch, and so she would do what witches always do. She would push back on fate like she could single-handedly alter the course of the mighty Swift River.

Miria pulled the glass-like red bead she kept strung around her neck from where it was tucked under her bodice and ran her fingers over it. The heat of old anger washed across her skin—sharp and dangerous. Her nana had taught her there was power in that, but Miria didn't wear the charm for power. She wore it because reliving the anger reminded her of who she was.

Adaline hadn't needed to ask, because of course Miria would help. She *would* change Adaline's fate.

All it took was a single beaver to muck up a current and flood a farm, after all.

The first step was discovering who the Overseer's son was so she could study him. It was common enough knowledge in town that the witch had cures for illnesses, spells to let you speak to the dead, charms to bring you luck, and more. All Miria had to do was figure out what he desired most and entice him with a trade. Magic for a broken engagement to a woman he didn't know. He would walk away assuming he got the better end of that deal.

It had seemed like an easy task this morning at breakfast, but Miria hadn't lived in town since she was five, and her visits, though they occurred more often than the townsfolk believed—mainly because people believed they never happened at all—had not yielded that information. One thing Miria did know, however, was that all marriage announcements had to be posted at the town chapel. Surely, that was her best bet, and that was how she had found herself a sad witness to a child's funeral, one of the few events that could distract her, temporarily, from her own problem.

Miria tucked the anger-filled charm back into her bodice and touched a second bead around her wrist. This one was a milky pink that a casual glance might mistake for a lump of quartz, and she kept it close to her skin at all times. Its magic was a constant soothing presence that way, but the feelings it filled her with were more potent still when she purposely touched it. Its sensation, though also warm, could not have been more dissimilar to the first charm. This was the warmth of holding hands, of soft lips, and a heartbeat blooming like a rose in her chest. While Miria wore the red charm to remember herself, she wore this one to remember Adaline.

The feelings refocused Miria, and she checked herself over quickly. With her hair braided tightly around her head and the rest of her dressed unremarkably in plain skirts and an equally uninspired bodice, no one would glance at her and see a witch. Her rough hands and lightly freckled, sun-touched skin marked her only as any woman who worked—a fishmonger, a weaver, a brewer. Even a woodcutter's daughter. Nevertheless, she retrieved a couple drops of dew she'd collected that morning from a vial in her purse, and she touched them to her face, a bit of magic to disguise her features, just in case there was one among the mourners who might recognize her.

Far be it from her to ruin the ruse they all clung to—that the witch never ventured into town. That if they stayed far away from the Shadow Wood Forest, they were safe.

While Miria rarely left the woods, she nonetheless knew that safety was a convenient illusion for them. The most dangerous place was often home. The woods were wild and the woods were free, and that carried risk. But it was behind painted facades and locked doors, in the eyes of those you were supposed to be able to trust, where true evil lurked.

Stories told otherwise, of course, whether they were the ones in plays and books or the ones people told each other. Once, Miria had believed those stories herself, including the ones poured into her ears at the chapel. But the thing about stories was that they were never just stories—were they? You had to watch who told the stories and ask yourself why they did. Stories could be filled with truths, but just as often, they were filled with lies.

Hitching up her skirt, Miria stepped out onto the dirt path leading from the cemetery to the chapel, her boots kicking up dust as she walked. In the woods, she could have hidden herself, but in town it was more difficult. Fortunately, the short, bald man, who Miria guessed was the priest based on his vestments, had arrived to provide a distraction.

With him was another woman Miria didn't recognize. She was tall—and not just in comparison to the slight-statured priest—but it wasn't her height that drew the eye. It was the way she carried herself, with a self-assurance that spoke of wealth, if not power. For a moment, Miria wondered if the woman was related to Adaline. Adaline's uncle was the Lord of Gawfrid, the province that enveloped Swiftdok, and his manor was a great sprawling estate that sat on a hill above the town—and Adaline was tall herself.

But that was where the similarities ended. On longer inspection, the woman's clothes, though finer than most, were not fine enough to count her among the local nobility. Miria knew nothing about current fashions, but even from this distance, she could tell the woman's gown had no lace and limited embroidery. The sleeves were fastened with ties instead of buttons. She had money, especially in comparison to the rest of the mourners, but she was not on the level of Adaline's family.

Miria moved on, not planning on paying the mourners any more attention, but the priest's voice rose above the din in a way his head could not, demanding it. "We did all we could, but the church cannot counter such vile magic on its own. We must pray for order. Justice is order, and the Divine Order will aways triumph over human-made chaos and destruction, if not in this life, then in the next."

Miria's steps slowed. She was almost to the chapel, and she should keep going, search for the wedding announcement and return home. But she couldn't help herself. Previously, the mourners had been sad and subdued, but with the priest's words, the air rippled with agitation.

"It's true then?" an elderly woman asked.

The priest had taken the hands of a young woman to whom he was speaking more softly, so the tall, wealthy woman answered. "It's true. He'd been losing blood and vitality for months before his death."

Somewhere among the assembled mourners came a wail, followed by hushed voices and dark murmurs. The time for sorrow was quickly being replaced by the time for vengeance. Miria could sense it like a hot breath on the breeze, lifting hairs on the back of her neck.

"We know some of you have sought out the witch," the tall woman said, more loudly, making full use of everyone's attention. "And you see what it's done? Another family is grieving. Your bargains with the witch have caused this. There is no small magic, nothing harmless about her power. Her magic is fed by our children's blood. Those of you—"

At this, the priest cleared his throat and placed a soft hand on the woman's arm, cutting her off. "Perhaps, Rosmilda, this is not the time."

Miria could not see the woman's face, but she could tell by the way Rosmilda's posture stiffened, then forcefully relaxed, that she was displeased to be interrupted in the middle of a satisfying rant. "Of course, you are right." Then she clasped hands with the same woman the priest had. "My dearest, Freda. I am so sorry."

The voices quieted, anger burning out like ashes in the fireplace, leaving only the cold emptiness of sadness once more.

After a moment, Miria, too, returned to the task at hand, but her thoughts remained divided between Adaline's letter and what she'd overheard.

It was no surprise that people would blame a child's death on the witch. They'd been doing that since long before Miria was born. Everyone knew the witch stole children's blood for her magic and turned the men who dared cross her into clay. Just like everyone knew the witch never left the woods. Lately, they'd even taken to saying the witch herself feasted on the children's flesh after she'd drained them of their blood, and that rumor was especially galling because Miria knew the boy (now a man) who had spread the lie.

But no matter how wrong they were about everything, it was inescapably true that more children had either disappeared or died of a mysterious wasting illness over the last several years than Miria remembered happening when she was younger. It was concerning, but not a problem she knew how to tackle or whether it was something she should attempt in the first place. Miria was proud to have helped some of those vanished children disappear, but trying to solve a problem while being blamed for it was exhausting. Her nana would have told her to keep her head down, and at the moment, it didn't seem like bad advice.

Besides, she currently had another, more pressing, problem to work on.

The chapel's sturdy oak doors were propped open to allow in the breeze, and Miria stepped inside, blinking twice until her eyes adjusted to the dimness and her nose to the potent incense. She'd been no more than waist-high the last time she'd been inside the stone building, but it retained a sense of familiarity like a cruel whisper in the back of her mind. She couldn't quite place it, but she recognized it and didn't care for it.

Light poured into the main chamber—surely it had a name, but Miria didn't know it—from several tall windows, but here in the antechamber, the space was lit only by flickering candles. Nevertheless, the notices pinned to one wall were legible, at least to those who could read.

The first to catch her eye featured a crude drawing of an old woman in a hooded cloak. *Warning*, the text read. *Only those with business in Shadow Wood should enter the forest. It is forbidden to seek out the witch.*

And below it: *Anyone with information about the blood-wasting illness should contact the Overseer immediately.*

Miria shook her head at the wildly ridiculous illustration and moved on. It took her a minute to find the wedding announcements, and she wondered, briefly, if Adaline's would not be listed since it sounded as though the arrangement had been made in haste. But there it was, along with all the others for the current moon cycle.

Lady Adaline, daughter of Sir Alberik and Lady Brunhila of Waeremund to Hans, son of Garulf, Overseer of Swiftdok.

For a moment, the room spun around Miria. The chapel dissolved into a blur of color and candlelight, a sulfur and smoke nightmare that left her dizzy. Then she breathed deeply and her hand once again grasped the charm she'd tucked into her bodice, letting its furious heat wash over her.

Ground her. Focus her. Fill her veins with clarifying, purpose-giving rage.

Hans, son of Garulf. Garulf, Overseer of Swiftdok.

The Overseer was her father. Which meant Adaline—beloved keeper of the witch's heart—was supposed to marry her brother. The boy who'd abandoned her. The boy (now a man) who'd lied about his escape from the woods and embellished the tale, giving more children and parents nightmares for his own gain.

Miria loved her nana with an intensity only matched by how much she hated her blood family, but the old witch hadn't been infallible, and this time, Miria should have trusted her instincts. Those blackbirds had definitely been an omen.

Chapter Four

One Month Before the Wedding, Continued

Miria stumbled out of the chapel, her head spinning too quickly for her to focus on walking, but her pulse pounding too hard for her feet to slow down. Somehow she avoided tripping, but she didn't stop moving until she reached the end of the chapel's lane and the bustle of town demanded she pay attention to her surroundings.

How was such a rise in her father's station possible? A wish spell was powerful magic, to be sure, but all magic had its limits. That Miria's father could have wished himself from a poor woodcutter who could barely feed his children to Swiftdok's Overseer? It wasn't possible, or so she would have thought.

Her memories of him had clouded with time, but before she'd put him out of her mind, she had fitted together some of his pieces and glued them into a picture with the bits her nana had filled in. He'd been proud but poorly educated. He'd resented Miria—then Greta—for her birth killing his wife. In the years before he sold her, drought and then floods had driven food prices high. What few specific memories Miria had of him were not happy ones. He was quick with punishments and completely lacking in affection except for the occasional praise he offered her brother. Mostly, she remembered being scared of him and of always being found wanting. Once, Miria recalled asking Hans why their father was angry all the time, and Hans responding, "Because he deserves better when he works just as hard as everyone else."

Miria, to this day, could not argue with that, but she found it profoundly cruel that he'd taken that anger out on a small girl. But then, when people could not hit a lord or a king or an unfair system, they inevitably reached for the nearby people who couldn't defend themselves, didn't they? Her father was far from the only person in Swiftdok to do so, and Miria couldn't conjure much sympathy for any of them.

So how did a man who felled trees for a living, a man who Miria wasn't entirely sure could read—at least not when she'd known him—end up in charge of Swiftdok? The Overseer was responsible for the day-to-day running of the town. Maintenance, law and order, even tax collection were within his purview. It was one of the highest government positions a man could rise to if he was not born to a noble family.

The Overseer was appointed by the province lord, in this case, Adaline's uncle. Lord Sigmun would not simply have handed the position to Garulf. To even reach a high enough status that the lord would be aware of his existence, her father would have needed to climb over a hundred wealthier, more powerful men. Then he would have needed to win the lord's favor.

Miria did not recall her father possessing an abundance of charm any more than he'd possessed an abundance of coins. So how?

She took one deep breath, then another. The speed at which she'd exited the chapel had momentarily chased away her anger, but her confusion couldn't hold it at bay for long. The how wasn't important. What would she do about it—*that* was the important issue.

The fury burning in her veins was hotter than the stones beneath her feet at midsummer. Her plan—to trade with Adaline's future groom—had been swept away like the ashes of her old life. Her father had traded his five-year-old daughter for power beyond anything Miria would have believed possible. That, in the end, the trade had benefited her was irrelevant. He had left her with the witch, not caring whether she lived or died, and no doubt assuming it would be the latter.

Her brother was scarcely less to blame. Yes, he'd been left too, another victim of their father's heartlessness. But Hans had obviously known more than he'd shared at the time. He'd had a plan—one she'd improved upon—but not the will to ensure Miria's safety. He'd called for her, held out a hand as he'd run, and that was something—a memory Miria had held onto, believing it was the best Hans could have done at the time. But she'd stopped lying to herself years ago. He could have waited for his younger, slower sister. Just for a moment. He could have come looking for her later, using the pebble trick again if he feared getting lost.

But Hans had done none of those things, and Miria had eventually learned why. When Hans had reunited with their father, Garulf had laughed and laughed. Hans's escape from the witch had finally—truly—made their father proud. Garulf had believed he and his clever son had outwitted the terror of the Shadow Wood, and Hans, basking in their father's approval at last, had grown up content with what Miria's sacrifice had bought him.

Together, her father and Hans had betrayed her in a way no child should ever be betrayed. They'd taken her love, her trust, and her home.

One thing was certain: They would not take the woman she loved, too.

Miria would do whatever it took to prevent that, and she would not play fair. There would be no trade to prevent Adaline's marriage. There would be only vengeance. Once she was done, there would be nothing left, no family of hers, for Adaline to be forced to marry into.

Without realizing it, her feet had begun moving again, carrying her into town. Miria jumped to the side as a cart rattled past at an unsafe speed, eliciting cries of alarm and annoyance. When was the last time she'd been so much in the center of this madness? Miria couldn't remember, and she'd clearly forgotten much. The air was thick with dissonant snippets of conversation, the clack of wheel axles, and barking dogs. The smells were just as loud—bodies baking in the sun, fish frying over coals, horses being horses. The violence of it all overwhelmed her senses, as accustomed as they were to the quiet harmony of the forest.

It was hard to believe she'd grown up in this and considered it normal. There was a reason the witch rarely left the woods; she preferred it there.

A couple attempts to obtain an answer to the question, "Where does the Overseer live?" finally resulted in directions. Miria wasn't entirely sure she wanted to see the new family home or what she might do when she arrived, but she headed up the hill to where the richest houses overlooked a quiet canal.

The streets calmed as the elevation rose. Miria's mind drifted once more now that it was safe to do so, dreaming of curses she might inflict on her father and brother, and scheming of how she might pull them off.

Yali had warned her against using magic for evil. All magic took something out of a witch, and it left a little something in return. Magic used for good—to heal, to help, to protect—healed and protected the witch. Magic used to harm or for other ill intentions had the opposite effect. Any curse Miria cast on her family would blow back on her. She had to consider whether those repercussions would be worth the price.

But also, if cursing her family helped Adaline, wasn't that worth any price?

Miria's hand tightened around the fence post in front of a three-story home along a quiet, winding street. The shutters were painted a soothing blue, and bright pink and purple flowers overflowed from the window boxes. Easily, three houses of the size she'd grown up in could fit on each floor.

No one appeared to be around, so Miria opened the gate and walked up the short path. If she were to curse her family, she would need something of theirs to use, and a stolen pansy or lobelia from a window box would not be sufficient. She needed to get inside.

Although Miria hadn't planned on doing strenuous magic today, she had come prepared. Even without hearing the woman at the funeral or seeing the notice posted at the chapel, she knew better than to risk being discovered. In case of emergency, she always kept a few tricks upon herself. This hardly counted as an emergency, but anger rarely made anyone rational—not even witches.

From the purse tied around her waist, Miria pulled out a blue chicken feather. It was slightly crumpled from being stuffed in the purse, but it would do. She pricked a finger on a pin, smeared the drop of blood on the feather, then blew on it to let it catch the breeze. Before the feather could fall to the ground, she snatched it again and tucked it into the braid woven around her head.

When people looked at the chickens, they saw what they expected to see. When they looked at her, they would also see what they expected to see. Hopefully, inside the house, that would be nothing. It wasn't as good a camouflage as her forest cloak provided, but as long as she moved quietly, it should be enough.

The house's side entrance was unlocked, and Miria crept into a dim, narrow hall. It had to be a servants' entrance, and the shock of her father being able to afford servants hit her anew. Voices carried from her right, along with the scent of baking bread, so Miria stayed to the left. Eventually she found herself in the front of the house, which was thankfully deserted, allowing her to gawk in peace.

Growing up, Miria's father had owned a real bed, but she and Hans had slept on straw mattresses on the floor. During the winter, there were advantages to that arrangement; Miria could pull hers closer to the fire for warmth. But it had never been comfortable. What other furniture they'd owned had probably seen better days, though Miria remembered nothing of it other than that they hadn't had a lot. A table with two benches. A chair that her grandmother had claimed until she'd died, and then her father had claimed afterward. There had been a chest for storing blankets and coats and heavy winter clothing during the summer. A set of shelves had held the cooking implements. Her father's axes and saws had been stored by the door, making it easy for him to choose the tools he needed when he left early each morning.

In this room in the new house, there were no tools or signs of manual labor to be found. The main room boasted an ornate stone hearth and a long table of fine wood before it. Instead of benches for seating, there were ample chairs. A white runner, embroidered with strawberry blossoms, split the table in two like a line of frosting, and atop it sat a crystal saltcellar and spice chest in the shapes of apples. Two silver candlesticks gleamed in the sunlight through the window. Even the mantel was sprinkled with tiny ceramic flowers—a red rose and a white, a pink blossom and a yellow—like cake-toppers. Curtains framed the windows in shades of gold, and a vase of fresh irises added purple to the colorful décor.

Hearing no sounds coming from the next floor, Miria climbed the stairs, noting the banister, too, was polished to a rich shine. Her hands shook as she paused on the landing. She was more overwhelmed by the home's opulence than she'd been when she'd nearly been struck down by a reckless driver.

This sitting room was grander than the dining room, boasting not merely plain chairs but upholstered ones. More candlesticks covered the mantel and small tables. Perhaps not all were silver, but there were so many. Tapestries hung on the walls, and heavy curtains on the windows. There was a rug before the fireplace and paintings in carved wooden frames.

One painting in particular caught Miria's attention, and she drew a sharp breath. Her father had enough funds to pay for a family portrait; that alone was shocking, though perhaps not surprising given everything else she'd discovered. What was far more intriguing was that the family in the portrait was not hers. Not entirely, or not as she'd known them. Her father must have remarried. She had a stepmother and two sisters.

Despite not having seen her father's face in years, and despite him being considerably better groomed and dressed than he'd been in her last memory, Miria would have recognized him anywhere. Gray shaded his neatly trimmed beard, but his face was every bit as hard as she'd always recalled it. Not even a new wife or newfound wealth could soften him.

Her brother's features were more recent in her mind, and they were not much changed since the last time she'd seen him two years ago, so possibly the portrait was several years old. His hair remained that indeterminate shade between blond and brown, always lighter than Miria's or her father's had been. Otherwise, he much resembled their father in this painting, more than Miria thought he'd done in reality.

The woman who was presumably her father's new wife drew most of Miria's interest. She looked vaguely familiar, although Miria couldn't place her, and the two girls could have been no more three or four years old. They looked uncomfortable in their fancy dresses, and Miria couldn't blame them for that. Adaline complained loudly at times (at first in person, and more recently in her letters) about stiff fabrics and heavy layers and itchy lace. (And then, in the next breath, she would exclaim how beautiful the gown she was describing was, because Adaline's contradictions were part of her charm, or they were if you were Miria.)

Miria squinted, trying to discern any resemblance between her sisters and her father, but aside from the dark hair, she could not. It was possible they weren't actually related by blood, that the girls' mother was a widow and they were the product of a marriage before she'd met Miria's father. But that possibility didn't stop Miria's heart from beating with a softer emotion than the ones that had driven her here.

She had sisters she'd never met, and the bits of her insides that didn't burn with a need for vengeance bled a little with the realization of yet another loss. Sisters were another thing her father had stolen from her, and Miria's imagination flew with the missed opportunities—games she could have taught them, hair she could have braided, hours they could have spent perfecting their stitching together.

Where were the girls now? The house was quiet, and Miria was grateful for it, but part of her couldn't help but want to take a peek at her new siblings.

And still you must find something to use to curse your father and brother, the anger in her heart whispered, and those missed dreams crashed into reality.

The options for that were endless now that she was in a house filled with small luxuries. But if Yali's warnings about the ramifications of cursing hadn't been enough to stop her, and they probably had not been, the possibility of any curse inadvertently hurting her sisters was enough to make Miria pause. What would happen to the girls if true harm befell their father? Could they lose everything? Miria had lived hungry for her first five years. Her desire for vengeance at any cost wavered before the possibility of inflicting that pain on innocent children.

She would have to think about this, and she would have to be very careful. It was one thing to be willing to pay any price to protect Adaline. But if she shared that cost with innocents, then she became the monster everyone believed the witch to be. Adaline would not thank her for it, either, nor could Miria love her so much if she did.

Miria passed through a couple more rooms, letting her fingers trail lightly over fine linen table coverings and pretty furniture. As Overseer, her father most likely maintained an office in the house, and that seemed like her best bet if she wanted to steal a personal item for a curse.

At the sound of a door opening below, she slid into the stairwell and braced for potentially seeing her father, but it was a woman's voice that carried up through the floors. Miria couldn't make out the words, but the woman spoke authoritatively, and the sound scratched at her memory.

"Let me see the girls," the woman said to someone, and Miria ducked into a room on the third floor with an open door. "There's nothing like a child's funeral to make me appreciate my own blessings."

Miria, apparently, wasn't the only one to hear the woman's voice. A door at the far end of the hall creaked open, and a young girl stuck her head out.

Her resemblance to the children in the painting was passable. She was clearly one of Miria's sisters, though possibly the painter had been too kind. The girl's eyes and hair color were the same, but the girls in the painting were pink-cheeked and red-lipped, healthily solid. This girl's skin was pale and her frame wispy. Judging by her height, several years had passed. As Miria tried to guess her age, a second girl appeared alongside the first, looking very much the same in complexion.

They possessed one other unexpected commonality as well, which caused Miria to draw a breath with surprise. They both had magic in their blood.

It had been difficult for her to see it at first with their cheeks so bloodless, but as they shuffled out the door, she caught the faint shimmer of it beneath their skin. Her ability to recognize magic had been one of Miria's last skills to manifest, but once she developed the eye, magic's telltale signs were unmissable.

Yali had taught her that magic was often, though not always, passed through families, so both of the girls possessing it was not a shock. Miria having it as well suggested the magic came from her father's side if they were sisters by blood, but it was hard to say. Unless the proper spells were cast, magic faded with age. If Hans had ever had it when he was a boy, Miria would never know. She'd never asked Yali if that was one reason she had let Hans go.

The girls' wide eyes and cautious expressions made Miria long to wrap them both in hugs and force some hearty food upon them—although no doubt she was being silly and reliving her own childhood needs. With all her father's money, the girls couldn't want for food or anything else so tangible. She was merely angry and pained and looking for new reasons to despise her father.

Bustling on the stairwell interrupted Miria's musings. Her stepmother's voice—or the woman Miria assumed was her stepmother—had grown closer, and she wasn't alone. The stairs creaked as an older woman appeared at the top. Her gaze swept right over Miria and landed on the girls.

"Come," she said. "Your mother is home and wishes to see you. Are you feeling up to going downstairs?"

It didn't appear to be much of a question. Hands were taken, and the group slowly passed by Miria and down the steps. After a moment, Miria followed. Although her spell had worked so far, she remained cautious and waited until everyone had moved into the sitting room before peering inside.

The woman who'd brought the girls down was fussing about with setting up tea while the girls submitted to their mother's attention. Strangely, they showed little affect as they were doted over, their faces drawn. Miria could not recall ever being able to stand so still at their age. Either her stepmother was better at discipline than Miria's father had ever been, or perhaps she'd really been as uncontrollable as her father and Nana had always accused her of being. The thought made her smile, but the emotion only lasted a moment.

Her stepmother turned then, and Miria gasped. It was the woman from the funeral, the one whom the priest had called Rosmilda—the one who had blamed the witch for the child's early death.

So that was why Miria had thought the woman in the painting looked familiar. The painter hadn't quite captured her likeness well enough for her to make the connection before, but there was no mistaking it now.

As if she heard Miria's sudden breath, Rosmilda glanced toward the doorway. Her eyes narrowed, and Miria drew back, pulse quickening. Logically, she knew the odds of having been seen were low, yet it was best not to linger any longer. Hitching up her skirt, she retreated back to the stairs and down to ground level.

No one raised an alarm, but she paused only to grab the saltcellar from the dining table. The crystal bowl was mostly empty and deceptively heavy in her hand for its size, and the few grains it held scattered across the floor as Miria tucked it into her purse. Just in case. Having seen her sisters, Miria was nearly certain she could not go through with a curse, but it made her feel better to have possibilities—and to steal something of so much value from the man who'd already stolen so much from her and who threatened to take so much more.

Chapter Five

Twelve Years Before the Wedding

When she used to yearn to be taught more things, Miria would never have believed magic might be among them. But while she'd been thrilled by the possibility, she'd also have never believed that learning magic would involve so many mundane and tedious tasks.

Some of them Miria tolerated better than others. Every day, Nana sat down with her for several hours to teach her letters and figures. Yali had explained that knowing how to translate sounds and sums into shapes and to communicate them without speaking was a kind of magic, one that most people never learned and even fewer mastered. For that reason alone, knowledge was kept in books to keep it secret. Since Miria wanted every drop of magical knowledge she could inhale, she was determined to master these lessons.

Miria's other daily tasks involved chores, and those she was less excited by. She had imagined, erroneously it turned out, that a witch could use magic to accomplish all she needed done—that freshly baked bread might just appear in her oven, and her plants would provide her with fresh fruit all year round. If Yali could give Miria's father a spell that provided anything he wished for, why not give herself one that could do all of that?

Her nana had explained that magic was not an endless resource, nor could a witch produce something out of nothing, but to Miria, that was often what it seemed like. And so it was a cruel set of circumstances to discover that living with Yali meant Miria's workload had not decreased. In addition to fetching water and feeding the chickens, Miria was expected to clean and cook and weed the garden.

For a while, Miria did everything she was asked without complaining, certain that any day—once she proved she was useful—Nana would decide it was time to start her *real* lessons.

When summer had turned to autumn that first year without Miria learning a single spell, however, she began to suspect that her nana had simply wanted a servant, not an apprentice witch. And when she finally couldn't hold the thought in any longer and it burst out of her with a childish stamped foot, Nana had laughed.

"I already have a servant," she'd said, referring to the large clay man whom she called the golem (a very unsatisfactory name, in Miria's opinion). "You came here not knowing how to cook an egg or dry an apple. You couldn't tell a weed from a bean sprout or recognize your own name in letters. With every chore you do, you learn things you will need to know later. And the first thing a witch must know is how to take care of herself. If she can't take care of herself, she can't take care of others."

Chastised, Miria had dropped her chin to her chest and mumbled an apology. Her nana was right. She had not known how to do any of those things, although how most of them related to magic remained unclear.

Nana sighed, and her wrinkles deepened, softening her face. "Chin up, child. It's been a long time since I've worked with any so young. I forget, your patience is proportional to your age. I'll teach you a little spell now—how's that? The sun is setting earlier these days, so this will be a good one for you to know."

And so Miria had learned her first spell—how to conjure a bit of sunlight in her hand. It had taken her many attempts to achieve it, and her light was not nearly as magnificent as her nana's was, but that day had been the best of Miria's life.

Three years since, her magical repertoire had grown. Yali had taught her how to collect her anger in the emotions jar (as promised) and how to call a fog to conceal herself in the forest. Miria could ask the plants to bring her fruit and the stream to send her fish, and she'd never get lost in the woods again because the trees had become friends who would guide the way. She'd also, after a close call with a hungry boar and a daring rescue by Yali's golem, begged her nana to teach her the spell for creating her own clay man to protect her.

"You are a witch," Nana had said. "Witches do the protecting. You must learn to protect yourself so you can protect others."

"I can protect myself by creating a golem that will protect me and others," Miria had countered, and her nana had laughed and agreed that Miria had won the argument.

So, over the past winter, Yali had taught her the basics of the golem spell, and Miria had practiced writing the proper words. But the spell drew a lot of power and required a lot of focus, both of which she struggled with when she also had to concentrate on her writing. The best Miria had managed so far was to make her figure twitch. Today, though, her mood was lifted by the thick lilac scent and the buzz of the bees bumbling from flower to flower. She felt full of vigor and magic. And most importantly, determination.

The red clay was soft in her hands as she molded it into human form, and because she couldn't help herself, she used a sharpened stick to draw a happy expression on the figure's face. All of this, though, was mere cosmetics.

All magic demanded a witch's sacrifice, whether it was a drop of her blood, a strand of her hair, or simply the sweat of her labor. And magic like this—big, long-lasting magic—required sacrifice of the same order. Nana had told her that she would need to give up something precious of hers to do it. That part alone had stumped Miria for a time. She had little to give besides her blood, but blood was not enough for a working like this, its power consumed too quickly to sustain a spell that would last for years.

The answer had come to her several days later. The hair ribbon she'd worn the day her father had traded her to Yali was all that she had left of her old home. Not even the clothes she'd worn remained; her nana had taken them for scraps when Miria had outgrown them.

Most days, Miria didn't think much of her old life, and when she did, those feelings were deeply conflicted. She missed her father and Hans, and she hated them both a little, too, though mostly that emotion was directed at her father. Their betrayal burned in her heart, but it no longer raged like a wildfire. Her nana told her stories, sang her to sleep, and taught her amazing things, and that love was soothing water, dousing the flames in her chest. And when on occasion that fire flared, sparked by a memory or a scent or something too ephemeral for Miria to place, she added the fury and pain to her jar like Yali had taught her. With every passing moon, the flares grew less frequent and less intense.

Despite that, the ribbon felt like a lifeline tying her to the last remnant of Greta and any happy memories that girl once had—a brother's kindness, a grandmother's hugs, even games with the other children in town. As much as she wanted to let go completely, it hurt to do it.

Miria retrieved the ribbon from a pocket in her tunic. This wasn't her first attempt to use it in the spell, and those previous attempts showed even though she'd carefully washed the ribbon after each one had failed. Taking a deep breath, she wound the ribbon into a tiny ball, then pricked her thumb on a pin and smeared it with her blood as she said the proper incantation.

Then Miria pressed the balled-up ribbon into the golem's chest where its heart should be. Continuing to chant, she molded the clay around it to cover it up. Next, she picked up the sharpened stick again and carefully wrote out the enchantment on the figure's body. She could feel the power flowing through her fingertips as she did, and sense the golem's bundled ribbon heart beat beneath the clay.

Once. Twice. Grasping for a semblance of life.

Miria closed her eyes and blew on the figure, willing with everything she had for the golem to wake up, for her life's air to breathe animation into its form.

She opened her eyes only when she felt a tap on her hand. Despite her best attempts, the golem didn't have proper eyes or a mouth, but its face and its gestures made it clear—it wished to be set down.

Shrieking with surprise and delight, Miria placed the clay man on the ground, and she watched in amazement as he inspected his form. Unlike Yali's golem, who towered over Miria, hers was tiny, no more than a foot high. Miria had never thought to ask Yali about anything as trivial as size, and it was too late now. The golem was prancing about, flexing his arms, and—to Miria's eyes—looking quite pleased with himself. As pleased, in fact, as she was with herself. Though he was small, he was surely mighty, and she felt a rush of fondness for her lumpy creation who was already stretching his form into a more symmetrical and appealing shape.

Yali had been out back, hanging the linens to dry in the breeze, and at the sound of Miria's yelling, she hurried around the house. Her own golem trailed behind her, carrying the wash basket.

"Well," her nana said, placing her hands on her hips. She looked as surprised by this development as Miria felt. "I knew you were powerful, child. Well done."

Miria thought her grin would never leave her face. "He's very small. Will he grow?"

Yali considered the question while the little golem approached his much larger brother. The two inspected each other curiously. "Yes, if you will it. But it's best that it's small now. Remember, you need to instruct it."

Miria nodded. They had gone over that during the winter—how to give the golem commands so that he might act of his own accord and how to care for him.

Miria scooped him up and set him on the garden wall so they were closer to eye level. "You will obey me," she told him, though she knew he would do that anyway, as she was his creator. "You will also obey my nana."

The golem bowed his head. Yali's golem could communicate verbally with her, but Yali had warned Miria that she might not have the same experience. Each bond between a witch and her golem was personal, but Miria hoped that day would come later.

More specific instructions could come later, as well. As would, perhaps, a hat. Nana would remind her that he wasn't a doll, but Miria would argue that sewing tiny clothes would help her practice her stitching.

"I will call you Tulip," she decided.

"What?" Yali asked.

As with all the other practicalities for creating a golem, Miria had given this one much thought. "There are two. They need names so we know who we're talking about. Mine will be Tulip, and yours will be Azalea." They were two of her favorite flowers.

Her nana shook her head. "Golems don't have names, child. They're not people."

Yali had made the same argument before, when Miria had tried wrapping Yali's golem—Aza, as he was becoming in her head already—in a blanket before he went to fetch more firewood during a snowstorm. Logically, she knew the golem didn't feel the cold, but it had only seemed a kind thing to do. She would make him a hat, too, if she could. His head would require a lot more scrap yarn than Tulip's.

"Dogs aren't people either," Miria pointed out, "but we name dogs."

"Yes, but dogs are family. Our golems work for us."

"Dogs work for people, too, and so do servants. And they both have names."

Nana rolled her eyes, but she smiled. "Fine. They are so named." She started to say something else, but the breeze shifted, and her face turned toward the east.

Miria felt it, as well. A sensation on the air that tickled her mind, unlike anything she'd felt before. Birds fluttered about in the trees, their songs changing to unfamiliar tunes.

"Someone nearby is in trouble," Nana said. She lifted her hands and cast the spell for the trees to part. The cottage's path lengthened, stretching out into the forest and dredging up memories that Miria preferred to keep buried.

She had no time to dwell on them, though, as the golems needed to be sent behind the cottage so as not to scare a potential visitor. Azalea already knew this, but Tulip did not, so it became the next instruction.

Miria had just finished seeing them off when a girl appeared far down the path. She was dressed simply, but her skirts, shoes, and shawl were new-looking except for mud around the skirt hem, not an unexpected finding during a spring walk through the woods. Her blonde hair was pulled to the side in a braid, and her face had the round softness of someone who hadn't had to suffer through an empty larder in the winter. For all that, though, fear was written on her face. When her gaze landed on Miria, some of the fear lifted, as though Miria's presence made her situation less frightening.

Nana had gotten her cane again, and she made a show of leaning on it. By now, Miria had learned that the cane was mostly an affectation. Nana rarely needed it when they were alone.

"Welcome, child," Nana said, and it was odd to hear her refer to anyone else that way. But it was also odd to think of the visitor as a child. As she'd gotten closer, Miria's thoughts on her age had changed. She would have guessed her to be an adult. Not an old one, but old enough. Perhaps to her nana, though, anyone without wrinkles was a child.

The visitor glanced around, and her brow furrowed. "Are you the witch?"

"I am." Yali nodded toward Miria. "She's my apprentice. Come inside. Let's have some tea and talk."

Miria started the water boiling while Yali cleared off a spot around the table. Seemingly dazed, the woman simply sat where indicated, and she stared at her hands until the tea was ready. Up close, Miria could see signs of struggle that she'd missed previously—bruises on the woman's arms, dirt beneath her nails, a cut on her cheek near her ear. Questions bubbled on Miria's tongue like the water in the teapot, but she held them in, letting the silence stretch out.

"What's your name?" Yali asked at last, sliding a cup over.

"Betra."

Yali, Miria noted, did not offer her name in return. "And what is it about the child you're carrying that I can help with?"

Miria's eyes opened wide along with Betra's. How had Yali known that?

After another breath, Betra burst into tears. Silently, Yali handed her a handkerchief from the pile of clean cloths while Miria stood awkwardly by, unsure of what to do.

Finally, Betra wiped her face. Her hand trembled as she folded the handkerchief into a neat square. She didn't speak again until she'd finished and her breathing had slowed. "The merchant guild-master's . . ." She lowered her head, as if even those few syllables had been a challenge. "I was his wife's personal maid."

"And you are no longer because of the child?" Nana asked gently.

"I am no longer because her son . . ." Betra squeezed her eyes shut.

"I see."

Miria frowned, because she did not know what her nana saw, but this didn't seem like the moment to ask questions.

"You spoke of this to your employer?" Nana asked.

Betra shook her head. "No, I spoke to no one at first, but the cook guessed. She told me her former assistant, who had been fired last year, was let go for the same reason. So I found her, and I spoke to her, and I learned there were others, too. And then I got so angry, I did something foolish—I went to the magistrate. I thought, if there were many of us, they must believe me and would help."

Yali said no words, but her grunt said much.

"The magistrate refused to believe me. He told me Wilmur—that is the guild-master's son—is a good man, and I was wicked for accusing him of such an awful thing. So I went to the chapel, but the priest told me the same. He said Wilmur would never violate the Divine Order in such a way, and I was only feeling guilt for my own transgressions." Betra's hands curled into themselves. "The magistrate and the priest—*they* spoke to my employer. And now I'm fired, too, and no one will hire me because they believe I would lie about a good man."

Her voice quivered, but Miria saw fire in Betra's eyes. She wasn't quite following this tale, but she thought she knew what Betra was feeling, and she wanted to scream on her behalf. It seemed unfair to Miria that children were allowed to scream their rage, but adults were expected to shed it more quietly. At least, adult women were.

"He is *not* a good man," Betra said, looking at Yali a little wildly, as though afraid she, too, would disbelieve her. "He has done this three times, perhaps more, and he will again now that he has confirmation he can get away with it. But meanwhile I cannot find work, and this child . . ." She rested a hand on her stomach.

"Miria," Nana said, and Miria startled out of her thoughts. "Fetch me a chrysanthemum blossom from the garden. One will have bloomed this morning, aware that we may need it."

Miria nodded. She was reluctant to leave the conversation, but Nana wouldn't have asked if it wasn't to help Betra, and Miria wanted to help. She raced to the garden where she found a single chrysanthemum was blooming, just as Yali had said it would. Its petals were such a dark purplish red they almost appeared black, and Miria would have sworn she hadn't seen it last year. Still, Miria thanked the plant for its offering, then she hurried back to the cottage.

"I don't blame the others for their silence, given what happened to me," Betra was saying. "But would it have helped if they'd spoken?"

"Hard to say." Nana took the blossom from Miria. While she'd been gone, her nana had brought two jars to the table. One contained what Miria knew to be some kind of healing potion—Yali had taken it to town for women before. The other jar was one Miria had never seen, black with an unbroken wax stopper.

Yali arranged the two jars and laid the chrysanthemum down behind the black one. "You have three decisions to make," she told Betra. "Do want to keep the child? Do you want to stay in town? And do you want to make sure Wilmur never again does what he did to you, no matter the price? You don't need to answer immediately, although I suspect you already know your mind, or you would not have found your way here."

Miria suspected that Yali also knew the answers, and that was why she'd been sent to fetch the chrysanthemum, although she didn't know what it was for.

"No and no," Betra said. "And yes. No matter the price, I will not let him ruin another life if there is something I can do about it."

Nodding, Yali opened the first jar and poured a drop of bright red liquid into Betra's teacup. "For the first answer. Drink this, then you will lie down on the bed for the afternoon until it works. For the second, while you are resting, I will make preparations. And for the third." She broke the wax seal on the black bottle with a knife and dropped three petals from the chrysanthemum blossom into it. Purple smoke rose from the jar before forming into a beautiful sphere that shimmered in the air. It settled on Yali's hand, and she placed it on the table. "Before we leave tonight, you will cast this into the wind with Wilmur's name."

Betra drank her tea, and Nana showed her to the bed while Miria cleaned up the tea accessories. While Betra slept, Miria inspected the sphere. It was much larger than the wish spell and looked infinitely more fragile, like the finest glass she'd ever seen.

"Do not touch," Nana said, and Miria jumped back.

"What is it?"

"A very dangerous spell in the wrong hands. Not your hands," she added when Miria glanced at her palms, "but you're too young to burden with this kind of magic. It is nothing that should be used easily or without strong reasons. That's why I do not keep it fully prepared."

"What will it do to Wilmur?"

Yali pressed her lips together, considering. "Justice. Of whatever type Betra chooses, as is her right."

Miria filed this away without comment. "Where are you taking Betra?"

"To another town, far from here where no one will know her past." She unlocked the small chest near the hearth and added several coins to a purse.

Miria counted them and guessed the journey must be far if Nana was taking so much money. Then again, despite how simply they lived, Nana had no shortage of coins. "Will you be gone long?"

She heard the way her voice wavered, and so did Yali, for her nana playfully flicked her braid. "No, child. Do not worry. I won't be gone more than an hour. Another witch in that new town will help Betra settle when she arrives."

Miria had heard Yali talk about other witches before. Yali said there were witches near all towns of sufficient size and in all countries, if you knew where to look. Miria had never met any of them, yet she knew her nana corresponded with some. Letters would arrive, sometimes by birds and other times seemingly out of the air.

"Can I come?" What was happening here today, though she might not understand it fully, struck Miria as exceedingly important. Nana had said a witch's job was to help, and so she needed to learn how to do this, whatever it was.

Nana kissed the top of her head, which was becoming difficult. In another year or two, if she kept growing, Miria would be the taller of the two of them. "Not this time. When you are older and ready. You have much to learn first."

Chapter Six
One Month Before the Wedding

Miria stomped toward the town gates, recklessly heedless of the traffic or any strange glances that might be tossed her way. The fury in her veins needed to be burned off.

There were no farms along the footpath between the woods and the town. Just a field, currently thick with summer grasses and brimming with purple and white wildflowers that dotted the green like decorations on a cake. It was as though everyone tried to maintain a buffer between civilization and the line of trees that marked the beginning of the Shadow Wood Forest. No doubt that was because terrible creatures lived in the forest. Witches, mainly.

The irony, of course, was that witches were everywhere if you knew where to look.

Everywhere except where Miria longed to be—at Adaline's side, comforting one another, scheming together.

Miria had followed Yali that day she'd given Betra a full coin purse and walked her through the woods, watched as her nana had cast the portal spell. It had been several more years until she learned that spell, longer before she mastered it, and yet for all that magic available to her, she was here and Adaline was several days away. Unreachable.

"This rock is a portal?" Adaline had pressed her hand against it, jabbed it with a finger, and finally flung her entire body atop it while Miria had laughed. "Sometimes I think you're teasing me, you know."

Miria pulled her up, and Adaline shrieked with surprise. "You're lucky it doesn't work that way, or it could have swallowed you, and you'd be on the other side of the country by now."

That thought had seemingly never occurred to Adaline, judging by the startled expression on her face, and that was hardly a surprise. "You would have stopped me if that were the case. Right?"

"Oh no, I'd have let you fall through it. You might have learned a lesson in being more cautious."

"Miri!"

She couldn't hold in another laugh. "And then I'd have gone through and rescued you, as I have a tendency to do."

Adaline scowled playfully and poked Miria in the arm. "You would have let me fall through it. I believe that. So does this rock—" she narrowed her eyes at it as though still questioning whether Miria was playing a prank "—take you anywhere? Could you visit me at home this winter?"

Adaline's light tone faltered beneath the weight of the question, and Miria's good humor faded within her chest.

"Not anywhere," Miria said. She drew her finger down the rock face, and the spell hidden on its surface rippled gold beneath her touch before dissolving into nothingness again. "There must be a similar portal on the other end, and not just any portal—one where I've already been so I can add my magic to the spell. My nana's taken me to many places, so now I can go to them on my own, but there's no portal in Waeremund."

"But it's the capital."

"Probably why. Such overt magic around so much nonmagical power is dangerous." Miria smiled sadly.

Adaline sighed. "I'd be angry that you witches are all such an antisocial bunch except I understand why you must be. I hate it. I don't want to spend all fall and winter without you."

Miria leaned into her then, and they held each other silently for a minute because the unfairness of it all was too much. Being a witch had made Miria believe she should be able to find a solution to any problem, and being a wealthy lady had likely made Adaline believe the same. Once. Before they'd grown up and discovered their power—all power—had limits, and theirs was especially small compared to that of kings and men and institutions.

"It's only fall and winter," Miria said, pressing her cheek against Adaline's. "You'll be back in the spring?"

Adaline nodded. "I hope. By summer at the latest."

Only she'd been wrong. Instead of six or eight months passing, nearly two years had come and gone. Adaline still wasn't here, and now the people who'd kept them separated all that time conspired with Miria's family to keep her away forever.

She wouldn't allow it.

Miria emerged in the cottage's clearing not an hour later, her thighs and feet burning with the exercise and sweat running down her back, but her head clearer. Tuli—as she'd come to call her golem over the years—was leaning against an apple tree, perfectly motionless beneath the first small signs of fruit. Was he asleep? Did he dream? Did he even have a mind with which to think when Miria wasn't addressing him? She'd never gotten satisfactory answers to those questions from either Yali or her books.

Tuli had a bit of a personality, though, or so Miria chose to believe. More than Aza did, or rather, more than Aza once had. Her nana's golem had returned to the earth along with her nana, and even now, just remembering that she was here alone, without the woman who'd saved her and raised her and loved her, made Miria's heart ache.

She had half a mind to rouse Tuli for the company, but the golem seemed peaceful doing whatever it was he did when he was like that, so she resisted. She did not need his assistance with the course of action she'd decided on during her walk, so she let him be.

Inside the cottage it was blissfully cooler than it was out, and Miria tossed off her layers, remembering how Yali had so often called her wild. Not that her nana had dressed like a proper lady without cause, but Miria had always taken clothing as more of a loose suggestion than a strict rule, particularly during the hottest days of summer. If a child was raised in the woods, no one should expect her to act civilized.

Stripped down to a loose linen tunic, her legs and feet bare, Miria settled at the cottage's long table. The red charm, dangling on its cord, bounced against her chest as she swung her legs beneath her, but Miria ignored it. She'd dwelled much on her anger during the walk from town, considered deeply all she'd learned and the options before her, and she hadn't made a decision regarding her family yet.

Now that she was home, it wasn't her family that she wished to think about at all, but their lives were entangled with Adaline's. She had no choice.

Somehow, she had to devise a plan that would help Adaline and serve her own vengeance without harming innocent children. To do that, Miria needed more information. She could write to Adaline and hope Adaline would provide it—and she *would* do that—but Adaline could not necessarily be counted on to provide exactly the details Miria required. That was only partially due to Adaline's faults as a correspondent. The rest of the fault was Miria's; she didn't exactly know what to ask.

Fortunately, for that, there was magic. It could not solve all problems, but this was precisely the sort of problem it excelled at.

Miria pulled a shallow glass bowl closer. It had once been Yali's, and like so many of her belongings, Miria had inherited it. The apprentice had become the witch, though there were many days when Miria felt far from qualified for the job. Many times when she wished her nana were around to answer questions or provide guidance or simply to lend a shoulder to cry on.

Never was that more true than now, when the biggest act of magical work she had to complete was for the most personal of issues.

Taking a deep breath, Miria removed the bracelet with the pink charm from her wrist, recalling the day she'd given an identical one to Adaline.

"This is magic," Miria said, tying the pink stone around Adaline's wrist. "It will keep a piece of my heart with you at all times. Not literally!"

Adaline's shoulders relaxed. "How am I supposed to tell with you?" She wrapped her fingers around the charm and smiled. "It's warm. It . . . it feels like you."

"Exactly. I put my feelings for you in it. Whenever it touches your skin, and especially when you touch it on purpose, you can remember me. It should also protect you because love is protective." She felt her cheeks burn with the admission,

"Like I could forget you." Adaline threw her arms around Miria and squeezed so hard Miria thought she might crack a bone. "It's perfect. It's the best jewelry I own, even if I'll have to hide it. But what about you?" She released Miria and stepped back. "Can you make one with my feelings in it? Would they protect you?"

Miria had hoped to do just that, but she smiled mysteriously since it amused Adaline. "I could do that, I suppose."

For the moment, she snipped a lock of Adaline's hair to keep with her. "With this, I'll be able to scry for you. Find you. If you ever need me, I'll come to you."

The light on Adaline's face faded at that, and she pulled Miria close again. "I'll always need you, but I know what you mean. I don't want to leave."

Miria said nothing to that, for there was nothing to say. They'd repeated the same words to each other time and time again, but words without actions rarely changed fate. Instead, she held Adaline, pressed cheek against cheek, threaded her fingers through soft brown waves, tried to memorize every detail of Adaline's face from the tiny moles on her neck to the curve of her hip against Miria's own, to the honeysuckle and lavender scent that clung to Adaline's hair. Soon enough, words—though written on paper—would be all they had left.

Almost all, Miria amended to herself. She had this charm, and Adaline hers, and they were also a connection. Adaline couldn't use the one Miria have given her for the same purposes that Miria could, though. Purposes that Miria tried not to use it for too often since they were rather invasive of Adaline's privacy. Under these circumstances, however, Miria assumed Adaline would forgive her for prying.

She placed the bracelet at the bottom of the bowl and poured just enough water to cover it and then a little more. Grasping the edges of the bowl, Miria called on her power and focused on the dilemma at hand.

"Show me what I need to know."

The water shimmered like a thousand lights sparkled from beneath it. Then the magic settled, and Miria found herself looking at Adaline.

Her heart fluttered in her chest. No matter how many people she might meet, Miria would never find another woman as beautiful, could never imagine that seeing anyone else would make her feel so much joy.

Adaline, however, was not looking at her. It was unclear when the scene unfolding in front of Miria's eyes took place. It could be the present, although that seemed unlikely. It could have been this morning, or yesterday, or a week ago. Based on the date of Adaline's letter, Miria doubted it was much further in the past.

Adaline stood on a stool, her spine rigid and her hands curled into fists. Her long, brown hair was darker than it used to be, as yet untouched by the sun, and pulled up in that way that could only be achieved by a lady's maid with a small armory of pins or (in Miria's case) a bit of magic. Without even a single loose tendril to fall on her high cheekbones, Adaline's large honey-colored eyes seemed to take up most of her face.

The last time they'd seen each other in person, the sun had freckled Adaline's pale cheeks and turned strands of her hair to gold, but Miria knew from Adaline's letters that she hadn't been permitted to run freely outdoors for the past year, and her unblemished skin and darker hair were proof of it. Not that Miria minded the effect. Adaline's skin looked soft and dewy sweet, and she imagined what it would be like to rub their cheeks together. (Nor, to be clear, had Miria minded when Adaline's skin had browned and freckled in the sun. It was still Adaline's skin, and therefore perfect in whatever state it happened to be in.)

There was the sound of a soft grunt by Adaline's feet, and with some effort, Miria dragged her eyes away from Adaline's face. After two years of not seeing her in person and five months since the last time she'd scried on her this way, Miria hated shifting her gaze. But the magic had answered her call with this scene, so she'd best pay attention to all of it.

A woman slid about on the floor by Adaline's stool. She had several pins stuck in her mouth, and she was fighting the fabric around Adaline's ankles. Only then did Miria realize what she was watching: Adaline was being fitted in her wedding gown.

Surely, it *had* to be a wedding gown. Miria could not believe that even the queen's cousin (which Adaline was) could have need for so fine a gown otherwise. She'd been too enamored by Adaline's pretty face and detailing its changes to take in the dress before, but Miria allowed herself a moment to feel awed and possibly a bit intimidated. It was one thing, after all, to know that Adaline's family was nobility, that one of her uncles was the Lord of Gawfrid and one of her cousins was married to Waere's king. It was another to be reminded of what that meant.

Truly, being raised in the woods had made Miria feral. Social stations and money were abstract concepts to her normally.

The gown was a light blue, as bright and bold as a perfect sunny day. Nearly every inch of it was embroidered, and the bodice was so covered in sapphires and pearls in the shapes of birds that the dress sparkled like a river in the sunlight that streamed through the window to Adaline's left. Additional jewels flashed around the neckline and sleeves.

The dress was both stunning in its beauty and offensive for the same reason. Though dazzling, it overshadowed Adaline's natural beauty, and Miria couldn't tolerate that.

Adaline, on the other hand?

Things Adaline professed to love: pretty dresses, swords, and Miria. Though not necessarily in that order. Regardless of her opinion on the wedding, Miria was certain Adaline adored the gown.

Miria mentally pulled back further from the vision, trying to gain a wider perspective on the scene. The room Adaline stood in was richly furnished in a way that made Miria's father's new house look shabby, but the fine trappings were not nearly so interesting to Miria when they were found somewhere she expected them to be. It was the difference between seeing a deer in the woods and finding one in a sitting room.

"Do you not like it? Stop looking so glum." Adaline's mother hovered at the edge of the scene, on the cusp of Miria's scrying bowl. She darted in and out of Miria's view as she paced.

"It's stunning. Of course, I love it." Adaline fidgeted, seeming to only be holding her arms in place with great difficulty. "It's not the dress that's making me glum. It's marriage to a stranger."

"You met once. Therefore, he is not a stranger."

Adaline rolled her eyes.

"Don't make that face at me," her mother snapped, which was a rather impressive observation since she wasn't looking in Adaline's direction. But Adaline's response was exceedingly predictable. "Did you think you wouldn't have to grow up one day? That you could play soldier with the boys forever? Your father should never have indulged your peculiar habits. I told him you'd become incorrigible."

Adaline crossed then uncrossed her arms as the seamstress gently cleared her throat in way of admonishment. "I thought you'd give me more time."

"Time for what? Your beauty won't last forever. This is a good match—your bloodline and his money. Your uncle Sigmun recommended it strongly, and you will only get richer now that he has secured your future husband land and a title from the crown for your wedding gift. That took no small amount of effort. Be grateful."

"If this family needs money that badly, I don't see why we couldn't just sell a few of the jewels from this dress." Adaline raised her wrists so the sapphires flashed in the sunlight.

She had a point. Miria might be feral, but she nonetheless knew enough about money to know that just a few of those jewels could probably feed the average Swiftdok family for a year.

Her mother sighed. "Don't be ridiculous. You are the queen's cousin, and you should look like it. I suppose you'd rather be traipsing through the mud in men's clothes again."

"Now that you mention it." Adaline grinned.

"That's exactly why we didn't tell you until everything was arranged. You need to grow up, Adaline. You have duties as a lady. You can take it up with the Divine Order if you're angry you weren't born a boy, but ask your brothers—even boys have their duties."

"I don't want to have been born a boy. I just don't want to marry one."

In spite of everything, Miria smiled. Adaline appeared so close, it was as if she could press her finger into the water and touch her. But the water shimmered again, the scene fading from view until Miria was left staring at nothing but a wet charm.

She plucked it from the bowl and pressed it to her lips, hoping Adaline could feel that on her wrist, assuming she was wearing the charm. Beneath the swaths of blue silk she had on, it had been impossible to see.

Returning the charm to her own wrist, Miria's gaze fell on Adaline's letter, and it reminded her of why she'd scried in the first place. It was time to put the lonely wishes of a lovestruck girl aside and focus on a witch's task.

Show me what I need to know.

What had that scene shown her that was helpful? There was nothing to it that Adaline hadn't mentioned in her letter.

Miria dried her fingers off against her tunic and picked up the letter, reading the words for what was probably the hundredth time. Another reading didn't make them less painful, and it certainly didn't change anything.

Or did it? *I'm to be married to the Overseer's son at midsummer,* Adaline had written, and Miria sucked in a breath. Of course. That was what the scene had shown her.

Lord Sigmun's gift to Adaline and Hans was to be nothing short of land and a title for Miria's brother. Hans would cease to be the Overseer's son, and become . . . well, something. Adaline's mother hadn't said what the title was, but it hardly mattered. It was a title, and that was enough. Her family—her selfish, greedy, traitorous family—was to be granted status. Far more than they'd already snatched for themselves.

Whatever her father had done with that wish spell, even his grasping hands could not have anticipated it would bring him so much. His son would be titled. His future grandchildren would be counted among the nobility. All he'd had to do to win such a prize was give up a daughter, leave her to what he'd believed was her death.

Miria's blood thrummed with a bloodthirsty tune as she tossed the scrying water onto the ground outside. She wanted to throw the bowl as well, smash it to a million pieces like her heart had been smashed that day she'd been abandoned.

But the bowl had been her nana's. To Yali, it had been a treasure from her home country, a land she'd last traveled to when she hadn't been much older than Miria currently was; it was a piece of her heart. To Miria, the bowl was a reminder of the woman who'd picked up her broken bits and put them back together, which also made it a piece of *Miria's* heart. So Miria took the bowl back into the cottage, searching for the calm she'd felt earlier. The peace she'd felt looking at Adaline's face.

Her heart was whole again, healed by Yali and entrusted to Adaline. She'd survived, and more—she'd thrived, as Yali had promised.

But so had her father.

That would be no longer. Miria understood what she had to do, and it was so simple. So elegant. Her father had risen as far as a man born without a title could rise, and he must believe his son would rise even higher. So what if he'd tossed aside a daughter to do it and would ruin another woman's happiness, as well? It wasn't like he cared about hurting girls or women.

But Miria did. She would be the *so what.*

All she had to do to ruin her father's plans was stop the wedding. Dash his hopes to the ground and shatter them like glass. And when she was done, she would make sure he knew that she was behind it. Make sure he knew his cruelty had created his own destruction.

The best part was that Miria's sisters could not possibly be harmed by this plan, and Adaline would be saved. There was no need for curses. Miria would not have to suffer at all for her vengeance, and Adaline would be an eager participant, even if she did not yet know the entire extent of Miria's motivation.

For the first time since Adaline's sparrow had delivered her letter this morning, Miria felt . . . not happy, but perhaps content. In spite of the unseasonable heat, midsummer was still a few weeks away. Adaline's family would not arrive until close to the wedding, so there was ample time to plan and prepare.

But first, she had to dry Adaline's tears and give her hope. Miria grabbed her quill, but before she could begin writing, she set it back down. These were dangerous words to write.

With her other letters to Adaline, there was always a risk, but Miria assumed Adaline could explain away the correspondence if unanticipated eyes discovered it. Telling Adaline she had a plan to stop the wedding would be a lot harder to explain, and perhaps as importantly, the day's events had awakened a longing in Miria's chest, one that was as ever-present as her shadow but mostly ignorable like a shadow, too. Only the shadow wasn't mindlessly trailing behind her today. It stretched and waved its hands and grasped at her coat-tails.

Adaline's tear-stained letter. The shock of the marriage announcement. Seeing Adaline in the wedding dress.

Writing of her intentions to Adaline was no longer enough to satisfy Miria. She needed to see Adaline. Really see her. Talk to her.

Miria's fingers twitched at her sides as she consulted the spell books. All this time, she'd stuck to writing letters with Adaline because it was simple, but there were other methods to keep in touch. None of the witches Miria knew used those methods regularly because of the heavy magical toll and the complications for all involved, but perhaps . . .

She pulled the book she needed from the shelf, telling herself she wasn't being silly. There was a real danger in committing her thoughts to writing. But the truth was, today had broken Miria's patience. While revenge couldn't come soon enough, one month provided plenty of time for her to plan. She could do something silly and magically costly in the meantime.

Chapter Seven

One Month Before the Wedding, Continued

It took Miria four days to arrange the spell, gather the supplies, and cast all the necessary steps, and she still didn't know if it would work. Adaline would have to be available at the correct time and at an appropriate location. This, Miria reminded herself repeatedly as she worked, was why witches typically stuck to letters like everyone else.

She had, in fact, sent a letter to Adaline, explaining what Adaline needed to do on her end, but while Miria was fairly certain the letter would have been received in time—four days was ample for her network of birds to carry it to the capital—she had no guarantee Adaline would be able to follow the instructions. All this work, all this energy she'd spent, could be for nothing.

Miria stifled a yawn as she paced in circles around the cottage. It was closing in on midnight, and normally she'd have been asleep ages ago. Even the anticipation of seeing Adaline wasn't much of a match for the exhausting work she'd been up to earlier.

Candlelight set the walls flickering and bathed the rooms in a golden hue. If Miria stilled her mind for a moment, she could almost transport herself back to the late nights she'd spent with her nana, working spells that could only be performed during the darkest hours. During those sessions, Yali would brew them both a fragrant tea to keep their minds sharp as the sun set.

Miria had some of the blend left, part of the last batch her nana had made. She'd considered brewing it earlier but decided against it. Without her nana to pour it into the tiny teacups that she kept especially for this brew, the ones she'd painted herself with owls and bats and other nocturnal birds, part of Miria wondered whether the tea would even help. Was it the leaves and herbs in it that had kept her sharp, or Nana's stories as she brewed it and the subtle way she'd quiz Miria on her preparations for what was to come? Was it the desire to prove herself and exceed Yali's expectations?

Besides, if she brewed the last of it, it would be one more part of her nana that was lost forever. Yali would laugh at her for thinking that way, but it was too easy to be melancholy when the sun set.

Miria shook off these thoughts and returned to the main room. Adaline was where she needed to focus—Adaline and a future that could be changed, not a past that was permanently scribed in time.

The air in here was thick with the scent of the herbs she'd been burning all day in preparation—bay and anise, rosemary and thyme. She propped open the door slightly to let in an exchange of air and glanced up. The moon was high, peeking its glowing face through the mottled clouds as they drifted past. It had to be nearly time.

Sure enough, when she returned to the hearth, the last piece of her spell had finished. Miria drew a finger though the ash left at the bottom of her cauldron. It should have been hot after smoldering all day, but it was pleasant to the touch as she drew the appropriate symbols through it. Before she even finished, she felt the ash shift and begin to solidify, and when she was done, what remained was a crude wooden key. Miria carried it to the scrying bowl, which was filled with the water she'd also prepared earlier, and she twisted the key about in the water like it was a lock. The key disintegrated, turning to ash once more, and as the ash settled on the bottom of the bowl, the water shifted.

Miria had never cast this spell or any like it. All she knew was that it was similar to the portal spells witches used to travel, but—for all its complexity—it was still far less intense and complicated than those spells. She'd expected the water in her bowl to act like it did when she scried, but the change was faster, almost violent in its power. One moment she saw the bowl's bottom, the next, it was as though a hole opened in its place, revealing a scene in a room Miria had seen only in visions a couple of times before—Adaline's bedchamber.

Was the hole a small portal? Could she send something through it? Miria had so many questions, but then Adaline's face appeared at the other end, and Miria's desire to experiment vanished along with the bowl's bottom.

Adaline screamed. Then swore. Then clamped her hand over her mouth, her large brown eyes growing wider as she gazed in astonishment.

Miria couldn't help but laugh, and her laughter drove away the sleepiness that had been encroaching over her. "If you wake your household and I did all this work for a spell and then don't even get to explain why, I'll . . ."

She had no idea what she would do. Seeing Adaline in real time left her too happy to think, and a grin split Miria's face in two. Despite all that work, maybe she should have tried to do this on at least one other occasion in the past two years.

Adaline glanced fretfully around her, but her face took up the entire bottom of the bowl, so Miria was in the dark as to anything else going on. "It's fine, I'm sure. Everyone retired long ago, and oh, this is amazing. Miri, I can't believe I'm talking to you. Why did you never tell me you could do this before? Why haven't we done it? Is this like the portals you told me about? How else have you been holding out on me?"

"I haven't been holding out on you, I promise." Miria tucked a curl behind her ear. Leaning over a bowl like this was not ideal. On the other hand, Adaline's hair was loose and flowing over her shoulders, and it seemed to be falling toward Miria. It was so deceptively close, Miria thought she could reach out a hand and touch it. "I never attempted this before because it's a lot of work, and I don't know how long this spell will last. Not long, I suspect. But I didn't dare write to you about the wedding."

"The wedding." Adaline groaned. "Don't talk to me about the wedding. You're here. Or, well, I can see you, so it's close enough. I want to talk to you about anything else. Miri, I miss you."

Miria's heart skipped. Adaline wrote as much frequently, but hearing her say it was something else entirely. Both sad and sweet, the words filled Miria with warmth even as they made her chest ache.

"I miss you, too," Miria said, "but I need you to know—I have a plan. I'm going to prevent your wedding."

Adaline opened her lips—full lips, whose touch Miria was suddenly missing more profoundly than she'd missed them in a while—then she closed them. Her gaze turned serious as she seemed to contemplate this news. "I suppose if you're going to insist on talking about the wedding, that is the way to do it. I don't want you to do anything risky, though. I didn't ask for your help because I couldn't live with myself if something happened to you while you tried to help me."

Miria waved off Adaline's concern before realizing that Adaline probably could not see her hands, just as she couldn't see Adaline's hands. "You don't have to ask. My motivations aren't entirely selfless, you know."

Actually, they were less selfless than Adaline was likely to imagine.

Adaline laughed, but her humor was clearly strained. "I hope not. I would be very upset if you weren't jealous of me marrying someone else."

Jealousy. The word hit Miria like a stone dropping into the water, an intruder disturbing the stillness. It was funny, but Miria hadn't spent much time feeling jealous. That Adaline would have to marry someone else one day had always been a given, a fact as immutable as the sunset. She and Adaline had never really discussed it, because what was there to discuss? It was only a topic that could sadden and infuriate them both, and Miria had never really considered what marriage would mean beyond that it was unfair to force Adaline into a situation she didn't want to be in.

But now she did think, and worse she imagined. Someone else kissing Adaline's soft lips. Someone else running their fingers through those long, brown waves of hair. Someone else's fingers tracing the contours of Adaline's silky skin.

Miria dug her nails into her palms. It wouldn't just be some nameless, faceless *someone else* if she failed, either. It would be her brother.

Fury overpowered the jealousy in her gut. Miria wasn't sure if that was any better. In retrospect, Adaline had been in the right to not want to talk about the wedding. Miria would have rather rejoiced in seeing Adaline's face.

"Miri?" Adaline's voice returned her to the moment. "Are you all right?"

Miria realized she was scowling. "I feel more anger than jealousy," she admitted. "It's not as though you want to marry someone else."

Adaline made a horrified expression. "Heavens, no. And I'm sorry. I'm only teasing you because it takes my mind off everything. When I dwell on the situation for too long . . ."

She cried. Miria had noted the tear stains on Adaline's last letter, but she wouldn't bring them up.

"I'll have the situation in-hand by your arrival, I promise," Miria said instead. "I'm working on a plan. I just needed you to know so you could stop worrying."

Adaline made a skeptical noise. "As amazing as I believe you are, I'm not sure you possess enough magic to make that happen. But it does make me feel better to know you're scheming. As long you do nothing that will put yourself at risk."

"I can't promise, but I'll do my best."

Adaline sighed heavily. "Fine. I'll accept your help in that case, but only because I really do not want to get married."

"Oh, do not let me force my help on you." Miria snorted. "Perhaps you already had a plan for getting out of it?"

"Well, yes." Adaline adopted her most haughty voice, the one she used when entertaining Miria with stories of the ladies at court. "Since you mentioned it, I was thinking of this play I once saw. The princess in it disguised herself as a boy and ran away to join a ship's crew in order to avoid marriage. The ship got overrun with pirates, so she became a pirate herself, and eventually she captained an entire pirate battalion and overthrew her own family. What do you think? Should I try it?"

Miria thought of Adaline teaching her how to use a sword and of Adaline fighting with her parents to be allowed to spar with her father's guardsmen. But she also thought of all of

Adaline's very feminine curves that she couldn't see in the bottom of her bowl, and she pretended to examine Adaline's long lashes and delicate chin. Then she shook her head solemnly. "I think you would very much enjoy being a pirate, but you would make a terrible boy. You're far too pretty."

Adaline's face fell, but she couldn't contain a smirk. "True. It is a challenge being so beautiful."

"And modest."

"Also true. Humility *is* one of my many virtues."

Miria's attempt to keep a straight face finally failed, and her laughter made Adaline laugh as well. She'd missed all the stories Adaline knew, and the way she'd mock the ambitious and backstabbing people she had to deal with at court. But mostly, she'd missed the easy way Adaline could make her laugh.

"This is the part where you're supposed nudge me in the side or give me a light shove," Adaline said, "and I'm supposed to throw myself at you and kiss you until we're not laughing anymore." As she said it, her smile faded. "I take back what I said earlier. Seeing you but not being able to touch you might be worse than just exchanging letters. It's too strong a reminder of what I can't have."

For a second time during this conversation, Miria's cheerful mood slipped away. "Considering the effort I went through . . ." Then, seeing Adaline start to apologize, she quickly continued. "No, I'm not being serious. I know I could have put everything I wanted to say in a letter, but I was too impatient to see your face again after the news."

"And I'm so happy to see yours, even if it also makes me sad."

"Don't be sad. I'll see you in a month when you will *not* be getting married."

Adaline took a deep breath. "Right. We will make it so, or not make it so. Now stop bringing up my wedding-that-will-not-happen, so I can enjoy this time with you. You can put your plans in letters, and we can scheme together. Your birds are very discreet, and I'm very good at keeping them safe. I promise. No one has found one yet."

Miria glanced at the saltcellar down the table, and despite her alleged reasons for this spell, she buried her intentions to explain more. Adaline was right, and she knew it. There would be time later to tell Adaline about who her intended groom was. She should enjoy the moment.

"No more wedding talk then," Miria agreed. "Tell me about anything else you've left out of your letters. I've missed your voice. Your stories."

"You may be the only person to miss my voice," Adaline said, perking back up. "The rest of my family constantly tell me to be more quiet and demure. It's no wonder I miss you so much."

Miria closed her eyes for a moment to fight back the tears that suddenly threatened, the pain as sharp as Adaline's sword tip in her chest. But she opened them quickly, not wanting to waste a second when she could be drinking in Adaline's presence.

"I would never," Miria said, and she happily let Adaline fill the conversation with more pleasant topics until the spell fizzled out.

When her eyes closed for the night, she laid her head down with the sound of Adaline's voice in her ears, and she slept, clutching the bowl close.

Chapter Eight

Ten Years Before the Wedding

Yali was inside, wiping down her scrying bowl when Miria dashed through the doorway. "There's smoke in town!"

Ever since Nana had taught her the spell that allowed her to transform into an owl, Miria dedicated time each day to working on it. She couldn't maintain the form for long yet, but she was getting better, and that was how she'd seen the smoke from high above the treetops.

"Yes, it appears someone knocked over a lantern near one of the taverns," Nana said, seemingly unconcerned. "It will be bad."

"Can we help?"

Yali put the scrying bowl on a shelf. "Not with this, child, I fear. There will be many dead and too many injured for us to make much difference."

Miria frowned. Yali had insisted many times that a witch's duty was to help. She didn't see why they should only help when those in need sought it. What if other people didn't know they could ask? Besides, her nana helped children all the time without them even knowing it. What if there were children who needed help in town?

Miria raised these objections, but her nana was stubborn. "If you go to town, you will find many people suffering, many people in need of your help. You will want to help them all, and you can't, and it will upset you. A witch can only expend so much magic in a given time, as you're discovering whenever you fall out of the sky. If you expend all your power, if you leave not a single ember burning inside you like a coal in the fireplace, you won't be able to replenish it. And then, you will die, as well. Your heart is kind, but not yet wise. Sometimes, a witch directs fate, and sometimes she should stand back and let fate do what it will. Learning to decide when to do these things is never easy, but it must be done."

"Well, I won't," Miria said. She had, after all, mostly learned to stop herself from falling out of the sky. She was certain she could stop herself in this manner, too. "I think we should do *something*. I want to go."

She half expected Yali would stop her as she filled her magical purse with healing spells and supplies, but her nana did no such thing. When Miria turned around, Yali was watching her with an odd expression.

"Perhaps you need to go," her nana said. "But wait another hour. Let me make sure the fire is under control and you won't be rushing into danger. Then let Tulip or Azalea carry you to the edge of the woods and wait for you there. Save your strength, and I will keep an eye on you in case there's trouble."

Miria didn't like waiting when people might need help, but Yali had a point about the fire being dangerous. Miria could control small fires and prevent herself from burning, but if the town fire was large and violent, she would be no match for it.

She did what her nana insisted, and by the time she arrived in town, the fire had been mostly put out. But Swiftdok was in an uproar. An entire block of businesses and homes was gone, and the reek of smoke, of charred wood, burned straw, and more was almost too much for Miria to tolerate—almost enough to make her resolve falter and accept that Nana had been correct and she should have stayed home. This was too much. What could she possibly do?

All around, people were shouting about places and objects and names that Miria didn't know. Children cried and men cursed. Most people were too lost in their own distress and panic that they paid one ten-year-old girl no mind, but that girl saw them all and heard their anguish. Miria knew she'd continue to hear them later when she was far away, safely tucked into bed. Their pain and loss would haunt her. Maybe that, too, was why Nana had told her not to go.

Eventually, Miria navigated through the chaos until she found a street where the injured had been taken, and she wandered among them, trying not to choke on the stink of smoke and their open, raw wounds and burned flesh as she searched for those to whom she might be of use. Some of the people she passed might have been dead already, or they were too close to it for any help but to be offered that relief. Others, older girls or women were already assisting with water, tinctures, and bandages.

Miria put a magical poultice on the burned arm of a man whose glazed eyes barely seemed to see her, and she gave a sip of a healing potion to a woman who could not stop coughing. Her hacking fit ceased immediately.

"What is this?" the woman asked.

"Clean water," Miria told her, for Yali had taught her that some lies were necessary, especially for witches.

Miria moved on, tending another burn victim and a woman who'd broken an ankle jumping to safety, until she found a boy near the end of the street, breathing hard. Like most of the people nearby, his face was darkened with smoke and ash, but beneath it, Miria could tell he couldn't have been more than a few years older than her. He seemed to be trying very hard not to cry, and it was no wonder. Part of his left pants leg had burned away, and the exposed skin was blackened and bloody.

Miria knelt next to him and rummaged through her dwindling supplies. "What happened?"

She meant mostly to distract him so he wouldn't notice what she pulled from her purse, but his blue eyes were shrewd when he turned to her. "There was a cat. I had to save her, but then the ceiling . . ." He closed his eyes, but only briefly. "I got her, though."

"You were very brave," Miria said. She found another burn poultice and began cleaning and wrapping his leg. She couldn't see his face while she worked, but the way the tension drained from his body as the magic took effect and eased his pain was obvious.

It was more so when he grabbed her arm. "What are you doing?"

"It's just a poultice."

"It's magic," he whispered, and Miria finally looked up. His face had regained its color beneath the grime, and his breathing steadied. But his every nerve was on alert. "I can feel my leg healing. You shouldn't do that."

Miria yanked her arm away, annoyed. "I shouldn't heal you?"

"Not here, not like that." He glanced down the street, but everyone else was lost in their own suffering. If it was stares he feared, Miria didn't see why he bothered. "Thank you, but you should go before you're caught."

"But . . ." But she wasn't tired, not yet. She had plenty of power left, and there were still so many people injured.

Something in the boy's expression and tone, though, rattled Miria's bones. His fear was contagious.

"People will not thank you for using magic to aid them."

Miria raised her eyebrow, ignoring the new tension in her gut. "You did. The people who come to the woods seeking help do."

The boy shook his head. "I did, but now I owe you. Don't you see? Those who go to the witch choose that debt. None of us here chose."

"You don't owe me anything." Why would he think she required something in return? It was true that many people paid Yali for her magic, but Yali helped many who could not.

He closed his eyes again and took a deep breath, like she was the one acting irrationally. "I do, though, and you should go before you're discovered. Don't make me owe a debt to a dead girl."

"That's not how it works," Miria hissed. But the boy had shaken her, and there were more adults walking down the street. Some man had taken charge and was directing others. Miria did not want to be ordered about by a strange man.

As if sensing her displeasure, the man turned her way. "Girl, get out of here!" he yelled, and Miria scowled.

"You should do as he says," the boy told her.

Part of Miria was starting to wish she hadn't healed the boy since he was being so annoying about it, but no. If he'd saved a cat, he deserved to be saved, too. No matter how irritating he was or how worried he was making her.

"Fine." She stuffed everything back into her purse.

Had her nana known this would happen? Had there been yet another reason why she'd told Miria not to bother?

Miria left town the way she'd come in, unnoticed amid the chaos. By the time she'd conjured a small light to guide her path through the field and into the woods, exhaustion was setting in. Perhaps she'd expended more energy than she'd realized. She hadn't felt her magic run low, but with so many people to help, so much need urging her forward, making her heedless of her own condition . . . Perhaps she'd been lucky the boy had told her to leave.

When she returned to the cottage, Yali was sitting by the hearth, just as she'd been when Miria had left, with her sewing on her lap. She might have been dozing, but her eyes opened as Miria set down her purse.

"You should wash your face," Nana said. "You smell of smoke and blood."

Miria knew she was right, so she did. But the smoke lingered on her clothes. Tomorrow, she'd have to wash them.

"How did it go?" Nana asked when she finished drying her face.

"There was a boy . . ." Miria sat by Yali's feet in front of the hearth and picked loose threads on the rug while she formed her thoughts. "He told me people wouldn't thank me for using magic to help them. He insisted he repay me later. Why? You help people all the time, and if I chose to help, then I'm not doing it to expect something in return."

Yali sighed and inspected her handiwork. Whatever she'd been working on, it seemed to be made of white rose petals and thorns, and Miria hadn't seen it before. "Many people fear magic because they don't know it. You did, if you remember."

She did, of course, remember, but she'd learned a lot since then. As always, the more she knew, the more questions she had. "You said lots of people are born with magic. Why do only witches use it? If other people used it, they would know it and not fear it."

"Because the children who are born with power, if they stumble upon how to use it, are usually taught to fear it. Magic marks them as being different, and people don't like being different, so they suppress their power, often without even trying.

And because they feel like they must suppress it, they grow to hate it."

"But people trade for magic. They want it."

"Wanting things and hating those things you want often go hand-in-hand."

In an exchange that made little sense to Miria, that statement made the least. She got up, deciding it was time for bed. Maybe Nana's words would be understandable in the morning.

Sleep didn't come easily. Her mind fixated on the horrors she'd found in town. Teary-eyed, Miria silently climbed into Yali's bed some time later. Her nana didn't complain despite Miria's hair still reeking of smoke, and she didn't give Miria any of those frustrating looks that conveyed *I told you so*, like when Miria typically did something she'd been warned not to attempt. Yali merely pulled her blanket around Miria and sang Miria's favorite song, the one about the young girl who got lost in the forest and was raised by elves who made her their queen.

"Do you have a way to find the boy again?" Nana asked when the song ended.

Miria nodded. She had the cloth she'd used to clean his wounds. It was coated in his blood.

"Good," Nana said. "You should make him repay the debt. It will haunt him until he's done it. Now try to sleep."

Chapter Nine
Three Weeks Before the Wedding

Miria opened the chest at the foot of her bed and dug through years of accumulated items that she'd held onto on the off chance they might one day be useful—a feather from a snow-white crow, wool from a lamb born during an eclipse, a blue daffodil found lying on the forest path. At the bottom, wrapped in perfectly normal wool, was a dirty cloth, browned with a boy's dried blood.

Miria knew she should not have held onto it for so long, but she never had thought of any favor the boy she'd once healed could provide that would make for an adequate repayment. Every time she'd tried, a voice in the back of her mind told her that now—whenever now happened to be—was not the time.

When Miria held the bloodied cloth today, the voice—whatever the voice happened to be—was silent. They were in agreement at last; this was the time.

Three days later, Miria headed into town. It had taken her some effort to ensure she was using the boy's blood, and not someone else's, but once she was certain, the blood had revealed to her that the boy whose burned leg she'd once healed was now a man who served in Lord Sigmun's household guard. Furthermore, she'd ascertained that the man had a name—Otto—and he spent the two evenings a week that his schedule allowed at a tavern in town with several other guardsmen.

Since approaching him in town seemed safer than approaching him while he worked at the Lord of Gawfrid's manor, Miria had waited for the first opportunity. To be extra cautious, she'd donned the petal-and-thorn shirt that Yali had begun sewing on the very evening that Miria had met Otto. It was likely not a coincidence that she'd started it then; magic rarely was. The shirt fit snugly and invisibly beneath her dress, lighter and tougher than any leather armor.

Hopefully, it was unnecessary. *Probably*, it was unnecessary. But Miria was done being surprised while she was in town.

For that reason, she ought to be grateful that Otto and his fellow guardsmen spent their free evenings at the Bloody Goats Inn, which happened to be the only tavern in Swiftdok that Miria had ever stepped foot in. That, naturally, had been Adaline's doing.

"You've never been to a tavern?" Adaline had asked incredulously.

"No. Why would I?" Miria laughed. "I try to avoid going into town, remember? Why would you *want to go to one?"*

"It sounds exciting." Adaline put down the wreath of grasses she was braiding. "My uncle's men play dice, and they said there's music at nights, and they were singing the most bawdy lyrics they learned. I think it would be fun. Just to see what it's like, of course."

Miria had to admit the promise of music was tempting, and more to the point, she loved making Adaline happy (even, when convinced as she was now, that Adaline would not find a tavern so charming in person as it was in her imagination). Nonetheless, Miria magically disguised them both one day, and they bought lunch at a tavern rather suspiciously named the Bloody Goats Inn since that was where the lord's men liked to frequent.

There was no music during the midday meal, and the fish pies and ales Adaline bought them both couldn't make up for the lack of entertainment. Adaline, however, had been undaunted.

"What do you think?" she asked, leaning across the table.

The inn was three-quarters full, but no one paid them any attention. Miria had made them look a little older, and—in Adaline's case—much plainer.

"I think I can make a better fish pie myself," Miria said. "Is it everything you hoped it would be?"

Adaline danced in her seat, realized that drew some unwanted eyes, and quickly settled down. "It's perfect. I mean, the food is barely edible, and there's no music like I hoped, but look at us. We're having an adventure."

"Doing something most people would consider completely normal." Miria laughed, but Adaline wasn't wrong. Even disguised, eating at the inn was an act of bravery. People like them weren't supposed to be here, and given a chance, many people would make sure they knew it.

"Exactly. We're not normal, are we? But it's nice to pretend for a bit."

"It is nice, but I don't have to pretend when I'm with you," Miria said. "You always make me feel much more normal than I am. I never had a friend before."

Adaline's smile froze on her face a moment as though she wasn't sure what to make of that statement. Then she seemed to come to a decision, and her smile broadened. "Well, you make me feel anything but normal, and in a much better way. Every day with you is an adventure, even if we go nowhere."

Adaline's words had done something to Miria's insides then, although at the time she'd blamed the fish pie.

Miria pressed her thumb against the pink charm on her wrist, trying to ignore the ache in her chest that memory awoke. Although the inn's physical presence hadn't changed since that day, there wasn't much else about the moment that should have reminded her of it.

The evening crowd was far less subdued than the midday crowd had been, and the inn was packed, bodies pressed shoulder to shoulder around the tables. And while there were a couple of musicians this time, no one appeared to be singing any bawdy lyrics she could share with Adaline. In truth, Miria could barely hear their instruments over the din.

Miria clung to a spot of wall near the door, and she sighed in relief when Otto finally arrived. He looked much as she remembered, though his blond hair had darkened slightly and his chin was covered in straw-colored scruff. Miria discreetly took his wrist as he passed by with three others, all of whom had the same look about them—the brash confidence of men who trained all day with weapons but who were too young and naïve to be fearsome. Miria doubted Otto or his friends had ever used the swords they carried outside of a dueling circle.

Disguised as Miria was to resemble a gray-haired woman (the best disguise for being invisible without actually casting a spell for such a thing), Otto had walked right by without noticing her. But Miria let a touch of power flow through her fingers, and it seeped into his skin. When he turned, startled, she allowed him to see through the spell and hoped he would remember her. It would make things go more quickly if he did.

Luck was on her side. Otto gasped. "You? I've been waiting for this day."

Some of the color drained from his face, further de-aging him in Miria's mind. So much for his sword and training and for her armor. He was still that boy, scared of her.

"You do not need to be so alarmed," Miria said. "But you have a self-imposed debt, and I'm here to claim it."

Otto swallowed. "I don't want to hurt anyone."

"Convenient, then, that I'm not asking you to."

A serving woman pushed by them, her tray laden with drinks and bowls of a not-especially-terrible-smelling soup.

Miria tugged on Otto's wrist. "Sit with me a moment so we aren't in anyone's way. If your friends ask, tell them I'm an old family friend," she added when she caught him glancing toward the table with the other men.

Otto put up no fight as Miria took two seats near the door and asked a server to bring them each a cup of ale, figuring a drink might soften Otto's concerns. For a moment, she considered casting a spell so they wouldn't be overheard, but she decided it wasn't worth the effort. The tavern was loud with conversations and laughter, and the closest customers were deep in their cups already.

"I do owe you a debt," Otto said. He rubbed his hands together nervously. "My leg . . . I thought I would lose it for sure, but there's not even a scar from whatever you put on it."

It had been a simple enough healing spell, placed on a clean, fresh poultice. Cheap as far as magic went. But Miria did not point this out. "I'm glad. Anyone who tries to save a cat from fire deserves no less. But now I need your help, because there is someone I'm trying to save. I know you work for Lord Sigmun. I'm sure you're aware he is hosting his niece's wedding this summer."

Otto nodded, but his expression said he was wary. "'Course. It's a lot of extra preparations and nonsense we have to deal with, but it should be a good time. I'm told there'll be extra ale and wine for all of us to celebrate."

A good time for whom, Miria wondered. Not Adaline. "I need you to explain the layout inside the manor walls and grounds, and where the noble guests will be staying."

"I told you—I'm not doing anything that will hurt anyone."

The server returned with their drinks, and Miria quickly slipped her a couple of coins before Otto could do it. The last thing she needed was him thinking he could repay her by buying some questionable ale.

"No one will get hurt," Miria said a second time, after the server had wandered away. No one directly. And not if things went to plan. "You have my word."

Otto wrapped his hands around his cup, but he didn't drink. "I'm supposed to trust a witch?"

"Trust a girl who saved your leg and maybe your life had you gotten blood poisoning. Your skin was blackened as coal."

Her words hit their mark. Otto winced. "I can still smell it, feel it sometimes in my dreams. But look, I know you helped me and others that day, but what about all the children who are going missing and dying? What do you have to say for them?"

Miria sipped her ale (tolerable) as she decided how to respond. Of course she knew the witch was blamed when children disappeared, and it wasn't a rumor she wanted to entirely dissuade. For one, she *had* helped two runaways disappear in the last year. And two, it served her purposes for the townsfolk to be wary; it always had. Miria, like Yali before her, hardly wanted everyone scouring the woods for the witch on a daily basis.

"All the children?" Miria repeated, focusing on the implication. "How many do you mean have gone missing?"

Otto shrugged and drank some ale. "I don't know exactly. I hear things here and there, and I haven't kept count. But I heard at least three cases that I can think of recently—little ones who vanished from their beds, and then turned up dead months later. Near your woods. People are saying the witch or her evil spirits dumped them there."

This was news to Miria, both what happened to the children and the rumors. It helped explain the attitude she'd seen at the funeral a few days ago.

Miria didn't like it. These rumors could cross the line from instilling wariness in people to inciting violence. She didn't have time to deal with other people's anger when she had her own to manage, and she didn't like the possibility that someone might be harming children.

Otto was looking at her curiously. He didn't entirely believe she was innocent in this, but he wanted to. Naturally. No one wanted to be indebted to a child-killing monster. "Are you saying you haven't been sending evil spirits to take their blood and souls?"

"Of course not." Stealing souls? That sounded like a tale the church would tell. Miria recalled the priests being obsessed with the idea of souls. Vaguely, she wondered whether that was considered more horrific than the stories of the witch cooking and eating the children—the rumors her brother had started. "What's this about evil spirits?"

Otto shrugged. "Some kids have gotten sick with some blood wasting disease. I've heard the kids say evil spirits come to them at night. I don't know if it's true, but something is draining their life away. There was another funeral just a few days ago."

He had to be referring to the child's funeral that Miria had inadvertently stumbled upon. She refused to believe there might have been more than one so recently.

There were no such things as evil spirits, at least nothing like them that Yali had taught her about or that Yali's books described. Miria wanted to shake Otto and convince him to stop listening to such nonsense.

But there was something . . . A memory pushing its way through the woods of her mind, clawing for her attention like a sapling for sunlight. Where had she heard children talking about evil spirits before, and was it meaningful?

Miria tried to wash down the itch in her brain with more ale. She had her revenge and Adaline's rescue to plan. She didn't have time to investigate a rash of mysterious illnesses and deaths.

And yet the itch refused to be appeased. Surely, it insisted, she did not need to spend every minute of every day until Adaline arrived making plans and preparations. The witch helped children, always. More—the current witch had young half-sisters. With her family's wealth and her father's position, they were less vulnerable than most to any nefarious business that might be occurring, but still.

If she could recall the memory, Miria acquiesced, she could spare some time to devote to this mystery. Assuming the memory was of any use.

For the moment, however, she had to wrap up this conversation. The tavern was growing more packed, and Otto more fidgety. The drink hadn't done much to calm him down.

Miria pressed her hands flat against the table's scarred surface. Otto wasn't the only one who wished this conversation to be over. The sheer number of bodies crowding the room was making it hard for her to concentrate. Miria doubted even Adaline would have enjoyed their outing so much had there been this many people then.

"If there is anything I can do about these children's illnesses and deaths," Miria said, "I will try. But in the meantime, I am still owed something by you. Will you provide me what I asked for?"

With a sigh, Otto nodded. "I'll tell you, and I hope I won't regret it."

Chapter Ten
Seven Years Before the Wedding

Miria was tending to the illusion spells on the cottage when the stranger stepped off the path and into her presence.

Engrossed as she was in the magical working, she hadn't noticed the woods shifting to allow the woman's approach. Nana had left yesterday evening on a short trip to visit another witch. She did that more often as Miria had gotten older and could be trusted to maintain whatever passed for order around the cottage. Miria was proud of her new responsibilities, and a touch nervous about them, too. What if something important arose while Yali was gone? Could she really handle it?

So when the woman appeared in the cottage clearing, Miria's veins filled with anxious excitement. That the woods had just allowed this newcomer to find her way here was interesting. The spells naturally gave way to children or women in immediate distress, and sometimes to people who had been granted entry previously. Miria wasn't sure what to expect from this woman, who appeared healthy enough and whom Miria did not recognize from any prior business, though that didn't mean anything. Sometimes Miria was gone for hours at a time, doing one thing or another on her own, and Nana didn't call for her help unless she required it.

The woman didn't see Miria immediately, and she began to yell. "You lied to me! Your trade was no good. We did everything you asked, and we got nothing! You horrible, evil, cursed woman—how could you?" She picked up a rock and threw it.

Tulip and Azalea had been around back, working on the cottage walls, but at this assault they came charging forward. Miria felt their feet pounding the dirt before she saw them, and she couldn't stop them from running toward the woman as she detangled herself from her spell work.

The woman's yelling turned into screams.

"Tuli, Aza, it's all right," Miria said, running after them.

The golems stopped abruptly, ten or so feet from the woman, who had sunk to her knees. She glanced between them and Miria. Her face was white. Her anger had morphed to fear, and her fingertips dug into the dirt. "I'm sorry," she whispered. "I did not mean . . . Please forgive me."

Miria turned to the golems. "Everything is fine. Please go back to work." While the golems did as instructed, Miria tried to think of how her nana would handle this situation, which was a challenge since her nana would not likely have been in this situation in the first place. Yali would have noticed the shifting magic and expected a visitor, but since that possibility had passed, Miria was forced to settle for the next best thing.

She straightened her back and did her best to project her nana's calm, slightly intimidating presence. She neither wanted this woman fearful nor in such a rage that she was throwing rocks.

She also had no idea why she was furious to begin with, and that seemed like a good place to start. Unless this woman had willingly reneged on whatever bargain she'd made with Yali, there was no way Yali would have given her a faulty spell. Miria could not believe that. "What happened? Tell me everything."

The woman did not stand, and she gazed at Miria with wide eyes. "The healing spell you gave to my Pipin—it didn't work. I thought he might have improved, but he's sicker than ever."

She thinks I'm Nana. For a moment, the thought distracted Miria from the woman's words. But why not? Everyone spoke of the witch in the woods, not the witches. And why could a witch not be an old crone one day and a thirteen-year-old girl the next?

As Miria saw no reason to dissuade the woman of this notion, and a few to encourage it, she pushed her confusion aside. She had to focus on the relevant issue, and that was: What would Nana say if she told her that her healing spell didn't work?

The answer came easily: She would say the recipient was not sick.

"The healing spell was good," Miria said, trusting that without question.

She could leave the matter there. If this Pipin's condition hadn't improved, the woman needed to look elsewhere. But where? Miria's conscience was bothered. People only tended to seek out the witch as a last resort. The woman must have already exhausted her options.

"I don't doubt your skill, it's just . . ." The stranger hung her head.

"It didn't work. Right." Miria wiped her hands on her tunic. "May I see Pipin? There might be more to the situation than there appears on the surface."

"Would you?" The hope in her voice scraped the very edge of Miria's nerves.

She feared she was only going to disappoint, but Miria followed Pipin's mother to one of the farms south of town, determined to do what she could.

Pipin must have been about three or four years old, tiny enough to retain his baby features but with the first signs that he'd grow into a strong, stout man. Assuming he lived. He sat on a chair by a window, wrapped in blankets, although the room wasn't cold. His pale, freckled face split into a grin when he saw his mother, but it was a tired smile.

"He gets dizzy," his mother said. "Some days, he's too tired to walk across the room. And there are these." She picked up Pipin's arm. "I didn't think to mention them when we last met, but they seem worse now. Show her."

That was directed at Pipin, and he pushed up a sleeve. Miria bent closer for a look. Although it was early afternoon and the sun's angle was poor through the window, the red dots on his arm stood out starkly, even against his freckles. They made Miria think of dozens of puncture wounds, but their placement wasn't haphazard. They trailed up his small arm in what was almost a straight line.

"How did you get these?" Miria asked.

"I think it was the monsters." He whispered, as if fearing the creatures he accused could hear him. "They come at night."

"You dream about monsters?" Miria asked. She was out of her depth for sure if that's what this really was. Nana's books and tales spoke nothing of monsters that weren't of the human variety.

Pipin nodded, and his mother elaborated. "His father and I spoke to the priest. He thinks it's evil spirits sending the dreams, making him weak. But why would they attach themselves to my boy? He's a good boy." She wrapped her arms protectively around Pipin from behind.

He squirmed in her grip, but patted her arm, trying to reassure her.

"Evil spirits are more a matter for the church than for me," Miria said, recognizing the irony in those words. The church would likely say someone like her was the *cause* of the evil spirits. It was no surprise that Pipin's mother had gone to the priest first. What stung was that Miria doubted she could do any better than the priest had.

Still, she had to try. Yali had assumed the boy suffered from some medical affliction, but since her healing spell hadn't worked, it was possible her nana had been wrong. And since Miria couldn't craft a healing spell more powerful than Yali's, she would do something very different.

"I can create a protective charm," she said. "I don't know if it will work better, but it's the only other idea I have."

So Miria took some supplies from her satchel and wove one of her own hairs into a rough but functional bracelet of nettle, rose, and a chip of quartz. It made for a rather crude protection spell, but she'd packed with healing spells in mind, and so it would have to do. Her hair would ensure the magic lasted a long time, and when the spell settled, the bracelet resembled nothing so much as an unremarkable piece of twine with a slight crystalline shimmer if held near the light. She tied it around Pipin's wrist, and instructed his mother that she could always lengthen the bracelet if needed should he find it preferable to wear around his ankle or neck.

"As long as it remains on him, it will work," Miria said. Whether it would do what they hoped, she had less confidence.

* * *

That evening, after Yali returned home, Miria told her what she'd done.

Her nana had returned carrying food, and they sat around the table, each eating a small pastry stuffed with cheeses and mushrooms that was very different from Miria's normal meals, suggesting Yali had traveled far.

"You did well," her nana said, and Miria sat straighter, pride spreading out from her chest. "There are no such things as evil spirits, so your protection charm is unlikely to do much, but it cannot hurt, and may help."

"What do you think it is then?" Miria asked. She'd been pulling a corner off the pastry to see how far the strange cheese would stretch, but Nana's praise reminded her that she was supposed to be acting like the responsible witch she wanted to be seen as. That probably meant not playing with her food. "If the boy isn't sick, and it's not spirits?"

Yali sipped her cider, one wary eye on Miria's length of cheese. "I don't know. The boy might be doing it to himself. He has magic in his blood—I noticed it when his mother first approached me—and his fear of it could make him ill. If that's the case, your charm might be what he needs—both to protect him from his own power and from his own mind."

"He has magic in him? He could be a witch?"

"Could but won't be."

Miria chewed this over literally with another bite of her dinner. "He didn't seem afraid of my magic. And if he won't be a witch, then how does he know how to use his magic?"

"Remember—I told you some children may stumble upon how to use their power by accident," Yali said. "Strong emotions can bring it out, and young children struggle to manage theirs. If he did that, it might have frightened him. Whereas if you use magic, it does not matter much to him, so he's not scared."

Miria returned to her dinner, but her gaze fell upon the jar Yali had given her years ago. It had been a long time since she had felt the need to add anything to it, but it reminded her of what Yali had said that day Miria woke up in her bed. "You told me there was magic in my anger and grief. Do all strong emotions bring out power?"

"What do you think?

Miria tried not to groan. It had also been a long time since Nana had played the *what do you think* game instead of just answering questions.

She wiped her fingers and drank some cider while she considered. After she'd impressed Yali with her actions today, she didn't want to disappoint. "I think . . . You never suggested I add any other emotions to a jar for their power. There must be a reason for that."

Yali's lips did more than twitch this time. She chuckled. "I can't fault your reasoning, but all emotions do contain power." She reached beneath her blouse and pulled out the blue charm she always wore around her neck. Miria knew it was magic, but she'd never asked what it was. "I don't usually bother with emotion magic, but a sister witch made this for me with the happiness we shared one time."

"What does it do?"

"It keeps me feeling younger than my years." Yali's smile was mysterious as she tucked it back under her shirt. "Most of our emotions will never contain enough power to make them worthwhile for magic, yet when they do, they can be very effective. Strong love for someone, for example, can provide strength or protection. Intense joy is useful for certain types of healing spells. Fear can be handy if you wish to curse someone, although a witch should never do that. And anger . . ."

Yali steepled her fingers, and glanced toward the shelf with Miria's jar. "Anger is the most potent emotion for magic because of its very nature. Anger is a sense of injustice, and injustice is the universe in chaos. When an injustice is corrected and justice obtained, that is making order from chaos. And what is magic?"

"Magic is making order from chaos," Miria said. It was one of her nana's first lessons.

The universe constantly moved toward chaos. Miria had known that before she'd met Nana. *Everyone* knew that because the church taught it. People fought against the chaos—they built houses, wove fabric, were simply born—itself an act of defiance. But wood rotted, fabric decayed, and people died. That made witches like knights in the great cosmic battle against chaos. They had special skills and the training to fight.

All of this, too, Miria had known for a while, but she was finally arranging these facts in her head, and they were not stacking neatly. "I don't understand why the church doesn't like magic when the church is also about order."

Nana let out a strangled kind of grunt. "That's because the church doesn't truly care about order; it cares about what benefits itself. Divine Order says humanity should submit to the church, that women should submit to men, that those with common blood should submit to those with noble blood, and royal blood rules over them all. Why is a woman's loose hair a sign of chaos? Why is questioning a priest? I'll tell you—because it's not about order; it's about control. Control that benefits the church and those who run it."

Yali was getting into her rant, and she stood, pacing in front of the hearth. "Anger is about justice pushing on injustice; order pushing on chaos. That makes anger the purest form of power a witch can draw on. And that is why the church tells women and children to suppress their anger, that there's something wrong with them if they act upon it. They don't want any of us to have power. Only them."

Miria wished dinner hadn't been so good. A stuffed stomach did not help her brain form clear thoughts, and Nana had given her much to think over. She'd known Yali disliked the church, but Miria had thought it was just because the church did not like witches. While that still seemed to be the case, it sounded like the reasons the church did not like witches were complicated.

Yali took a seat on the bench next to Miria, and she clasped her closest hand. "No more questions? That's unusual."

Miria hadn't realized how long she'd sat, pondering Yali's words. "I don't know where to start," she admitted. "There's so much I don't know."

She'd been feeling so proud of herself for what she'd done today, so responsible. So ready to be a true witch. But as usual, the more she accomplished, the more she discovered she had to learn. She barely knew anything—not just about magic, but about the greater world and how she fit into it.

When she admitted this to Yali, her nana squeezed her hand gently. "That's half of what it means to be a witch, child. To question everything and never stop learning."

"What's the other half?"

"To push," her nana said. "To use what you've learned as you push against the chaos."

* * *

Although Miria wondered whether Yali was humoring her when she said Miria would never stop questioning and didn't need to know everything to be a witch, she discovered soon enough that her nana had been telling the truth. It was on a crisp autumn day that Yali declared Miria had finished her apprenticeship and was ready to be initiated—as long as Miria was sure that was what she wanted.

"No one is born a witch," Nana told her. "A witch is something you must choose to be. By now, you know most of what it entails, and what this life will ask of you. If it's not what you want—"

Miria hadn't even allowed her to finish the sentence. It was all she'd wanted for years.

Her nana had nodded, clearly not expecting any other answer. "Think on your reasons," she'd said. "You will make that choice official later, but more—there is still a lot for you to learn and a lot of work ahead of you. You can't know all of it until you become one of us, so you must be willing to go forward on trust, and I know you have good reasons not to trust anyone."

"I trust *you*," Miria said. Her nana was the only person she trusted, so if Yali trusted the other witches, that would have to be good enough.

"You trust me, or my basket of raspberries?" Yali asked, but Miria could see the way Nana's lips quivered with emotion as she smiled, and she pulled Miria into a tight hug.

"Why did you become a witch?" Miria asked after Yali let her go.

It felt like a daring question, one Miria wouldn't usually be bold enough to ask.

Her nana doled out bits of her past in unexpected ways, and usually at times when Miria least expected them—singing a song she'd grown up with as they washed clothes, their attempt to recreate a cake Yali remembered from her youth because she'd gotten a sudden hankering for it, the saga of how she'd obtained her chickens when one escaped the garden (it involved an ogre, a riddle, and some magical beans, and Miria still wasn't sure if all of it had truly happened or if her nana had been teasing her). But Miria rarely got an answer to a direct question, and as she'd grown older, she'd realized that Yali possibly didn't like thinking of her past any more than she liked thinking of her old family.

Under the circumstances, though, Miria thought *Why?* might be a fair question.

Nana had been in the process of braiding grasses that they would dry over the winter, and she didn't speak until she'd tied off her current braid. The braids would be useful in all sorts of spells from cleaning to healing.

"When I was a little younger than you," Yali said at last, "a plague swept through the city where I grew up. Doctors couldn't stop it. The people said all the death must be as the gods willed it. Now, the gods where I was born are the not the same gods as we have here, nor is the church the same church—not in name anyway, but they are much the same in other ways, just as people are much the same everywhere even if they look or sound different. That church claims magic belongs to the divine, and to use it is to argue with the gods."

Nana closed her eyes as she sank into the memory. "There was one woman in town who could cure the sickness, but my family, like most people, wouldn't take her cure when they got ill. Whether they believed the church that using magic meant you were fighting the divine will, or whether they were afraid of the mortal consequences, I don't know. But I snuck out to this witch and begged for the cure for me and my baby sister, and it worked as promised. We got better. We lived. After that, I decided that if death and suffering was the will of the divine, then I had a duty to argue with the gods. No one should suffer when a person has the power to alleviate their pain."

To argue with the gods. To push against the chaos. Miria was almost sorry she asked Yali for her *Why* as the weight of the responsibility being offered to her pressed against her chest.

"Did that woman become the witch who trained you?" she asked, needing a lighter topic.

"Eventually, yes. I was older than you were when I started my training." Nana playfully brushed Miria's nose with the braided grass. "Do not look so somber. There's plenty of joy in a good argument."

If by a good argument, Yali meant there was joy in performing magic, that was true. And if she meant she enjoyed a good rant, that was certainly *also* true.

But, because Miria was curious, she had to ask: "What would happen if I said no to becoming a witch?"

"Then we would find a home and vocation for you," Yali explained, "and over time, your magic would fade like anyone else's."

And so, on the thirteenth full moon of Miria's thirteenth year, she became a fully fledged witch.

It was the first time Miria got to meet other witches, these mysterious women who Yali occasionally visited, who lived in lands she'd never seen, and spoke with accents she'd never heard before—or, at least, several of them did. A couple appeared to be as old as her nana, and one didn't look as though she could be much older than Miria herself. The rest spanned the decades between.

They were every bit as disparate in their appearances—short and tall, slim and round, some with skin paler than Miria's own and others with skin as dark as the darkest owl or sparrow's feather. Only twelve traveled through Yali's portal for the initiation, though it sounded like there were dozens more around the world. Nana explained that it took thirteen witches to anoint a new witch.

One of the witches, a woman named Sarel, had arrived two days before the others. She was tall, with olive skin, amber eyes, and a friendly dimple when she smiled. Miria took a liking to her immediately, and the feeling seemed mutual, which was a relief. Yali had explained that Sarel would be the one to perform Miria's initiation; Yali herself should not do it since Miria was her apprentice. Since Sarel was the first new witch Miria had met, she wanted to pepper Sarel with questions about where she was from, but for most of those two days she was shooed away from the cottage. Sarel was helping Yali prepare the spells for the ceremony, and Miria was not allowed to learn them until she'd been initiated.

The winter night of the ceremony was silent and frosty, and a layer of snow shimmered under the moonlight, sparkling like the stars above. The evergreen branches hung low with it as though they'd dressed in their best finery and were bowing before the group of women who'd assembled. Someone had added fragrant herbs to the bonfire, and the cold air smelled as spicy as the mulled wine Miria had been given to drink.

Yali, Miria learned, had already presented her reasons for initiating Miria into the witches' sisterhood, and this was why she'd been gone so many times over the past year. She'd told others of Miria's knowledge and skills, and—just as importantly—of her curiosity and empathy.

"Why do you choose to be a witch?" Sarel asked as a way to begin the ceremony.

After her nana's instruction, Miria had put some thought into her reply. "Because one day, another girl might be left in the woods like I was, and she'll need someone to care for her and fight for her like someone did for me."

Nana looked teary-eyed, and Miria thought her heart might burst with how much she'd grown to love the old woman. The witch she'd once foolishly feared had become the mother she'd never known.

"To be a witch is to live on the edges of society," Sarel said. "A few people will appreciate your gifts and value you for who you are. Most, if you are fortunate, will tolerate you because you are useful to them. But to others, you will never be anything but evil. And yet, a witch doesn't bend toward chaos, even though that's easier. She protects the vulnerable, she defies the tyrant, and she strives to always be a shining light in the darkness. Despite these burdens, you chose to make this your path. It's not your power that makes you a witch; it's what you do with it. Magic is merely the tool we've perfected. And now that you've made your first choice on your path, we'll ensure you retain your ability to use it."

Chapter Eleven

Two Weeks Before the Wedding

Even if she hadn't told Otto she would look into whatever mysterious affliction was killing the town's children, Miria would have felt it was necessary once she recalled where she'd first heard the story about children seeing evil spirits. She'd never heard again from Pipin's mother, so she had no idea if the boy she'd tried to help all those years ago was alive. Although she dreaded the most likely answer to that question, intuition (or, more honestly, the lack of any better ideas), told Miria that finding out was her best lead.

Her preparations for helping Adaline (and by extension, getting revenge on her family) were coming along. She had time to investigate.

It had rained most of the day, and a thick evening mist blanketed the woods, the town, and the rolling hills around them when Miria flew to the farm. The sun was beginning to set, and thanks to the clouds, the light was dimming earlier than usual.

In the fields, the farmhands hurried to finish their chores before the light was too far gone.

The scent of dinner cooking wafted out an open window as Miria knocked on the farmhouse door. Behind the sturdy wood, she heard sounds of a minor commotion and unintelligible voices. Then the door opened, and Pipin's mother stood there, looking just as Miria remembered her, though maybe with more gray threaded through her reddish-brown hair than she'd had previously.

"You?" She swallowed audibly.

"Me," Miria agreed. "It occurred to me that I never learned whether the charm I made for your son helped. I hoped . . ."

Here, she faltered as it dawned on her that the topic she'd brought up was not a casual one. There was only one outcome she could hope for, but speaking it raised the possibility of another. Miria did not believe that speaking things could magic them into being—yet another misconception Yali had cured her of—but she didn't wish to draw attention to it either. Although, if Pipin had died, then surely Miria's mere presence would be enough to pain his mother. Had she already done more damage here than she'd intended?

Perhaps she should have sought the outcome of Pipin's fate another way, but it was too late. If it came to it, though, she supposed she could make Pipin's mother forget their conversation, and let her grief fade away once more.

Fortunately, no such spells were required. A beautiful smile lit up the woman's otherwise plain face. "It did! Oh, it did. You must come in. I should have returned to thank you. Excuse my manners. Please." She gestured into the house, suddenly as flustered by Miria's unexpected appearance on her doorstep as she'd been that day she'd tossed rocks at the cottage.

"You made a trade. There was no need for additional thanks," Miria said. She was still unclear what the trade had been. If Yali had told her, she'd forgotten. All that was important was that the woman didn't believe she owed Miria anything additional.

Well, except perhaps, some information, but she'd already provided that.

But Pipin's mother was espousing dinner, ensuring Miria that she'd never eaten anything as fine as her roast, and if she would just come inside . . . Out of politeness, Miria stepped through the doorway, and she couldn't deny that the dinner smelled wonderful. But being seated with company was not only far beyond her comfort tolerance, it would be a distraction. She had to think.

Her charm had worked—why? That was the question she needed answered next, and what did that mean with regard to evil spirits and child deaths?

"The illness never returned?" Miria asked after refusing another dinner entreaty.

"No, or I should say yes." The woman rubbed her hands against her apron. "It did once, when I removed the charm you made. You see, Pip had recovered, and I thought 'Oh, the Overseer should know about this' because I'd heard of other children being similarly afflicted. But he and the priest said I'd made a mistake. Your magic was dangerous, and I should remove the charm. I confess, I allowed myself to be persuaded, but not long after I did, Pip took ill again. I'd never actually tossed the charm—I have *some* sense—so we put it back on Pip's wrist, and he's been fine since. You'll see. Pipin, come here!"

A groan came from somewhere in the back of the house. "I just got in from helping Da with—"

Pipin's voice broke off as he stomped into the room and noticed Miria. The years had changed him far more than his mother, but Miria could see the tiny boy's chubby face lurking beneath the fine layer of dirt he sported over his ten-year-old cheeks.

He inhaled sharply. "I remember you."

"I remember you, too," Miria said. What she did not remember was that his blood hummed with magic, but then, she hadn't been able to see it in others seven years ago. Nana had told her Pipin had the power, though. She recalled that much. It was possibly the reason why her protective spell had worked. And also possibly why he'd needed it in the first place. "I'm glad to see you're well."

He grinned and held up his wrist where he wore the charm. Its magical shimmer was hidden by the years of imbedded dirt that no washing could remove, and the length had clearly been added to so that it continued to fit his wrist. But just as clearly, Pipin was one child in Gawfrid Province who did not fear the witch in the woods.

The thought made Miria smile, but her mind raced. She asked a couple more question, then gracefully (she hoped) backed out of the dinner invitation again as she heard men entering the house around back.

At home at the cottage, Miria paced in circles around the central hearth as her nana had on many an evening. She'd obtained the information she wanted, but she wasn't sure what to make of it. Pipin had once said something about evil spirits attacking him as the cause for his illness, but had other children experienced the same bad dreams that he'd had, or were evil sprits an excuse the adults were using to explain what was happening? Were the evil spirits bad dreams at all? Just because they weren't real, that didn't mean there wasn't another phenomena that was being attributed to evil spirits. And aside from a mysterious illness, was there anything Pipin had in common with the children who hadn't been as fortunate to wear a protective charm?

Magic might be able to assist Miria with that last question, so she dutifully set up the scrying bowl and cast her spell. The key to magic of this type, however, was knowing the precise questions to ask, and Miria could only refine hers so much with what she knew. Children in Swiftdok, in the province, in all of Waere died often with all sorts of illnesses. Sometimes the symptoms made the culprit clear—flu, whooping cough, the poultry plague. Other times, the illness was obvious but the cause was nebulous, and in those cases, it wasn't at all uncommon for folks to blame the illness on spirits or magic or a witch.

Miria kept at it for an hour until her head began to ache too much to continue. She pushed the bowl away and realized she should eat. Without more to go on, there were far too many deaths to ever hope for her to find a pattern, and the whole endeavor was making her feel hopeless and depressed for reasons that had nothing to do with her futile search and everything to do with visions of so many tiny gravestones.

She made herself a quick and easy dinner of eggs and herbs from the garden, plus some leftover bread, and she was sprinkling salt over the eggs, courtesy of the saltcellar she'd stolen from her father, when a new thought hit.

"Are you feeling up to going downstairs?" The woman—a nursemaid perhaps?—in her father's house had asked that of her half-sisters. And hadn't the girls looked a touch wan? It could mean nothing—Miria hoped beyond reason that it meant nothing—but her sisters and Pipin did have one thing in common. They all had magic in their blood.

Miria ripped off a hunk of bread and chewed without tasting. Surely, it was a coincidence. Many children had magic in them, more than most people would believe. Just as many became sick with perfectly common illnesses. In fact, Miria didn't even know if her sisters had been sick when she'd seen them.

But it was something to think about, although it made her stomach twist with worry. Especially when her father, the

Overseer, seemed determined to hand out terrible advice to the town inhabitants, judging by Pipin's mother's reports of their conversation.

Miria finished her dinner but barely, and only because she couldn't bear to waste food. This new task she'd given herself was becoming as personal as helping Adaline was, and this development did not please her, particularly as tackling it was going to be a lot more work than she'd anticipated.

It figured that given how straightforward and simple her plan for vengeance was, the universe had needed to push her into something far more complicated to keep her on her toes. And yet, when she closed her eyes for sleep later that night, Miria could practically hear her nana's voice in her head: *The universe does no such thing, child. It's witches who push.*

PART II

THE LADY WITH THE SWORD

Chapter Twelve

Two Years Before the Wedding

Miria was searching for mushrooms, which was, perhaps, one of the more boring and tedious magical tasks that she'd been forced to undertake in a while. But there was one particular type of mushroom that only appeared around the full moons that occurred between the spring equinox and the summer solstice, and only after a warm rain, and—well, she happened to need it. Not at this very moment, but Yali's stores of it were running low, and once the window of opportunity passed, it was gone for a whole year.

Yali had planned to go foraging with her, but Miria could see she'd been tired, and so she'd encouraged her nana to do a task that required less walking and went alone. Nana tired more easily these days, and as much as it saddened Miria, it frustrated Yali more. Miria didn't know how old Yali was, but she knew it was well over a century, and she suspected humans were not meant to live that long, not even witches who knew all sorts of magical ways to extend their lives.

As long as there was something Yali could do closer to the cottage, however, it was easy enough for Miria to gently persuade her to do that rather than whatever chores required physical exertion. Gone were the days when her nana could spend several hours seated, teaching Miria how to read and do calculations, but the cottage—probably like all houses—required constant upkeep, and so did the garden and the chickens. Miria was just glad she was around to tackle the bulk of the tiring work these days.

Even when the work was as dull as wandering the woods in search of rare mushrooms.

Had Yali been with her, allowing them to cover more ground, the task might have ended hours ago, but Miria finally struck fungi gold around the time her stomach started rumbling for lunch. She'd packed some dried fish, but she ignored her annoying organ for long enough to fill her sack with the purple-and-orange mushrooms she needed. Once she had a couple of pounds worth and was debating whether to eat now or return to the cottage, she realized the forest sounds had changed.

She wasn't alone.

Miria was deep enough off the forest path that she hadn't worried about running into human visitors. She'd also lived here long enough to identify various bird calls, and she could pick out the difference in sounds between a squirrel or a mouse or a vole, never mind a larger creature like a deer or a boar. Even if she wasn't paying attention, it would be difficult for any of the forest's normal inhabitants to sneak up on her. But the sounds coming from the east definitely did not belong, nor were they familiar, and Miria placed a hand on the nearest tree, asking what it knew.

Trees did not communicate like humans, but this particular oak left her with the impression of two creatures, neither of whom appeared particularly threatening, at least not to a tree.

The snapping of twigs and underbrush grew louder and closer, and finally—grew more recognizable. Although she could see nothing as yet, Miria was positive one of the creatures was a horse. She slung her bag of mushrooms over her shoulder and headed uphill toward the noise. The girl who'd once needed help protecting herself from a wild boar was long gone. A horse—even if accompanied by a lone soldier—didn't worry her. To be safe, however, she wrapped her forest cloak around her shoulders.

The cloak was created from a beautiful patchwork of leaves—maple and oak and birch and more in every shade of green—and they were still as supple as the day Miria had collected them. But the cloak's real magic was that it could conceal her in the forest. When she wrapped it tightly and pulled up the hood, she faded from view like a caterpillar among the grass. Yali had one just like it, and the day she'd taught Miria how to make her own had been almost as exciting as the day she'd begun teaching her how to create Tuli.

Concealed in this way, Miria walked until she found, as anticipated, a horse. She didn't know much about them and had never ridden one, but even she could tell this horse was beautiful—tall, pure white, and regal. An equally expensive-looking saddle sat atop the horse's shiny coat, bearing an unfamiliar crest stamped into the leather. But that was all Miria noticed about the horse, because then a young woman appeared around its far side.

Of all the scenarios that had run through her head once she'd identified the sounds of a horse, that its companion would be a girl near her own age had never been one of them. A lost woodsman, a guard or constable searching for someone, an unfortunate traveler—they were all men. Women, especially young ones, did not go wandering the woods alone. And if they were the sort who could afford a fancy horse and saddle, they especially did not do so. Women like that did not work; they were sheltered and guarded.

If there ever had been guards or a guardian with this woman, however, they must have also been lost. The woman's face was pinched with worry. Withdrawing her cloak, Miria started forward, and the sound of the leaves crunching beneath her boots drew the woman's attention. She turned sharply, one hand reaching for the sword at her waist—yet another incongruity that Miria was only just noticing—and she gasped.

"Hello?" Miria said, although it came out more like a question than a statement. The sword was muddling her already confused thoughts.

The woman's shoulders relaxed, which was as sure a sign as any that she did not immediately assume Miria was a witch. "Hello?"

Her accent marked her as someone who had not grown up in Swiftdok, but that wasn't a surprise. Perhaps wealthy women in other parts of the country didn't behave like those in town? Miria rather doubted that—Nana had told her that rich people everywhere were the same—but it would be *some* explanation for a number of inexplicable things that started with the horse and the sword and that ended with the gleaming gold buttons on the boots peeking out from beneath the woman's skirts. Her dress, overall, was simple and cut for riding, but what it lacked in lace and pearls it made up for in quality and elegance.

Perhaps the woman's clothes didn't need much adornments, Miria decided, given her oval face was so naturally pretty. Her chestnut brown hair was braided to the side, and her wide brown eyes were framed with thick lashes. Both her lips and cheeks were red with exercise or the sun.

Miria swallowed, suddenly wondering what she must look like in contrast—a girl (barely a woman herself) wearing nothing but an un-dyed linen tunic and a man's leather leggings with a cloak of leaves draped over her shoulder. She'd done her hair in two braids down her back this morning, but wispy black curls were already breaking free around her face, which was probably covered in a healthy layer of sweat or dirt. Certainly, there was plenty of dirt beneath her fingernails. Miria never thought much of her appearance except for when she needed to disguise it, but she doubted anyone would describe her as pretty, despite Nana saying she had eyes like emeralds. A nana was supposed to say things like that.

Miria mentally shook herself. She had no idea why she was thinking about such silly things. If this woman was offended by her appearance, that was not Miria's problem. *She* was not the one clearly lost in the woods, and as such, despite the other woman's wealth or appearance, Miria had the upper hand.

Actually, that seemed like a good way to continue. It was her turn to speak, after all.

"Are you lost?" Miria asked.

The woman nodded. She appeared to be trying to put up a brave front, but her left hand gripped her horse's reins tightly and her lip trembled.

"You're a far way from the path," Miria continued.

"Something spooked Pearl," the woman said, shooting her horse an affectionate but exasperated expression. "By the time I got her under control, I had no idea where the path had gone."

"Behind you, if this is the direction you've been walking in."

"Thank you." Some of the woman's tension dissipated from her features, but then she bit her lip and seemed to assess Miria the same way Miria had been assessing her.

Miria curled her fingers into her palms, more aware of the dirt beneath her fingernails than she cared to be. "I've been foraging for mushrooms," she said by way of explanation for an unasked but obvious question. "I'm Miria."

"Oh, right. My manners. Forgive me." The woman's pink cheeks deepened in color. "My mother would kill me for being so rude, but she'd also kill me for being out here alone and getting lost and . . ." She shook herself and curtsied. "Lady Adaline of Waeremund."

Miria nearly tripped over a tree root, and Miria never tripped over tree roots. This woman was not simply wealthy, she was nobility. The only noble family in the area belonged to the Lord of Gawfrid, which meant she must be a relation. Miria should have guessed that was what the crest on her saddle meant.

"Um, I'm just Miria," she repeated.

"That's an unusual name," Adaline said. "Are you not from around here?"

"I am. It's a . . ." She stopped herself before she could say *It's a witch name*. What was a witch name anyway? Yali had told her Miria was a good name for a witch, but Miria had never questioned why. She'd liked it, and so had gone along with it. A new name for a new life. She made a mental note to ask her nana about the origin of witch names later.

"It's a family name," Miria said, figuring that was true enough.

"It's pretty. I like it. Adaline is a family name, too. We always have to be named after someone in the family. Heavens forbid one of us is allowed to be her own person." She clasped a hand over her mouth. "I can't believe I said that aloud. You won't tell anyone, will you?"

Miria laughed. "Who would I tell? If I showed up wherever you live, someone would chase me off—with a broom if I'm lucky and likely a crossbow if I'm not."

Adaline's face fell. "Probably. My mother's likely to use a broom on me if she hears what I've gotten up to."

"I promise not to tell."

Adaline grinned, and her stomach rumbled the way Miria's had earlier. "How far am I from the path?"

"Not far, but it's about a ten-minute walk because the ground is steep and footing will be treacherous for your horse. I can lead you, so you don't get lost again. If you like." Offering seemed like the right thing to do, but her motivations didn't feel entirely selfless. Adaline was interesting in a way most people Miria met were not. Probably, it was just because she was so different than most people—Miria had never met nobility before—but also the way her emotions were so plain upon her face was endearing, and something about her voice sparkled in an otherwise normal day, like the sun reflecting off a pool of stagnant water.

"I would like that very much." Adaline's expression suggested she thought Miria was as interesting as Miria found her. That wasn't especially surprising, Miria supposed. Under other circumstances, Adaline was unlikely to ever converse with the sort of person who foraged for mushrooms.

And, come to think of it, Miria's path in life had never led her to a woman who carried a sword before. She had questions.

"I'll lead you," Miria continued, "but you need to tell me how it is that you have a sword. Do you actually know how to use it? Can I see?"

Witches were supposed to be helpful, yes, but they also traded. Maybe her motivations would seem less complicated if she asked for something harmless in return. Or maybe she was just trying to justify her curiosity.

Adaline's grin broadened further. "I can. I've been taking lessons—another thing my mother can't stand, but my father approves, so she doesn't have much choice about it. It helps that I'm the youngest daughter. My two older sisters are very proper ladies, and until my brothers were born, I got to be the boy. I mean, not really, and I had to persuade my father at first, but then he liked the idea. And my mother has my other sisters to dote over, so I don't see why she has such a problem with it." She finally paused for breath. "Do you really spend all your days out here in the woods by yourself, without protection?"

Miria fought down a laugh. "I'm not as unprotected as I appear. I just lack a sword, and I've never seen a woman carry one before."

"I think it's very unfair. When I was younger, I told my father he should allow girls to join the household guard, and he told me none would want to. But obviously that can't be true. I would want to, so I can't be alone. Do you want something to eat?"

"Oh, um . . ." She was hungry, or she had been until finding Adaline had distracted her.

"Or do you need to get back to work?" Adaline asked, as though it just occurred to her that she might be diverting Miria from something else. "I'm sorry if I'm interrupting you."

"No, it's fine." Even if she'd been busy, Miria suspected she'd have given the same answer. "I picked all the mushrooms I need."

Adaline stopped and pulled a wrapped bundle out of one of her horse's saddlebags. She handed Miria a large pastry. "I brought a ton of food. I'm always hungry. Here, eat with me."

"Thank you." The bread was golden, and it smelled deliciously spicy. Miria took a giant bite out of it, and she was delighted to discover it was stuffed with well-seasoned meat that reminded her of a stew Yali sometimes made. It was much more satisfying than the dried fish Miria had brought to nibble on.

She glanced over at Adaline, and heat rushed to Miria's cheeks as she realized Adaline had not taken a bite straight from her pastry. Instead, she was breaking off small pieces and delicately putting them in her mouth. Was that how a well-mannered lady ate? Miria swallowed her most recent bite and did her best to mimic Adaline's behavior, but the piece she tried to tear didn't pull off easily, leaving her with two pieces, each too big for a single bite. She stared at them, perplexed as to how Adaline had managed to even eat prettily, until she felt the other woman's eyes on her.

Adaline was clearly suppressing her laughter, and Miria's cheeks burned hotter this time. "Honestly, you've got the better way to do it," Adaline said, and she stuffed the remains of her pastry in her mouth and tore off a chunk with her teeth. "Heavens, it even tastes better this way," she added with her mouth full.

Miria snorted, and she felt her cheeks return to their more normal hue. "I'm not totally feral, I don't think. This is just fancier food than I normally eat while I'm walking."

Since manners didn't seem to matter anymore, she followed Adaline's example and bit into one of her too-large pieces with abandon.

Adaline giggled. "My mother tells me I'm feral all the time. She doesn't say feral, though. She calls me incorrigible and barbaric and disappointing. I can't believe I've been denying myself the chance to truly act it. This is so much more fun." She dug the remaining filling out of her pasty, leaving a hollow in the bread. "What's more simple for eating in the woods? That's what these are cooked for."

Miria shrugged. "I have some dried fish. It's less complicated. Do you want to try some?" She wasn't sure why she offered when her simple meal didn't come close to comparing, but Adaline had shared food with her so it seemed only right to share her own.

"Sure." Adaline shoved the last of her bread in her mouth, and Miria dug out the packet of fish she'd wrapped this morning. She handed a piece over, wondering if someone like Adaline had ever eaten anything so plain, but Adaline's eyes lit up as she bit into it. "This is really good. Much better than what our cooks do."

Adaline's cooks had to rely on purely mundane methods for drying and smoking whereas Miria and Nana used some magical assistance. Although Miria had thought the magic just made the process easier, perhaps it did more, too. She'd never eaten smoked fish any other way that she could remember.

Adaline hadn't been exaggerating about packing a lot of food. She pulled out some small cakes next, each studded with dried fruit and nuts, and they began walking as they continued eating. Miria hoped Yali hadn't prepared lunch for her; she was too full for anything else.

"What kind of mushrooms were you picking?" Adaline asked.

"My nana calls them witch's friend, but they probably have another name." They almost certainly did.

"So not eating mushrooms then."

Miria laughed. "No. I wouldn't recommend it. Are you in town visiting someone?"

"My uncle is Lord Sigmun?" She sounded hesitant, as though unsure whether a feral woman in the woods would know who that was, and Miria nodded in assurance. "He's my mother's brother, and we haven't visited here in a few years, so it was time to come again. I don't mind, really. The capital is so hot and stuffy in the summer. It's much better being out here where there's space to run around. Not that I'm supposed to run anymore, but no one will stop me if I say I want to go for a ride, as long as they don't realize how far I'm riding."

"Which, I assume, they won't if you don't tell them you got lost in the woods?" Miria smiled and pointed up ahead where the path was now visible. Part of her had wished to conceal it, to take Adaline on a longer than necessary walk and draw out their time together. But she didn't wish Adaline to get in real trouble with her family either, and she should head back to the cottage herself.

Adaline sighed, her smile one of pure relief. "I don't know how I'd have ever found it again without you."

"I'm sure you would have eventually," Miria said. Regardless of Adaline's navigation skills, a woman her age lost in the woods was the sort of situation that would trigger one of the many protective spells Yali (and now, Miria) had erected. It might have just taken some time.

"I don't know." Adaline bit her lip. Since she wasn't local, she probably had never heard about the witch who guarded the woods. "I owe you."

"You do actually." Miria twirled the end of a braid around her fingers. "You were going to show me how you can use a sword."

"Oh, right." Adaline glanced upward through the clearing in the trees to where the sun was sliding across the sky. "Are you often in the woods?"

"Invariably."

"Then I'll do better than share. I'll teach you. I can come back every day if you want and give you lessons." Her excited expression turned hesitant. "If you'd like, I mean. I'm sure you have other things you must do, mushrooms to harvest or whatever. But you should know if you're out here by yourself. Even with other protections." She glanced around, obviously dubious as to what other protections Miria might be concealing.

Especially when she was in the woods, Miria hardly needed a sword to protect herself, but she saw no reason to admit this to Adaline and every reason to keep that knowledge to herself. Surely, Adaline wouldn't return if she knew Miria was a witch, and Miria wanted nothing more than to see Adaline again. To possibly have a friend. How long had it been since she'd spent time with someone her own age?

The question quietly shook Miria. Those she helped didn't count for much. They knew she was a witch, and they feared her, and that was fine. But it meant their company was limited and based on nothing more than need.

Adaline, on the other hand, certainly found Miria strange, but she wasn't afraid of her. She'd smiled and laughed and shared more about her life than Miria would have dared to ask. So much, in fact, that Miria felt a little badly about all she was hiding, but she told herself it was necessary. Perhaps if—no, when—she saw Adaline again, she would share more.

"Summer days are long," Miria said. "I have plenty of time to do my chores and spend a few hours each day learning how to use a sword. I'd like that."

Adaline's grin rattled something in Miria, lighting up her face and warming Miria internally. It made it all the more clear how much Miria wanted a friend. "Then tomorrow. Where should we meet?"

"Stick to the path," Miria said. "I'll always be able to find you."

Chapter Thirteen

Three Days Before the Wedding

For over a week before Adaline and her family arrived, Lord Sigmun's manor bustled with wedding preparations. Nobility and other important people from around the country would be descending upon it for the festivities, and rumors flew that even the queen herself might show. Adaline dismissed that possibility in one of her letters, but given all the activity around the lord's estate, Miria wouldn't have been surprised. As she waited impatiently for Adaline's arrival, she circled the skies above the great manor and its grounds, watching wagons filled with supplies climb the road from town and the steady stream of merchants, carpenters, and hired hands transform what was already wealth beyond measure into something grander still.

Miria did not happen to be present when Adaline's carriage rolled through the main gate, but she saw the additional livery on display when she did her early evening flyby that day, and her stomach swooped so that she felt like she was falling out of the air. Tomorrow then, would be the day their plan went into motion. She and Adaline had discussed the details in their letters (or rather, Miria had told Adaline what she'd planned and allowed Adaline to object, which she hadn't). Adaline had been as eager to flee into the woods as Miria had been to help her.

While Miria had counted on Adaline's enthusiasm, she hadn't counted on the wedding commotion, and in retrospect, she could have saved herself a lot of worrying if she had. The constant influx of people through the gate made sneaking into the grounds ridiculously simple. Miria had disguised her features and prepared a story should one be necessary, but no one questioned one more seamstress making a delivery of alterations.

From there, her plan became trickier. Thanks to Otto's assistance and some details Adaline had filled in, Miria knew where to find Adaline's rooms inside the manor demesne, as well as the fact that Adaline's activities were being heavily monitored. Apparently, she'd already made one unsuccessful attempt to run away. The only thing that surprised Miria was that Adaline hadn't gotten farther before she'd been caught.

No matter. Miria would ensure that Adaline's second attempt would be successful. What they would do after that, she hadn't put as much thought into. That Adaline would stay with her, having vanished seemingly into thin air, until after the wedding was obvious. No one would think to look for Lord Sigmun's niece at the witch's cottage. Adaline would be spared her matrimonial fate, and Miria's family would be humiliated and cheated out of their promised prize. But later?

Miria told herself that would be Adaline's decision. She certainly couldn't expect that Adaline would wish to continue staying with her. A lady, even one as terrible at it as Adaline, was used to luxury and servants and expensive meals. Miria had nothing to offer but a cozy cottage, a clay golem who handled the hard labor that magic did not, and some magical chickens.

And, well, her heart. But Adaline carried that wherever she went. Her physical location wouldn't change anything.

Miria swallowed past the anxiety these thoughts raised. She'd already dwelled on them for too many nights leading up to this day. Now was the time to focus on the task at hand. If she couldn't sneak Adaline away without being caught, she would have a whole new set of worries to fret about.

After entering the demesne through the servants' entry, Miria ducked into the first secluded corner she could find and cast the same spell that she'd used to sneak about her father's house a few weeks ago. She needed to conserve her power for the magic she intended to cast on Adaline, but while disguising herself as a seamstress was good enough to get her this far, a place she was reasonably expected to be, she'd next be entering parts of the house where she very clearly did not belong.

Mostly invisible, Miria navigated her way through the maze of rooms, hoping her memory and Otto's directions wouldn't fail her. She made it to the hallway where she believed Adaline's rooms were located without incident, and she was feeling confident about her success until she saw the guard by the door. That was to say, the guard himself wasn't precisely a problem. Adaline had warned her there might be one. The unanticipated wrinkle was that the guard appeared to be slumped over, asleep at his post.

Miria couldn't say why this made her uneasy as otherwise entering Adaline's rooms undetected would have been more of a challenge, but it was unexpected, and unexpected things were never welcome when a witch had plans.

Biting her lip with trepidation, Miria unlatched the room door and slipped inside. The guard didn't stir, although he let out a great snore.

In addition to guards, Adaline had also warned Miria that there might be an attending lady or two in her room on babysitting duty, so she suppressed the urge to call out Adaline's name while she took in her surroundings. The air was scented with perfumes—the same notes of honeysuckle and lavender that Adaline used to favor predominated, but they mixed with florals and spices that were less familiar to Miria's nose. Beyond the scent and all the fond memories it evoked, the room was furnished in gold and pale blues with a comfortable seating area, vases filled with an assortment of freshly cut flowers, and a small table and chairs. On the table was a tray of tea implements and a plate stacked high with pastries.

There was also a woman's head. Her eyes were closed, and her lips hung partly open.

Miria held her breath for a moment, creeping around the table for better angle, until she saw the woman's chest rise and fall, and then she exhaled with a cringe. It appeared whatever fate had struck down the guard outside also had affected Adaline's finely dressed companion, and that suggested . . . Miria darted past the dozing woman into the bedroom.

The room was empty. Adaline was gone.

With a groan, Miria dropped to the opulent bed and ran her fingers over the silk brocade coverlet. Not only was this unexpected, it wasn't the plan. This was, rather, the plan freefalling out the third-story window into what should be (based on the Miria's map) an interior garden below.

Inside the satchel Miria carried, along with her spell supplies, was a change of clothes for Adaline. The almost-invisibility spell Miria had used on herself wouldn't work on Adaline since it depended on people not expecting to see the invisible person. So Miria had planned to disguise Adaline as a servant—another seamstress-for-hire—with plain clothes and an altered face.

Then together, with Miria scouting the way to the servants' stairs, they would walk out of the manor just as Miria had come in. No one, Adaline had assured her, would question people leaving. It had been so simple once Miria had realized all she'd needed to do. Only now . . .

Miria shook her head, torn between amusement and annoyance. She'd known Adaline was impatient to leave, but she couldn't have stayed the entire day? Had she really needed to stick a sedative in the tea? Whatever she'd done, it hardly mattered. Miria needed to know whether she'd escaped the manor grounds on her own or if she needed assistance.

"Oh, Adaline," she muttered under her breath, taking a quick search of the room. It would be handy if Adaline had left a note or a clue, but Miria didn't see anything that looked likely and she wasn't sure what she might be searching for. It wouldn't make sense for Adaline to leave anything that someone else might stumble upon.

She checked the small writing desk, beneath the bed pillows, and every flat surface she could find. As Miria's fingers trailed over the back of a chair, her gaze skimming the clutter of perfume bottles, brooches, and barrettes scattered atop the dressing table, she found something else interesting.

Miria's brow furrowed as she picked up the gold necklace. Seven delicate pink sapphires sparkled from the rose-shaped pendant, and tucked among them—masquerading as yet another jewel—was a charm. Also a pale pink, it was indistinguishable from the sapphires at first glance. For someone who was not a witch, it was doubtful they would have noticed it. Exquisite craftsmanship had gone into its creation, ensuring it blended in seamlessly with the real jewels.

It was very unlike the charms Miria wore around her neck and wrist, charms she hadn't even thought to shape into more than vaguely spherical lumps.

Where had it come from? Who had given it to Adaline and why? What did it do? Miria had so many questions she didn't hear the sound of the woman in the other room stirring until a chair scraped over the wood floor.

Despite being nearly invisible, Miria instinctually stepped away from the open doorway and backed herself around the far side of the enormous four-poster bed. Her fingers were still wrapped around the pendant, and she slipped it into her satchel so she wouldn't forget to ask Adaline about it later.

"My lady?" The woman sounded groggy, which was no surprise, and she half stumbled into the bedroom, apparently having discovered the sitting room was empty.

Miria breathed lightly, trusting her magic but only so far. If she bumped the dressing cabinet or rustled the bed hangings, it could draw attention.

"Oh." The woman made a few unhappy noises. She spun around and even checked beneath the bed. Not finding Adaline, she nervously picked at the pleats of her yellow skirts.

Miria only stirred when the woman retreated into the other room, and she heard the door open.

"You! Get up!" A grunt followed, and Miria peeked around the doorway. The woman was shaking the sleeping guard. "Lady Adaline is missing. What have you done?"

"What?" The guard shot to his feet, shaking his head as though he could shake off the residual effects of whatever Adaline must have drugged him with. "Why are you asking me? You were having breakfast with her."

"I was napping," the woman snapped. "I'm permitted to do that. You're not. I'll alert her family. Go search the house and grounds for her. Be quick."

Miria sighed. If it was to be a manhunt, she hoped Adaline had a good head start. It wasn't as though the lady didn't have plenty of experience running away from her uncle's estate, but

Miria was fairly certain she'd never attempted it under these conditions. Just to be safe, though, once the door closed and Miria was alone, she rummaged through her satchel.

It was just like Adaline to throw all of Miria's plans off course.

Chapter Fourteen

Three Days Before the Wedding, Continued

A witch, Yali had once taught Miria, would be wise to always carry some basic spell supplies with her: a means to heal, a means to harm, a means to hide, and a means to figure out which of the aforementioned options was the most prudent.

Miria was more grateful than usual for that advice, though neither healing, harming, nor hiding were currently among her objectives. Scrying, however, had multiple uses, and she unwrapped a small circle of highly polished silver from the enchanted silk she used to store it. It was less convenient than Yali's glass scrying bowl, but far more portable.

She had no doubt she needed to move quickly. Even if she had time before anyone returned to Adaline's room, she was racing against men who knew the demesne and all the assorted buildings on the manor grounds far better than she did. The need to conserve her power by using a more involved but elegant spell warred with her need for expediency and brute force, and expediency won out. Miria found a light brown hair tangled in Adaline's comb and wrapped it around her hand. She pricked a finger and smeared a drop of blood over the silver, muttered the proper words, and focused on Adaline's hair.

The blood vanished from the silver's surface, revealing Adaline with a furtive expression on her face. Her hair was hidden beneath a deep blue hood, and a cloak that would only be considered plain to someone of her wealth was draped around her shoulders. The room she was in was sparse and poorly lit from high windows, and Miria couldn't fathom where she might be until Adaline crept in farther. Weapons were neatly stored along the wood wall in front of her—swords of varying sizes, mainly, as well as polearms sporting a variety of wicked blades to her right.

It was an armory then; Miria should have guessed, though she'd hoped Adaline had simply made a dash for her freedom. Her odds of success seemed like they would have been higher without entering one of the rooms in the estate mostly likely to be occupied by the people searching for her, but then, perhaps that was the very reason no one would think to search there.

In all of Miria's scheming, she hadn't scoped out where the lord's armory was. Clearly, that had been poor planning when her friend was so enamored of stabby metal objects. Miria couldn't blame her too much, though. In Adaline's place, she wouldn't want to run and hide in the woods for days without her satchel of basic spellcasting supplies. Girls and women, be they witches or ladies, deserved to protect themselves.

Unfortunately, this was going to cost Miria something extra. Adaline didn't appear to have company, which meant time remained in which they could escape without being noticed if they were fast enough. The plan wasn't lost yet.

Miria drew on more of her power, her fingernails digging into her skin as she angled the silver toward the window so that it caught the sunlight. "Take me to her."

The gleam of light that reflected off the metal shivered once, then it rose into the air, hovering inches from Miria's face. No one would be able to see it but her, but she still had to navigate to the armory unseen, which meant she couldn't drop the illusion spell she wore either.

"Lead the way," Miria commanded the light, and she hoped the magic would sense her intentions and take her on the least populated path rather than the most direct.

Aside from a brief run-in with a very perceptive chambermaid who caught Miria's reflection in a mirror, screamed, and ran, Miria made it out of the demesne undetected. She was a little uncertain as to the consequences of the maid's reaction, but if all went well (that seemed optimistic given nothing else had so far), she would be long gone before the woman could talk about visions of ghosts in the mirror.

Despite her pounding heart and every instinct screaming at her to do the opposite, Miria strolled across the grounds outside like she deserved to be there. After all, the spell worked by making people see what they believed should be present, and someone who seemed like they belonged would therefore go unnoticed. To Miria's relief, Adaline must have left the armory, because the light led her to the lord's stables.

Like the armory, they were mostly deserted. A couple of stable hands leaned against the outside of the building, sharing a drink, and they paid Miria no mind as she slipped through the doors. Inside the building was cooler and smelled of horses and fresh hay, and Miria found Adaline immediately, no light required any longer. She dismissed it with a flick of her wrist as she dashed over to her friend.

Adaline startled at the sound of feet, and she spun around with guilt plastered over her face. It melted away in an instant, replaced by such joy that Miria's heart skipped a beat.

"Miri!" Adaline half whispered, half screamed, abandoning the saddle she'd been buckling to Pearl and charging over.

Miria allowed herself a moment of relief and comfort and dizzying happiness. She buried her face against Adaline's neck, melted into her warmth and breathed in the honeysuckle and lavender scent of her perfume. In some dark, anxiety-plagued recess of her heart, she must have worried that after two years, things would have changed too much between them. That her attempt to rescue Adaline would satisfy her need for vengeance but not her other, less bloody, needs. That her body would no longer respond to Adaline's like it used to, and worse—that Adaline would no longer wish it to.

It was a fear that not even talking to Adaline a month ago could allay. There was just something different about breathing the same air, about touching each other's skin. But Adaline's arms around her were fierce, and when she finally let go to touch Miria's cheek, her eyes shimmered with tears.

"I missed you." Miria wasn't sure which of them said it first, and it didn't matter. All that mattered was that they were together again.

"We need to leave," Miria said at last. She could have stood here, pressed against Adaline and reveling in her closeness forever. "The plan . . ." The plan had neither called for Adaline stealing a sword nor taking her horse, but here they were. The sword, Miria could work with. The horse was something else.

Adaline's eyes opened wide as she guessed something was amiss by Miria's expression. "Did you not get my last letter? I wrote that I wanted to take Pearl with me."

"You wrote? No." Miria shook her head. "I didn't get any letter."

Adaline swore. "No wonder you look so confused. You must be furious with me. I thought that since you hadn't written back, you were fine with everything, or if there wasn't time for that, you could write to me once I arrived, and—"

She cut off at the sound of the stable doors opening.

"Everyone in the house is searching for you," Miria whispered, ducking low. "I can't disguise you *and* your horse."

But perhaps that didn't matter anymore. Voices behind them rose in alarm. Adaline had been spotted.

Amid cries of "There she is!" and "My lady, what are you doing?" and variations thereof, Adaline finished attaching Pearl's saddle. A sinking sensation in Miria's gut told her the plan was about to veer even more wildly off course than it already had.

Miria could hear the guards running toward them, and Adaline swung herself onto Pearl in what Miria was certain was not an appropriate fashion for a lady, even one in riding skirts.

She stretched a hand down in Miria's direction. "Come up here with me."

Miria didn't move. Adaline had tried teaching her to ride two years ago, and she had not been a fan. And since all attempts at subterfuge were gone, she saw no point in subjecting herself to discomfort when she had a better means of traveling.

Miria shook her head. Her friend bit her lip, ignoring the men who were entreating her to return the manor immediately where her family was worried for her, banquet preparations were under way, and other such pleas that were cast aside like dust.

Seeing as Miria wasn't budging, Adaline finally snapped her attention to the guards. "I'm going for a ride. You can tell my parents that."

The most authoritative looking of the men, one who had a slightly fancier uniform than the others, stepped forward through the stall's open door. "I'm afraid it's your father's orders, my lady. You do not have his permission to ride today. Please come in, and you can discuss it with him."

Adaline let out a scream of frustration. "I am so tired of men telling me what to do." And with that, she took off through the stable, sending the surprised guard stumbling out of the way.

In the confusion that followed with the men shouting orders at one another, Miria crouched farther out of sight and shifted into her owl form. If the guards had noticed her at all while they pleaded with Adaline, once she was out of sight, she was out of their minds. Cries were going up around the stable, and Miria heard one of the men announce they would stop Adaline at the manor gate.

Not if Miria could help it.

Miria took flight, bursting through the open barn doors and circling the building until she'd adjusted to her new vantage point. Below, the bustle around the grounds had taken on a sense of urgency. Word was spreading faster than Miria would have thought possible, and Adaline was charging for the gate.

Which was closing.

Miria swore to herself. She had to keep the gate open long enough for Adaline to pass through. Had to keep the guards who were already on her tail from catching up. Neither of these things were ones she could do in her owl form. She needed magic, and it would not—could not—be subtle.

In her haste and with her preoccupied mind, she landed gracelessly on the grass outside the manor and returned to her normal form. The illusion spell was gone—she couldn't maintain two such magic-intensive spells at once—and people yelled out in surprise and fear as the witch materialized nearby. (To be fair, many people were already yelling thanks to Adaline's commotion.) Miria didn't have time to worry what the ones who'd seen her might do; she merely hoped that none of them aimed a crossbow her way.

First, the doors. Miria raised her hands, calling on the wind, and it answered readily. Too readily. Nature was always eager to lend itself to magic, but Miria needed this gust to be contained and refined—enough to make it too hard for the guards to close the gate but not so much that it stopped Pearl from racing through the opening. Wind whipped her hair and clothes about her as Miria grasped the very air itself, directing and focusing it. The gate, which had been almost shut, was flung wide. Miria thought she could hear a horse wailing, but the sound could have come from any number of horses.

Just a little longer, she thought, struggling to keep the wind focused. Then Adaline charged through the gate, her face buried in Pearl's mane to shield her from the wind.

With relief, Miria dropped the spell, but she had no time to rest. Adaline had spotted her, and Miria waved her on down the road toward town and the woods. Guards were following. The ground rumbled with their horses' hooves as they pounded closer. Miria had to stop them, preferably without anyone getting hurt, and she didn't have much time to think about how. Her body was growing weary with the strain.

An illusion to distract the horses? She had the supplies for that, and while she didn't have the power left to disguise or hide a moving target, she could create something static that blocked Adaline from the guards' view.

But as Miria wracked her mind for an idea, new cries were rising from the manor grounds. "It's the witch! She bespelled Lady Adaline!"

With a shock, Miria realized some of the guards were not coming for Adaline at all. They were aiming for her. Whatever good ideas she might have conjured if given the time to think them through fell to the wayside. She had to act quickly, so Miria called forth the first illusion she could think of that would accomplish everything she needed.

She set the grounds and the manor on fire. Fake flames erupted from the grass, the gate, from every direction. Horses and humans alike screamed, and chaos descended upon the area for real. Despite the fire having no heat or substance, it swept through the crowds, consuming everyone's attention and causing all to flee.

Miria wrapped herself in the fake fire, disappearing into the flames and escaping those seeking her. Adaline, she hoped, would not turn around and come racing back in fear. If she turned at all, Miria hoped Adaline would be able to guess what Miria had done and thus keep running. She held the illusion as long as she felt able, knowing she was far from finished with magic for the day. Once the confusion sounded as though it were dying down, Miria took to the sky again, and the fires vanished as quickly and painlessly as they'd appeared.

Miria didn't look back. Her owl's eyes sought out Adaline, and she kept pace above once she found her heading into the forest. Adaline wisely hadn't stopped, and she finally slowed only as the woods closed in around her, easing Pearl into a trot. She brushed the horse's head and whispered encouragement while she checked over her shoulder to see if she'd been followed.

Miria dropped to the ground and shifted back.

"Miri!" Adaline dismounted and ran toward her, and Miria leaned into her embrace but only for a moment. "You're trembling. Are you all right?"

Miria lifted a hand, dismayed to discover Adaline was right. "I've been expending a lot of power. I need to rest."

"Well, we're in the woods," Adaline said, wrapping an arm more sturdily around Miria's body. "We're safe, aren't we?"

"Not yet. We must get to the cottage. Your uncle's household knows I'm involved, and they'll look for you here. I can hide us, cut them off from the path."

"All right." Adaline wiped road dust and sweat from her forehead and helped Miria over to Pearl. "But you should ride. I know you're not a fan—" she interrupted Miria's protest "—but you need to conserve your energy. Let me walk."

There was logic to that, much as Miria disliked it, so she allowed Adaline to help her onto the saddle, and she led the way to the cottage. What she would do with a horse there, for however long Adaline stayed, that was another question entirely.

Miria's mind drifted on the journey, but she pushed the worry about Pearl aside. She had more pressing issues to contend with. Since the original plan was no more, her work had compounded. The lord's niece being abducted by the witch was not an action that would go without consequences. Even those who believed Adaline might flee were unlikely to believe she might flee in that way. People were already claiming Miria had bewitched her.

Part of Miria didn't mind. In some ways, her revenge was all the more satisfying if her family knew the witch was behind the disappearance of Hans's bride. They might not know their relationship to the witch, but such a happenstance might force them to remember their history of dealings with the witch and the little girl they chose to abandon. Perhaps a touch of guilt would flavor their anger and their fear for Adaline's well-being.

On the other hand, the Shadow Wood would soon be crawling with guards from Adaline's family. From the cottage itself, Miria could keep them hidden, but although it would be easier there, it would still tire her. She would need rest eventually, and a lot of it.

But until then . . . She glanced down at Adaline, who chose at that moment to glance up, and Adaline's smile was radiant. She was covered in dust, her hair sliding out of its many pins and sticking to her cheeks, and tiny worry lines creased her forehead. But she looked beautiful and more—alive in a way she hadn't truly appeared in the visions Miria had scried of her. It was as if when she'd fled her uncle's manor, she'd escaped some of those invisible chains of propriety and duty that were dragging her down. She looked—finally—hopeful.

Miria knew beyond a doubt that she couldn't bear letting her leave again. She might not have used evil magic to get revenge on her family, but just as surely, the repercussions of this plan would end up hurting her as badly as the magical blowback would have done if she had.

Because how could Adaline ever stay?

Chapter Fifteen

Two Years Before the Wedding

Miria had half expected that Adaline wouldn't return to the woods, promised sword lessons or not, but she'd shown up around the same time every day for the past week, save for yesterday when her aunt and uncle had been entertaining guests.

"They had an archery competition set up for the boys, but of course I wasn't allowed to participate," Adaline was saying as she popped another raisin in her mouth. "I had to spend the entire day with the ladies. I mean, it wasn't all bad. We sang and played piano, and I like that. But then my grandmother brought out embroidery, and I was reminded how rubbish I am at it."

"You should have told her she'd be more impressed by your archery." Miria smiled as she adjusted her grip on Adaline's sword.

She'd led them to a clearing near a small stream. Tall pines and firs surrounded them, and the ground beneath was carpeted in lush, fragrant needles. It was a favorite spot of Miria's. Between the scent of the trees and sweet trickling sound of the water, it felt almost otherworldly, though unlike some other spots in the woods, no magic had gone into its creation.

Adaline grinned. "I did say something like that, and you should have seen the look my mother gave me. It would have frozen molten steel. Here, pull your shoulder back a touch."

Adaline's hand was gentle on Miria's arm, but that didn't stop the prickling sensation on her neck or nervous flutter in Miria's stomach. The sensations were annoying and distracting, and they'd come more often over the last few days. Miria would have thought they'd go away as she and Adaline became closer and grew more used to one other, but the opposite seemed to be happening. Sometimes, she felt them just by thinking about her new friend.

"I don't see why I'm supposed to be good at embroidery just because I'm a woman," Adaline continued. "I can sing, I can dance, speak three languages, and I can shoot straighter than half the men in my father's guard. Seems like that should be enough for any one person to be considered skilled. There, that's better. Now run through your forms."

Adaline removed her hand from Miria's arm, but the heat from her touch lingered. Miria ignored it as she demonstrated the parry and block techniques Adaline had showed her. The sword was lighter than she'd expected, but it grew heavy in her hands after too long. Adaline had initially been surprised by how strong Miria was, but Miria supposed that was because Adaline didn't spend much time with girls and women who were accustomed to manual labor. Still, Miria didn't have the proper muscles for swordsmanship since she'd never needed to use them that way before.

Miria ran through the exercises twice, then Adaline picked up her arms and repositioned her again. Miria's pulse picked up as well. She only half listened as Adaline maneuvered her body into positions that didn't feel at all natural. Adaline's face was so close. Her cheeks were so smooth and pale, her lips so pink, and her eyes so kind. They reminded her a bit of Yali's eyes in that way, but only in that way. How was Miria supposed to concentrate when someone like Adaline was touching her?

Clearly, that was the issue. Miria wasn't used to touching anyone except her nana. She wasn't even used to talking to anyone for so long except her nana. But Adaline could talk and talk, filling Miria's head with stories of a life Miria could scarcely imagine—the capital in all its enormous glory, and dramas involving people who Miria would never meet but that made her laugh anyway. After five days of conversation, Miria had learned more about what life was like for a woman of Adaline's station that her previous eighteen years had ever taught her. None of it affected her in the slightest, yet she hung on every word.

"It's good I don't need to rely on this thing," Miria said after several more minutes. She dropped her arms and let the sword swing toward the ground.

Adaline was watching her with an intense expression, and Miria hoped she wasn't offended by her less-than-careful consideration for the cherished weapon. But Adaline wasn't looking at the sword, she realized. She was staring at Miria, and Miria shifted self-consciously.

She often wondered what Adaline truly thought of her, the feral woman living in the woods. Of course, she hadn't actually said she lived in the woods, but it had to be obvious. Then there was the way Miria dressed. It wasn't that Miria didn't know how to dress the way a normal woman her age did—Yali had made certain of it—it was simply that she wasn't used to it and didn't care for the less practical clothing.

Nor did she own more than a single "town-ready" outfit (as her nana called them). She had a proper shift and overdress, both of which she could alter with little glamour spells that required scant effort if she needed to, but Miria had worn those clothes twice and used magic on them once. That had seemed more than enough. Adaline couldn't seriously expect the sort of woman who wandered the woods by herself to own more clothing. So rather than continue to wear her "good" outfit, by the fourth day Miria had decided to stick with her normal linen tunic and leggings. They were less heavy, making them more comfortable in the heat, and easier to move about it in when practicing with a sword. Besides, Adaline had already seen her dressed that way on the day they'd met.

But whether Adaline commented on Miria's strange appearance or not (and so far, she'd opted for not, though how long her silence would last worried Miria), she'd definitely noticed. This was not the first time Miria had felt Adaline's gaze fall heavily on her, although the only words Adaline had ever spoken about it was to say it must be nice to have so much more freedom of movement. When Miria had pointed out that Adaline's clothes were much prettier, Adaline had laughed and twirled her skirts about, admitting that she did love a pretty dress. That had led to her describing the glorious green silk her mother had bought to make Adaline a dress for her eldest sister's upcoming wedding, and the matter of Miria's clothes had been dropped.

Adaline jumped up and took the sword from Miria, their hands brushing a moment, then she stuck it in the sheath. "You would get better with practice, I promise."

Miria made a noncommittal noise. "Like you and embroidery?"

Adaline let out a scream and clasped her hand over her heart. "How dare you! I thought you were a friend."

"I'm just surprised you don't like it." Miria laughed. "It involves repeatedly stabbing fabric over and over with a pointy object."

"Do not think my sister, Dagna, didn't try to encourage me by using that same line. It also involves something like visual artistry, however, which is a gift I do not seem to possess. One of the *few* talents I appear to lack, that is. I can't be expected to be perfect at everything." She flung her braid over her shoulder.

"It would be unfair to the rest of us if you were good at everything."

"Precisely." Adaline stuck her hands on her hips. "Embroidery is my sacrifice for the sake of every other lady's pride. But since we've discussed my faults, I demand to know what yours are."

"I think mine are clear—I will never win a swordfight."

Adaline scowled through her laugh. "I set you up for that easy answer, didn't I? Fine. What are your talents?"

"My talents?" Miria's brain raced, searching for a way to deflect and alter the direction of the conversation.

"Talents," Adaline said, undeterred. "And do not say foraging for mushrooms or I will challenge you to that swordfight."

"Harsh." Miria spun around, seeking inspiration, something she could say that was neither a lie nor the truth.

A tiny, reckless corner of her heart toyed with the idea of saying "magic," partly to see Adaline's reaction and partly so she could stop hiding her true self (such behavior didn't seem conducive to friendship), but Miria knew better. Adaline might tolerate her being strange, given that Adaline was a bit strange for a lady herself, but witches were something else.

"The forest," Miria said at last. "My talent is knowing the woods. I can identify every bird call and every tree, every leaf. I know where the best wild berries grow, how to beckon the fish to my traps, and I could find my way through these woods if you blindfolded me."

Magic, naturally, helped with all of that, but even without it, Miria knew these woods better than anyone save Nana. Her answer was true enough.

Adaline was uncharacteristically silent a moment, seeming to contemplate this response. Then she nodded slowly. "That's a good talent, useful. Is that how you've managed to stay hidden in the woods so long? I mean, not that I think you're hiding, but you've never told me you live in town or what you do or anything really. I swear, I don't think you're a fugitive. Unless you are and want to tell me a secret? I won't tell anyone. I read a story once about a group of thieves living in the woods much to the north of here. They were led by a knight who was wrongfully accused of some great crime by the crown, and they would rob the rich travelers passing through and give the money to the poor, until he fell in love with a noblewoman, and . . ." She paused for breath. "Have you heard that one?"

Miria shook her head, which was something she would have done even if she had heard this tale, seeing as it had distracted Adaline from her initial questions. "What happened?"

"Oh, he courted her, and she fell in love with him, but before they could figure out how to run away together, her brother found out and set a trap. The knight and all his fellow thieves were killed or captured, and the magistrate seized everything they had stolen from the townsfolk and left them even more destitute. Then he married the lady himself." Adaline frowned. "It's a horrible story. I wish I hadn't thought of it."

"Truly!" Miria raised her hands in despair. "Why would you share that? You need to read happier books."

Adaline rolled her eyes. "I'm sure it was given to me to teach me some kind of lesson."

"Obviously no falling in love with men you find in the woods."

"I am quite certain that won't be a problem." Adaline affixed the sheathed sword to Pearl's saddle and turned back to Miria with a sly expression. "What about thieves, though?"

"I wouldn't advise that either. They're completely untrustworthy and could steal your heart."

"I mean," Adaline said, "are you a thief?"

"Oh." Heat crawled up Miira's neck. She was almost positive the logical thread in this conversation had broken. If she tugged on that thread, it sounded like Adaline was suggesting . . . Miria pushed aside her confusion and the warmth it stirred. "I promise I'm not a thief."

"Good to know."

"I'm something far worse."

Adaline's face lit up. "A spy? A murderess? A heretic?"

"A wild and uncivilized woman."

Adaline clapped her hands together. "My favorite kind."

* * *

Adaline left that afternoon while the sun was high, and Miria returned to the cottage to begin dinner. She'd picked up fresh cream earlier, and that plus some early shoots from the garden and her cheerful mood, put her in the mind to bake Yali's favorite savory pie to go along with the fish she'd caught.

Her nana raised an eyebrow when she saw Miria stirring the thick cream sauce, but she said nothing until they sat for dinner. "I thought you were going to practice the portal magic today."

Miria blinked. She had meant to do that this morning. The portals that allowed witches to travel long distances were complicated spells that required regular maintenance. Miria had learned how to cast them, but that didn't make her proficient at it.

"I'm sorry." She lowered her head. "I lost track of the time."

"You don't need to apologize to me, child. I've just never seen you so distracted before."

Miria dipped her bread in the sauce and swallowed. "It's nice to have a new friend, but I won't forget my responsibilities."

"It's good that you don't," Yali said. She poured herself more of the elderflower wine before continuing. "I don't mean to discourage you being friends with this girl, but you must remember who she is. You've tried so hard to remove yourself from your old life, from the world outside these woods, and that's partly on me. I encouraged it."

"I'm not *completely* feral," Miria said, unsure if she was trying to convince herself or her nana this time.

Yali snorted. "Not completely. Possibly you're too sheltered to be so. Lord Sigmun's niece might be a lovely girl, but she's connected to powerful people, and powerful people are dangerous. Especially for outcasts like us."

The *I know* danced on Miria's tongue, but did she? Had she been too glib with Adaline earlier, joking about who and what she was as she tried to make Adaline laugh?

Nana seemed to read something of these thoughts, because she nodded. "You are so different from the girls in town, and even more different than Adaline. I'm glad you became friends despite that, but you must be prepared for the likelihood that your friendship won't last, through no fault of your own. I don't want you to be hurt."

Miria swallowed. Her nana did not want to specifically remind Miria of the pain when those you cared for—and who you thought cared for you—abandoned you. The warning, however, was clear, and she'd be wise to heed it.

"And I do not want to accidentally bring harm or unwanted attention to you by being careless," Miria said, also choosing to avoid the subject directly. "I'll be careful. I promise."

Unfortunately, promises, like plans, were sometimes impossible to keep.

* * *

Miria tried for as long as she was able. She made Adaline a tea to ease the discomfort of her monthly bleeding and didn't tell her that magic was one of the ingredients. And once, when Pearl got a hoof stuck in a tangle of unfortunate thorny plants, Miria discreetly healed her injuries. But one day Miria went to meet Adaline along the forest path and discovered she wasn't alone.

Adaline had followed Miria's lead as best as she was able, and she'd taken to dressing in more simple attire. For the past week, she'd abandoned her lady's fine riding dress, opting instead for an undyed linen underdress and a drab bodice and split skirt—an outfit even plainer than the one Miria wore into town. She told Miri she'd secretly obtained the clothes because they made it easier for her to sneak away from her uncle's manor and she no longer had to explain inconvenient things, like mud stains, to anyone. With her perfect posture, soft hands, and fancy braids, Miria thought Adaline managed to make her clothing appear regal regardless, but it was true that no one would guess she was the Lord of Gawfrid's niece from a simple inspection.

And surely that was why two men who could not be more than a few years older than Miria had the audacity to be heckling Adaline on that day.

They both had axes slung over their shoulders, and their shirtsleeves were rolled up as high as they could go. Patchy stubble covered one's chin, a reddish brown that made his face appear dirtier than it was. The other was taller and thinner, with a gangly look that years of swinging an ax might or might not cure. There were no logging sites nearby, which meant they'd run off from wherever they were supposed to be.

"Did you steal that horse?" the taller one yelled at Adaline. "No way a girl like you owns it."

"And the sword," said the other young man. "What's a girl doing with a sword?"

"Think if we took 'em back, someone might reward us nicely for them, yeah?"

They'd crowded around Pearl, making it difficult for Adaline to continue riding, at least not if she didn't wish to hurt them, which she clearly didn't. Not yet. "Move along," she snapped, her voice laden with the weight of her station.

"Move along." The shorter boy imitated her tone and snickered.

Miria studied the two for a moment longer, searching for any potential resemblance to the face of a brother she barely remembered and deciding there was nothing of her own in theirs. Surely then, neither of them could be Hans.

She stepped off the path, letting her cloak slip across her shoulders as she did. Adaline was busy kicking away the taller of the boys who'd made a grab at Pearl's reins, but the shorter man nearly jumped out of his skin as Miria seemed to appear out of thin air. He cursed and took a step backward.

"She said move along. Now go." Miria's voice lacked Adaline's casual authority, and she knew it, but she also knew hers carried a different sort of power. Especially in the woods, hers was a voice of a witch in control of her domain.

The shorter, red-haired man, the one whom she'd startled—sensed that power immediately. He rubbed the back of his ruddy neck nervously and didn't move closer, yet he still eyed with her suspicious hostility. His friend was more oblivious or too interested in harassing Adaline to notice anything strange about Miria. He did, however, stop making a grab for Pearl's reins long enough to turn his attention Miria's way.

"What is this?" he asked, spitting on the path. "Upside down day? We got a girl with a stolen sword and another girl dressed like a boy."

"Miri, be careful," Adaline said. Pearl had a clear path to break into a run, if Adaline needed to escape, but Miria knew Adaline would never leave if she thought Miria was in trouble. She would stay and prove she knew how to handle her sword.

Miria nodded to indicate she heard Adaline, then she pointed down the path in the direction from whence Adaline had been riding. "Leave."

The short man neither moved closer nor moved to follow her directions, but the taller one laughed. "This your forest to go around bossing people about?"

"Yes, it is actually."

Tall Man shoved his companion on the shoulder, nudging them both closer to Miria. "You don't even got a sword, girl. You can't order us around just 'cause you're wearing clothes that don't belong to you." He tapped his fingers over the handle of his ax. "Maybe someone's looking for you *and* her?" He motioned toward Adaline.

He was getting close enough that Miria could smell the stink of sweat and old beer on his clothes, and her pulse quickened as she realized her dilemma. It would be so easy to make them not merely leave, but run, but to do so would require revealing more to Adaline than she was supposed to.

The sound of boots hitting the path directed Miria's attention to Adaline. She'd jumped off of Pearl and was pulling her sword from its sheath. "If you think I don't know how to use this, you're mistaken," she said.

"Is that so?" Apparently the shorter man thought this was funny enough that however unnerved he was by Miria, he was able to grin. No, *leer* through his snickering. "I do like a girl who knows how to handle a man's sword."

The other man clearly thought that was the height of wit, and they shared a laugh that made Miria's hands curl into fists.

"What about you?" he asked, turning to Miria. "You know how to wear a man's clothes, but do you also know how to work a man's sword?"

He snaked an arm over Miria's shoulder, and Miria decided she'd had enough. Adaline wasn't going to be able to intimidate these men by brandishing the sword, and while she was good with it (in so much as Miria could tell these things), Miria didn't know how she'd fare against two men armed with axes if it came to actually trading blows. Nor did she want Adaline to experience the trauma of finding out, regardless of the outcome.

Just as importantly, one of the men had touched her, and she did not like it one bit.

"I said LEAVE." Miria summoned her power to her fingertips and tongue, calling upon the trees to aid her.

A crack reverberated around the treetops, and a large branch dropped from above. It landed between the two men, mere inches from them both, sending them each shouting as they scattered backwards in alarm. Miria sliced through the air next, calling on the wind, concentrating it, focusing it—easy in her anger—and the gust knocked them both to the ground. Dirt, pine needles, and leaves landed on them like a burial shroud. The men scrambled for purchase and found none as the wind shoved them another ten feet down the path, their bodies careening over roots and loose stones.

Miria heard Adaline cry out behind her, but as she'd already gone this far she saw no point in leaving the job half finished.

"Conceal us," she whispered to the forest.

And the forest did. The fog rolled in from all sides. The trees seemed to close in around her, Adaline, and Pearl. The breeze hushed and the woods creaked, the men's muffled grunts and groans were swallowed by the silence. Then Adaline's horse made a sound of fear, and that told Miria she needed to stop. There was nothing left for her to do anyway. The men were gone.

Miria lowered her hands, and only now that the threat was gone did her heart start to pound. Now she had to face Adaline.

How did she explain this? Did she assure Adaline the men would be fine, if a little bruised and scraped? That they'd lick their wounds and likely concoct a fantastic tale that painted them as heroes to share with their friends over cheap beer? Did she lie to Adaline, try to make her disbelieve the evidence of her own senses? There were spells she could cast to help her forget.

No, she couldn't do that. Not to a friend. But she had to say something, so Miria turned, wishing she had a spell to help her craft honest but acceptable explanations or excuses. Ones that would appease and not frighten Adaline.

She should have known better.

"Are you the witch?" Adaline asked.

Miria gaped at her. Adaline had never given any hint that she'd heard about the witch in the woods. Miria hadn't even thought word of the witch would ever reach the lord's manor.

"Is that a bad thing to ask?" Adaline rushed on. "Do you not like to be called a witch? What about sorceress or enchantress—are those better? Please don't be angry at me! I already suspected it, but I didn't know how to broach the subject, and what you did was amazing. Like something out of a story. Truly. Can you show me more magic?"

"Um," said Miria when Adaline paused for breath. "Are you all right? Did those men harm you before I arrived?"

Adaline stared at her a moment as though she'd already forgotten the men. "Oh, those wretches. Yes, I'm fine if you are. I don't care to think more about them. Honestly forget *them*. Tell me about *you*. Are you the . . ." She trailed off, allowing Miria to fill in her preferred term.

Miria took a deep breath. As often as she'd wished she could tell Adaline the truth, she'd never imagined how she would do it. It wasn't something she'd allowed herself to seriously contemplate. "Yes, I'm the witch. A witch anyway. I didn't tell you because I didn't want to frighten you."

"You didn't. Don't." Adaline belatedly seemed to realize she was holding her sword, and she re-sheathed it. "I mean, I've heard stories about witches being awful, hideous old women who steal blood and eat babies, but you've never been awful, and you're not hideous or even old, and you eat just like I do. You've never given me any reason to be afraid. So once I started to suspect, I realized that if you're the witch, then the tales I've heard must be wrong." Adaline drew a deep breath. "Which is hardly surprising. You should hear the nonsense people say at court; they'll lie about everything if they have something to be gained by it."

In spite of everything, Miria's lips twitched. Yali would, no doubt, warn her to be very careful, and she ought to impress upon Adaline the need for secrecy, but Adaline's excitement was infectious—as it usually was. In this moment, Miria had a hard time worrying.

"You're nothing like I heard a noble lady would be," she replied. "I suppose we can't believe everything people tell us."

Chapter Sixteen

Two Years Before the Wedding, Continued

Miria had never had anyone to show off to before, and she quickly discovered that her delight in Adaline's admiration for her magical skills was surpassed only by Adaline's delight in seeing them demonstrated. Adaline gasped, clapped, and screamed with unrestrained enthusiasm for spells Miria had come to think of as mundane, and her heart swelled with every exclamation she elicited from Adaline's lips.

She knew she ought to keep her head about her and be discreet, but she'd never had an audience so willing to be pleased. Encouragement and compliments from Yali were different somehow. Miria wished for her nana's approval, but Yali's appreciation was couched in her mentorship and it grew Miria's confidence in her skills. She liked pleasing Yali because her skill was a reflection of her nana's skill. Likewise, thanks from the townsfolk and farmers for her assistance were different, too. Miria required no such praise from them, and their fear often made them loath to give it. Still, she liked helping them because helping people was a good thing to do.

She liked pleasing Adaline because . . . She liked Adaline. Making Adaline happy made Miria happy. She would lie in bed at nights thinking of new ways to accomplish it.

Not all those ways were magical. Sometimes it was as simple as making her favorite cake to share or picking Adaline a bouquet filled with the colorful flowers that only grew in the cottage garden. But her other thoughts tended toward magic—spells that wouldn't simply impress Adaline but delight her. A tea Adaline could take with her to relieve her monthly pains, a charm to place beneath her pillow to ensure sweet dreams, a needle that would guide her stiches and help with the dreaded embroidery. Miria would have cast any spell Adaline requested, but Adaline never asked anything of her that way. All she wanted, she said, was to spend the rest of her days with Miria, and there was no spell to make that possible.

Today, Adaline had brought Miria another book of stories for her to share with her nana, and that meant Miria wanted to share something equally exciting—showing Adaline how she could fly.

She kept her flight short so as to not unduly tire herself, and she shifted back to her human form as her feet touched the ground. For once, Adaline made no sound as Miria demonstrated her spell; she sat motionless, her eyes wide and jaw hanging slightly open.

"An owl?" Adaline said at last when Miria took a bow. "That is the most amazing magic you've shown me yet. Can you change into anything else?"

Miria shook her head. "The spell allows for only one form. Once it's cast the first time, that is all."

"That's . . ." Adaline jumped off the log she'd been sitting on. "I can't actually say it's disappointing because it remains anything but." She sighed. "I wish you could teach me spells like I've been teaching you how to fight."

"I wish I could, too," Miria said, meaning it. "But it's a rare talent. My nana says it's about as common as having blue eyes."

"Which neither of us have." Adaline bit her lip. "Though yours are such a pretty green, like the moss after it rains. Mine are just a dull brown, like my hair."

The compliment made Miria flush, although she couldn't say whether it was at all accurate.

"Your eyes are a beautiful brown. They're the color of honey." And large and kind and . . . simply breathtaking. As was Adaline. Miria wanted to say all of that, but she couldn't bring herself to form the words, so she switched the topic. "You need not covet magic when you have so many other skills."

Adaline blew a strand of hair out of her face. "But not enough skills until my embroidery impresses my grandmother."

"If that's your concern, you shouldn't worry. I don't think magic would impress your grandmother either. Even those who benefit from what it can do fear it often as not. There's a reason why I live in the woods rather than in town."

"That's unfair. It's ridiculous. Rude." Adaline kicked a twig and sent it flying into the underbrush. "Why can't we be allowed to live our lives how we are? You should live wherever you like and be compensated for your skills and the work you do to help people, and I should be allowed to follow my own interests, whether that's music or dueling or embroidery."

Miria understood the sentiment, but upsetting Adaline was the opposite of what she'd been aiming for with today's demonstration. "You don't need to get worked up on my account. I like living in the woods, and I have no need for much money."

"But it's not fair that you're denied the choice," Adaline said, not calming down in the least. "None of us are allowed choices.

We're told that the world is supposed to be a certain way, and we must all twist and mold and shrink ourselves to fit it. And I realize I say that as someone who has luxuries that many people would kill for, but I am not immune to those pressures. My cousin, the queen, is not immune. Her entire purpose in life is to produce royal babies, and perhaps she likes that purpose but perhaps not, and she will certainly enjoy every comfort while fulfilling her duty, but the point is that it doesn't matter whether she likes it or not—*she had no choice.*"

Miria said nothing, for she hadn't ever considered that a queen's life might be chosen for her in much the way Miria's life had been chosen when her father had abandoned her. Or more so really. Miria could have died in the woods if she'd been unlucky, but ultimately, she'd chosen to become a witch. Perhaps she'd been given more freedom and power than a queen.

Adaline had no trouble filling the silence. She pulled her sword from its sheath and swung it as though she were doing battle with an invisible enemy. "You are the only person I can even express my frustration around. If I object too strongly at home, no matter what the reason, I'm scolded for my tone." Swing went the sword. "A lady doesn't raise her voice." Thrust. "A lady doesn't contradict her superiors." She returned to her starting stance. "*A lady* does not indulge in something as base as anger." Swing again. "Or wish for violence." Thrust. "She just puts up with whatever shit life throws at her, apparently." Adaline jabbed a killing blow into the forest floor.

"My nana told me that society doesn't want women to indulge their anger because there's power in it."

"My power is supposed to be in my station," Adaline said. "In my ability to control and manipulate those around me. That is what a lady does."

"It is a form of power."

Adaline retrieved her sword. "Yes, to be fair. But it's also restrictive. Sometimes I just want to scream, too. Or stab something. It all comes back to how we're denied choices."

"Well, you have choices here," Miria said. "Here, you get to be in control. What would you do if you had all the choices in the world?"

Adaline sheathed the sword, and she froze abruptly. "That's the thing—how can I know? I've been exposed to so few options. But I would tell you what I would *not* do." She stuck her hands on her hips.

Miria couldn't help but smile at her change in attitude. "And what's that—embroidery?"

Adaline snorted. "Yes, true. But also I would not be married off for the most suitable offer."

Something dark and unpleasant twisted inside Miria's gut. Some part of her had known that would be Adaline's future, but she'd managed to avoid thinking of it. Avoidance, however, was one luxury Adaline was denied.

"Would you marry at all?" Miria asked, and then she mentally smacked herself for probing a path that only left her feeling poorly.

Why was she feeling this way? (She knew why.) But why had it never occurred to her to think so much about this topic? (She knew that, too.) It was because there was nothing she could do to alter this fate. To be a witch was to push, but a witch could only do so much. Adaline would leave at the end of the summer, and Miria might never see her again. To even hope for more than she had now was silly; it was setting herself up for pain. Her nana had warned as much.

"I might marry," Adaline said, interrupting Miria's unwanted thoughts. Her mood shifted again, her face taking on a dreamy expression. "If I could marry whomever I chose, which I cannot. So I guess, no, I wouldn't marry. But if I could choose anything, then I would choose to change what makes marriage impossible. Then it wouldn't matter that I wasn't like the other women I know. It wouldn't matter that I don't think about kissing men like they all do."

Miria realized she hadn't breathed for a moment, and she slowly let out her air. "All? You know me, and I have never dreamed about kissing a man."

Adaline's gaze sharpened, and heat crept up Miria's neck from the way Adaline watched her. "Never?"

"Honestly, I never thought about kissing anyone until . . ." Until just now. Just now, when it had occurred to her to think about kissing Adaline, and Miria's pulse took off at a sprint, leaving her lightheaded.

"Until?" Adaline pressed with increased intensity, and suddenly, like magic, she was standing so close. Miria didn't understand how it happened.

"Until today when you started me thinking about kissing," Miria said, which was truthful, if not the entire truth. She was half a breath from taking a step back, from fleeing as though her life depended on it. But she couldn't. Her feet were rooted to the ground, and her heart felt tied to Adaline's. If she ran, it would tear from her chest and she'd collapse.

Adaline must have sensed her warring needs. She reached out and touched Miria's bare wrists, further locking Miria in place. Her terror abated slightly, but her blood only raced faster.

"Who are you thinking about kissing?" Adaline asked. "Me?" Miria couldn't form words, but she didn't need to. Adaline frequently had words for them both, and Miria had never been so grateful for it. "I've been thinking of kissing you since the day you rescued me when I was lost."

Miria drew a deep breath. The woods were alive around her, but all she could see were the way Adaline's eyelashes curled, the smudge of dirt on her left cheek, the pink of her lips. Her nose was filled with the honeysuckle scent of Adaline's skin and hair, and she heard nothing but the way the blood pulsed through her ears. Outwardly, she couldn't move because her insides were flying.

"You can, you know," Miria said once her mouth worked again. "If it's not beneath a lady to kiss a mere woods witch."

She expected some quip from Adaline, but Adaline, for once, abandoned words. She released Miria's wrists and cupped her cheeks instead, drawing their faces together until together was all Miria knew.

Miria closed her eyes, and the sensation of flying did no justice to the swooping and rushing feeling that coursed through every part of her, but it was the closest comparison she could make. The first time she'd lifted her wings, felt the earth fall away beneath her, felt her body catch the air and the giddy joy of weightlessness—it was much like that. Miria coasted high above the trees, only she was not weightless at all this time. She'd never been more in her body, attuned to every sensation, every tingle, every bit of heat and magic spreading through her.

I would change what makes marriage impossible, Adaline had said, and Miria wished for that power. Not that she could ever marry Adaline, a woman like her—a witch and an outcast who was happiest covered in dirt. But to have the possibility available if they'd met under other circumstances . . .

The church said marriage was reserved for men and women; any other combination defied the Divine Order. Miria had never thought much of it. As a witch, her very existence supposedly defied the Divine Order, so why should she care what the church thought about anything else? But now she couldn't help but recall the way Yali always fumed over the convenience of the Divine Order being whatever served the church and (occasionally, though less importantly) the crown.

"Recall," Yali had once said a few years ago, "the church says the Divine Order means men should have power over women, and so if

women could join forces with other women instead of men, men and the church would lose their control over them. Any time someone with power says 'Divine Order' ask who it benefits. It's always about the powerful maintaining or increasing their power."

"Or money," Miria had added, feeling like she understood this.

"Money is a form of power," Yali had said.

The memory flashed through Miria's mind in the half second in which Adaline withdrew her lips, leaving Miria a swirling tempest of emotions. Elated and furious, she barely knew what to do with herself.

Then Adaline smiled uncharacteristically nervously, and it was so charming that Miria was compelled to throw her arms around her and kiss her again. Adaline laughed when their lips parted this time, and it was Miria who felt shy.

Adaline tucked the hairs that had fallen from her braid behind her ears, but she did not step back. "Do not take this the wrong way, but I need to correct you on one thing."

A bit of the swooping sensation returned to Miria's gut, but in a less pleasant way than it had a moment ago. "Did I do that badly? You're an excellent teacher, and I would be happy to have more lessons."

Adaline pretended to look shocked. "What are you implying? Do you think I have so much experience kissing other women?"

"I wouldn't say for sure, but you certainly can't have less than me."

"That's fair, seeing as you are a bit of a hermit. But." Adaline held up a finger. "I was not about to critique your kissing, although I am happy to keep practicing with you. What I was going to say was that I object to you calling yourself a mere woods witch. You deserve a better title."

Relieved that she deserved no critique and with the promise of more kissing in the future, Miria relaxed again. "I'm afraid titles are reserved for people like you."

"An informal title," Adaline said, "given by me, so it's the only sort that counts. I hereby name you Miria, daughter of Yali the Wise, second Witch of the Shadow Wood, Sorceress of Gawfrid." She solemnly pressed her palms to Miria's cheeks and kissed her forehead. "What do you think?"

"It's catchy. Perhaps I will make myself a family crest."

Adaline grinned. "As long as you don't ask me to embroider one for you."

Chapter Seventeen

Two Years Before the Wedding, Continued

The summer solstice arrived that year with less excitement than it usually held for Miria. All four of the year's solar holidays and all thirteen of the lunar ones were busy times for a witch. Each marked an occasion that was favorable for a different type of magic, so on the solstices and the equinoxes, Miria and Yali would be up earlier than normal, preparing, casting, or tending the necessary spells.

But even if Miria could sneak away for a few hours, she wouldn't see Adaline today anyway, for the Lord and Lady of Gawfrid always graced Swiftdok's town solstice festival for a few hours in the morning to toss coins and gifts at the townsfolk before retreating to their manor where they celebrated the holiday in whatever extravagant fashion nobility did. Afterward, the town continued their celebrations without them, with music and dancing, and the customary sweet treats and costumes.

Miria didn't remember much of it from her "before" time, but after the day's spell work was completed, she and Yali would make an appearance each year (disguised, of course), and discreetly hand out small spells to those who seemed most in need, as was customary for witches. A sprig from an apple tree for the girl who needed help getting over a broken heart, a tiny wreath of tansy blossoms to temporarily take the pain from an elderly woman so she could dance for the day, an egg from one of the magical chickens that would fill the belly of a hungry boy for a week. These were relatively small magics, created or collected over the course of the preceding year (or, in the case of the egg, the preceding day).

Miria typically looked forward to all the festivities, but this year, a day without Adaline's company felt less exciting. Still, the larger magical workings she and Yali had cast had gone well, and now that the sun was well past its zenith, there was nothing left to be done but to enjoy the holiday.

Miria set the plates filled with the traditional cakes and piled high with sweet strawberries and fresh cream on the table. Nana had been sorting through the spell trinkets they would take into town, and she pushed the remaining items toward Miria.

"Are you not planning on carrying any of them this year?" Miria asked, grabbing a strawberry. The weight would be nothing, not even for someone as old as Yali.

Her nana stretched her legs out. "I do not think I'll go into town this year."

Alarm washed over Miria, her good mood swept away in an instant. "Are you feeling all right? Should I stay, too? Do you need anything?"

Following the alarm was guilt, like thunder followed lightning. She'd been spending so much of her spare time with

Adaline lately when obviously her nana needed her. What kind of witch—what kind of *daughter*—was she?

Yali shook her head and swatted away the concerned hand Miria laid on her wrist. "I'm going to see a friend, or rather, a friend is coming to see me. You and your friend have made me realize I should see my own more often, too."

Miria was silent a moment as Yali blotted up some cream with her cake. She sensed there was more to it, but not whether pressing the matter would result in any knowledge. Nana always fussed when Miria fretted over her.

Sensing her concern, Yali sighed. "The point of having an apprentice is so I may offload some of my work. Yes, I'm old and my feet tire more quickly than they used to, but that's all the more reason to give you more to do." She cackled. "You do not need me to go into town and hand out gifts, and I do not need you hovering. Go, and maybe you'll find your friend."

"She won't be there," Miria said, picking at her food. "They'll have returned to the manor by now. And I don't hover! I just want to be helpful. I've been neglecting you."

"You are helpful, but you are also young and very sheltered here. You deserve to live a little, too. We see each other for the greater part of every day, child. You don't need to feel guilty about spending time with other people."

Was there some magic Yali had yet to teach her about reading people's mind and emotions, or were hers so clearly written over her face? Miria flushed. "If you truly don't require me here, then I'll go into town."

Nana nudged Miria's dessert until the bowl pressed against her hand, an admonishment to eat. "I require you to go into town so I do not have to. Is that better?"

Miria rolled her eyes, but she speared another strawberry with her knife. It would have to do.

* * *

It seemed everyone in town had taken the day off of work to celebrate, but logically that couldn't be true. Certainly, the doors to the inns and taverns were thrown open to entice patrons with drinks, and the bakers had spent untold hours concocting sweet cakes and pastries to sell to the revelers. The farmers in their fields and the men and women who served the wealthy continued to toil, as well. Around the main market square and the town green, it only looked like a giant party if one didn't look too hard. It was those people, along with the ones too poor to indulge in strawberry cakes and peach tarts and raspberry-filled donuts, into whose pockets and hands Miria slipped spells as she detected need.

She'd nearly emptied her satchel of gifts and had already begged off two boys asking her to dance when she paid for an ale and leaned against a stone bridge to rest. Streamers on the trees flew in the wind, and a band nearby played a danceable tune. Even the tiny boats in the harbor, visible below from her perch, had colorful cloths flying from their masts.

"Well it just seems wrong." A woman's voice caught Miria's attention, and she glanced left to where a group of three women walked arm-in-arm. Older than her, though far younger than Yali—Miria assessed them quickly. Something about the speaker's tone warned her of trouble. They were dressed in the plain clothes of working women, much as Miria was, but with bright gold scarves tied about their heads like solstice crowns. They began to cross the bridge in Miria's direction.

"What is she to do? Neglect her other children?" asked a second woman. "It's the solstice. Let them enjoy what they can of it."

"The girl's been missing for only two weeks," the first woman said. "If my daughter was taken by the witch, *I* would not be out two weeks later, buying my other children treats."

"Seems unfair to the other children who deserve a bright spot." That was the third woman.

They moved on, the discussion continuing much the same way, never realizing the witch was right there, frowning at them.

Miria sighed, though not because she was being blamed. Another child who'd run away possibly, but not toward the woods and to help. Or possibly, another child who'd died under who-knew-what circumstances. Miria would hope for the former option. That one did not guarantee a tragic ending.

Miria finished her ale and followed after the women into the thick of the revelry. Their conversation had reminded her of a reason to be in town for the day—learning news. The witch did not get involved in town gossip or pay attention to politics, but her time in Adaline's company had started to make Miria see there might be utility in learning more about the world beyond the Shadow Woods's borders. If nothing else, it seemed wise to know what the townsfolk were thinking about her.

She hadn't gotten far with this endeavor before a group of rowdy dancers, who'd clearly drank a bit too much, jostled the passing crowd. In the commotion to get out of their way, a young man bumped into Miria's side.

"I'm so sorry." He placed a strong hand on Miria's arm to steady her.

"It's . . ." The *fine* withered on Miria's tongue as she took in his features. The high cheekbones and light brown hair that shone golden in the sun—those were common enough among the population. But the strong nose and tilt of his brow were familiar, and his eyes . . . There was no way around those eyes. Miria had never spent much time examining her own appearance until Adaline had burst into her life, causing her to think of such frivolous things, but she'd stared at her own reflection enough over the last few weeks to recognize her eyes in this stranger's face.

Only this man was no stranger, was he?

Surprise was all that kept Miria from blurting out her brother's name. She wasn't sure she even could. The combination of vowels and consonants, sounds that she'd once clung to in her childish love as she'd yearned to see her brother again, were not sounds she'd spoken aloud in years. As the memories had faded and her pain had grown duller, so too had her desire to acknowledge him or dredge up any of the past. To say Hans's name out loud was to muddy the peace she'd made internally.

But now that he was here, looking at her, not recognizing her (she couldn't blame him for that; it had been her goal when she'd disguised herself), Miria found that her internal peace was more fragile than she'd believed. It shivered and dissolved like the glassy surface of pond water, muddy emotions bubbling to the top.

"Are you all right?" Hans asked, and Miria realized she'd stared a touch too long.

She struggled to compose her face, to shove all the mud back beneath her surface. "Apologies," she said. Then, before she could stop her tongue, she added, "You look very familiar. Do you have a sister?"

Miria immediately wished to take the words back, but something inside of her needed to *know*. To know he still thought of her. To know he regretted not saving her. To know that she could, at last, let go of all the pain and resentment and rage that she'd stored inside Yali's magical jar over the years. A shared burden was all she needed to release it for good.

All Hans had to do was look sad and show remorse. Admit he missed her. It didn't seem like a large ask of the universe.

Yet the universe—her brother—did not oblige.

"I did," Hans said, and he didn't sound sad, just surprised.

Miria gave him the benefit of the doubt. It must be a most unexpected question. But surely, he would show something more akin to regret next.

"The witch stole her away, years ago," Hans continued.

A lie, but perhaps that was the way he remembered it. And hadn't Yali said her father could speak the truth of the matter to no one? Perhaps Hans had been taught to conceal the truth. Miria would overlook this, too.

"I'm sorry to hear that," Miria said after a moment. One ought to say something, even if she was the witch who recognized the lie. To not do so would seem strange. And besides, she wanted Hans to keep speaking until he gave her what she craved.

"It was a long time ago," her brother said, and rather than sorrowful, he seemed unconcerned. Dismissive of her condolences. "I tried to save her from the witch and her horrible oven, but I was only a boy. In the end, it might even have been a kindness. She was not a very useful girl—always daydreaming, very stubborn and willful. My father would not have been able to accomplish nearly so much with her underfoot and causing trouble."

He uttered a few more excuses and platitudes after that, but Miria didn't hear them. Her heart pounded, and the fury that had simmered into a mild heat with age reignited into a wildfire, the sound of which drowned out the commotion of the solstice festival around her. It burned hotter and brighter than the sun on its longest day.

She shouldn't have asked, but how could she have not when she'd asked for so little? Just a hint of regret and sadness; that was all. How could he not even spare a single drop of concern? What had happened to the brother who used to sneak her extra bread, who'd whispered stories to her in the dark when she was frightened, who'd held her hand tightly as they'd entered the woods that fateful day?

How could he have turned into their father? Callous. Compassionless.

But then, how could he have not done so when it had been just the two of them for the past thirteen years? When their father, alone, had been allowed to mold him into the man he'd become?

For thirteen years it had been the two of them, and the one wish spell bought by her life.

If Hans had regrets that day, if he'd later begged their father to return for Miria, how long might it have taken for Yali's magic to distract him from his pain and soothe his heart? How long until he agreed with their father that the trade had been worthwhile?

Not long, she realized. Not long at all. He might pretend he'd tried to save her that day, but he hadn't waited for her. He'd ran and saved himself, and left her behind without a backward glance. In the years since, she'd mostly forgotten. And "her horrible oven"—what did he even mean by that? It was lies piled onto lies.

Miria was burning from the inside out. Power was building under her skin. She hadn't come close to losing herself in rage for years. Not only had time healed her (only temporarily, apparently), but she'd grown up. Eighteen-year-old women did not throw tantrums like five-year-old girls did. More to the point, nothing had challenged Miria's self-control in such a way in years.

She'd been happy, but only because she'd been able to forget. And in forgetting, some part of her had been able to cling to scraps of a delusion.

Miria stormed through the crowds who were descending upon the town green, her hands curled into fists at her sides as she struggled to hold in her power. She had no recollection of how she'd ended the conversation with Hans, and that was as it should be. If only she could have no recollection of him at all. Her skin felt hot, and sweat beaded on her neck. The last time she'd felt so feverish, Nana had tucked her into bed and given her magical tea to drink. But she was not sick this time, not in the same way.

Miria made it through the town gates and trampled partway through the wildflower field toward the woods before she let out a scream. Power rushed out on her breath. She had no means to capture it here, no way to save the magic and stuff it into the jar on the cottage shelf, and it rose up on the wind.

The sky rumbled. Dark, heavy clouds churned out of nothingness. The temperature dropped, and the light dimmed as the sun vanished behind the growing storm. With a louder crash and a flash of light, the clouds unleashed their rain. Fat, cold droplets smacked Miria on the head and turned the field to mud beneath her feet.

It cooled her, too. Smothered the fire in her blood, though not completely. Just enough that she could breathe again. Think. Do more than rage.

The storm didn't let up for her entire walk home.

* * *

Yali didn't chide Miria for summoning a storm, though Miria was certain her nana knew what she'd done. A storm like that was not natural, after all. But chiding was not Nana's way, and perhaps she knew that it would only further foul Miria's mood.

Neither of them spoke of the incident until that evening. Miria was tired from the long day and all the spells she'd cast in the morning, and mostly she was worn down because anger was exhausting. She had enough power left in her for one more spell, though, and she was determined to cast it this day—one of the most powerful days for magical works—before she crawled into bed.

Yali's friend had left hours ago, and her nana sat before the hearth, taking advantage of the longest day's light to make annotations in one of her many books. She looked up as Miria took her jar of emotions from the highest shelf and carried it over to the table, marking her page but not yet inquiring as to Miria's purpose.

Ever since Yali had shown her the blue charm she wore around her neck, Miria had been intrigued. Over the years, she'd peppered the older witch with questions about how to create such a thing, and after her studies, Miria was convinced she could do the same.

Her goal was simple: if she wore her rage and her pain around her neck, she could never forget. With a tangible reminder that would burn her when she touched it, she would never feel so caught off guard—so utterly shocked—by her family's betrayal again.

This charm that she would create would have a practical purpose, too. If she couldn't forget, she would be less inclined to lash out when she was reminded of what happened. No more letting her power get away from her. No more unintentional storms.

The spell was not complicated, but it did drain the last dregs of Miria's remaining magic. She would sleep deeply tonight, despite her troubled mind.

"It is cruel to yourself to carry so much pain around with you," Yali said as Miria held up the red stone. "But perhaps is it not unwise."

Miria had the grace to blush. "I hope I didn't ruin your outing with your friend."

The charm glowed faintly in her fingers, like there was truly a fire inside it, and its heat seeped into her skin. She could feel the fury and pain churning beneath the smooth surface—strong enough to remind her, muted enough to ignore if she wasn't focusing on it.

Her nana waved off her concern. "It was only water. Will you make a bead of it, so you may wear the magic?"

Miria nodded but found she was too tired to attempt even such a minor spell. "I'll do it tomorrow."

"Here." Yali held out a hand. "Let me do it for you."

"I can do it."

"I know you can, child. But let me. And you can come sit with me and read me some poetry."

Ah, so that's what this was. Miria smiled. She handed the charm to Yali and curled up next to her like she used to do when she was younger and still learning her letters, and her nana wrapped a thin arm around her while Miria read until the solstice light finally dimmed.

Chapter Eighteen
Six Months Before the Wedding

Miria and Adaline had both counted on Adaline's family visiting her uncle again the following summer, but a tear-stained letter from Adaline had arrived in the spring, telling Miria they were going to be traveling abroad instead. Reading between the lines, it was clear Adaline's parents were beginning to look in earnest for suitable and advantageous matches for Adaline's future husband. But since Adaline never spoke of it, Miria didn't either.

The next summer passed into winter, and Miria barely enjoyed it before it did. Without Adaline's personal form of sunshine to brighten her days, Miria felt as much a golem as Tuli or Aza, going about her duties without complaint or joy. Though, that was probably not fair to the golems, who Miria was still convinced thought and felt more than they were capable of letting on. Tuli, for example, had an uncanny knack for trimming the flowering hedges and bringing Miria the cuttings on days when she was feeling especially despondent.

Adaline's letters never stopped, regardless of where she was. Through them, Miria learned that her mother had finally put her foot down and forbidden Adaline from sword and archery practice. The number of dances and social engagements she was forced to endure had increased, and though dances had once been a source of entertainment and joy for Adaline, she lamented that they now came with expectations of her spending time conversing with men in whom she had little interest—and whose interest in her made her most uncomfortable.

The M-word was first broached in a letter Adaline sent on a particularly sunny but bitterly cold winter day. Miria found the bird waiting for her when she returned to the cottage after picking up some supplies in town.

Yali was counting out pine needles for a healing potion in front of the fire. She never opened or read any of the letters from Adaline, but she did always seem surprised when one arrived.

Miria set down her satchel and took the letter eagerly, only the years of good manners drilled into her head by Nana making her reach for some seeds to feed the letter's feathered carrier before she broke the wax seal. The sparrow pecked away contentedly at its meal, warming itself by the fire, but Miria felt anything but content reading Adaline's latest words.

"Are you all right?" Yali asked.

Miria sighed. "I'm fine, but Adaline sounds miserable. I wish there was something I could do."

"You are a witch," her nana said. And Miria heard the rest of the reminder as clearly as she smelled the pine needles. *It is a witch's calling to push.*

But push what in this case? Adaline was a lady and several days' journey away in a place Miria had never been. She could not—would not—leave her nana, especially in the winter, and even if she left . . . It wasn't as though Miria could marry Adaline, was it?

"I cannot push against the whole country, the whole church, and win," Miria said.

"No, but do not doubt the impact of small pushes when timed correctly. Even a single beaver can alter the course of a mighty river if their dam is placed just so."

Miria began unloading her satchel. A bag of pepper corns. Two new needles. Such tiny items worth their weight in gold or magic. "I would not know where to begin to place such a dam."

"That only suggests the time is not yet right to build one. Come child, it is not like you to be so gloomy."

It wasn't, and Miria tried to shake off the mood. It should have been easier with the dazzling sunlight reflecting off the snow outside, plus the crackling fire and warmth in here. But it wasn't only Adaline's letter that weighed on Miria's heart. The colder months were not being kind to her nana. She seemed to grow weaker with each full moon. Yali herself did not seem upset by this, albeit frustrated at times, but Miria's heart ached with what she knew was inevitable.

And then there was the news from town, which did not help.

"There's apparently a wasting illness taking children's lives," Miria said, settling in the other chair before the hearth. "Strange, isn't it, that we've had few entreaties for help all winter? At first, I thought it must be the weather keeping folks in town, but the more I heard people talk of it today, the more it sounds as though it's been going on for the last couple of years. Shouldn't we do something, even if we're not asked? Look into at least? Try to find a cure?"

Yali rested a soft but firm hand on Miria's own. "You are young and full of vigor and heart. I know you want to help, but if no one has come to us, there might be a reason. Illnesses are cyclical, and so is fear. And fear is dangerous. We cannot save everyone, nor is it our duty to try. We do what we can, but we must protect ourselves, too. If we poke our heads out too much, even with the intention of helping, we might find someone swinging an ax in our direction, and then where will we be when needed? We are convenient people to blame for others' problems. Despite your noble friend, you are still only a woman and an outcast."

Miria lightly squeezed her nana's fingers. The older woman's skin felt dangerously thin beneath her own. "I know you are right, but it does upset me."

"Of course it does. You would not be here if it did not."

Miria let the topic drop. Yali was right about one thing—she could not save everyone, and she had enough worries about the two people she cared about most. For Adaline, she hoped her letters provided comfort or an outlet for Adaline's feelings, and she bided her time, wishing that one day she might be able to do more.

For Yali, she could—and did—do more, ensuring her nana was always comfortable and that she got plenty of rest. Miria prepared her favorite foods, invited her witch friends over as often as she could, and generally did her best to prove to Yali that she was smart and strong and responsible. That one day, she would be entirely capable of carrying on the legacy that had been gifted to her.

If she cried sometimes while she slept, no one else needed to know.

When Yali died in the spring, Azalea returned to the earth along with her. She lost not one family member, but two. But the other witches came without needing to be called, and they ensured Miria did not have to endure the pain alone. Some were her nana's friends that Miria knew only by name, but others were witches she'd met before. Sarel came, and another witch, Nalki, who'd also been present at Miria's initiation. They cooked and cleaned, and they helped Miria bury her nana in the spot Yali had requested. They sat with Miria and told her tales about

Yali (some new, some well-loved), and they collected her tears and strung them on a chain that sparkled like the morning dew. The tears were beautiful, they said, because Miria's love for her nana was beautiful. When Miria drew her thumb across them, her favorite memories of Yali were as clear in her head as the tears themselves. They made her cry harder, but they also made her smile.

For thirteen days, someone stayed with Miria at all times. For thirteen days, they mourned together and welcomed more witches whom Miria had never before met but who had come to pay their respects. They brought more food and gifts of little spells, and invitations to visit that Miria could respond to when she felt up to it.

Then life had to return to normal, or something like it.

After thirteen days, Miria was without human company for the first time in her life. She tucked the crystal memories away, checked on how the other women had packed up Yali's personal belongings, and fed the chickens. The garden and the spring repairs kept her too busy to wonder what was going on in town, but Adaline's letters couldn't let her forget everything beyond the cottage.

Miria hoped her friend would be able to visit again this summer, but it was a hope she couldn't spend much time dwelling on. The old witch in the woods was gone, and the young witch had very powerful shoes to fill.

PART III

THE GIRLS WHO PUSH

Chapter Nineteen

Two Days Before the Wedding

Things Miria remembered: convincing Adaline they could not keep Pearl with them safely and to send her back on the path through the woods toward town; calling on the trees and the mist to hide the cottage, building the protections thicker than she'd ever built them before; Adaline's arms holding her up as exhaustion made her knees wobble.

Things Miria did not remember: how she'd gotten into bed.

Miria rolled onto her back, blinking slowly into consciousness. Her head ached and her disorientation was stronger than it normally was when she emerged from sleep. She'd drained her magic far more than was wise, but she'd had no choice.

She lay still for a moment, fighting through the fog in her brain to understand why her present state felt strange, and her fingers rubbed the familiar patchwork of her blanket.

After Yali had died, it had taken Miria several months to move from her smaller bed in the third room into her nana's bed. At first, Miria couldn't bear to remember that her nana's bed was empty. Then, she'd taken to curling up in it occasionally, seeking out the scents of cedar and mint—Yali's scents—that permeated even the wooden frame, its soft mattress, and blankets like a hug that reminded her of its former occupant. Finally, practicality told her that it was silly to leave the bed empty or to sleep in it only on random nights when she felt morose. So, a couple of months ago, Miria had moved her bedding to the larger bed and had turned her old room into storage where she kept a chest of Yali's belongings that she could not bear to part with.

It was in Yali's—now Miria's bed—that she found herself, unsure of how she'd gotten there, and not alone. That, possibly, was what was strange. Adaline lay curled up next to her, her back toward Miria.

Miria wiggled her bare toes beneath the quilt. Who had pulled off her boots and stockings and tucked her in? Adaline or Tuli? More importantly—how much time had passed since?

That question raised fear in Miria's heart, but as all appeared quiet inside the cottage and no one was pounding on the door outside, threatening its occupants with violence, Miria decided they must be safe for the moment. Feeling slightly better, she sat up and draped a hand over Adaline's shoulder.

Beneath her, Adaline stiffened, giving Miria the impression that she hadn't actually been asleep. When she turned around, her eyes were red like she'd been crying, and Miria no longer felt better about anything. Her heart jumped to her throat.

Adaline was upset. She regretted what they'd done. Miria had to fix this immediately.

"I can take you home if you want," she said, pushing the words through her sadness and disappointment.

To her surprise, Adaline shot upright, her tear-stained face turning panicky. "What? No. Why?"

"You've been crying. I assumed you decided this was a mistake."

Adaline shook her head, and more brown waves dislodged themselves from her pins, joining the mess spilling about her shoulders. Miria fought the urge to remove the pins entirely and comb Adaline's hair with her fingers.

"I . . ." Adaline gripped the quilt as though she was afraid Miria would tear it from around her body. "No, I'm sorry. I'm just so useless. I don't know what to do. Before you went to sleep you were saying something about tea, but I don't know where you keep anything, and I don't even know how to boil water or how long to steep the leaves. When you fell asleep, I laid down next to you because I didn't know what else to do, and I'm sorry. I'm afraid *you'll* think this was a mistake."

Relief swept over Miria, and she wiped sleep from her face before wrapping her arms around Adaline. If *that* was all . . . Adaline melted into her, and she felt so good. So right. Miria wanted nothing more than to lie back on the bed with her and simply breathe for a few moments, basking in their success at getting as far as they had.

But despite the quiet, despite the temptation and her relief, there was no time for that.

"You are not useless," she said into Adaline's hair. "You merely have different skills. Put me in a room with the Lord of Gawfrid and you would see how hopeless I am."

Adaline sniffed and her attempt at a smile wavered. "I don't believe my dancing skills will come in handy while I'm here."

"You don't need to be handy here. You only need to *be* here." She kissed Adaline, and for a moment, let nothing more concern her mind. Then Miria climbed out of bed before the temptation to remain became too strong to ignore. "There are things I should tell you, though. Or best yet, show you."

As she spoke, Miria realized she'd probably collapsed before she could give Adaline a spell to let her properly see the cottage. She had no idea how it must appear to Adaline, but it would not be as it truly was. That had to be her first task. Before the confessions and assessing the state of their plan, she had to make sure Adaline was settled.

Tiredness slowed Miria's movements as she shuffled into the main room. Tiredness and thirst and hunger. Working so much magic had taken its toll, regardless of her sleep.

"How long did I sleep for?" Miria asked, searching among the bottles on her shelves. Luckily, she had a spell already prepared that would help Adaline. She couldn't possibly cast one otherwise until she'd eaten.

"I don't know for sure," Adaline said. She followed Miria warily into the room. "You fell asleep fairly quickly once we were inside, and the sun was setting. It's now morning. The sun rose maybe an hour or two ago."

So it hadn't been as long as Miria had feared. She hadn't lost a whole day.

"You must be starving, too. Here." Miria poured two drops of a clear liquid into a clean teacup. "It will show you everything here as it truly looks."

"As it truly looks?" Adaline asked, yawning.

"I don't know if the spells on the cottage affect the inside, but without magic in you, the outside would definitely appear false."

"Oh." Adaline drank the potion without further questions, which Miria considered both reckless of her and trusting, and quintessentially Adaline. It made her heart happy as she grabbed the teapot, checked that it was filled with water, and placed it on the hearth.

Miria didn't bother with magic to heat the coals, preferring to save her strength. When she turned, Adaline was spinning in place, scrutinizing the room. "Any different?" she asked.

Adaline rubbed her eyes. "Actually, no, but I wonder . . ." She dashed to the door, ran outside, and whooped with delight. "The outside matches more closely what I'd expect from the inside. I was so confused yesterday. Although, it still does seem bigger inside than it should. Magic, I assume?"

"Of course." While the water heated, Miria grabbed a basket. "I'm going to get eggs. You must be starving."

"Oh, well, actually." Adaline's stomach rumbled. "A bit."

"I'm sorry I was a terrible host and fell asleep on you yesterday without making sure you had any dinner or something to drink."

"You were exhausted from saving me!"

Now it was Miria's turn to equivocate. Adaline still didn't know that Miria's plan to "save" her overlapped with her plan to get revenge on her family. While she would have helped Adaline anyway, the convenience of two merging goals was offset by the feeling of guilt they created. As though Miria's motives for helping Adaline were less pure because they aligned with other, less noble, ones. Miria told herself she was being ridiculous, but was she really? It sounded like a question for the philosophers Miria had read during Yali's tutoring sessions.

"Why must I read these dull men?" she'd once asked her nana. "Can't I practice reading with the spell books?"

"Knowing how to cast a spell is not enough," her nana had replied. "A witch should know when and why to cast a spell—or not."

"But no one talks about spells in these books, they use twenty words when ten would suffice, and they always sound so confident of themselves when I'm not sure they should be."

Yali made a triumphant noise in her throat. "Then they are teaching you the ways of men, as well. Another good lesson to learn."

Despite her situation, the memory made Miria smile.

"There are things I need to tell you," Miria said, redirecting her thoughts to the present. That conversation was something else she couldn't bear to do without tea and food in her stomach. "Let me prepare us breakfast first. Sit, and I'll be back."

But Adaline would not sit. She wanted to help Miria collect the eggs, and she wanted to learn how Miria made the food and the tea so, in her words, she could be less useless in the future.

"You're recovering," Adaline insisted. "I want to be able to take care of you. Besides, I've been nothing but coddled and fussed over for the past year. I've been forbidden from practicing my swordsmanship or archery, and I spend most of my days confined to one chair or another. If I'm allowed out, it's only with a companion to take slow walks on foot or horseback. Nothing fun."

"I'm not sure I'd call making eggs or kneading bread fun," Miria said, pouring the tea.

Adaline shrugged. "It's a novelty to me, so it is in a way. And anyway, it allows me to be active. I have energy that I've not been permitted to express, and you are clearly in need of more rest, so let me be your servant and caretaker."

That, Miria had no trouble believing. Nor did she doubt that Adaline wanted to make herself useful. So even though everything took longer because she had to take the time to show Adaline where items were stored and how to prepare food (and she could use no magic to help with any of it), Miria obliged. Besides, Adaline's insistence on being her hands meant Miria could ask Tuli to keep an eye on the woods, and she felt safer knowing the golem would be keeping lookout. Nonetheless, her hands trembled with exhaustion by the time they sat and ate, but the food and the tea helped.

"What is it you need to tell me?" Adaline asked as she sopped up honey with her bread. It would have taken too long to start a fresh loaf, so Miria had cut thick slices of yesterday's leftover bread, warmed them, then slathered them in butter and honey to soften them again.

There was no putting it off any longer, and without knowing if or when Adaline's family might make it past Miria's spells, she knew better than to delay. She just wished she was more prepared mentally. Emotionally. Although, to be fair, Miria doubted more rest would help either of those things.

"I never told you how I became a witch," Miria said, wondering where to start.

Adaline blinked, as though Miria had said something more like, *I never told you how I became a human.* "I just assumed it was the usual way, like how I became Lady Adaline. I was born it."

Miria understood that. If she hadn't become a witch, she probably would have thought the same. "That is one way, I suppose. But very few things just are."

She was sounding like her nana, and though that pleased her, Miria didn't mean to lecture Adaline on the nature of change. She was simply procrastinating because this confession was difficult.

"There are many ways to become a witch," she said, starting over. "They all require you to be born with magic in you, but as I've explained, while that is uncommon, it is not exceptionally rare either. In my case, I became a witch because my father traded me to the former witch, my nana, for a spell."

"Traded you?" Adaline gasped and almost knocked over her teacup. "Gave you away?"

Miria nodded.

"So your nana was not your nana. She accepted you as payment?" Adaline spit out the word.

Miria cupped her hands around her teacup, letting the heat seep into her skin. All the salt and the sugar she'd consumed were slowly making her feel better, but this conversation would be as draining as casting a significant spell. "Yes, but do not think badly of her for it. She was helping me. She was my nana in all ways but blood, which is the least important way. My father was very poor, and I was very young at the time. My mother and grandmother had died. I had no one to raise me properly as a girl. My father considered me useless. Even my brother, who was many years older and capable of learning my father's trade, was of little more interest to him. At least not then. He traded us both, or tried to."

Adaline flinched at the word she'd been using to describe herself all morning.

"He thought the witch would likely kill us, use us for our blood or some nefarious magic," Miria continued. Although she could reflect on the circumstances that had led her to Yali with more perspective these days, perspective didn't numb the feelings of betrayal. Perhaps nothing could numb a person to the knowledge that someone close would trade your life for gain. Not even the charm around Miria's neck could contain all of her emotions. "My nana didn't like that about him, and she saw my potential. She took me in, and she let my brother believe he escaped so he could return home. She saved me. Saving children is part of what a witch does, and she needed to train a new witch."

Miria provided Adaline with a bit more about her childhood, the way Yali had cared for her, the lessons she'd received in this very room. How she'd never gone looking for her family, especially the man who hadn't cared whether she lived or died.

It was hard reliving these memories, particularly with Yali's death so recent, but it was harder still to get the rest out. Miria knew she was delaying, waiting for Adaline to ask the inevitable question.

But Adaline didn't ask it as quickly as Miria thought she might. She fumed on Miria's behalf instead, paced about the table and pulled Miria into her arms the way Yali once had, as though she could make up for all the love Miria had been owed by her blood relatives. Miria didn't need the sympathy or indignation, but she didn't mind the hugs.

Finally, however, Adaline found the question Miria had been waiting for. "You've never even been curious what happened to your father and brother? I don't know if I could have refrained from searching for them. It's best that I'm not a witch because I would have turned all my magic against them. You are a better person than I am."

"I tried to pretend they didn't exist, mostly. I saw my brother again for the first time that summer you were here last. Do you remember that day I got so angry that I called down a storm? That was because I ran into him. *That* was why it was better I ignored them." Miria's teacup was empty, and she considered making another pot, but that would just be another excuse to delay speaking. She pushed her empty cup away. "I can't ignore them any longer."

She grasped Adaline's hands, recalling her nana's words about Adaline and timing and pushing on fate. "I am not a better person than you, though I've been a more patient person. Until now. It seems our lives are more entwined than not. Maybe me finding you lost in the woods the day we met was a coincidence, or maybe there is a greater story here. But the way it stands is this—the man your family has arranged for you to marry—he is my brother."

Chapter Twenty

Two Days Before the Wedding, Continued

"Your brother?" Adaline jerked back as though Miria had just performed her most shocking spell yet. "The Overseer's son is your brother? The Overseer of Swiftdok is your father?"

Miria merely nodded. She had a hard enough time wrapping her mind around it herself.

"But. . . ." Adaline shook her head. "You said your family was poor. Why would such a wealthy man . . ." She trailed off, apparently unable to form the words *sell his daughter*.

"I believe he's only achieved that post in the last few years," Miria said. "I don't know when he achieved the wealth that allowed him to rise to such a position. He was nothing but a woodcutter when I was growing up. It was skilled work, but not so well-paying that we didn't suffer without the money my mother and grandmother would have brought in. My nana gave him a very powerful spell—a single wish. She wanted to ensure he didn't change his mind and that I did not have to stay with him. He may not have been kind, but he must have been clever enough to use the spell well."

Adaline pursed her lips. Color had risen to her cheeks with indignation when Miria had told her story, but it drained away. She looked a little queasy. "He must have used it very well for my uncle to think so highly of him and ignore his background. Although, his wealth certainly helps with that. My family has titles, but my father's gold has been running thin."

Because of her rare but occasional scrying on Adaline, Miria knew that already. Adaline's uncle's coffers were reputedly flush, but those of Adaline's immediate family were less so. Gold might be the only reason they would consider marrying Adaline to someone so far beneath them. Miria's father, greedy to raise his children high, and Adaline's father, simply greedy, would benefit from the arrangement. Naturally, only Adaline and Miria would not.

As always, the girls were an afterthought. In the end, they were just objects for a man—something to be bought and sold, whether to a witch or a richer man.

But not this time. Miria had vowed it.

"My brother," Miria began, but she cut herself off. What of him? Did she want to assure Adaline that he must be kinder than her father? She wasn't sure of that herself anymore, and if Adaline—when all was said and done—was forced into the marriage, Miria didn't want to give her false hope.

"I don't really know him," Adaline said, filling the silence. "I met him and your father only briefly. But . . . Oh!" She raised her hand to her mouth in surprise. "Some of my uncle's staff have called your brother a hero—the only child who ever escaped the witch. I thought it was just more silly tales since there's no need for anyone to escape from you, but that would explain it, I suppose."

Miria grimaced. "Yes, after that day we met in town, I tried to learn more. He spun a good story for people, claiming the witch tried to cook him and his sister, and how he managed to be clever enough to get away but couldn't save her. No doubt his lies helped bolster my family's reputation. As if anyone needed more tales of how awful witches are—we'll steal your blood and bones for magic, we'll turn you into clay, and we'll cook and eat you, too. We must be very clever to do all of that and leave bodies behind."

"Oh, Miri, I'm sorry. Your brother seemed pleasant when we met, and I can't say your father made enough of an impression to stick with me. I wish he had. I wish people who did horrible things came with some sort of warning about them—spiteful eyes or an oily voice or ugly features like they do in children's stories." Adaline sighed. "My time has mainly been confined to other women. Your father's wife, though, I suppose she's your stepmother? I've been in her company much more."

"What is she like?"

Adaline twined her fingers together almost nervously. "Rosmilda is gracious. Helpful. She apparently does a lot of charity work in town and with the church. But I admit there's something about her that I've never trusted. There was a girl I was friends with for a time back home. She was the one who always knew everything that was going on around court. She had the best ideas for fun, was always helping others, and we all wanted her to like us. But finally I started noticing that ideas other people had eventually somehow became her ideas, and sometimes her help actually made things worse, but you were criticized if you pointed this out and *ill luck* often followed. She didn't want you to be her friend; she wanted to be your benevolent queen, only she was more self-serving than benevolent. Something about Rosmilda has always reminded me of her."

That didn't sound promising, and Miria tried to reconcile Adaline's impression with what she'd seen. Rosmilda's words at the funeral—the way she'd stated her opinion so forcefully—there might be something to it.

". . . they always sound so confident of themselves when I'm not sure they should be."

"Then they are teaching you the ways of men, as well. Another good lesson to learn."

Miria frowned. Yes, something about Rosmilda had reminded her of that conversation again. Though surely it was normal for a woman of her status to act like she had power. Because she did.

Miria didn't like it, though. While it didn't seem right that a man like her father should have married a sweet, gentle woman, for the sake of her half-sisters, Miria had wanted to believe it so. "What about their children? I have two sisters. Have you ever met them?"

"No, I'm sorry, although I've heard Rosmilda speak of them on many occasions. She's said their health is poor. They don't leave the home often, and every time I've seen your family it's because they were expected to travel to my uncle's. The girls don't come with them."

"Of course," Miria murmured. Adaline's family would not go to the Overseer's home, no matter how nice it was relative to the other houses in town.

She stood wearily, though more fortified than she'd expected earlier. Adaline jumped up with her, her arms poised as though to catch Miria should she fall over.

"I'm not that feeble yet." Miria swatted Adaline's hands away with a laugh.

"I just want to be sure. I want to help." Adaline closed the distance between and cupped Miria's cheek, and Miria's eyes closed. This was all the help she needed, knowing Adaline was here with her.

But she wouldn't be here long if Miria didn't continue to work, and the thought snapped Miria's eyes back open. She clutched Adaline's hands and reluctantly removed them from her face. "If you want to help, you'll remove the rest of the pins from your hair and braid it. I'm waiting for one to fall and stab you in the eye."

Adaline stuck out her tongue, but she also touched her head and winced. "I must look awful."

"A touch feral, but that's nothing we aren't used to around here. And you're still the most beautiful woman I've ever seen."

"Hmm." Adaline wrinkled her nose, picking out the remaining pins. "I'm not sure how many women you've seen, hiding in the woods like you do, but I'm too vain to argue the point. Will you braid my hair for me, and then let me help with something real?"

"I suppose I can find another use for you," Miria said. "Now sit."

Another use turned out to be asking Adaline to clean up after breakfast, a chore Miria typically loathed but which Adaline took to with the gusto of one for whom cleaning up after herself was an interesting novelty. Miria hoped she'd retain that sort of enthusiasm over time, but that led to the question of how long Adaline could possibly stay with her (and the answer being: never as long as Miria would want), and so she put the mundane chores out of her head to contemplate something more important, if not exactly more cheery.

Miria had magical tasks to see to. Tuli was circling the cottage perimeter and hadn't reported back with any signs of disturbances, so that was good, but she should consider strengthening the concealment spells around the cottage, just to be safe now that she was feeling strong enough again. She should also unpack the magical implements she'd brought to the manor yesterday and consider refilling her satchel with fresh supplies that would be handy in case she and Adaline needed to make a hasty retreat at a later time. That was the less tiring of the two tasks, so Miria set to it first.

One by one, she retrieved items from the satchel. Her feather. The bit of silver. Something unexpected? Miria pulled her hand out of the bag and gazed at the pendant she'd stolen from Adaline's room. The pink charm, masquerading as a sapphire, glittered up at her. She'd forgotten all about it until this moment.

Adaline had taken the wash bucket to dump outside, and Miria was still contemplating the charm and what it might be for when she returned. "Is that mine?"

Miria held it out to her. "I imagine so. I found it in your room. Do you know what it is?"

"An extremely generous wedding gift," Adaline said. "Why?"

"One of these sapphires is actually a charm." Miria tapped the fake jewel. "That's why I took it. I wasn't trying to steal from you, I promise."

"First of all, you *should* have stolen from my room. What if we need money to escape from my—*our*—families? I took some gold with me, but more is always better. Second of all, you mean that's magical?"

"You didn't know?"

Adaline shook her head and stepped closer, squinting at the pendant. "It all looks the same to me."

That was interesting, and potentially revealing. Why would someone give Adaline a charm and not tell her what it was? Sapphires were expensive, but to anyone who was not a witch, magic was worth far more. And that meant Miria could only think of nefarious reasons for keeping the charm's presence hidden. Who had given it to Adaline with no explanation?

That question, she could ask momentarily.

"It's well disguised, but this one here—" she touched the charm among the sapphires "—it's not a jewel. It was crafted in a similar way to the charm I gave you, although I doubt it serves a similar purpose."

Adaline stuck her foot on the table's bench and flexed her ankle. "I wear yours, always. Only I had to put it around my ankle so no one would see it. My mother would have torn it off me if she had, but no one sees my bare feet except my maid."

Miria smile and kissed Adaline's cheek. "Clever. But my charms were not half so clever as whoever made this one. It's exquisite work. You could have worn it and no one would know what it was."

Adaline let her foot drop to the floor, her smile fading. "But what does it do? Why give it to me?"

"The first qucstion is—who gave it to you?"

"Your family." Adaline frowned. "The other night, an early wedding present, like I said. Rosmilda said it had belonged to her mother, and she hoped I would wear it for the wedding. I thought it was such a generous gift, and I was surprised, but . . ."

Rosmilda? Miria flipped the pendant around in her hand, and pressed the jewel to her palm. Warmth washed over her, but not the heat of anger or the familiarity of Adaline's heart. Something resonated within her, though. Something was familiar about it.

Adaline bit her lip while Miria pricked a finger and drew a drop of blood over the charm. Listening. Feeling. It wasn't old, this charm. Whether the pendant itself was as Rosmilda had claimed, Miria couldn't say, but she was certain the charm was new.

There was an art to discerning an unfamiliar spell's purpose, and it was one Miria didn't have much practice with since she'd never had much cause to use it. Witches worked together, or at least they did not work at cross-purposes. It was far easier to simply ask a witch about an unfamiliar spell she might encounter than it was to try to learn its power on her own.

Nothing about this situation made sense, though. Rosmilda was not a witch.

Miria placed the pendant on the table, more disturbed than ever. "I believe, although I could be wrong, that the charm contains a love spell. One that would make you fall in love with my brother."

Adaline shivered. "I knew I didn't trust your stepmother."

"How did my stepmother get such a thing?"

"I don't know, but I'm glad you stole it so we can destroy it." Adaline shoved it farther away, then wrapped her arms around herself. "They tried to put a spell on me!"

Miria tucked the pendant in a cloth and set it on a shelf. Casting a spell on a person without their permission violated every lesson her nana had taught her. Adaline had every right to be horrified, and Miria's blood fumed along with her. Selfishly in part. Someone had tried violating Adaline's heart, and in doing so, steal Adaline away from her.

Miria grasped the red charm around her neck and poured her anger into it. It felt hotter for a moment before resettling against her skin. The act did nothing to ease Miria's feelings. Pouring her emotions into the charm (or the jar before it) did not take her anger away; it merely conserved some of the power in it. But the act had taken on a ritual quality, merely doing it calmed her and allowed her to think more clearly. And she had to think. She had so many questions.

"It's gone now," Miria said, "and we'll find out who and how. I promise. I don't know where Rosmilda came from before she arrived here, but it cannot be beyond Waere's borders. I've heard her accent. I'll send an inquiry to the other witches I know. Maybe one of them can explain how she obtained it."

Adaline nodded, but she looked unsettled. "I'm glad I didn't try it on. I almost did, but I was so focused on escaping that I did nothing but fret over our plan."

"*Your* plan," Miria said, playfully nudging her in the ribs and hoping to settle her nerves. "I had no idea there was to be a change in *our* plan."

The tactic succeeded too well. Adaline let out a low whine and another apology, and Miria had to assure her that everything had worked out fine. Although, truthfully, she wasn't certain of that in the slightest.

Eventually, though, Adaline returned to cleaning while Miria wrote a quick letter, which she sent off to all the local witches she knew. It was around noon when she finished. She hadn't heard a report from Tuli yet, and it was well past the time when Miria wanted to know what was going on. She needed to strengthen the protections, summon Tuli back, and figure out her next steps.

Calling for Tuli came first because it was the simplest, and Miria began collecting sticks of hawthorn and oak for the protection spells while she waited for him to arrive. He appeared a few minutes later, approaching the cottage from the south.

Adaline, who was helping Miria gather wood, startled at his approach. Miria had noticed that Adaline often seemed a touch unnerved around the golem, though she tried to hide it. "He surprised me is all," Adaline said, catching Miria watching her. "I thought he was coming from the other direction."

Miria was about to ask why when the woods answered for her. From the northeast, a flock of birds suddenly took to the sky, screaming.

Miria dropped her sticks, and Tuli paused.

"That's unusual, isn't?" Adaline asked, sounding as if she wanted to be corrected.

It was extremely unusual, and Miria grabbed Adaline's hand and pulled her back toward the cottage. In the distance, trees began shaking. The ground rumbled, and Miria's muscles tensed. A hundred invisible, magical threads were snapping and shrieking, the vibrations as loud as thunder in Miria's head and unlike anything she'd experienced before.

Something was coming through the forest from the direction of town. Something big. And given the way Miria's protections and wards were reacting, it was extremely unfriendly.

Chapter Twenty-One

Two Days Before the Wedding, Continued

Miria felt the thing before she saw it. A cold, slimy kind of power slithered over her, reminding her of congealed fat at the bottom of a dirty cookpot. Foul magic. Magic like she'd never experienced before. Yet beneath that terrible layer was something familiar, the building blocks of a spell Miria recognized even if she couldn't place it. The mechanism for the spell was not unknown to her, even if the source of its power felt wholly wrong.

Whatever it was, it was aiming straight for her. For the cottage. All of Miria's wards, the concealment spells—they were meant to keep out unwanted people or dangerous animals or violent weather. A magical attack had never been something she'd considered, nor had Yali before her. There had never been a need to protect the cottage from another witch.

"Do you smell that?" Adaline asked, and it was Miria's first clue that some of the foulness she was experiencing wasn't magical in nature at all. Whatever was coming was fueled by magic, but it was no ethereal spell.

Then the creature burst through the trees, and fear and shock wrapped icy fingers around Miria's heart. Adaline screamed out in language that certainly no lady was supposed to use, but Miria could not find words. There *were* no words for this thing, except perhaps one—abomination.

That was why Adaline could smell its rot and Miria recognized the spells beneath the twisted magic. Someone had created a construct. But unlike Tuli with his clay body and loving heart made of a cherished ribbon, whoever had done this had set out to create a nightmare and powered it with hate.

It wasn't large. It stood no taller than Miria herself, but somehow that made it all the more horrifying. Size, Miria understood. An imposing presence was naturally something that could be fearsome. But the fear and disgust this construct engendered were nothing natural.

It wore the head of a boar over the decaying torso of what might have once been a brown bear. Its left eye was missing, and its mouth was pulled wide to display a set of mismatched teeth. One leg was gray fur. Another brown. A third had no fur left at all, just flesh peeling off bleached-white bone. Flies hovered about it, and squirming patches in its filthy fur suggested colonies of maggots had made it their homes.

It stood on its haunches, more humanoid than animal, a creature of a dozen or more corpses. Hooves and claws. Bones and rotting flesh held together by unseen bonds and rage. It let out a howl of triumph and focused its single eye in Miria's direction.

Vomit rose up Miria's throat. But fear and revulsion, probably shock, had left her too stunned to move. For a moment, her world narrowed to nothing more than herself and the abomination. She forgot Adaline. Forgot Tuli. Forgot why this thing might be here in the first place. There was only it and the certainty of death.

But Tuli, either sensing the evil that swarmed around the construct like the cloud of flies or Miria's reaction to it, didn't hesitate, and Miria's world expanded once more. Her golem picked up a large, fallen tree branch and charged forward, a clay knight to the rescue. Miria marveled for a second before remembering that this was literally one of the tasks she'd created him for. One of the first commands she'd given him after obeying her was to protect her, her nana, and the cottage. The marvel was merely that Tuli didn't need a reminder after so many years of never being called upon to do so, nor did he need explicit instructions.

Miria felt a surge of pride, less so for her magical skills and more so for Tuli himself. If Yali were here, Miria knew her nana would tell her she was ridiculous, that a golem was nothing more than an extension of her power. But Miria had considered Tuli (and Aza) family for as long as she'd known them. What her adult mind knew couldn't override what her child's heart felt.

And in that heart, she recalled her power and her reason for fighting.

Tuli swung at the construct and landed a solid hit on its side. Bones cracked and flesh splattered, splinters and viscera falling to the dirt. But though the creature stuttered, it did not fall. It fought back. One claw-like appendage reached out, swiping at Tuli, who batted it away.

Seeing the construct attack Tuli roused Miria the rest of the way out of her stupor. Whatever magic powered that thing was clearly strong, possibly as strong or stronger than her own. She needed to act, not gawk. That meant she needed supplies.

In her years studying under Yali, Miria had cast many kinds of spells, but never ones meant directly to harm. She didn't even know ones like that. But like a fallen tree branch could provide a handy seat for a woman or be turned into cudgel for a golem, so too could many normally harmless spells be used offensively. She just had to think this through and choose wisely. Her power was stronger than it had been, but she was far from her best self.

"Ada!" Miria threw open the cottage door, but she needn't have worried. Adaline was right behind her. "Tuli should be able to hold that thing off," Miria said, searching her supplies and hoping that was true, "but I'm going to give him some help."

"So am I." Adaline unsheathed the sword she'd insisted on bringing with her yesterday, her face determined.

"You should—" The words faded on Miria's tongue. Telling Adaline to stay inside was pointless. "Have you ever fought something for real?"

Adaline flexed her hands and arms a couple of times. "Something like that? Never. Should be exciting!" Then she was out the door before Miria could question her word choice.

Miria took a deep breath. Two against one was better odds, but now her two favorite people in the world were locked in battle with powerful magic. She had to get out there and help them. All she needed was some nettle and twine.

There. Miria grabbed the piece of rope that she'd packed into her satchel earlier and charged for the cottage door, but she never made it. All around her, the cottage was dissolving, swirling away like dirt in a stream. First the door, then the walls, even the floor. Miria reached out a hand, as though she could seize whatever magic was doing this, but nothing about this spell was recognizable in the way the horrible construct's magic was. That had been simple to understand—a spell twisted and turned vile. This was something else altogether—an amalgam of spells, each a whisper in Miria's mind. Each too small to grasp on their own and untangle.

Miria cried out as she fell to her knees, a floor—a new, strange floor—forming beneath her. Frantically, she scrambled to her feet, searching for the person who had done this, but she appeared to be alone.

But where was she? Miria wracked her memory, trying to recapture the sense of magic as the spell had wrapped around her. It hadn't felt like a transport spell, like the sort of thing she and the other witches used to traverse distances. And yet the cottage and her woods, they were gone.

She stood in a small, sparsely furnished room. A single table took up the bulk of the space, its top polished from use but roughly made. It had no chairs, but benches were on either side. The hearth was simple and unadorned. A set of unpainted shelves filled with cooking implements sat to one side, and Miria ran her finger over a ladle, wondering why it seemed familiar. Behind her, near the door sat a pair of well-used, heavy boots that had seen better days, and hanging above them . . . She inhaled sharply. A set of axes.

Now, she thought she understood. She remembered.

"So it's not real," she said, wanting to hear her own voice. "You took me nowhere except into my memories."

Whoever was doing this to her was powerful, but perhaps not powerful enough to transport Miria against her will. She took some confidence from that. Her fingers pressed into the gouged tabletop. It felt solid beneath her skin, but that, too, was a memory. If she focused, she could tell how distorted her former home was as the spell struggled to make sense of a child's perspective merged with a twenty-year-old's body.

Hunger. Cold. A hole in her heart as she snuggled inside scratchy wool blankets, pretending they were a grandmother's loving arms, someone to hold her and love her. Somone who cared.

"You're a useless girl. What have you done to help us today? Stop your crying and go fetch some water. Move faster."

The memories surfaced again and again, ripples in a pond cascading out, each triggering a new one. But they were less than water, easy to let slide between her fingers. Miria acknowledged the pain, and it passed. That girl had food now and warmth. That girl had found someone to snuggle against on a winter's night. She had people who cared. She did not have to be sad anymore. Sadness was not helpful.

Miria wrapped her fingers around her red charm. That girl had abandoned sadness for her anger, and her temper was rising. She was sick of this game.

"Show yourself, you coward," Miria said. "Or are you incapable of it?"

Truly, she had no idea what was possible with a spell like this. She was beginning to put together the pieces of how this one had been constructed, but she'd never attempted anything like it. A little goading, however, felt good. It gave her a sense of control, and if it cost the person behind the spell power to call Miria's bluff and show themselves, even better. That could make it easier for Miria to break the spell.

"What? No tender feelings for your old home? Did the witches strip that all away from you?"

Miria spun around, but she already knew who she'd find before the spellcaster emerged from the shadows. She'd only heard that voice twice, but it made so many pieces fall into place.

"Rosmilda," Miria said, staring down her father's second wife.

She looked younger here than Miria recalled, possibly a trick of the spell. Sunlight that did not exist in Miria's memory illuminated her hair, cast her in a fake golden glow. Perhaps she thought it made her appear more beautiful or powerful, but Miria did not conflate those two things like the bards did in their songs and stories. Power was her nana's wizened, spotted hands. Beauty was Adaline's unrestrained laughter.

"So you're the witch who's causing me trouble," Rosmilda said. "I always thought the witch in the Shadow Wood was old. Imagine my surprise when I learned it was you."

"You speak like you know me," Miria said. As she talked, she moved around the table, placing it between her and Rosmilda. Let Rosmilda believe she was using the table like a shield. Beneath the tabletop, Miria's fingers danced over the spell's threads of magic. Since she understood the pieces that constructed it, she stood a chance of tearing it apart.

"Oh, I do know you, the parts that matter." Rosmilda tilted her head to the side, studying Miria. "I can even see bits of your father and brother in your face. Did you think I couldn't put it together? You were in my house."

Miria was too surprised to adequately hide her scowl. So she *had* been seen that day. She wasn't certain how Rosmilda could have figured out who she was, but she wasn't certain of many things. Like how Rosmilda could do magic in the first place. She was no witch, and she'd possessed no power that Miria had seen.

"And, now you're attacking my home?" Miria asked. "That's a rather strong retaliation. You could have simply asked for the saltcellar back."

Rosmilda laughed. "You can keep the saltcellar. Once your brother has married Lady Adaline, such a paltry item will be meaningless. You can't hide her forever. As long as Adaline is near you, I will always be able to find her, because I will always be able to find *you*. The blood bond between a parent and child, or a brother and sister, is strong enough that I don't need your own blood to scry for you."

Blood. The word jostled a memory.

It was her third autumn in the cottage in the woods. Miria had been mending the winter clothes Yali had brought for her—wool tunics and leggings that promised to be warm and luxurious when the weather changed—and her thumb was bleeding.

"Not yet," Yali had said when Miria asked (again) to learn a mending spell. After placing a fresh log in the fireplace, she held out a hand, and with a brush of her own thumb, she soothed Miria's

injury. "The strongest magic comes from sacrifice. What do you think that means?"

What do you think? *was the question Yali often asked when she wanted Miria to understand something. As though learning wasn't just supposed to be Yali putting information into Miria's head or showing Miria how to do a new task, but something Miria was supposed to figure out on her own.*

"Blood is a sacrifice?" Miria guessed. Nana had explained that the most powerful magic required blood, and the way Nana had healed her thumb was certainly meant as a clue.

"Blood is a form of sacrifice, yes. It is not the only form, merely a convenient one. Time and energy are sacrifices, too. What that means is that the more effort you put into your work, the stronger the magic you produce will be."

"So that's why people are wrong when they tell tales about witches taking people's blood for magic," Miria said. "That's not how it works."

"It's not how it should *work," her nana said. And then, seeing the way Miria's brow pinched, she added, "A witch who knows what she's doing can take magic from others' blood if they have any magic at all in it, but spells cast that way will never be as powerful as those cast by a witch who sacrifices herself."*

Miria chewed this over, wondering why a witch would ever bother using someone else's blood when she had her own. None of the spells Yali had taught her so far had required blood, and she'd assumed that meant the stories about the witch stealing blood were completely false, but apparently it was a half truth at best. Since coming to live with Yali, Miria was discovering that the truth was always far more complicated than what she'd been told.

She glanced down at the sewing basket and sighed. "But why does that mean I need to sew?"

Her nana removed her magical cloak from the peg next to the door, and Miria inhaled sharply. "The power in my cloak's magic comes from me stitching it by hand," her nana said. "To create one for yourself, you must be able to sew the leaves together and infuse each bite of the needle with your magic." She returned the cloak to its peg and clasped Miria's hand. "And if you jab yourself with a needle and lend it the magic in a drop or two of blood, even better."

Miria strove to keep her face neutral, but her mind buzzed. Though she still did not entirely understand how Rosmilda was doing this, the memory had given her an idea.

"Perhaps," Miria said absently in response to the scrying problem Rosmilda raised. There were ways to block scrying, though they took effort. Surely, Rosmilda knew that. Or maybe she didn't. Since Miria couldn't figure out where Rosmilda had learned magic, it was best not to make assumptions, and wiser to say little lest she give away something Rosmilda didn't know.

Frankly, Rosmilda already knew more than Miria liked. She needed to keep Rosmilda talking, though. Long enough to distract her while Miria undid her spell. Long enough that maybe Miria could finish piecing together the rest of the puzzle Rosmilda posed.

"You make an awful lot of assumptions." If Rosmilda knew anything about witches, she ought to know that helping women and children to safety was what they did.

"Like that you will keep Adaline close?" Rosmilda asked, taking the bait. "Of course, you will. A witch would never harm an innocent woman, no matter what the stories say. Ironic when it's so easy to blame you all for the harm others do. But no, you will not harm Adaline, and you can't let her go if you mean to stop the wedding. That means it's a matter of time before I help her uncle get her back. Save the poor lady. Be their heroine."

Save her? Of course, the men had assumed Miria had bewitched Adaline. She'd heard them say it yesterday. More interesting were some of Rosmilda's other words. The jibe, the attempt to taunt her, dredged up more memories that Miria hadn't thought about in a while. They clicked in her head, like another piece of the puzzle snapping into place—and this one was a puzzle Miria had been thinking about for years without seeing a connection between the pieces.

Heat rose in her blood. The slow, simmering anger that someone would dare attack her home began to boil into fury. This wasn't just about her. Not anymore.

Miria did not have all the threads of Rosmilda's spell untangled yet, but the horror and rage that was dawning on her gave a boost to her power. She'd untangled enough. She could rip.

This was her memory, her head. Rosmilda had made a mistake (one of many, Miria noted in the back of her mind). Miria controlled what existed in this space, and she summoned an image of the supplies she needed. Thread and a silvered knife manifested in her palms. Beneath the table, she wrapped the thread around her hands, pulling it taut.

Rosmilda seemed to realize what Miria's hands had been up to beneath the table, but she was too late. Focusing her power on the knife, Miria cut through the summoned thread—the threads of Rosmilda's spells—and broke them in pieces. The image of her old home snapped away with a violent shudder, and Miria stumbled a few steps in her cottage, reeling physically from the force of her own power and Rosmilda's colliding.

She took a deep breath, then another, willing away her disorientation. Adaline, Adaline, Adaline. Miria silently repeated her name until she could focus once more, fully back in her body.

Something crashed outside and jolted Miria's heart. She scrambled for the spell supplies she'd been gathering before Rosmilda had interrupted her and threw open the door, fearing the worst.

"Adaline!" But it was not Adaline on the ground, nor Tuli.

Her golem was a little worse for the battle that had raged while Miria was bespelled. A chip was missing from his head, and his left arm was only partly attached—both injuries Miria would fix once this ordeal was over—but Tuli didn't notice or care (Miria wasn't sure which, or either). The golem swung his tree branch with one arm, further flattening the abomination into the dirt.

Adaline stood off to the side, holding her sword at the ready. Luckily, she seemed in better condition than Tuli, though her braid had come loose and her skirt was half shredded. She wore a victorious smile and flushed cheeks, and she glanced in Miria's direction as Miria charged forward.

"Where have you been? You missed me being your gallant knight." Adaline jumped as Tuli whacked the abomination again, then turned back to Miria. "With help, I mean. Tuli and I make a great team."

Feeling half as dazed as she had when Rosmilda magically attacked her, Miria dropped her hands to her side. "Cut off its head."

"Happily." Adaline held up a hand toward Tuli. "I've got this part, Sir Tulip."

As though recognizing Adaline's station, Tuli bowed and stepped away, which the first time Miria had seen him do something like that, and she would need to evaluate this scene again later. Apparently, fighting together had created an unexpected bond between them. It made her happy, but it confused her.

Also, the foul construct was moving, trying to put itself back together. She had no time for questions about magical eccentricities.

Adaline stepped forward and, with a great swing of her sword, she cleaved the creature's decaying boar's head from its motley torso. It twitched once and fell still. Miria cringed.

Adaline whooped, and even Tuli seemed extremely pleased with himself, judging by his posture.

Miria pushed all this nonsense aside and crept closer. "It must have some magic inside, powering it. A heart of sorts. I need to destroy it."

It took a few minutes of rooting around inside the chest cavity to find it. Adaline and Tuli stood over Miria's shoulders, stabbing or whacking anything that twitched, but that did not make the task any less grim or gory, and Miria winced her way through it.

"This must be it." Miria used a hawthorn stick to poke at the black lump. She didn't know what to expect, but her find seemed likely. The ribbon she'd placed in Tuli to give him his power would have transformed with him, and when Yali had died and Azalea had returned to the earth, his magical heart had vanished with him. The person whose magic was powering this creature, however, was alive, and so its heart thrummed with power. Miria could only guess what her own golem's heart looked like, but she could not believe it was like this—reddish black, like a ruby but ugly. The oily, unpleasant magical sensation the creature gave off—unrelated to its very physical rot—stemmed from it.

As though reading her thoughts, Adaline glanced between it and Tuli. "Is that . . . ?"

"No," Miria said, letting her conviction hide her ignorance. "Tuli was created with love. This was created with something else."

She made quick work of it, sprinkling salt over the magical heart until its color leeched away. Within seconds, the rest of the abomination fell to pieces around them. Unlike Aza had, it did not crumble to clay, for it wasn't made of clay, but the bones and flesh collapsed to the ground as magical bonds broke.

"I think it smells worse," Adaline said, covering her nose. "Tuli is lucky he doesn't have a nose to smell it."

In Miria's mind, Tuli chuckled at that.

"We should bury what's left," she said. "With its foul magic, not even the carrion eaters will want to feast on it, I don't think. And perhaps they shouldn't, to be safe."

That was the sort of task for which Miria was especially grateful for Tuli's help. She easily fixed his head and his arm, and while the golem dug a pit and buried the disparate decomposing body parts, Miria repacked her supplies. More than ever, it seemed wise to be ready to flee at a moment's notice.

Her mind was so occupied elsewhere, between her task and what she'd learned from Rosmilda, that she almost forgot Adaline was there until her friend spoke up. "I thought you were right behind me when I ran out of the cottage earlier. Don't get me wrong—I'm glad you stayed inside until Tuli and I had won the day, but warn me next time so I'm not looking over my shoulder to make sure you're safe."

Adaline had been uncharacteristically silent since the fight, and she looked tired. Miria realized she must not have gotten much sleep last night—the excitement and stress would have kept her awake. She'd been so concerned for her own recovery and why it was necessary that she'd glossed over Adaline's. And, to be fair, Adaline had powered through the morning, trying to act like all was fine. Because of course she had.

Miria set aside her satchel and sat next to Adaline. She wrapped her arms around her, let Adaline's body sag gently into her own. She wanted to protect Adaline, and Adaline wanted to protect her, and Miria didn't even know what they were protecting each other from. Yesterday, her plan had been so simple. The villain of both their stories so obvious. The past hour had changed everything.

"I was behind you," she said. "Until I was attacked. That creature was a distraction, I think."

She filled Adaline in on what Rosmilda had said and done, and Adaline was soon out of her seat, weariness melted away like so much snow in the heat of her outrage. "She's the one who created the charmed necklace then. She must be. Miri, this isn't safe. If she can do that to you. . . . I should return. I know you want revenge on your family, and you deserve it. But now that I know doing this puts you in danger, I can't let that happen. Maybe there's another way. Maybe—"

"Absolutely not." Miria jumped up too, and she took Adaline's shaking hands. "There was always a risk with this plan. But revenge aside, you are worth any risk. I just need to rethink things. Rosmilda is a problem, and I have a duty to deal with her, regardless of you or my family. But it will be tricky."

"What do you mean?"

Miria grimaced, because the next part confused and pained her. It was what she'd been dwelling on since Rosmilda's magical attack. Saying it out loud might help her think it through, but it was unpleasant, and she knew what Adaline's reaction would be.

"Rosmilda is not a witch," Miria said. "I've seen her in person, and she had no magic of her own. I would have been able to tell. But the spells she used—they were like twisted versions of the spells I learned from my nana. Rosmilda altered them, which means she was trained by a witch. I'm positive of it."

Adaline bit her lip. She'd cleaned her sword while Miria packed after the fight, and she ran a finger over its smooth steel, clearly thinking about what she'd like to do with it next. "How is she casting spells if she has no magic of her own? Do you think she's working with someone?"

"It's a possibility, to be sure. But I don't think so. I think she's been up to something else for a while, and I never noticed.

Or more accurately, I noticed but never figured out what was happening."

Miria realized she'd been pacing in front of the hearth the way Yali once had, and she forced herself to pause. Her hands grasped the back of one of the chairs, and she squeezed until her knuckles whitened. "For years, there's been a mysterious plague affecting children in Swiftdok and the outlying farms. Specifically, I believe it's affecting children with magical blood. Even Rosmilda's own children—they looked frail when I saw them briefly, and you were told they were sickly. I think Rosmilda has found a way to use the magic in those children's blood as her own. A spell cast with ill intentions brings illness back on the witch. My nana warned me against casting evil magic for that reason. Rosmilda does not feel the effects of what she's casting, but those she stole from do."

Adaline stared at her, struck speechless, which was truly a feat and one Miria would have laughed at under other circumstances. There was nothing humorous here, however, and Miria shoved the chair away from herself with the force of her fury. "It's been her the whole time, and yet it's me, and witches like me, who are blamed for the perverted blood magic she's using. *She* called it ironic and convenient. *She's* been pushing that rumor herself. I heard her."

Being a scapegoat for Rosmilda's crimes infuriated, but only half so much as knowing what Rosmilda was really up to. How many children had gotten sick or died because of her?

Yali had told her the sickness was probably nothing and to leave it alone. It was not a witch's place to get involved unless their help was requested. Certainly, it was safer that way; Miria had learned that lesson. But circumstances had changed, and Miria couldn't help but wonder if she'd gotten involved sooner, spent more time trying to find the cause of the mysterious illness, how much suffering she could have prevented. She didn't fault Yali for the position she had taken, but she was no longer certain she could take it herself.

Nor would she be expected to. Adaline's eyes had grown as wide as they had when Miria had confessed the truth about her family this morning, and she reacted much as Miria had assumed. She picked up her sword and adjusted her grip around the pommel. "If what you say is true, and I believe you, then it's time to bring this fight to my would-be mother-in-law."

Chapter Twenty-Two

Two Days Before the Wedding, Continued

Miria swallowed. While she understood (all too well) Adaline's sentiment, this was not a battle that should be fought with a cudgel, like Tuli had beaten the abomination. She would need to be as sharp and subtle as Adaline's sword edge to prevent additional damage to innocent people.

"We can't," Miria said, reluctantly. "Or not so quickly anyway. Anytime Rosmilda attacks us with magic, she's drawing on some child's power, and that child is feeling the repercussions. It's slowly killing them. We need to avoid that, if at all possible."

She said if, but there was no *if* about it. If she was correct, two of those children were her half-sisters. They both had magic in them, and Miria didn't believe for a moment that a woman who was so ready to harm another woman's child would draw the line at her own. She might be more careful, which was why Miria's sisters were still alive, but they were too convenient a power source for Rosmilda to ignore.

She had to get them away from Rosmilda, for their sake and her own. If she could bring them to the cottage, she could wrap them in spells to protect them from Rosmilda. The other children, whoever they were . . . Miria would help them, too. But for now, she would start with the ones she knew about.

Small steps. A beaver's dam might alter the flow of a river, but it was built with one log at a time.

"How do we that?" Adaline asked, interrupting Miria's thoughts. "Can you block her?"

Miria blinked until she recollected what Adaline was referring to. "I don't know. I wrote to the other witches this morning. Hopefully, I'll learn more when someone writes back. In the meantime, I'm going to start with what I do know. I need to rescue my sisters."

"*We* need to rescue your sisters," Adaline said, already reaching for her sword belt.

Miria braced herself, because Adaline was not going to like what she was about to say. "Not you. It's—"

"Daughter of Yali the Wise, first Witch of the Shadow Wood, Sorceress of Gawfrid, if you think I'm staying here and sitting on my ass while you embark on a dangerous rescue mission, you do not know me half as well as I thought you did!"

In spite of everything, Miria had to fight down a laugh. It had been a while since Adaline had called her that, and in light of Yali's passing, she'd adjusted the title. Good memories relieved some of the chill in Miria's blood and soothed the frayed edges of her heart.

But they didn't change anything. "It's not that I don't want a valiant would-be knight with torn skirts to accompany me, but remember what I said. Every time Rosmilda draws on her power to attack, we risk her harming an innocent in the process. Two of us together are more of a threat, thus it's more likely that she would lash out. If I go alone, I might be able to avoid that kind of confrontation."

Ideally, she could avoid Rosmilda entirely and sneak her half-sisters away without their mother noticing. But now that Miria knew her stepmother had been aware of her sneaking around her house once, Miria would not put it past her to figure it out again. This time, Miria would be smarter and look for magical wards or other traps that would give her presence away.

Adaline pursed her lips, her arms crossed. "I concede the point. But tell me this isn't just about you trying to keep me safe when I could be helpful."

It was about keeping Adaline safe, which despite recent events, was something Miria was best able to accomplish with Adaline at the cottage. It was also about what Miria had explained, though. "Any help you could give me is outweighed by the potential harm. I need to attempt this on my own first."

With a sigh, Adaline removed her sword belt and tossed it on the table. "Keeping you safe is important to me too, you know."

Miria pulled her close. "I know, but I'm much safer in town today than you are."

Adaline grunted in response. "If my future wedding wasn't in question, there's a strong likelihood your family would be at my uncle's manor for pre-wedding festivities. There were parties and gatherings planned for all the out-of-town guests. Who knows what's going on now, but it's possible they're there anyway, scheming together."

It would make Miria's life easier if they were, but she was committed regardless. "Let's hope they are holed up at your uncle's since my sisters aren't likely to be with them."

"I can't imagine they are. Their names are Winda and Katline, by the way. In case you didn't know."

She hadn't. Winda and Katline. Miria tried the syllables out a few times. "They're good names. Strong names."

She hoped the girls were stronger than they looked.

It was early afternoon by the time Miria was prepared for the trip into town. She'd packed supplies, including as many premade spells as she could, and she'd taken the extra time to scry on her father's house for whatever information it had to provide. Everything appeared quiet on the outside, which was all she could see. It suggested Rosmilda had some wards around the building to prevent being spied on, and Miria would need stronger magic or a better means to learn more.

Adaline consoled herself over her inaction by turning Tuli into her sparring partner and assuring Miria that she would figure out how to cook dinner while Miria was gone, a promise that gave Miria something else to worry about on her journey into town—namely, that Adaline would burn the cottage to the ground.

Miria had expected to discover men searching the forest for Adaline as she walked, but to her surprise she found none. It was unlikely they'd given up, which suggested that Rosmilda's attack meant she and Miria's father really were working with Adaline's family. Where the men had failed yesterday, magic took over. Although Miria doubted Adaline's family was aware that magic was being used.

Still, she was grateful for the quiet; and disguised, Miria entered the town without trouble. Any part of this plan that did not require her to use magic was a gift. Once she found her sisters, she would have to quickly wrap them in protective spells. If she had to fight Rosmilda on top of it, Miria feared tiring herself out as much as she had the day before—a possibility she hadn't shared with Adaline since it would only worry her.

She kept her eyes open for signs of trouble as she made her way toward her father's home, but although the townsfolk she passed seemed especially tense, nothing else stood out of the ordinary, and especially tense wasn't surprising given what happened yesterday. Word would have spread through the taverns and town square. Even those who had previously turned to the witch in the woods for help expected her to *stay* in the woods—to not make trouble.

For the witch to have made such a bold appearance, to have openly attacked (from their perspective) the Lord of Gawfrid, the world would have turned upside down. If someone as powerful as Lord Sigmun was threatened, so were they all. It would have been stranger if no one was on edge.

Miria patted her satchel of supplies for reassurance. At least if anyone saw her looking anxious, she had a good excuse.

Acting like she had every reason to be there, Miria strolled up to her family's home. Today, there would be no hiding herself. Her sisters needed to see her, and she couldn't risk casting any spells she didn't absolutely need to. When she found the girls, then there would be time for magic.

Miria held that thought firmly in mind as she inspected the servants' side door for wards. None had kept her out last time, but there were as many kinds of wards as there were needs for protective magic. Rosmilda had known Miria had come here before, which suggested Miria had set off something.

She ran her finger around the door frame, hoping no nosy neighbors were watching. When she found nothing, she turned her attention to the stones beneath her feet. There, in the center of the path right before the door, she found what she was looking for. One of the flat walkway stones was giving off power, faint but enough to tickle her palm. If Miria hadn't been searching for it, she'd never have noticed it. No doubt she'd stepped on that stone during her last visit.

After another glance around, she knelt and flipped the stone over. Sure enough, a sigil had been painted on the bottom in a reddish-brown ink that Miria suspected was dried blood mixed with other substances. It was a simple warning mark, not too unlike the ones Yali had drawn around the cottage and which

Miria maintained. Only the power in this one was cruder. Rosmilda had known what to draw, but she hadn't perfected the technique for powering it, nor did she have the strength to make it invisible. Although perhaps she simply hadn't bothered. The fake sapphire she'd given Adaline suggested Rosmilda had skills when it was worth her while to employ them, but most people wouldn't be picking up the stones.

Miria removed a jar from her satchel and sprinkled its contents over the ward. The mix of salt, forest dirt, herbs, and a drop of Miria's own blood worked instantly. The sigil faded from view, and Miria felt its power vanish. She quickly replaced the stone and wiped her hands on her skirts.

No one had stopped her or called out to her yet. Luck was on her side, perhaps. She inched open the servants' door and slipped inside. Although she heard a few voices from the direction of the kitchen, and the scent of roasting meat and baking bread filled the air, she encountered no one, and she crept up the stairs, holding her breath.

Surely, her sisters weren't left alone all day while the rest of her family did . . . whatever they were doing. Wedding festivities or wedding scheming. A rich man like her father would have tutors or a governess for his daughters.

Miria had counted on additional company, and she'd come prepared to deal with any such person. But as she climbed the last flight of stairs toward the girls' room, the lack of voices was more concerning than a chorus of nursemaids or guards would have been. Something was wrong. Could Rosmilda have expected her? And if so, why had she not sprung another trap? Even if she were too tired from her earlier spellcasting attack to use magic (and Miria did not know whether stealing other people's power would tire her out), she could have stationed guards and told them she expected trouble.

Miria set her jaw as she headed down the hallway. It had seemed so unlikely that her father or Rosmilda would have taken the girls to Adaline's uncle's for the day, but what if she'd made a mistake? She'd been hasty; she knew that. Her suspicions had overpowered all of Yali's cautious teachings. She'd wanted to get her sisters and not waste time planning. But as Miria opened the door to the room where she'd last seen the girls, it appeared all she'd done was waste time. No one was there.

This was clearly Winda and Katline's room. It was filled with the pretty comforts Miria had not even known to dream about when she was a child. Two beds, each piled with lovely blankets and soft pillows. A plush rug between them. A basket with dolls and wooden games. Fine hairbrushes and silky ribbons.

But it was also filled with an air of sadness, as though these signs of wealth and privilege were more like decorations than objects meant to be enjoyed. The girls in this room were loved and cared for to the extent that they were useful, but no more. It was no different, really, than what Adaline had spoken of, although their "use" might be very different to their respective families. A gilded prison was still a prison.

Anger surged in Miria once more, and she dug her nails into her palms.

She spun on her heel, discarding her first failed plan for another as quickly as her heart beat. What of the tools Rosmilda was using to cast her stolen spells? She must have supplies somewhere. If Miria could steal those, she could halt Rosmilda's spells, even if only temporarily.

They would be hidden, obviously. Locked away in a room where no one would stumble upon them. That meant the public rooms on the lower floors were out. A bedchamber perhaps?

Miria opened a couple of other doors until she found a likely room, decorated in florals, the air tinged with the scent of old perfume. The bed in the center was finely carved and covered in richly dyed blankets and lace. At the foot of the bed sat a trunk. Thinking at once of her nana's trunk, Miria rushed over to it and cast a simple spell with a half-copper coin to pick the lock. Expectantly, she pulled back the lid only to discover nothing but mothballs and heavy winter clothing, polished leather boots lined with wool and soft furs.

Grimacing, Miria shut the trunk after searching through to the bottom. She should have known her spell had worked too easily. She stood, taking a closer inspection of the room, and her gaze settled on a small, silver box on the dressing table. It might be nothing more than a jewelry box, but Miria brushed a finger over it, and her skin tingled faintly like it had with the path stone.

The box itself did not appear to be bespelled, but some of its content were. It, too, was locked, unsurprisingly. Gritting her teeth because she was annoyed at needing to cast again when she was trying to preserve her magic, Miria picked the lock and flipped open the lid.

She'd expected to find charms, perhaps a premade potion. What the box contained was more disturbing—small scraps of parchment, each labeled with a name or description, each colored with the distinct ruddy brown of dried blood. Just a splotch, no larger than the half-copper coin in Miira's hand. But Miria could sense the power in each magically stolen drop.

This was Romsilda's stash. This was how she maintained her connection to the children whose power she somehow siphoned from afar.

There were eight of them, and the names meant nothing to Miria, though she noted her sisters' names did not appear on any. But then, Rosmilda didn't need to go to such lengths with her own daughters. They lived with her; their blood was easily available whenever Rosmilda needed it.

Miria's own blood quickened as she debated. If she took all of these, she would cut Rosmilda off from her victims, or all of them but her own children. But for how long? And if she did that,

Rosmilda would know what she'd done. Would she rely more heavily on hurting Winda and Katline until she replenished her supply?

With the names and their blood, Miria could find each child and put protective spells on them, but that would take time—days to protect all of them since Miria didn't dare weaken herself too much. Nor were these eight likely to be the only children in Swiftdok with magical blood. They were simply Rosmilda's current choices.

Miria swore to herself. She wanted to protect her sisters above all else, but she knew she shouldn't put her own family above these unknown children. They were a start. This was something. Even if Rosmilda sought other children to replace these particular ones as soon as she realized what Miria had done, Miria would have helped those she could.

And perhaps . . . Miria stared at one of the names. If Rosmilda had found a way to draw on a child's magic from a scrap of stolen blood, perhaps she could find a way to protect a child from afar, too. Rosmilda clearly knew a thing or two about magic that Miria didn't, but Miria refused to concede that Rosmilda might be more clever than she was.

Miria didn't like the possibilities presented, but she liked doing nothing even less, so she placed the bloodied parchment pieces in her satchel and closed the silver box, being sure to put everything back as she'd found it. She cast a last glance around then returned to the hall.

If she found a means to cast a protective spell from afar, she would need something personal from her sisters in lieu of blood. A strand of hair would be ideal.

She slipped back inside the girls' room and immediately headed toward the brushes and combs on their dressing table. Had their hair been the same color? Miria unthreaded a strand of light brown hair from the brush as the door opened softly behind her.

Chapter Twenty-Three

Two Days Before the Wedding, Continued

Miria spun around, a spell on the tip of her tongue should she need it.

Rosmilda strode into the room, her face smug, and Miria's stomach sunk. Either she'd been expected or she'd tripped another unseen ward. It hardly mattered. The risky and reckless rescue attempt had failed, and her luck hadn't held.

Well, this time she was not unprepared to deal with Rosmilda magically, if it came to that. The spell danced about in her mouth, ready and eager, but Miria held it in. She set the brush down behind her back and lightly pushed it away so Rosmilda wouldn't know what she'd been up to. She wanted to hear what Rosmilda had to say.

"I'm surprised to see you again so soon," Rosmilda said, and Miria noted she paused just past the doorway. Her face was smug, but her body emanated tension. "Did you come to return my saltcellar?"

If she were Adaline, she'd have a witty comeback for that, but Miria hadn't grown up at court. Verbal sparring was not among her talents. She preferred bluntness. "I came to confirm it was you who's been making the children in town ill."

"Oh, that." Rosmilda's brow pinched, as if she were genuinely confused and surprised by the accusation. But also unconcerned. "What did I say to make you figure that out?"

"Many things actually. Do you take blood from your own daughters, too? Do Winda and Katline suffer so you can have magic?" It was another risk, letting Rosmilda know she knew her sisters' names, not letting Rosmilda underestimate her. But despite her expression and earlier arrogance, Rosmilda seemed a lot more wary of Miria in person than Miria had anticipated. If there was a chance she could intimidate Rosmilda into behaving for a while, the risk seemed worth it.

Rosmilda's smugness faltered a moment, and she glanced at the girls' empty beds with something that could have been tenderness. "It is unfortunate, but their power will fade in time. I can't seal it into them the way it was sealed into you. And when they are older and that time has come, I will make it up to them by teaching them to do what I do. For a small sacrifice now, they will be strong and powerful later. I'll make sure of it."

Miria tried to take heart that Rosmilda had ambitions for her daughters beyond them being a power source, but it was hard. Yet maybe it meant Rosmilda was not as horrible as Miria assumed. Maybe there was something good in her, something Miria could work with.

"And the other children?" Miria asked. "What of their lives? They never got to grow up."

"That's also unfortunate, but there are not enough children in this town born with magic to always spread my needs out adequately. I tried to convince your father that we should move to a larger city, but he had his plan, and I can't say it was a bad one. Look at where it's gotten us." She spread her arms wide, then dropped them harshly. "I go to their funerals. I say the prayers with their families. It comforts their parents that someone of my position would take the time to do that."

On second thought, maybe there was nothing good.

Miria scowled. "So kind of you to pretend to mourn those you killed while you point fingers elsewhere. The Overseer's wife must appear to be such a benevolent woman."

Rosmilda shrugged. "People need someone to blame. You shouldn't take it to heart. The witch is not a person to them. She is a figure. A symbol. She bestows favors and ill fortune like the gods, but while blaming the gods for your misfortunes is dangerous for your soul, the witch cares not about your soul. She doesn't control your afterlife. She's a safe place to put the blame when you have no one else."

Safe for the townsfolk, perhaps. Not for the witch. And if people did not blame the actual source of their problems, if they were too distracted by lies to seek out the truth, then their lives would never improve. But Miria let all of that slide. "Yes, you give them an easy answer to accept. One that requires no effort on their part, and which conveniently deflects the blame that should go on you."

"Should it?" Rosmilda suddenly snapped alert, like a string had been pulled in her spine. "When a king's army tramples over a foreign town, he is a powerful leader securing his people's future. When a man slaps his wife, he is just ruling over his household as the gods intended. Men leave a trail of casualties in their wake for their ambitions all the time."

"And what of it? None of those things are good."

"Such is my point." Rosmilda's sharp gaze bore into her, and Miria sensed the older woman was as confused by her perspective as Miria was revolted by Rosmilda's. "The world is not good or just, and it is especially not so to us women. I come from a background much like you. The witch who took me in tried to tell me I could have a purpose. For a while, I bought all of her noble bullshit, but then I grew up. Why should I waste my talents helping people who never cared for me? Why shouldn't I help myself the way men do?"

"We're not men."

"No, we're not." Rosmilda finally took another step into the room, animated by her anger. Finally, *that* was something Miria understood. "Men have power. Even a poor man, like your father was, had power solely based on the luck of his birth. Why? Because the church decrees it. Even the crown, the supposed ultimate power of this land, clings to the church for the power it gives them. And the church clings to its gods for the justification. Power is always granted by affiliation with more powerful people. That is why witches, for all their magic, have none. They are women, alone."

"So you latched onto my father to legitimize your power."

"Yes, he'd used that spell he traded you for well, but he'd never have come this far without me." Rosmilda picked up a child's volume of stories from the table by one of the beds and ran her hand over it reverently. Miria didn't know how much a book like that cost, but she knew it wasn't insignificant. "Don't think that half the women in this town wouldn't murder my family to take what I have. We all have to look out for our own. I'm doing what I can to protect my children; it's what a mother *should* do."

Miria couldn't help but scoff. "It's not what my father did."

Again, something softened in Rosmilda's face like it had when she'd glanced at her daughter's bed. "A father wouldn't for a girl, it's true. But a mother would. It's a shame you did not know yours."

"I had a nana, and she taught me to be better than that."

Rosmilda groaned. "She taught you to be content to live within a world that despises you when you have more innate power than the people who wield social and political power do. Is that why you came here? To try to shame me for not being content with that lot?"

I came here to stop you, Miria thought, but she held in the words. She could not, would not fight more with Rosmilda until she knew her sisters were safe from their mother's spells.

"I came here to reason with you," Miria said instead. "Leave me be."

"I would, happily, if you had not abducted Lady Adaline. Witch—Greta—that was your name, was it not? Your brother has told me so."

Miria flinched at the name she hadn't gone by in so many years, but she did not correct Rosmilda.

"Greta, I do not wish to fight with you, and I believe that you do not wish it either. I think you're smarter than that. You wish to avenge yourself on your father, do you not?"

Miria said nothing, unsurprised that Rosmilda had figured out one of her motivations for stealing Adaline away.

Taking her silence for the agreement it was, Rosmilda set down the children's book and pressed on. "I would as well, in your place. That's why I know you aren't unreasonable. You *want,* too. But put aside your grudge for long enough to think clearly. Think bigger. Just imagine how much we could do once your brother is wed to Lady Adaline—a woman with a direct connection to the throne! I cannot even credit my own spells for that good fortune. We were lucky she has earned such a reputation for being difficult that her family was willing to consider our match. It's a chance that must be seized upon, and you could be a part of it."

"It is tempting, I grant you, to dream about having the political power to reshape this world for the better." Miria couldn't deny it.

When she thought about the children in town whose bellies went empty, the women forced to flee their homes because of the quiet violence inside, every person forced into a role they would not have chosen. Even the rich and allegedly powerful like Adaline, sold off into marriage for someone else's gain. A single witch could help a single person. A group of witches could help a few more. But it took more power than any sisterhood of witches to change a country, a culture. Miria could dream of myriad ways to help so many more, no more redirecting a river like a beaver slowly stacking one log against another, but with all the power of a kingdom's army engineering a dam of stone.

But that wasn't the power Rosmilda dreamed of. A woman who would trample on the helpless to rise so high would continue to tread upon them once she reached her aim. And the higher she rose, the larger her boots would be, the more who would be crushed beneath them.

Some dreams could only ever be that. Even a wish spell had limits, and a witch was wise to know hers.

Besides, in this scenario, Adaline was reduced once again to nothing but currency for someone else. Regardless of any other failings Miria found with Rosmilda's ambitions, she would see a hundred hard, hungry winters of her own before she let Adaline's fate be determined by anyone other than Adaline.

Still, these thoughts lingered in her mind long enough for Rosmilda to see something there, and she grasped at it, assuming she had won the day. "People like us, we're forced to fight over scraps, and I refuse to settle for that. Hardworking, skilled, clever people deserve more."

Not for the first time during this conversation, Miria was forced to concede that Rosmilda was not wrong. But nor was she entirely right. *Everyone* deserved more than scraps, not merely the most clever or most ruthless, and that Rosmilda disagreed only hardened Miria's resolve to stop her plans.

"Your offer is generous," Miria said, though it was anything but. It had probably seemed like a generous offer to the other woman, but the truth was—Miria had magic and Rosmilda wanted it. If there was anything honest in Rosmilda's offer, it had to be driven by fear. She was worried Miria could thwart her, and Miria hoped she was right to be. "I will not be a part of any plans that have relied on the deaths of innocent children to come to fruition. When you plant a seed in poisoned soil, all you get is poisoned fruit."

Rosmilda sighed. "You must realize you can't hide Lady Adaline forever. I found you today, and I can do it again."

"You and your creation failed today, and would do so again."

"It hardly matters." Rosmilda waved away this reminder with a well-manicured hand, but Miria saw the way her cheek twitched. "We have all the resources of Lord Sigmun and Sir Alberik on our side, and do not think for a moment that Adaline's family isn't on *our* side."

Miria did her best not to react, but the way Rosmilda said the words certainly hinted that she'd placed them under a spell. Miria should have expected as much. Was it more charms like the one she'd tried to give to Adaline, or something harder to remove? Whatever it was, it meant more challenges for Miria.

Two days ago she'd really believed her plan to save Adaline and get revenge would be simple. Miria didn't know whether to laugh or cry.

"Lady Adaline's family is so anxious to have their sweet, headstrong daughter back," Rosmilda continued. "If you refuse to cooperate, they'll eventually retrieve Adaline by force."

Forget laughing or crying. Screaming would do. Rosmilda's threat was nothing Miria hadn't anticipated, but her stomach twisted all the same.

She glanced around the room and back at Rosmilda, who stood some ten feet or more away. Rosmilda had never dared get closer, but Miria doubted she was defenseless, and to be certain, she reached out with her power, trying to sense any magic upon Rosmilda's form.

It was tempting to try subduing Rosmilda here, while they were alone. But Miria hadn't planned for a direct confrontation. She had spells to defend herself and spells to escape should it come to that, but fighting with Rosmilda had never been her intention. Not until she could free her sisters. If Rosmilda was defenseless, though, Miria might risk it.

Unfortunately, as expected, Rosmilda did not appear defenseless at all. When she concentrated, Miria could feel power hovering around her body, the same sort of magic that had fueled the sigil on the stone path. It was an unnatural sort of power, stolen from others, and Miria let her focus shift back to normal, determined not to provoke Rosmilda into using it. Eventually, she would have no choice, but she'd be patient. Today's lack of patience had gotten her nowhere; lesson learned.

Or perhaps not nowhere entirely, but she'd not accomplished her goal, which was frustrating.

Either way, it didn't appear as though she was going to accomplish more here. She needed to return to the cottage quickly, fortify her defenses, and make new plans. And she had to warn Adaline of everything she'd learned.

"You can try to take Adaline by force," Miria said, inching closer to the open window. "But I do not recommend it."

"Brave words for a girl without a lord's guard at her disposal."

"I don't need a lord's guard. I'm a witch, not a woman clinging to a man for her power." The shot landed, and Miria had the satisfaction of seeing Rosmilda's placid mask crack just a fraction. Adaline, she thought, would be proud of that verbal bolt.

Then Miria transformed into her owl form and flew out the window.

Chapter Twenty-Four

Two Days Before the Wedding, Continued

Her verbal triumph did not carry Miria for long. She'd scarcely cleared the town walls when the air filled with unsettling shrieks. She landed on the nearest tree and turned to witness the sky filling with black shadows, and a chill ran down her spine.

Winged like ravens but so much larger, the shadows circled the town, their cries a desperate, haunting sound that drowned out every other noise. Then, as one, they swooped down, vanishing from Miria's line of sight but not from the world. She heard the townsfolk yelling in fear, doors and shutters slamming.

These were the creatures the farmer's son had seen coming for him, the ones who took the children's blood for Rosmilda's magic. Miria was positive.

That meant this was her fault. Although she'd promised herself she would not provoke Rosmilda into using more magic, she'd done it anyway. She should have gone along with Rosmilda's offer, pretended to consider it and buy some time. But she was as arrogant as the other woman had insisted, and her refusal must have made Rosmilda feel threatened, and so she was gathering her resources, just as Miria had been planning on doing.

Miria swore to herself, thinking of all the children in trouble right now. The parchment with their blood sat in her satchel, worthless in the moment. Tomorrow, maybe, she could use it to find Rosmilda's victims and cast the protective spells that would free them from Rosmilda's clutches. But promises to protect those children tomorrow did nothing to help the ones whose magic was being drawn upon today. Even if she flew back immediately and confronted Rosmilda, it would be pointless, Most likely, Rosmilda's magical thieves would be gone by the time she got there. Already, the yelling in town was dying down. Miria could guess the threat was literally vanishing before people's eyes.

Adaline would have known better. As brash and reckless as she was, Adaline was better skilled at dealing with people. A lady had to be. A witch did not.

Witches stayed in their woods or their bogs; they kept to their hollows and caves or the lonely windswept moors where it was safe. They did their work from afar. Miria was growing less and less certain that was as wise as they claimed. If she'd been in town more all these years or had taken a more active interest in the lives of those who lived around her, she might have assembled the pieces of Rosmilda's puzzle sooner. With that greater familiarity, some people might have been less inclined to blame her for it. Not all, certainly. People were always in need of a scapegoat, and anyone who was different, for whatever reason, made for a handy one. That was the risk in being known, but was it any more of a risk than what she'd been doing?

Miria didn't know yet, but her lack of knowing how to work with people was a weakness she vowed to correct.

When she made it back to the cottage, she found Adaline rolling dough. Flour coated her arms and face, which were shiny with sweat, and she wore an expression of grim determination.

Adaline looked up as Miria closed the door. "I went hunting for rabbits for our dinner, but then I didn't know how to prepare them because someone else had always done that part when I went hunting back home, so Tuli did it, and they're roasting in the oven out back. And then Tuli showed me how to make pastry dough so I'm—" She cut off as though suddenly remembering why Miria had left. "What happened? Where are the girls?"

Miria let the questions hang for a moment as she tried to take everything in. "Tuli showed you how to make dough?" When in the world had her golem ever learned that, and how was it that he was teaching Adaline these things?

"He doesn't normally cook for you?" Adaline asked.

"No. He doesn't eat so it never seemed right to ask him to help unless I needed his strength for a task."

Adaline's bit her lip. "Should I not have asked? Although he did kind of volunteer."

Miria set down her satchel, amazed at how Adaline could keep making her smile under any circumstances. "I do not think you could make Tuli do something he doesn't want to. Only I have the power to do that, and I hope I never use it. Although, my nana would say a golem doesn't want anything, so . . ."

She let the thought trail off, recalling Rosmilda's admonishment about Miria wanting things. Not that Rosmilda had meant it as an admonishment. More like a compliment, probably.

It didn't bother Miria to want. Rosmilda's view of witches was as twisted as her views of everything else. How many times had Yali warned her about expending too much magic helping people? About protecting herself? No, witches weren't supposed to be self-sacrificing to the degree Rosmilda had implied, and they were not immune from normal human desires, nor were they expected to be.

But the reminder refocused Miria's attention on the most pressing matters, which unfortunately did not involve Adaline's burgeoning culinary skills nor Tuli's surprising knowledge of pie-baking.

Adaline's rolling of the dough took on a bit of extra force as Miria recounted what had transpired. "So you didn't find your sisters, and Rosmilda has bespelled my family. That was probably a waste of her magic. My family wants your family's money. I'm sure they'd go along with Rosmilda's schemes just fine of their own accord. As for your sisters . . ." Her anger melted into an expression of concern.

Miria shared it, and tried—again—to take some comfort from the knowledge that Rosmilda meant good things for her daughters in the future. In the meantime, it was the town's children who were in particular danger. "Your family may not be as keen on Rosmilda's and my father's tactics as you think. People fear magic as much as they crave it."

"I know." Adaline ran her flour-coated fingers through the stray hairs lining her face, turning them white. "I'm speaking from frustration."

"I know the feeling well." She brushed the flour from Adaline's hair, letting the other woman's closeness soothe her aching heart.

She wanted a moment, nothing more, to kiss the flour off Adaline's lips, run fingers over her bare skin, make the most of every moment they were finally together again. But every moment she entertained such luxuries was a moment she could be working to lengthen Adaline's company. It was a cruel dilemma.

"Miri." Adaline murmured her name as she kissed Miria back, and Miria floated beyond the confines of her body, overwhelmed with the sensation of Adaline's fingers drifting lazily down her hip.

She stumbled backward into the table, and her hand collided with something hard. Her family's saltcellar.

Her body burning with more want (you see, Rosmilda—so much wanting), Miria pulled away. Her body and her brain needed two different outlets, and her brain was winning this battle.

"Rosmilda is preparing for something," Miria said, turning away so she didn't see her own unfulfilled desires reflected on Adaline's face. "I can't hold off your uncle's entire guard and whatever mischief she has in store forever, and if I'm going to work protective spells on the children I found, I need to be even more cautious about how I spend my energy. But if I scry on Rosmilda directly, I might figure out what she plans and direct my defenses most effectively."

"Sensible," Adaline said with a frown. "Not as fun as kissing you, but I suppose we should be practical now to allow time for more enjoyable pursuits later."

Miria nodded. She would hold that promise close to her chest and hope she was not too tired later to follow through.

While Adaline went back to making her pie, Miria retrieved the scrying bowl and got to work. The saltcellar was a direct connection to Rosmilda and to her father. A more personal object would have been better, but it was a valuable item, and its worth to them would count for something magically.

She thought so anyway, but after several minutes of trying to spy on Rosmilda or her father, all Miria had was a headache. She collapsed onto the bench and rubbed her temples.

"Are you all right?" Adaline darted over and clasped her hands. "Has she done something else to you?"

"I'm fine." Miria extricated herself from Adaline's grip and poked a finger in the bowl of water in frustration. "She must be blocking me. All is see is darkness, like a door has been slammed shut."

"She can do that?"

"Oh, yes. She's quite skilled for someone with no power of her own. I thought the saltcellar would be enough to find her, and it is, but its connection to her and my father isn't strong enough to overpower whatever spell she cast."

Frowning, Miria plucked a strawberry from the bowl Adaline had gathered earlier. It was perfectly ripe, and red juice rolled down her fingers as she withdrew them from her mouth.

"Blood." Miria sat up straighter and wiped away the juice. "That will have to work."

Adaline watched in alarm as Miria cleaned her knife and pierced the fleshy pad below her thumb. A single crimson drop splashed into the scrying bowl, and Miria placed a clean cloth over palm to staunch the bleeding.

"Blood ties me to my father and brother," she explained, seeing Adaline's worried expression. "It's possible Rosmilda could still block me, but the connection is so powerful, I doubt she's capable. I won't be able to find *her* this way, but I can scry on my father, and perhaps through him I'll find her."

Adaline nodded and picked up the strawberries. "I suppose it's too bad you didn't think of that before you went to find your sisters."

With the tip of her knife, Miria swirled the drop of blood in the scrying bowl, watching the red dissolve into the clear water. "True, although that wasn't a total waste of a plan. I don't scry much, though," she added sheepishly. "I should have remembered what Rosmilda said to me earlier, but it was only the strawberry juice that jogged my brain."

"You don't scry much?" Adaline smoothed the layer of strawberries out on the pie crust. "Did you never even scry much on me?"

"No. It seemed invasive. I wanted to give you privacy." In the pause that followed, Miria put aside her knife and realized Adaline was shaking her head. "What?"

"Did you never think that maybe I wanted you to invade my privacy?" Adaline asked, raising an eyebrow.

The question flummoxed Miria. "I . . . No."

Adaline groaned good naturedly. "You create men out of clay, weave lace with spiderwebs, and build ladders from morning glories, but sometimes you have no imagination." She smiled mischievously and leaned across the table. "You could have watched me while I took a bath. I often thought of you when I did, especially that day we went swimming in the river."

Miria felt her cheeks warm. "I don't lack *that* much imagination. The thought crossed my mind. But that's why I felt you should have privacy!"

She needed to return to the task at hand, but here was Adaline again, laughing and tempting her to dwell on those *more enjoyable pursuits* now instead of later. Before she could remind Adaline that thinking of her naked was not (unfortunately) conducive to scrying on her father, Adaline went on.

"More seriously, I always liked to think you were keeping a constant eye on me," she said. "That every time I felt like I was being watched, it was because of you. Wasn't it?"

"How often did you feel watched?" Miria asked.

"Constantly, because I was." The last of the mischief and good humor slipped from Adaline's face. "I was at court. Oh, if I could scry, I'd have been watching people all the time there. Court is run by gossip. I know I've said it before, but it's a good thing I'm not a witch. I wouldn't have your restraint."

Miria pushed away her remaining lascivious thoughts and pressed her hands around the scrying bowl. It was too bad she hadn't known Adaline's wishes before, but they could discuss that later among the more pleasurable things.

"Nor will Rosmilda," Miria said, partly to remind herself what she was up against. "It will be a bad thing then, if she ends up at court with you."

"Right." Adaline squared her shoulders. "I will stop distracting you so you can spy on her."

Miria wondered how long that would last, but she followed Adaline's example. She straightened her spine, closed eyes for a moment, and called upon her power. Her blood was both the connection to her father and a potent sacrifice for the magic. Still, for a moment, she feared it wasn't enough. The same blackness that had blocked her previously clouded the water. But as Miria held her breath, the blackness dissolved like her blood had, and a scene spread out before her. She closed her eyes again, thrusting her mind into the liminal space between her cottage walls and the room in which she found her father.

He looked much as he had in the portrait on his wall, though his hair was grayer and his face was harder, as if even in the few years since the painting had been made, he'd shed more of whatever little gentleness he'd ever had. His clothes were fine and rich, his fingernails short and clean, and the years of calluses he'd earned through his labor softened, either by time or intentional grooming.

That detail somehow struck Miria as the most absurd. He looked every inch the town's Overseer from his hair down to the soles of his boots, but clothes could be changed. His hands were how he proved to the world that he deserved to walk among the other men in his company, and Miria's old fury rose to the surface of her skin, prickling with power. She alone could see the real dirt on his hands, the filth he couldn't wash off or scrub away with a bit of pumice.

Hans stood next to him, his arms crossed and fingers tapping nervously against his shirtsleeves. His expression was less dour than their father's yet still grim. Worry lines creased his brow, and Miria wondered if any of that stress were for Adaline's safety or if it was all for his uncertain future.

The two were joined by four other men whose names Miria didn't know, though Adaline would surely have recognized them. Judging from their attire and adornments, one must have been her uncle and the other her father. Miria thought she could detect some resemblance there—in height and in coloring. Both of them also appeared worried, but something was off in their eyes, as though some light had been dimmed. Miria's first thought was that it was their worries, but she recalled Rosmilda's words, and that made far more sense. A father and an uncle determined to retrieve Adaline should not appear dullish. They should be fired up. But Rosmilda's magic clouded their minds.

Miria saw no traces of that dullness in the final two men present, but they appeared to be of lower station, dressed in the family liveries. Guard captains, if Miria had to guess. There was no need for Rosmilda to expend energy on them since they would presumably listen to their superiors.

"We could be back out there," the younger of the two captains was saying.

He paced before a shelf filled with more books than Miria had ever seen in one place. The entire room was filled with polished wood, heavy tapestries, and fine furniture, but it was the books Miria wished she could inspect.

The captain drew his finger around on the table, and Miria finally noticed that a large map had been spread open on it. It showed all of Gawfrid Province, from the mountains to the north, to the farms east of the Swift River, and the Shadow

Wood Forest to the west. A line cut through the woods—the true path, the actual road that would take people west to a town on the other side of the forest that was called Wulfton. Her path—the witch's path—could appear anywhere off that road.

"We've searched no deeper into the woods than this," the captain said, circling a spot along the road that did not go very far, but which did go far enough that it covered Miria's cottage. "We should have expanded the search today."

"I told you, there is no point," Miria's father said. "The witch cannot live so deep in the woods as all that. She comes to town too often for such a long journey."

Did her father know she was the witch? What, if anything, had Rosmilda told him?

"My lord?" the other captain looked at the shorter of the two nobles, the one who was probably Adaline's uncle. "They say the witch can fly. I'd reckon she can travel pretty far."

"We trust Garulf on this," the Lord of Gawfrid said. "The witch has never dared cross us before, but those in town would know of her and her capabilities."

Not likely, Miria thought, but for once, men's arrogance suited her purposes.

The guard captains exchanged weary looks, but their employers did not seem to notice.

"We must be patient, your men rested," Adaline's father said. "Trust Garulf. He has a plan."

"I thought there was a plan today," the second captain said. "Begging your pardon, but I thought the plan—"

"We suffered a minor setback today," Miria's father snapped. "My wife is correcting her error as we speak, and our second attempt will not fail."

The two captains looked skeptical at the mention of a woman, but Adaline's family didn't flinch, which was proof enough that Rosmilda had bespelled them.

Correcting her error—Miria didn't like the sound of that. She searched her father's and brother's faces for more that they weren't saying, but they gave little away.

"And when will this second attempt be ready?" the younger captain asked.

"Tomorrow, I was told," Hans said. His knuckles were white as he gripped the table, making his thoughts on the delay as obvious as the guard captains' were. He did not press their father, though.

Did *he* know she was the witch? If Rosmilda was using her father's or brother's blood to track Miria, then one of them must, if not both. Most likely, it was her father, but she would not make the mistake of believing her brother a better man. Not again.

"You will not find the witch's home without my wife," Garulf said. "When she is ready, your men should be, too. We will lead you right to the witch."

With another abomination. It was the only thing that made sense. Tomorrow was not a lot of time. It might be enough for Miria to fortify her wards around the cottage so strongly that no animals, never mind humans, would ever find it. But another construct, like Rosmilda's horrific golem that was magically guided with a sample of her family's blood—that was a creature Miria's wards could not keep out forever.

And this time Rosmilda and Miria's father would be smarter and not send it alone. That had been the error her father had spoken of. Rosmilda had assumed if she attacked Miria with magic, she would not be able to stop the abomination from retrieving Adaline. Neither of them had counted on Adaline not wanting to be retrieved, nor Miria having a golem of her own to defend her.

"Just so," Sir Alberik said. "Tomorrow, you will take a large contingent of men to the woods, rescue my daughter, and burn the witch's home to the ground. Then we will have much to celebrate at the wedding."

Chapter Twenty-Five

Two Days Before the Wedding, Continued

Miria tried to hold onto the vision, but her mind raced, and so did her heart. She snapped back to herself and didn't know how long she'd stared into a bowl of bloodied water until Adaline slid a teacup her way and the fragrant scent broke her thought loop.

"I can make tea now, too. See?" Adaline's smile was forced, and she sat next to Miria and guided her hand to the cup. "Drink and tell me how bad what you saw was. Your lips are dry, and your face is scaring me."

Miria drank. She didn't particularly want the tea, but Adaline had chosen a blend with the proper herbs to ground her. Was it luck or intuition?

"Rosmilda is creating another abomination," she said finally. "When it's ready, your family's guards will follow it through the woods. It will lead them straight here, the same way the last one found us."

Adaline shook her head vehemently. "My father's men would never follow such a creature. They would look at it and know it's a work of evil."

"Your father is bespelled by Rosmilda," Miria reminded her. "And if he orders them to, would they not do whatever it takes to rescue you?"

Adaline scowled, but she twisted her fingers uncertainly.

Miria sipped her tea, her thoughts racing. Where were the other witches she'd written to? She knew it was foolish to expect an immediate response, but she could really use one.

She could really use help, truthfully.

"One day doesn't give me much time to prepare," Miria said. "I'll have to choose—do more to fend off our families, or protect the children Rosmilda's magic harms. Protecting them might slow her down, but it won't be enough to stop her. I'm certain there are others she can draw from."

Adaline bit her lip. "Can you block her magic? You're more powerful, a real witch."

A real witch—Miria considered the phrase. What was Rosmilda? Her original assumption—that Rosmilda had obtained the charm she'd given to Adaline from a witch—was no longer likely. Rosmilda had created it. A witch had taught her, but that didn't make Rosmilda a witch herself. And what, if anything, did that suggest about her capabilities?

Miria traced the green vine painted on her teacup with a finger. "I doubt I can block her. It's the blood connection, the same way I was able to overcome her blocking me from scrying on my father—it's too strong. As long as my father and brother are with her, she can use their blood as proxies to find mine."

"I see." Adaline folded her restless hands together and stared at them.

Miria stared, too. At the tiny mole on the back of Adaline's left hand and the gold signet ring she wore on her right. Strawberry juice stained her delicate fingers. The longer Adaline stayed, the more she and Miria's father would trade places. Her hands would grow coarser, more like Miria's own. But her time here was seeming like it would be even shorter than Miria had feared. Far too short for that to happen.

The wedding was in two days. If their families' plan succeeded, Miria would fail herself and fail Adaline.

Then Adaline jerked in her seat as though reaching a decision. "It appears that as long as I'm with you, I put you in danger. I should leave so you'll be safe."

"What?" Miria grabbed her hands. "No, that's not an option. We'll think of something."

"Miri, listen to me. The only reason you're threatened is because I'm here. I can't stay and let these men and Rosmilda come for you and possibly destroy your home." Adaline wet her lips and stood. "I know you want to stop the wedding, and so do I. I probably want it more than you do in spite of your plans for vengeance. But if there's something I can do to protect you, I'll do it. I'll leave tonight, and they won't attack tomorrow."

Miria stood, as well, too agitated to stay seated. "*Maybe* they won't attack tomorrow. Nothing is certain. Forget my vengeance for a moment. There will be others ways I can get that. This is about you."

And it was, she realized. Her fury was a fire that deserved quenching, but Adaline came before all else. Vengeance had waited nearly fifteen years; it could wait another fifteen if required. But Adaline did not have that time.

"You deserve better than to be married to my brother," Miria said. "To be married into a conniving, scheming family that thinks nothing of using any means at their disposal to get what they want. Who would harm innocent children for their own gain. I can't let that happen."

Adaline laughed ruefully. "Your family will fit in perfectly at court with values like those. It's nothing that I'm not used to and everything I've been trained to expect."

"That doesn't make this any less terrible."

"It doesn't, but at least your brother is not three times my age, and he's never treated me with disrespect."

"You've hardly met him," Miria pointed out. "You said so yourself."

"All the reason I can be hopeful." Adaline sighed. "Miri, you have helped me more than I ever expected and in ways I never expected. You've shown me wonderous things and made me feel like I was allowed to be the person I am without judgment. You've made me feel love and have shown me love that I never dared hope would be reciprocated. This is the least I can do for you. Let me be useful to you."

"I can not let you go back there unless . . ." Miria swallowed.

"Unless?"

She wasn't sure where the word had come from. It was a wild hope, dragged from her bleeding heart before her brain could truly consider it. "Unless your return is not the end. Unless I know you won't have to go through with the wedding."

"You have a plan?"

She had an idea, an inkling, like a seedling too delicate and young to be called a plant. It needed time to grow and mature, time for Miria to determine whether or not it would root. Time she didn't have. Besides, any plan she might come up with would not be one she'd like. There would never be one Miria liked if it involved Adaline returning to her family.

"Let's plan then," Adaline said. "You're right. There must be a way for me to protect you and to stop the wedding. We'll just need to get more creative."

"Anything we attempt is likely to be dangerous. Rosmilda bespelled your family. She tried to bespell you, too. She'll certainly try again."

"But we'll outsmart her. I know we can." Hope brightened Adaline's face, and her eyes gleamed like her sword flashing in the sun. Her steps grew stronger, surer, as she paced. She might be a lady, but Adaline was a warrior at heart. She'd sacrifice herself for others but not without a fight, and her words confirmed every thought running through Miria's head. "You'll outpower Rosmilda, and I'll out maneuver her. I much prefer the straightforward simplicity of stabbing my enemies, but I haven't endured years of lessons in being a lady for none of them to stick. I was raised to protect me and mine in the viper's den of court and to give up my body in marriage for my family's sake. I would much rather risk it for yours."

Miria closed her eyes, struggling to hold onto the spark of hope amid her despair. The idea for a plan was far from being an actual plan, but it might be the only compromise she and Adaline could both live with. "I would prefer you not risk at all."

Her eyes opened as Adaline wrapped her arms around Miria's torso. "That bird flew the moment we agreed to try to stop the wedding." She kissed Miria's cheek. "Or perhaps it flew the moment you rescued my pathetic lost self two years ago, and I fell in love with a witch." Gentle fingers tilted Miria's chin so their lips brushed. "There's no story in which a lady and a witch can be together without risk, no matter how odd the lady or how powerful the witch."

"I fear I'm not as powerful as you need me to be."

"You are everything I need you to be, and more than I ever dreamed you would be."

She kissed Miria's mouth then, so tenderly that Miria's brain finally stilled. Worries were smothered beneath the press of Adaline's body against hers. Words were stolen from her tongue with the touch of Adaline's own.

Her practicality could only fight so long, and with the end of their time together looming closer than expected, Miria gave in. They could figure out a plan later.

Miria pulled Adaline with her into the second room, reveling in the sensation of Adaline's hips swaying beneath her hands as they walked. It was strange how the feeling of someone walking, of muscles moving and contracting beneath layers of fabric, could make her pulse pound. When the backs of her knees hit the bed, Miria sat. She wanted to pull Adaline down with her, but Adaline slipped from her arms.

"Wait," she said. "I want to remind you of what you missed all those times you were too honorable to spy on me in the bath."

Miria attempted to respond to that with something witty and failed utterly as she watched Adaline untie her overdress. She'd already abandoned her shoes and stockings in the summer heat (Miria's feralness was, apparently, contagious), so it didn't take long for Adaline to disrobe completely.

Miria's breath hitched. She'd thought she wouldn't forget how beautiful Adaline was, but her memory had failed her. Then Adaline was before her again, kissing her, and Miria reached out to glide her hands over so much soft skin.

But Adaline pulled away again. "Your turn. I'll help."

"I can do that myself, you know," Miria said as Adaline worked to remove her boots. Adaline was going too slowly, torturing her.

"The more you talk, the longer this will take."

Miria rolled her eyes but allowed Adaline to remove her boots and stockings and pull her layers over her head. When she was finally as naked as Adaline, Adaline seemed satisfied enough to join Miria on the bed.

"You should lie down so I can kiss you," Adaline said, pressing Miria's back into the covers with her body.

"Are you this demanding with your servants?" Miria asked. But she did as requested, not that she had a choice. Adaline was hovering over her, and Miria's eyes were hungry with the sight of her, though not so hungry as her mouth was to kiss her again.

"Hardly. I've never wanted to climb naked into bed with one of my servants." Adaline considered a moment, her fingers pausing their journey down Miria's chest and making Miria squirm. "Well, I did desperately want to kiss one of my maids when I was fourteen, but I never did, of course. Nor even suggested I wanted to. She was my age and terrified of me. I felt awful about it. Now, stop asking questions because I need to kiss you, Miri."

As soon as Adaline's lips grazed her throat, Miria couldn't speak anyway.

* * *

Some time later, as Adaline lay curled up next to her, Miria winced as she pulled at a strand of her own hair. The pain lasted only a second, barely noticeable in her current contented state, but the pain added to her sacrifice. Her spell would be stronger for it than if she'd merely used a strand of hair that had naturally fallen out.

"What are you doing?" Adaline raised her head, and her legs, which were entwined with Miria's, shifted.

Miria paused doing anything because the sensation was distracting.

"Protecting you," she said once she could refocus.

Adaline shifted positions again, this time tracing her fingers around the curve of Miria's breast. "There's time for that later. You should be kissing me again."

Rather than wait for Miria to do that, she took the initiative and lowered her lips to the hollow at Miria's throat. Unfortunately for her, Miria was too ticklish for the ploy to be successful.

"Later." She was unable to suppress a laugh, and she wiggled in Adaline's arms. "Later only exists if you don't leave tonight. Stay until morning so we can plan."

"I'll stay until morning so I can kiss you," Adaline said. "But yes, plan, too. Fine. I'll leave at first light in the morning."

Unless Miria could revise her tentative plan into one that didn't require Adaline leaving at all, it would do. "Let me finish this. Lift your hair. I'm going to do my best to hide the spell."

"Fine." Adaline sighed in an exaggerated manner, but she smiled and positioned herself as Miria instructed.

Adaline's hair was sweaty, as were they both, but that made it easier for Miria to weave. She braided her strand into a tendril of waves near Adaline's neck, whispering a protective enchantment as she worked. When she finished, she smoothed Adaline's hair down and combed it with her fingers.

"Will that protect me from Rosmilda's magic?" Adaline asked.

"I hope so. It's some protection anyway, and more powerful than the first charm I made for you. Combined, those two spells will need to be enough."

"Good. I trust you." Adaline spun around. "Now can I kiss you again?" She pressed her finger to Miria's lips. "Then we'll plan while we eat. I promise."

Miria was about to agree, but a warning brushed her mind, and she held up a hand. "Someone is outside."

Chapter Twenty-Six

Two Days Before the Wedding, Continued

Adaline stiffened, but Miria relaxed, even as she threw on her tunic. As anxious as she was, the ward being tripped had caught her off guard for a second, but it wasn't an alarm. The wards knew who had tripped them and were welcoming, and Miria allowed herself to feel hopeful.

"It's all right," she assured Adaline, as she crossed the cottage, belting her tunic in place. In the interest of time, she cast a spell to pull her unruly hair into a sensible braid around her head, then after some reluctance (she liked Adaline's hair down), she did the same for Adaline. Adaline let out a yelp of surprise and patted her head.

Once they were more or less presentable, Miria opened the cottage door. Three witches stood outside, including Sarel, the witch who'd performed Miria's initiation, and Nalki. Miria had not seen either of them since Yali's funeral, but she'd corresponded with Nalki semi-regularly since then. The blonde witch was older than Sarel, and she seemed to have taken it on herself to continue providing Miria with some irregularly timed but gentle guidance. Although it was no replacement for her nana, Miria did not mind the mothering, especially since Nalki was an excellent cook and liked to share recipes in her letters.

The third witch had been examining the wards on the trees, and she turned at the sound of the door opening. She was the only one of the three unfamiliar to Miria, with dark skin and gray hair she wore shorn close to her head. Miria had never seen a woman—witch or otherwise—with hair so short before, but it suited her.

"Sisters." Miria inclined her head. "You received my message?"

"We did," Sarel confirmed. "And it was concerning."

Miria motioned for them to come inside.

Adaline was tending to her forgotten pie. She regarded the other women warily but curtsied with all the grace of her upbringing.

"This is my friend, Lady Adaline of Waeremund, Lord Sigmun's niece," Miria said, figuring the abbreviated but formal introduction might make Adaline feel more comfortable.

The witches seemed to find Miria's description of her relationship with Adaline amusing, though none of them quite smiled.

Sarel inclined her head. "Lady Adaline. You may call me Sarel, and this is Nalki," she motioned to the blonde witch, "and Dinia."

The dark-skinned witch—Dinia—nodded. "Your message was brief, and I suspect there is much more we need to discuss. It's near dinner time, so we've brought food. Let's talk while we eat."

Miria hadn't noticed the time before, but with Dinia's words her stomach acknowledged it. "We have some rabbits roasting outside to contribute and a pie in need of baking."

"I don't know if the pie will be any good," Adaline said nervously. "I've never made one before."

Nalki laughed. "No need to worry, m'lady. We have enough food between the lot of us for twice as many people. Witches never do a thing without food. It makes every task more tolerable."

Adaline grinned. "That, I agree with. Perhaps I should find Tuli and put this pie in the oven then?"

"You mentioned a charm in your message," Sarel said once everyone had been seated and food had been passed around. "Start at the beginning and tell us everything."

Miria swallowed the rosemary and onion bread she'd been eating and considered. Where was the beginning? Was it when she'd concocted her plan to stop the wedding with Adaline? When she'd first started learning about the mysterious illness plaguing the town's children? Or further back—when her father had traded her to Yali for a wish spell that had put this moment into motion?

In the end, Miria decided to start there.

She half expected when she finished that the other witches would scold her for wanting vengeance on her family or for meddling in Adaline's life at all. She definitely did not expect Nalki to moan in despair.

"This is my fault," the blonde witch said, burying her face in her hands. "She was my apprentice."

"Your apprentice?" Miria cringed, hoping her tone didn't come out accusatory. She was caught off guard, but Rosmilda had said she'd been taught by a witch. There was no reason to expect that Miria wouldn't have met that witch.

Dinia patted Nalki on the shoulder. "You did nothing wrong, lovely. Apprentices fail all the time."

"They do?" Miria clasped a hand over her mouth in the vain hope that she could stop asking silly questions. Her nana had never made it sound like failure was an option. Miria could have given up and quit before her initiation, but she could not have failed to be offered initiation.

"All the time might be a bit of hyperbole." Sarel cast a fond glance at Dinia over Nalki's lowered head. "We try to choose the children we take on carefully, but it certainly happens on occasion. And usually that is the end of it. We help the girl settle somewhere safe and her power fades. By the time she's your age, it is gone."

Nalki raised her head and drew a deep breath. "Lival—what did you say she goes by now? Oh, yes, Rosmilda. I believe that was the name given by her mother; she went by Lival as my apprentice. She was always a very clever girl. That ought to have been my first warning, and I ignored it."

"Being clever is a bad thing for a girl?" Adaline had remained quiet until now, but she looked indignant.

"Well, no. Not generally. I'm stating it badly." Nalki cupped her wine but did not raise the goblet to drink. "It was the way she was clever—always looking for shortcuts, less concerned with consequences than with outcomes. I thought her cleverness was an asset in spite of these tendencies, so I ignored them. I was convinced I could train the negative aspects out of her. But as she grew older, they only became stronger. She was convinced of her own superiority and believed she deserved more power. She always wanted more, and I finally had to admit that she would never be content with the life we were offering. She would not use magic to better the world unless it bettered her own situation. It made her a danger."

"That is exactly what she's been using magic for," Miria said. "Bettering her own situation with no care for the others she harms in the process. How did she learn to steal power like that?"

Nalki shook her head. "I don't know. I didn't know it was possible myself."

Sarel also seemed unsure, but Dinia templed her fingers. "Rosmilda is not the first false witch I've encountered, though seeing as this is the first I've learned of her in these many years, she's covered her tracks the best. People can easily overlook and ignore so-called coincidences and good luck when they benefit those who smile broadly in public. Everyone wants to believe that they, too, can be the person who wildly changes their fortune. It gives them hope, so they don't question when it happens to others who they mistakenly believe deserve it. It's the false witches who reach too far, too quickly, too overtly cruelly that draw attention to themselves sooner. This Rosmilda has been as clever as Nakli describes to avoid detection."

A memory flashed through Miria's mind, of Yali speaking to her father the day he'd traded her away. *A man who overreaches loses his balance and will fall to his doom one day.*

She fidgeted in her seat. This was all well and good. Miria was glad to have answers at last, but the hour was running late. She needed a plan and to know whether the other witches would help. Being reminded of her father brought her intentions back to the front of her mind.

"Adaline is supposed to marry my brother in two days," Miria said. "Rosmilda plans another attack here tomorrow. With your help, we can prevent both of these coming to pass. Tonight—we can stop her."

The three other witches glanced among themselves, and Miria already knew she would not like their response before Sarel spoke. "We will help ensure Rosmilda is brought to justice for what she's done to the children she's harmed. We owe the community that since it's our fault they're hurting."

"My fault," Nalki interrupted, and Dinia laid a hand over hers.

"We are connected in this, a community." Sarel cast a glance at the witch next to her, but her attention remained focused on

Miria. "But Lady Adaline's marriage and your vengeance, while we understand why you feel like you do, it's not our place to be involved. Do what you will. We won't stop you. But Rosmilda is the focus of our work."

That was fine, mostly. For a moment, Miria had feared Sarel would give her a lecture about revenge. "I understand, and if we stop Rosmilda tonight—"

"Any attempt to stop Rosmilda tonight would be foolish," Dinia said. "I'm sorry. No doubt, she has increased any protections she might have after your encounter with her earlier. Every time she draws on her magic, she hurts others. The first thing we must do, therefore, is sever the magic she's using to draw her power. You said you know who some of those children are. Protecting them is our first step."

"How long will that take? I don't know how to do it myself."

"Time. If the four of us work together, we can finish it tomorrow."

Miria grimaced. "And if the three of you do it while I increase my wards here to stave off her attack?"

Dinia shrugged. "Longer."

Adaline wet her lips. "It's no good Miri. They're right. Protecting the children comes first."

"She'll find others. There must be others in town."

"We can only do what we can do," Dinia said. "If we can help some, then we should."

They were making the right choice, the ethical choice, the choice she'd intended to make herself before Adaline had become determined to leave. But they weren't the ones facing the result of that decision.

As if reading her thoughts, Adaline took her hand. "Even if you went after Rosmilda tonight, it may not be enough to stop the wedding. Rosmilda may have charmed my family, but if so, that was not the sole reason for the match. And I do not believe her sudden disappearance would deter your father or mine. They both stand to gain too much. I'll leave in the morning, and we'll continue with your plan."

Miria closed her eyes against the tears threatening behind them. For a moment she'd had hope that the other witches could make all her problems go away. But it felt like not much had changed. She would have help, but when it came to Adaline, she remained on her own.

"It's not much of a plan," she whispered.

"Well, the night is young," Adaline said. "And we have pie to discuss it over."

"Tell us what you're planning," Nalki said. "Just because we shouldn't interfere doesn't mean we can't offer guidance."

Chapter Twenty-Seven

One Day Before the Wedding

"Are you sure you want to do this?" Miria asked the next morning. If it could be called that. She'd set a magical alarm to alert them to the sun's first cresting above the horizon, but all was still dark outside.

It was dark inside Miria, too. Her sister witches had departed after they'd cleaned up from dinner, promising to return this morning with more help and supplies. After they'd left, Miria and Adaline had run through Miria's plan multiple times, looking for weaknesses and ways it could go wrong and finding too many for Miria's comfort. But Adaline had been undeterred.

"It's better than anything else we have," she'd insisted. "And unless you plan to abduct me in truth, then I'm leaving at first light to do my part."

Since Miria would not do that, as tempting as it was, she'd given up and gone to bed, allowing Adaline's lips and caresses to be a poor distraction. (Poor, not because they hadn't been pleasurable, but poor because every touch, every kiss, every whisper felt like a goodbye, so Miria could never forget what the dawn would bring.)

The dawn was here now, or something like it. Just a streak of blue velvet in the east made it clear that somewhere beyond the trees, the sun was, in fact, on the move. The air was chilly and damp, clinging to Miria like a second, unwanted skin.

And she was clinging to Adaline.

"It's never too late to change your mind." Adaline's hair muffled her voice as Miria spoke into her neck. "Until you reach the manor gate, you can always turn back."

Adaline squeezed her, hard. "There's a fair chance I'll run into my uncle's guards before I reach the gate, but I'll keep it in mind." With a last desperate bit of force, she released Miria and stepped back. "It's a good plan."

"It's a terrible plan."

"Stop being so pessimistic." She brushed a tear from Miria's face that Miria hadn't even noticed. "I know what I must do, and so do you. Even if everything falls apart and I end up married to your brother, there's nothing to stop me from running away later."

"Rosmilda might."

"But you and the others will capture her," Adaline said with a confidence Miria was too upset to share. "Whatever happens to me, I know she cannot stand against all of you."

"Is it awful that I care more about what happens to you than what happens to her? Does that make me as cruel and selfish as she is?"

"It makes you mine." Adaline tapped her right foot to her left ankle, indicating where she kept the original charm Miria had given her. "And I'm yours. And one way or another, you will have your revenge."

Miria raised an eyebrow. "How do you figure if I don't stop the wedding?"

"Rosmilda is your father's charm. Take her away, and he will have to work far harder to maintain his position and wealth. I wonder if he actually knows how without her magic bolstering them?"

Miria had to admit it was an interesting thought. "I suppose that would be a consolation prize, but I don't want merely a consolation prize. I want you."

"You will always have me." Adaline kissed her forehead, then she strapped on her sword. "Off to battle we go."

"Like a knight in one of your tales."

"A knight who triumphs." Adaline grinned, but even in the dim light, Miria could tell her face was pale and strained. She was pumping herself up, probably for both their sakes.

Miria owed it to her to project the same confidence, so she buried her worries as best she could. "I will see you again tomorrow."

"You will kiss me again tomorrow."

"As much as you let me." And every day after, but even if they were successful with this barely-there plan, Miria didn't truly know what came after. Her mood was agitated enough without dwelling on that, though. Nor did it do her any good to worry about a future that might not come to pass.

With a heavy heart, Miria lifted the mist so that Adaline could see as far down the forest path as the light from the magical flame she'd given her would allow. The flame would extinguish by the time Adaline got through the woods, but by then the sun would be her guide, and she'd be carrying no obvious trace of magic upon her. Nothing to suggest that her escape wasn't an escape at all.

When Adaline finally disappeared into the trees, Miria dropped the fog back in place, and her heart dropped with it.

This was it. The wheel was in motion, or—if Adaline was correct—it had been so since they'd met, and she'd simply not understood what they were spinning toward all this time.

A large hand landed on Miria's shoulder, and she turned in surprise toward Tuli. As lost in her head as she'd been, she hadn't heard him approach.

Miria gave one of his clay fingers a gentle squeeze. "At least we still have each other."

Tuli bowed his head in acknowledgment, and Miria thought she could detect sadness in his eyes.

Always, her golem replied. He didn't speak in her head often, but Miria was ever so grateful that he'd started after Nana had died.

"We'll get her back," she told the golem, somehow able to inject more confidence in that than she could a moment ago.

Tuli nodded, a determined nod. *I know.*

That was one of them. Two, if she counted Adaline. But the golem's confidence gave her some. She'd made Tuli with nothing but some river clay, a ribbon, and her own power and determination, and look at him now.

"We'll have visitors soon. Hopefully just friendly ones. Let's go prepare."

And eat something.

"Yes, and I'll eat something first."

A yawn rose up Miria's throat, but her nervous energy pushed it back down. She'd barely slept a wink, and there was no time to go back to sleep. But she could take a moment to fortify herself before the day's work began.

* * *

The other witches arrived as the sun peeked over the forest crown—Sarel, Nalki, Dinia, and a fourth witch with bright red hair and a lilting accent.

While Miria shored up her wards, the others worked on spells to break Rosmilda's magic. It was work that would have gone much more quickly if they could have come face-to-face with the children, but that came with its own risks. And once they were finished, they showed Miria what they'd done so she could replicate the spell on her own.

The others prepared food while Miria prepared additional spells, easier ones that she already knew how to do, for her plan the next day. Along with Tuli, they kept watch around the cottage in case Rosmilda and the guard attacked—in that, they were willing to intervene—but no one came. Whatever Adaline had said, however she'd convinced her family to leave Miria alone, it had worked.

When night fell, Miria was exhausted as she checked and double-checked her preparations for the next day. Despite her company and the forest chattering away as it always did, she felt so alone as she climbed into bed.

Chapter Twenty-Eight
Day of the Wedding

Miria brushed her thumb over one of the bloodied pieces of parchment she'd stolen from Rosmilda. She could see the traces of magic in it, but that meant nothing.

"You're sure you were able to protect these children?" she asked Sarel before placing the eight pieces of parchment into the purse tied around her body.

She would have preferred to take her satchel, stuffed with supplies for every contingency, but a satchel was easy to steal off her if a guard came too close. A purse could be tucked into her clothes. Today could go badly, and if it did, she intended to make herself as hard a target to catch as possible. Even her dress felt wrong for that purpose, but Miria needed to make people listen to her. As much as it bothered her, that meant she must try to blend in among them, look like one of them instead of the feral wood witch that she was. She mollified herself by wearing the petal-and-thorn armor Yali had made beneath it.

"Our spells should hold," Sarel said. "And it's certain Rosmilda knows about them if she's tried casting since."

"She might not have." Miria suppressed a yawn. Who knew what Rosmilda had been up to yesterday since she hadn't led a contingent of guards into the forest with another of her abominations?

"It might have been better if she had," Dinia said, giving voice to a worrisome thought that had occurred to Miria over breakfast. "She'd be tired today. Easier to control."

"Too late to worry about that now." The red-haired witch who'd joined them yesterday (her name was Hani) reminded Miria a bit of Adaline. Miria suspected she was itching for a fight, and she was entirely too cheerful this morning for Miria's mood.

While the other four witches debated the pros and cons of their situation, Miria strode on ahead. The wedding was to take place at noon, which was not so far away, and in the distance, the manor bustled. Few people were going in and out of the main gate, but between Lord Sigmun's and Sir Alberik's guards on duty, there wasn't an inch of wall uncovered. It was hardly a surprise given the scene she and Adaline had created only days ago, and it wasn't a problem that would be hard to overcome, but it also wasn't exactly welcoming.

As if anyone on the other side of that wall besides Adaline would welcome her. Miria had to quietly laugh at herself for having such an absurd thought in the first place.

The ominous sight of so many guards aside, colorful flags flew from the parapets, and someone had decorated the area around the main gate with garlands of flowers as though today was a joyful occasion. Miria longed to send a gust of wind to rip them down, but the time for a reckoning was coming in other ways. She would conserve her power for when it would be most effective.

Without thinking, she wrapped her fingers around the red charm dangling against her chest. Its heat was comforting. The rage she'd stored there familiar.

Today, she whispered to it in her mind. *Today we save Adaline and get our revenge.*

The charm grew hotter, but not unpleasantly so, and Miria tucked it back beneath her bodice.

The breeze picked up, blowing stray strands of hair into Miria's face, itching her nose and carrying with it the scent of smoke and horses from the manor. It would have been a beautiful day for a wedding, and Miria was certain the lord's kitchens had been conjuring a feast for all the guests. She hoped some of the staff got to enjoy the fruits of their labor later. As for those for whom the food had been intended, if she had her way, all they would be consuming for the rest of the day was chaos.

Nerves and determination had sped up her feet, and Miria paused to wait for the others to catch up. The guards along the wall and at the gates gave no indication they saw her or the women with her. Nalki had cast a variation on Miria's close-to-but-not-quite-invisibility spell on them all.

"Everyone know what they must do?" Hani asked for the third time that morning as they approached the gate.

"Hush," said Sarel. They were as close to invisible as they could get, but speaking might be enough to draw the guards' attention.

They didn't notice the women, though. Miria was about to breathe a sigh of relief as she passed by the unseeing guards, but her triumph was cut short by her walking into an invisible wall.

She stumbled backward, barely able to suppress her cry of surprise, and landed against Nalki. Hani had been next to Miria, and she, too, slammed into the same barrier. She wasn't as fast at catching herself from swearing, and between her voice and the commotion of bodies colliding, the guards stirred. Miria swore as well, but only in her head, and she pushed the other women to the side and out of the guards' line of sight.

"What happened?" Dinia asked softly.

"It must be a ward." Miria's mind raced. How long had it been there? Had Rosmilda erected it yesterday, after Adaline's return, in which case she might have tired herself out? Or had it been there since Miria's original escape from the manor?

"It felt like a stone wall," Hani muttered, rubbing her forehead. "You did a good job training this woman, Nal."

Nalki whined slightly. "I did warn you that she was clever."

Sarel had stayed behind at the gate, and Miria watched her run a finger down the seemingly empty space where the ward was. Her face strained, and she shivered before she ceased touching it.

The guards had wandered in the opposite direction of where Miria and the others huddled, and she assumed Sarel had done something to distract them. They were meandering back to their posts as Sarel rejoined the group.

"The ward will keep out anyone with magic in their blood, if I'm correct," she said.

"Well, that's a problem." Hani crossed her arms. "Not that we can't take it down eventually."

Miria gritted her teeth. She didn't have until *eventually*. The wedding would start soon, and she *was* going to stop it.

She glanced up to where the wall rose high above her head and into the clear sky. "How high do you think the ward extends?"

"You mean to fly over it?" Sarel asked. "If she's smart, she'll have added to it around the top of the wall. I would have."

Right, Miria would have, too. Yali had taught her how to create such a ward, but they took a lot of power to cast and maintain. The benefit was that they could be quite large if they were created at the correct anchor points and left to hang in the air, unencumbered by obstacles. In contrast, the wards around the cottage were simpler, even the ones Miria had strengthened of late. They relied on the forest's natural protections—the trees and their roots, the underbrush, even the wildlife. Maintaining them cost Miria little magic.

"If I can't go over it, I need to go through it somehow," Miria said.

"We could break through the wall," Hani suggested, and it was such an Adaline sort of suggestion—loud and violent—that Miria feared the trouble they would cause if the two of them ever met.

"I think that might give us away," Dinia said dryly.

If only she could travel through the distance magically, like witches did when they used their portals. But to do that required having set up a place on the other side to receive her, her spell already present. Miria was only able to travel through Yali's portals because her first time, Yali had taken her through. Once through, she'd cast her own spell on the other end so she would be able to travel without Yali in the future.

Miria clenched her hands together in agitation, and the charm she wore around her wrist—the one she'd made like Adaline's—peeked beneath her sleeve.

Wards were not where she excelled, but magic acted in patterns, and she turned to Sarel (who did appear to excel at them). "Could we confuse the ward? What if my magic brushes up against the ward from both sides?"

Sarel frowned. "If the ward is singularly directional, only meant to keep you out for example, then you appearing to be on both sides of it at once could make it falter. But the spell would need to be very similar, if not identical. Something cast before the ward was erected."

Miria held up her wrist. "Adaline wears a similar charm. Mine carries her emotions, and hers carries mine."

Sarel tilted her head, considering. "It might work, but it wouldn't allow the rest of us through. And how will you get her to bring it? They must be preparing her for the wedding."

"A bird." The same way she used to write back and forth with Adaline. Befriending creatures of the forest was the magic where Miria excelled.

Half an hour later, plus some borrowed ink and stolen parchment from town, Miria tied her instructions to a friendly sparrow who was only too happy to help.

She raced back to the manor where the others had continued to work on alternate methods for breaking down Rosmilda's ward.

"Anything?" she asked, slightly winded. The sparrow could fly much faster than a witch could run.

"Nothing from your beloved yet," Nalki said. She cast a glance to where Sarel and Dinia were working on breaking the ward. "Nor any success here."

"Yet," Sarel said, without glancing over.

Miria wiped her sweaty hands on her skirts and paced where she could keep an eye on the open gate. Would the wedding have started? They'd been wise to get here early, but even still, the sun was high in the sky. The trickle of people going in and out of the manor grounds had slowed to nothing. Miria wanted to throw herself at the invisible ward and scream in frustration. Rosmilda would not, could not, get the better of her when she was so close. Adaline might have been prepared to go through with the wedding if she needed to, but Miria was not prepared to let her.

Movement from the corner of her eye caught her attention, but it wasn't a bird carrying a charm in its beak. It was a guard. *The* guard—Otto—who had owed her a debt and paid it recently.

Otto glanced around nervously and nodded at one of the other men.

"Looking for something?" the second guard asked.

"Making sure everyone who was expected has arrived. M'lady Adaline was concerned someone might be missing." He raised his voice as he spoke and opened the palm of his left hand carefully, and there—Miria saw Adaline's charm.

Her heart leapt into her chest. This was odd, and Otto clearly didn't see her yet, but he was holding the charm out, trying to be discreet.

Miria darted over, and she could see the moment Nalki's almost-invisibility spell failed. It was predicated on people not seeing that which they didn't expect, after all. And somehow Otto had known enough to be here, to expect Miria.

His eyes widened, and his whole body twitched in surprise. Miria feared this would be all it took to alert the other guards, but one of the two was staring in the opposite direction, and the one who'd been talking to Otto appeared more concerned with teaching himself how to flip his dagger theatrically.

"What's that?" The guard dropped the dagger and motioned toward the charm as he retrieved it.

"What?" Otto shook himself. "Oh, found it lying about the wedding area. Figure it belongs to some girl, maybe one of the O'seer's daughters. Better pick it up in case."

The guard snorted. "Girls and their trinkets, eh. Looks like a fancy rock to me."

What was any precious jewel but a fancy rock, Miria thought. Her charm was something far more valuable. But this was not the time for it. Otto looked like he might pass out as she stood so close to him and pressed her own charm into the ward. With her other hand, she motioned for him to move his closer. He did, uttering some inane reply to his friend.

Miria stopped listening because as soon as both charms touched the ward, its power vibrated through her body. Her nerves tingled with it, her body hummed, almost violently at first, and Miria held her breath. Then the sensation calmed, her magic matching the ward's foreign rhythm. It was now or never. It had worked or it had not.

Miria crossed the gate's threshold. As soon as she was through, she felt the magic snap back into place, nipping at the hem of her dress. She let out her breath.

Miria nodded at Otto in thanks. Why or how he'd come to help would have to be a mystery to solve another day. She had a wedding to prevent.

But Otto snagged her wrist before she could run off. "Wait."

"Lady Adaline needs my help," Miria said. "I appreciate what you did, but—"

"You owe *me* now, witch," he said under his breath. "If nothing else, an explanation for why I just did that."

"Why *did* you do that?"

Reluctantly, she followed Otto into a secluded area. They were heading in the right direction. In the distance, Miria could see people in fine clothing milling about. It didn't appear as though the wedding had begun yet.

Otto ran his fingers through his hair, realized he still carried the charm, and thrust it at Miria. "Something is not right here. These people from town, the O'seer and his wife—they aren't right. You told me you would look into the illnesses plaguing the children in town. Did you learn anything?"

"I did, actually, and—"

"Does it have something to do with them? The O'seer's family?"

The question managed to strike Miria speechless for a moment. "How did you know?"

"Because I've worked for Lord Sigmun for years, and something has not been right around here for a while. Especially in the last week, m'lord and lady have been walking around like they're half asleep much of the time when there's been so much to do. Then you came flying through a few days ago, Lady Adaline disappears, and it's gotten even odder. The O'seer's wife struts about like she runs the whole place, and we've been told to let her be. A woman wouldn't do that unless she's a queen or a witch, and no way would Lord Sigmun allow it unless she *was* the queen. No offense."

"I'll consider it."

"I start wondering, then, what if she *is* a witch?" Otto said, talking over Miria's sarcasm. "So I snooped on her. I saw this thing she was working on, the thing m'lord and Sir Alberik said was going to help find Lady Adaline. It was magic, for sure, but not your kind of magic, if you know what I mean."

Miria did know. Though Rosmilda's golem and Tuli were not that different, magically speaking, she understood exactly what Otto meant.

"When Lady Adaline returned, claiming she fought her way out of the woods, I thought it strange again. And then, just now, I'm called in to assist the O'seer's wife. Seems Lady Adaline was found in possession of 'witch magic' as Rosmilda told of it. She said it was dangerous and gave it to me to dispose of. But Lady Adaline was distraught, fighting with her. There was a note with a ribbon. I'm sure Lady Rosmilda didn't care that I saw it because she doesn't think I can read, but I can well enough. I followed the instructions you left and came down to the gate. You tell *me* why now."

Miria had to take a moment to let this all sink in, and she took a deep breath, deciding how much she should share. She hadn't expected an ally in here other than Adaline, but Otto—even if his motivations were questionable and sexist—was not a gift she would overlook.

"Rosmilda blocked me from entering the grounds. You helped me break the spell she had to keep me out. She and my fa—the Overseer—are responsible for what's happening to the children in town, and I can prove it. Lady Adaline's marriage must be prevented from tying your lordship's family to the Overseer's."

"You're here to stop them?"

Miria pushed down the bit of guilt in her gut. It was true, after all. Even if her own motivations might be questionable, too. "I am. Will you help if I need it?"

Fear flashed over his face, and Miria regretted her words in an instant. He'd already done a lot, more than she would have expected, and she didn't even know exactly what she was asking.

"Forget I asked. Just watch out for Lady Adaline, will you?" she asked instead.

"Her ladyship and her family have my sword." Otto started away, then paused and glanced back with some trepidation. "Be careful."

"You, as well."

Miria let him return to whatever post he was supposed to have, and she tied Adaline's charm around her wrist. As she did, she touched her own, letting Adaline's emotions remind her what was at stake.

Her heart.

That was once ripped out her chest.

That was healed and then given over to another who needed her now.

Miria let Nalki's spell fall away, then she marched across the lord's lawn to a sham of a wedding and a moment fifteen years in the making.

Chapter Twenty-Nine

Day of the Wedding, Continued

The manor's north grounds had been given over for the wedding, showcasing opulence grander than anything Miria had ever seen before. There were garlands of flowers and colorful streamers everywhere she turned. The tables were laden with fine cloths and stacked high with delicacies she could not begin to guess at. To take advantage of the fine weather, the marriage arch had been erected at the far end of the lawn, rather than in the manor chapel, and it was completely covered in roses. A smaller table sat before it, holding the goblet of ceremonial wine and a censor of incense.

The only things finer than the decorations were the clothes worn by the guests themselves—silk and lace in a riot of color, jewels glittering in the sunlight, silver and gold gleaming in the ladies' hair. Miria was certain most of those gathered did not live in the area. They were other nobility, invited to celebrate and be entertained.

Well, she would give them entertainment. Miria's stomach swooped with the thought, but she would not be intimidated by wealth's power when she had her own. Rosmilda had reminded her of that.

Everyone seemed to be arranging themselves in some sort of order, and Miria stood on her toes, trying to see why. Moments later, the priest came into view, followed by her brother and father, both dressed in such a manner that no one would be able to tell they did not belong among the assembled men. Miria's hands clenched at her side.

So far, despite dropping the invisibility spell, no one had paid her much mind. There were few guards in the vicinity, and everyone's attention was on each other. Those in plain clothes or a servant's livery were beneath their concern. Miria might as well have blended in with the dogwood tree blooming behind her as she glared at her family.

"M'lady, there you are." A red-faced, harried-looking woman darted along the side of the crowd. "M'lord was wondering . . ."

"M'lord should learn some patience."

At the familiar voice, Miria snapped her head sideways. Rosmilda was ushering Adaline through a side door in the manor, Adaline's mother trailing a few steps behind. Her gaze didn't immediately turn Miria's way, but Miria braced for it. Rosmilda's voice was curt, and her lips were thin.

"We needed to make a last-minute alteration to Lady Adaline's hair," Rosmilda continued. "I trust her father wants her to be her best self for the ceremony."

The woman, whoever she was, must not have been important enough for Rosmilda to charm, because her back stiffened, as though she took offense at being talked to this way. But Adaline's mother made no move to correct Rosmilda's tone.

Another in her thrall, Miria concluded.

As for Adaline, she did look breathtaking, her hair curled and pinned and studded with pearls and more tiny flowers. Her dress was the same stunning blue embroidered silk that Miria had seen in her scrying, but Adaline was taking no joy in wearing it. Her face was blank, be it from fear or apprehension.

Miria unclenched her hands and stepped out of the tree's relative cover.

Rosmilda saw her the moment she moved, as though her vision was as keen as a cat's, as though she'd been expecting Miria to show her face. Although after what Otto had witnessed, perhaps she *had* expected something.

"Guards!" Rosmilda yelled toward the nearest men and pointed at Miria. "Remove that woman. She's a thief, not a guest."

A thief? Clever. Calling her a witch would scare the men, and this gave them reason to steal her purse. Rosmilda would know Miria carried necessary supplies within it.

Miria had no time to hesitate. She ran from the confused men who'd been called into action. Guests at the edge of the crowd—those who'd heard the commotion—whipped their heads in her direction. Voices rumbled in alarm.

Miria silently cursed the garments that slowed her movements as she skirted the edge of the gathering. She needed to get closer to the altar, to the men and the priest. To those who had the power she did not—if only she got near enough to break the enchantment Rosmilda had put on them.

It didn't take long for her to realize she wouldn't make it that far. More guards were closing in, forming a perimeter around those in charge. Brandishing swords.

Admittedly, Miria had not thought through the practicalities of this part of her plan very well. She'd been counting on Adaline raising her voice to assist, on whatever sway a lady of Adaline's status would have among those present. But if Adaline was trying, Miria couldn't hear her over the shouting.

She could hear Rosmilda, however, urging the men on and, from the sound of it, getting closer.

To her left, the priest was blustering; to her right, Rosmilda was pushing her way through the throng of well-dressed guests who were mostly standing around in confusion, and some of whom did look very entertained. All around her, guards crept in. Clearly none of them wanted to outright attack a presumably unarmed woman, but their reticence wouldn't stop them for long.

Since getting close enough to Adaline's father and uncle wasn't proving feasible, Miria skipped ahead to the next part of her plan. From her purse, she pulled out the pieces of bloodied parchment she'd stolen. She wasn't looking at Rosmilda, but at the men whose ears she was targeting. Nonetheless, Miria swore she felt Rosmilda's fury like a flame scorching her cheek.

"It's not me who needs to be seized, it's her." Miria pointed toward Rosmilda. "She's the one who's been behind all the children in town becoming sick and dying. The wasting disease, the evil spirits—they're hers. You see!" Miria held up the parchment. "This is the blood of the sick children, found in her house. Look!"

In the moment of distraction, Miria managed to dart closer to the priest and thrust out the parchment, but he skittered away. Coward. She placed the parchment on the altar. "Do you need more proof? You see this necklace she gifted Lady Adaline? There is a charm on it, and I can prove it. She meant to bespell Lady Adaline." Miria spun toward her brother, who stood near Adaline's father and uncle. "Your bride, your daughter."

She had people's attention now. Miria could sense dozens of eyes boring into her. Words floated by her ears like insects on the breeze—confusion, fear. Accusations of witchcraft were not something made lightly. Even the guards had paused, though it may have simply been to watch the spectacle.

Their reasons didn't matter. What mattered was that it bought Miria time. She reached into her purse, fingers grasping the spell she'd created yesterday to break Rosmilda's enchantment.

What also mattered was that Rosmilda had pushed her way through the melee, through the fine men and women who weren't sure whether to flee or laugh or turn on one of their hosts. And Adaline was behind her.

"Ad—" Miria caught herself, barely. "Lady Adaline, explain to them."

But Lady Adaline only stared at Miria with the same blank expression she'd worn coming out of the manor, and suddenly Miria understood.

We needed to make a last-minute alteration to Lady Adaline's hair. Miria cursed to herself. When Rosmilda had caught Adaline with Miria's note, she must have realized something was up. She *had* been looking for Miria when she came outside, and before then, she must have found the charm Miria had woven into Adaline's hair.

Nerves had powered Miria this far. Nerves and determination. But her heart began to pound with something more like fear. The uncertainty and worry she saw on the faces of the wedding guests was a pale imitation of the emotions flooding her veins. She had no Adaline to strengthen her voice. No sister witches to lend her their power. She was on her own.

She'd never been on her own before. Even after her nana had died, she'd had Tuli and a community of women to carry her through. She'd had the promise of Adaline's heart.

Now she had no one but herself.

Miria swallowed and hoped that Adaline had been able to carry out the other part of her plan, that she'd been able to place the protective charms Miria had given her on Miria's sisters so Rosmilda could no longer harm them.

The anti-enchantment spell felt like a rock in Miria's hands. Adaline and her family could be no more than ten steps away, but the distance felt vast.

Miria started forward, and a new voice joined Rosmilda's calls for the guard to grab her.

"Stop her, seize her. She has a spell in her hands!" Garulf raised his voice and tried to pull Lord Sigmun away. Did he know what was in Miria's pouch, or was it just a scoundrel's instinct for avoiding being caught?

"Put the bag down," one of the guards yelled. Miria recognized him from her scrying, the younger one. He held is sword out, but his eyes were trained on Miria's hands.

The guests were stumbling away. Miria could see the crowd writhing and shifting from the corner of her eye. The stench of fear was clouding out the scent of the incense and roses. Soon, she would have a clear path to the men if one of the guards didn't obtain some courage and run her through first.

"She is the witch!" Garulf said, stating the obvious. "Get her."

"Oh, yes, the witch." Miria spit out the words, her temper flaring. "And you are the man who sold your daughter to the witch. Do you not recognize me, Father? Do you not think I know exactly the kind of man you are? Did she tell you?" Miria pointed in Rosmilda's direction.

Someone gasped, the priest perhaps. Then something clattered to her left, and it was Hans knocking over an urn filled with rose blossoms. "It *is* you. Greta?"

Miria's lip curled. There was a soft wonder in her brother's face, something she could use, something she might need, but her temper was crackling like a fire, hard to reign in. "That name no longer fits me. Do you know what they've done—this family of yours? Are you fine with how they've used those around you, the lives they destroyed?"

Hans opened his mouth, but he grappled with nothing but air. Her words had hit something inside of him, but Miria didn't know what.

Nor did she have time to care. Rosmilda and Garulf were yelling again, and so was the rest of Adaline's family, those whose strings were tied to Rosmilda's dirty hands.

Perhaps it was the voice of Adaline's father or uncle joining in that finally got the guards to move. Suddenly, it felt as though Miria's world was shrinking. The last time she recalled such a claustrophobic terror was when she'd tried running from Yali all those years ago. But these were not benign trees or tangled vines or recalcitrant roots. They were grown men with swords, and Miria had only one move left.

She rushed forward, grateful for every lesson in swordsmanship Adaline had given her. For though she held no blade, those lessons had taught her how to dodge the hands reaching out for her arms, just as the wily forest floor had taught her feet to be nimble. Miria weaved through the men trying to catch her, leaning there, twisting here, her feet steady on the grass, and the distance between her and her targets closed as she raised the bag holding her spell.

There were more guards than she could avoid for long, though, and when a hand landed on her left arm, she flung the spell—a fine powder—toward Adaline's family with her right, and with her magic, she called on the wind to do the rest.

Chapter Thirty

Day of the Wedding, Continued

Without access to her supplies to cast a proper spell, the wind obeyed only half-heartedly, but it was enough—mostly. A cloud of amethyst rose into the air, and some of the spell dusted Sir Alberik and Lord Sigmun. People screamed.

Then Miria was jerked backward as more hands clawed at her arms. The moment was over, the spell's remains fluttering to the grass just like she was being forced to her knees. Miria blew into the breeze, wiggled the fingers that were pinned to her sides, but it wasn't enough to command the wind any longer.

The question became: would it be enough to wake the men, and would that help?

"Get her out of here. We'll deal with her later," Garulf barked as if he'd not heard a word of the accusation Miria had thrown at him only moments before. Some of the enchantment-breaking spell had landed on him, turning his face lightly purple, but there was no charm for it to break. The only spell he was under was one of his own making—the arrogant belief that he deserved more, by whatever means necessary.

But the guards still did not take orders from him or Rosmilda directly. They waited for word from their employers, and Miria remained on the ground. She struggled to catch sight of either Adaline or Hans through the bodies that encircled her, but all she saw were men's legs.

Her father snapped at the men again, then a new voice cut his off.

"Stop this. What is going on?"

And another. "You do not get to command my men, Overseer."

A hush followed. Then murmuring. Miria held her breath and cursed her inability to see. How quickly could Rosmilda recast the enchantment? Had any of the spell dust landed on Adaline?

"Explain this." Adaline's uncle, the Lord of Gawfrid himself, must have given some silent command, because the guards surrounding her shuffled, revealing an opening for her to see through at last.

"She is the witch," Rosmilda pressed through the crowd, dragging Adaline with her. Adaline, who still looked too dazed to have been affected by Miria's spell.

Miria's stomach sunk as low as her position. She needed to break the charm on Adaline, but her hands were bound too tightly to use. Her purse of supplies hung like a stone around her neck, and her red charm burned hot with her stored fury against her breast.

"She is the one who abducted Lady Adaline," Rosmilda continued, and Miria heard the note of fear that had crept into her voice, and it gave her hope. She could not re-charm these men so easily then. She had to regain control another way. "She's come here making wild accusations to stop the wedding for some horrible reasons of her own, no doubt."

"She said she is your daughter?" The priest remained in the back, and he spoke timidly.

"Of course, she did," Rosmilda spat out. "Witches lie. Everyone knows that."

Hans started to say something, but a look from Garulf had him closing his mouth.

Oh, how her brother continued to disappoint her. She'd given up on him years ago, yet the pain of that betrayal didn't ebb so easily. Miria glared at him. "I once thought you were so brave, Brother. You made me brave. But you're either a coward or as selfish and cruel as they are."

He lowered his head and backed out of view, and one of the guards raised his hand as if to slap her. Miria turned her glower on him, and he hesitated, his face white. So she still had fear of the witch on her side. It was a good thing they didn't realize she was mostly powerless at the moment.

"Ada, daughter," Adaline's father pulled Adaline in closer. "Is this her? Is this the witch who took you?"

Adaline opened her mouth slightly, but no words came out. Her face was no longer placid. It was strained, as strained as Rosmilda's face behind her, and Miria's pulse skipped. Adaline was fighting Rosmilda's enchantment. Rosmilda might have removed the protective charm, but Adaline had been prepared mentally for what might happen, and she was strong. Too strong and stubborn to make a proper lady, to hear her tell of it.

Hope pricked Miria's heart as she waited, staring at Adaline, willing her to succeed.

Sweat formed on Adaline's brow and she stumbled slightly, but a guard was there to help her to regain her balance. Otto again. When he removed his hand from her arm, he left a trail of amethyst dust.

Whether Adaline had nearly fallen because of her internal struggle or whether Otto had made it so as an excuse to coat her with the spell, Miria didn't know. But Adaline blinked slowly, and the cloud over her face lifted.

Adaline wet her lips and turned her head from Miria to face her father. "She is the witch, but she didn't abduct me. I ran, and everything she said about the Overseer and his family is true. I've seen the proof. You must listen to her. Rosmilda has had you under an enchantment—you can feel it now, can't you? Like your mind has been foggy for days?"

Adaline spoke softly but firmly, and yet the grounds had become so hushed that her voice must have carried. Miria could sense the gasps coursing through whoever remained nearby, as well as hear them. It was a collective shift in the mood, a tinge in the air. One of the guards loosened his grip on Miria's arms, not enough for her to move them freely, but enough for her to know Adaline's words were affecting people.

"If you'll pardon me for saying so, m'lord," said the guard holding Miria. "Some of your orders of late have been unlike you." Recognizing his voice as that of the younger captain, Miria turned to him in time to see the guard cast a furtive glance toward Rosmilda. "She and the Overseer have been taking an awful lot of liberties around here."

"This is preposterous," Rosmilda said, but there was more than that hint of fear this time, and her fingers were curling and uncurling at her sides.

She was going to cast another spell, and Miria couldn't stop her from the ground.

Adaline's father and uncle exchanged glances.

"Is this true?" the Lord of Gawfrid demanded of Rosmilda. "Did you place a spell on me?"

For a second, Miria thought Rosmilda would snap at him. Then the heat in her eyes dimmed. Her entire posture softened. The haughty woman, who minutes ago had been ordering everyone around like she owned the manor, diminished and became meek.

Rosmilda burst into tears. "Of course, it's not true. My lord, please. How could you believe such a thing? She's a witch. Lady Adaline confirmed it, and nothing she says can—"

"The pendant!" Miria motioned as best she could toward where the pendant had fallen to the grass. "You must have seen her gift it to Lady Adaline, and there is a charm in there. I can prove it."

"You gave my son's betrothed some nefarious magic?" Garulf stepped forward. "How dare you? What are these games you've been playing at, Wife?"

Clearly, her father had sensed the change in the air, too. And if Rosmilda had thought he would stand by her when times were hard, she was about to learn the same lesson Miria had learned as a child. Her father would never protect anyone but himself.

Rosmilda's face turned scarlet as fresh tears rolled down her cheeks, and these new tears—Miria could well believe these were real. They were tears of rage as the dagger of her father's betrayal drove into whatever hardened heart Rosmilda had. Having experienced her father's perfidy herself, Miria almost felt bad for the woman.

Almost.

"You ungrateful, arrogant . . ." Rosmilda tripped over her words before seeming to remember that pity was the better play. "After all I've done for you, Husband. My lord, if he has acted untoward, I know nothing of it. Will you let him accuse an innocent woman—a devout woman who has done so much for the church—like this?"

"Seize her," Adaline's father said at last. "We will get to the bottom of this."

"Seize both of them," Lord Sigmun corrected.

Garulf sputtered with indignation, but Rosmilda, seeing that her tears had failed, switched tactics. Miria saw it if no one else did—how Rosmilda's eyes closed briefly, the concentration on her face. She wasn't casting, so whatever she'd unleashed, it was something she already had prepared.

The guards let go of Miria, and Adaline was at her side in a flash, helping her to her feet.

"Are you all right?" Adaline asked, not pausing for an answer. "She found the charm in my hair. And the note you sent was . . ."

Adaline's voice was drowned out by an eruption of screams from the south. She and Miria spun around, searching for the cause. The grounds were devolving into chaos. The well-heeled guests were panicking, running straight at them.

"What in the world?" Adaline grabbed Miria's hand, and they dashed out of the way as the air whistled with a crossbow bolt sent from high above.

The yelling increased in volume, and on its heels came the sound of crashing and higher-pitched screams of terror or pain.

Miria sensed the cause first, then smelled it, the same horrific feeling of twisted magic that had charged through her woods only days ago. Another abomination. It had to be the creature Rosmilda had been working on to attack Miria but never used due to Adaline's return.

"Find a weapon," Miria said to her. "Anything. Quickly."

She didn't know if the abomination had been unleashed upon a specific target, but there were many possible people to choose from if Rosmilda had decided she was not going down without a fight.

Adaline didn't hesitate to pull up her skirts and produce a small dagger.

"Really?" Miria couldn't help but ask in disbelief.

"I wanted to be prepared," Adaline said. "I couldn't very well carry my sword. They took *that* from me."

Possibly she was better prepared for this sort of attack than Miria. The abomination charged into view as Miria searched her purse for any supplies she could use in this fight, but she'd had to limit herself.

Rosmilda's new creature was larger than the first—so much larger that Miria wondered where Rosmilda had been stashing it—and even more hideous, another amalgam of bone and rotting flesh, but this time, it was armored. Rosmilda had not intended for this creature to be brought down so easily. Thick hide was secured around its stinking torso and a metal band around its neck to prevent the most fatal of blows. For a tail, she'd attached a morningstar, and when it roared . . .

"Shit!" Adaline scrambled backward, and Miria went with her. "It's a dragon. Can she do that?"

Magical green fire singed the grass and sent putrid smoke into the air.

"I think she did." Miria's heart beat so hard it felt like it might burst through her chest. If the creature's head was lopped off and its body down, she could destroy the heart, forever ending the magic powering it. But she had nothing to stop it, no means of destroying its physical form. The guardsmen would have to do that.

Adaline glanced down at her dagger and groaned. "I really need a sword."

"You really need to stay away from it," Miria corrected her.

Adaline looked like she wanted to argue, but the beast swung its modified tail and another table went hurling through the air. Guards, who'd been trying to get close, darted out of the way. More crossbow bolts flew. A few hit the leather hide, but they did nothing to slow the creature down.

Miria pulled a knot of twine and nettle from her purse. "Let the guard handle it. Stay safe. If I can stop Rosmilda, that may put an end to it, too. Did you get what I need?"

Adaline snapped her attention away from the abomination. "Oh, yes! I was able to do everything as planned before she enchanted me. I gave your protective charms to your sisters when I met them this morning, so they should be safe, too, unless Rosmilda found those. Here." Adaline reached into her bodice and withdrew a strand of hair in Rosmilda's shade. "I can't promise it's hers, but I removed it from her gown last night at dinner without her noticing."

Quickly, Miria knotted the hair around her existing knot, whispering the words to the spell and hoping she was doing this correctly. Nalki had helped her with the steps yesterday, going as far as allowing Miria to temporarily bind her magic to practice, but Rosmilda would be fighting her, and Nalki had warned her that would make a huge difference. It was why they'd all come—to combine their powers.

But the other witches didn't appear to have made it past Rosmilda's ward yet, and Miria didn't have time to wait. The guests and the guards couldn't afford it.

One knot done, Miria scanned the grounds. She didn't believe Rosmilda would have gone far, and that had been too easy.

An ugly cry rang in Miria's ears, then Rosmilda's voice. "You stupid little witch. You can't bind my magic when I have no power of my own."

Miria didn't deign to answer her, if she even could. Rosmilda had learned much and taught herself more, but she didn't know everything, including that Miria could bind her ability to use stolen power by altering a normal binding spell. Like Yali had once promised her—there was always more to learn.

Miria began the second knot, but she before she could finish, a gust of wind knocked her over. Nearby roses climbed from their pots. They lifted into the air, and hurtled themselves at her in a barrage of thorns. Miria raised her arms to protect her face and skin, and Adaline jumped in front of her, taking the bulk of the assault.

"Keep going!" Adaline yelled. Blood dripped from her hands. "I see her. She's coming this way."

Miria completed the knot, and this time, Rosmilda's scream was not only in her head. Miria took a deep breath, channeling as much power as she could into the spell as she worked on the third.

The ground rumbled beneath her, and the abomination's stench grew worse. Adaline, covered in blood and with roses stuck to her hair and dress, yanked Miria to her feet. "Never mind. She's sending the thing this way. Run!"

Miria glanced over her shoulder as the abomination lumbered toward them, and she did as commanded. Sweat poured down her neck and slicked her fingers on the spell knot. Green fire lit up the grass and the air, almost pretty in its deadliness.

"I can't cast and run at the same time," she said, holding up her skirt as she and Adaline passed the wedding arch.

The abomination had slowed; it was favoring one side as it moved. The guards had done some damage, and they continued to attack.

"Look!" Adaline pointed.

Rosmilda stood along the stone terrace at the back of the manor. She'd woven a wall of thorns from the roses around herself, giving her plenty of room to cast, but enough of a barrier to keep anyone from getting close. It was a simple and elegant wall, but also weak.

Miria grabbed Adaline's arm. "Tell some of the guards to direct their attacks on Rosmilda. Perhaps they'll listen if it comes from you. We need to tire her out."

It went against everything Miria wanted if she was trying to protect the children whose stolen blood Rosmilda used, but she didn't see another way.

Adaline nodded and called out Miria's orders to the nearest guards. They didn't seem to like the idea, and Miria understood.

A magical beast was terrifying, but just a beast. A woman who controlled that beast was terrifying for entirely different reasons.

Still, if men thought they were the only ones who should be allowed swords and armor, they'd best step up to the responsibility. Adaline seemed to be thinking the same, because she grabbed a sword from an injured guard and charged toward Rosmilda herself, and that urged the others into action.

Miria abandoned her knots for the moment, pulled her feather from her purse, and summoned the wind. Two could play that game. With a slice of her arm, she sent a gust howling in Rosmilda's direction, causing her barrier of thorns and roses to go flying.

Rosmilda screamed with anger, but before she could retaliate, she saw the guards. They'd seized the opening Miria had given them and were sprinting forward. Quickly, Rosmilda changed tactics, and a gust hurtled the men backward.

Miria called upon the birds next. These were not the ones who knew her from the woods, but they heard her anyway and responded to her magic. The air filled with wings—brown, black, and gray—and the chattering and cawing of a small army. They swooped down on Rosmilda, but they never made it close. The air shimmered around her, and the birds at the front of the charge diverted at the last moment before crashing into a magical ward.

Miria saw the moment Rosmilda was forced to temporarily divert her focus from the abomination. It lasted only a second, but it was the sign she'd been looking for. Rosmilda was exhausting herself and her stolen magic. Creating a barrier of pure power as she'd just done without the aid of any supplies, even if only for a few seconds, would have been enough to knock Miria down for the rest of the day. Rosmilda didn't have to rely on her own magic so she wasn't as affected, but she wasn't immune to the cost.

If Miria was lucky, that hit to Rosmilda's power would have been long enough to weaken the wards around the manor as well, allowing Miria's reinforcements to sneak through.

"Again!" Miria called on the birds, the guards, whoever would listen.

Rosmilda was looking battered and tired as she tossed up her invisible shield once more, but this time she pushed some of that power at the guards. Several of the men went flying backward, colliding with each other and the stone walls.

Miria cast another knot. Behind her, it sounded as though the guards were finally beating down Rosmilda's creature, and Adaline let out a small cheer.

Confident that she had the upper hand, Miria closed the distance between herself and Rosmilda as the other woman staggered to her feet.

"You would choose their side?" Rosmilda sneered. She flexed her hands, seeming distraught at how little power they commanded. "Theirs over your fellow women?"

"I chose my side," Miria snapped. "Her side." She pointed to Adaline. "The side of the innocent people you've been harming, like my sisters. There's no room on your side for me. Your side benefits you, and you alone. Just as my father's side is for him alone. People like you don't care about anyone else, not even your children except as they are extensions of you and your wishes. I should have known you and Garulf would turn on each other the moment the need arose. You would have done the same to me."

Rosmilda grunted and reached for her magic again. "That was a mistake. Always witches have the same weakness. You were so busy protecting others, you forgot something very important. Since you've cut me off from drawing on others' power, the only person left with power I can take is yours."

"Except you can't take magic from me." Miria stepped closer, pressing her advantage. "Not without blood to draw it to yourself, and in this case, my brother's and father's won't help you."

"You may know more about witch magic than I do, but not about this kind of magic. With untrained children, yes. Blood is necessary. But with someone as powerful as you, someone who's spent years strengthening her magic, even a strand of hair would do." Rosmilda reached into her bodice and pulled out a single strand of dark, curly hair—the strand Miria had used to protect Adaline.

Shit. Rosmilda was right about one thing. Miria didn't know enough about this kind of magic, but she did know there was plenty Rosmilda could do with that hair. She'd been too busy working up to this moment to realize what it meant that Rosmilda had plucked it from Adaline's head.

Miria lunged, but she was too late. Rosmilda's shadow creatures rose from the terrace like an inky mist. They descended from the cracks in the manor's stones. They swirled around Miria in a black wind that darkened her vision and stole her breath.

She heard Adaline cry out, but the sound was so distant. Cold, the dreadful chill of a winter's nightmare enveloped her. Her skin prickled with it, the blood in her veins ran sluggish. Miria clawed at the shadows, but her fingers passed through them like the ethereal creatures they were. Closing her eyes, she focused her mind inward, reaching for her magic, for the pure rush of power that could overcome this spell, but even as she called upon it, it slipped through her fingers. She'd used so much already—too much, probably—and Rosmilda's spell was taking what remained, draining it before she could use it to fight.

Miria collapsed to her knees for the second time that day, bones slamming into stone, pain reverberating through her spine, her head. Exhaustion set in. In her chest, her heart beat heavy and slow. For so long, her magic had been a natural part of her, a sense as deeply ingrained in her any other. She barely remembered what it was like to not have access to it.

Unbidden, her memory of that first day in Yali's cottage passed before her eyes. *You have strong magic in you, and you will make a great witch if you choose to be one.*

Yet she wasn't strong enough. Perhaps she's never been strong enough. There was always someone tougher, bigger, smarter, more powerful to push her around. Sure, she was a witch, but Rosmilda didn't have to be one to win.

Her five-year-old hands slapped Swiftdok's dirty, cobblestone streets. Girlish laughter taunted her. And her brother's voice, still young and brave: *Next time, you get up and you push her back, and you retake what she stole.*

Useless advice from a boy who'd grown up to take what wasn't his, who hadn't cared to side with her, who was too selfish to do what was right.

Anger sparked in Miria's chest. *Against* her chest. The charm she'd made from the emotions Yali had stored for her burned her skin.

All your rage, all your fear—it's full of power . . . One day, it might be useful to you.

Miria wrapped her fingers around the charm. For fifteen years, ever since her nana had first captured her rage, she'd held onto those emotions. They were a reminder of who she was, of where she'd come from. They were as much a part of her as was the blood in her veins.

But she was not defined by her blood, not her ties to her father or her brother, nor the sad house where she'd grown up as hungry for love as for bread. She'd become something other. More. And she'd done it without hurting anyone the way her family and Rosmilda had. She'd made her own family; she'd shed the skin that had been Greta. She'd pushed back on her own fate.

She was a witch, and for the first time, Miria realized the witch did not need Greta's emotions reminding her of what she'd overcome.

She already knew.

Miria tightened her grasp on the charm and crushed it. Her childish fury, her anguish and betrayal, flooded her senses. The wails she'd let loose in the woods that day. The terror of being abandoned and the heartache. The absolute soul-crushing sense of cruelty and injustice set her entire body ablaze, and now she knew how to use it.

Injustice was the antithesis of magic. It was chaos, and magic loathed chaos, longed to mold it into something new and fantastic.

Miria threw her head back and unleashed her childhood power.

Magic burst out of her. Her nerves alighted with it. Her eyes were blinded by it. For a moment, she flew. For a moment, she could have scaled the manor walls, skipped from tree top to tree top. She was the fire, the storm, the Swift River roaring toward the ocean. She was unstoppable.

The shadows flung wide and dissolved into nothing. Miria heard a scream that might have been Rosmilda's, someone calling out her name that might have been Adaline. But her head felt detached from the rest of her. Then, a mere breath later, her body seemed to turn to stone. It became too heavy for her to hold up. All her magic was spent, and she crashed back to earth and collapsed into the ground. Her limbs were too shaky and tired to support her.

Vaguely, she was aware that the yelling around the manor had increased again, but she barely had the strength to raise her head. Rosmilda was running, her plans having completely failed, her stolen power entirely gone. She hiked up her skirt as new voices—the other witches—yelled for someone to stop her.

Miria grabbed the low wall around the terrace for support, so she was looking in the right direction the moment Adaline tackled Rosmilda to the ground. Rosmilda let out a muffled cry, but Adaline yanked her arms behind her and held Rosmilda in place in a very unladylike fashion.

"Next time," Adaline said, "Remember that truly strong women would never tie their power to a man's whims."

Miria smiled, thought: *I really love you*. Then her legs trembled, and she plopped back to the stones.

The next several minutes passed in a blur, a haze of pain and exhaustion that Miria questioned whether she would ever recover from. There was negotiating and more yelling (so much yelling, Miria longed for the quiet of her woods). In the confusion, Hani destroyed the abomination's heart, while Dinia and Nalki took custody of Rosmilda from allegedly powerful men who were only too grateful to have her become someone else's problem. They seemed much more inclined to deal with Garulf, who continued to protest his innocence in a way that no one sounded like they believed.

That was promising, but Miria needed to know what was going to happen to him, if he was to be held accountable for his part in everything, and what would become of her sisters. Winda and Katline needed someone to watch over them.

Through her haze, Miria attempted to relay all of this, but the wedding guests had fled and the guards wouldn't come close to her. Otto might have, but Miria didn't see him anywhere.

Adaline, too, had vanished in the time it had taken her to blink. Or perhaps she'd passed out for a moment; Miria wasn't entirely sure.

She leaned against the terrace wall, struggling to keep her eyes open, and her gaze landed on speck of sparkling red by her feet. Her fingers fumbled to pick up the piece of her spent charm. Somehow this shard had survived. Maybe she'd dropped it as she'd grown tired, or maybe the magic had burned through her too quickly, exhausting her before she could use it all up. The crystallized power glistened like blood on her palm, and Miria tucked it into her purse. Why, she wasn't sure. But instinct told her it wasn't wise to leave something so valuable and powerful for anyone to find.

Gentle hands helped her to stand. "I've got you," Sarel said. "We'll get a cart to take you home."

"My sisters . . ."

"I'm sure they'll be fine."

They won't be, Miria thought. *Someone needs to find them.*

It was so hard to form words, though.

"Adaline . . ." she started. Where was Adaline? Adaline could find her sisters, bring them to her. Then Miria could see them all, make sure they were all well.

But Sarel didn't seem to hear her, and Miria found her half-asleep self loaded into a cart. She would have thought the rocking motion would keep her awake, but she was fast asleep long before the witches reached the woods.

Chapter Thirty-One

Two Days After the Wedding

She slept for a day, so Sarel told her when Miria stumbled out of her bed. The cottage was strangely quiet. Miria had expected the other witches to be bustling about, deciding Rosmilda's fate, but it appeared to only be her and Sarel left. Of course, the others had their own territories to tend to, but where did that leave things?

"Sit," Sarel said. She was scooping something hot into a bowl. "I made you porridge. Not the most exciting meal, I know, but a good one when you're recovering."

Miria shuffled toward the table, trying to act like she didn't feel like she could sleep for another day, but Sarel wasn't buying it.

"Do not be surprised if it takes a couple of days to be back to yourself." Sarel slid the jar of honey and a bowl of freshly picked raspberries Miria's way.

Miria dumped enough berries into her porridge to drown out any other flavor. They remained her favorite food, even after all these years. "I don't have time for that. There's too much to do. Where's Rosmilda? My father?"

"We decided Rosmilda's fate yesterday while you slept."

"You should have woken me." She was annoyed by this but too worn out to say the words.

Sarel sipped her tea before responding. "You discovered her crimes, and you brought her down. You more than did your part. The rest should not have to weigh on you."

"And what is the rest?"

"There's a forest, about a week's journey by non-magical travel south of here. It was stricken with blight. The witch who tends it stopped the spread, but the forest was weakened. We've tasked Rosmilda with reviving the land. The witch will supervise her, and since Rosmilda knows how to use magic, she'll be provided with enough to heal the forest. She cannot leave it, though. She's been bound to the trees, her own vitality tied to theirs. Should she neglect her duty, she will die with the woods. On the other hand, should the spell we placed on her ever sense she has learned to feel true remorse for her actions and wishes to atone in another manner of her choosing, then the binding will be undone to allow it."

Miria scowled and swirled her spoon around the porridge bowl. The punishment fit, but it felt too good for Rosmilda when people had died. Still, Miria knew the witches would not kill her. They would want her to have the chance to make amends. If not for her own sake, then because she owed the world a debt for what she'd done.

"Do you actually believe she'll do good? She deserves far worse."

Sarel smiled. "If you're worried she won't suffer, don't. I have no doubt that she'll be miserable for a long time."

"And my father, my sisters?"

Adaline? Miria couldn't form her name without a lump rising in her throat.

"We made certain your father and brother could not help but speak the truth about their involvement in all that occurred." Sarel stood and began gathering the supplies she'd brought with her so many days ago into her traveling pack. "Since he isn't a witch, we've left your father's fate in the hands of those he wronged. Your brother, I'm sure you'll be relieved to hear, had no part in their schemes. The truth spell confirmed it."

He hadn't? That information didn't surprise Miria, but nor did it particularly relieve her. Thinking about Hans and her feelings toward him made her tired, and she was already exhausted. At least, if he hadn't been implicated, then he could watch over Winda and Katline. That was something, for now anyway.

"You're leaving?" Miria asked.

Sarel nodded. "I've been gone too long, but I wanted to be here when you woke up and not just leave you a letter explaining everything. You'll be all right?"

It wasn't really a question, but a statement of faith in her. A witch could take care of herself most of the time, and she knew when to call on others if she couldn't. Miria's time of need had ended.

Funny, then, that she still felt needy.

"I have Tuli to help." Miria hugged Sarel goodbye. "We'll be fine. Thank you for your assistance."

She walked Sarel the short distance to the door, but she was too weak to go any farther without pausing, and Sarel didn't expect it. They exchanged a few more words, and then that was that. Miria was alone.

Well, not totally. Tuli was in the garden, weeding, from the looks of it, and he waved when he saw Miria in the doorway.

Miria waved back and walked slowly outside. The forest was quiet, but only compared to the recent commotion she'd experienced. The leaves rustled in the wind, birds sang, squirrels and other small mammals scuttled through the trees and underbrush. It was peaceful. Delightful.

And quiet. It was what she'd wanted. Right?

Miria sat in a sunny spot on the ground, hugged her knees to her chest, and tried to enjoy it. But mostly, she thought about Adaline and wondered where she was and wished she didn't feel so alone.

* * *

Miria felt more like herself the next morning. Not well enough to do anything so strenuous as scry for Adaline, but well enough to make her own breakfast, feed the chickens, and use magic to rewarm her tea when it got too cold. She longed to venture into town to learn more about the aftermath of Adaline's disastrous wedding (and to discover the rumors that must be circulating about the would-have-been bride and groom and the Overseer), but that was asking too much yet.

A bath, on the other hand—she might be up for that, as long as Tuli accompanied her to the river to be safe. A bath felt sufficiently ambitious. If that didn't tire her out too much, she would see about making a plan for restocking her spell supplies. Yesterday, she'd taken note of what she was running low on, but her energy had run out before she could do anything about it.

So yes, she had a plan. She would not dwell on those things or people she could not control. She would be patient.

Miria was about to call for Tuli when the forest warned her of an approaching visitor. The person was neither a threat nor a stranger, but the woods weren't forthcoming with more information. It was enough to give Miria hope, though, especially when the path formed without her needing to call it.

Hooves clomped along the dirt, and the trees parted, revealing a white horse and hooded rider. Miria's heart beat with unexpected trepidation.

Adaline slid off of Pearl and barely tied her to a tree before rushing over and throwing her arms around Miria. "I'm so sorry. I wanted to come sooner, but so many things happened, and I couldn't get away. It's been madness. Are you all right? I saw the witches taking you away, and I feared you were dead, but they told me you'd be fine, but I hadn't received a letter from you or seen you in days, and . . ." She finally trailed off, burying her face in Miria's neck.

Miria appreciated Adaline's ability to keep speaking because it allowed her time to hold Adaline and emotionally regroup.

"I'm all right, I'm fine. I simply slept for a day." Miria laughed and realized tears were running down her cheeks, and she pulled away, wiping them off. "It's been happening a lot lately."

Adaline's eyes were watery, too, and she cupped Miria's wet cheeks. "You've been doing too much. You were incredible at my uncle's. I have no idea what you did, but it was amazing. You glowed for a moment, like a star. Like a goddess."

"Like a star exploding, perhaps," Miria said, smiling shakily. She'd read about such things in one of Yali's books about the sky. "I'm fine now but recovering. I suppose I should have sent a letter yesterday or this morning, but you'll have to forgive me. I'm still not thinking clearly."

"I don't need to forgive you for anything." Adaline threw her arms around Miria once more and squeezed so tightly that Miria couldn't breathe for a moment. "You'll have to forgive me, though."

The nervousness that had gripped Miria when Adaline first appeared returned. Was Adaline here only to say goodbye? After everything, Miria would not be surprised if her family had begun packing their carriages immediately.

"Forgive you for what?" Miria asked, not wanting to give voice to her worry.

Adaline knit her hands together nervously. "For intruding on you with no warning and begging you to allow me to stay?"

"Is that all?" The words burst from Miria in relief, with a laugh.

"I know, I am sorry. But my parents are distraught, and they're furious with me, as though I'm the one who was duped all this time by Rosmilda's magic when they were the ones who'd gone and gotten themselves enchanted! But I suppose it's only expected when everyone is so angry about all that happened, yet only certain people are allowed to be blamed."

"Only certain people?" Miria's laughter was brief. Tension once more surged through her veins. "I know what became of Rosmilda, but what of my father?"

Adaline wobbled on her feet, and Miria patted the cottage stoop for them both to sit. After doing so, Adaline pressed the wrinkles in her skirt with her hands before speaking. "After I explained to my father and uncle what I knew *multiple times,* I was banished from the discussions. Silly little me was not permitted to be part of the men's business, despite my significant role in it."

"So you don't know?" Miria couldn't tell if Adaline was stalling because she was frustrated that she had nothing to share or simply that she had nothing *good* to share.

"Oh, I know. Of course, I was not about to stand for that." Adaline gave her a good-natured admonishing look. "I just wish I had better news. Whatever spell your witch friends put on your father made him confess, but the spell wore off soon enough and well . . . He convinced my father and uncle that any role he had in everything was solely due to Rosmilda's influence. He claims he was corrupted by her, and he's thrown himself at the church for mercy and forgiveness."

Miria rolled her eyes, recalling how close Rosmilda had once been to Swiftdok's priest. "And the church will vouch for him because Rosmilda *corrupted* the priest as well, I assume? They will say that this is why giving women power is dangerous."

"I'm sorry to say it, but yes." Adaline sighed. "My family and the priest are eager to forgive him and absolve themselves of poor judgement. Due to his alleged weakness of mind, my uncle has stripped your father of the position of Overseer, but Miri, I strongly doubt he will face any worse punishments."

Miria doubted it too, but it would be a problem for a later day. "What of my sisters?"

Adaline smiled at this change in topic. "Your brother took them, the last I know. The witches' spell absolved him of any complicity. I don't know what he means to do next, but I do believe he cares about them, and they will be safe."

Miria wondered about that, but she would allow herself hope. At least until she was feeling strong enough to scry on them. "Then that accounts for everyone. Except you." She frowned, recalling Adaline's words of a moment ago. "Why are your parents furious with *you*? For defending me?"

"No, not truly anyway." Adaline took her hands, sensing Miria's confusion. "They're not even really angry with me, either; it's just that I'm a problem now. With so many guests at the wedding to witness what happened—Lord and Lady Eberhan, and Baron Filbert, and others—my parents fear that they'll never be able to marry me off due to the scandal. And while I'm pleased about this, they're talking of sending me to a convent and saying serving the church is the only thing left for me, and I refuse to wear those horrible dresses and spend my days serving men without even getting anything nice out of the deal for it, and so I packed some things and ran here and—"

Miria kissed her. She didn't really have the strength to kiss her with as much force as she did, but happiness and relief pushed her through the exhaustion, and then Adaline kissed her back and Miria could just follow her lead. She swayed slightly when they broke apart, and she gripped Adaline to say upright.

"Are you going to be all right?" Adaline asked.

"I'm never going to let you go again." Miria breathed deeply, and the scent of honeysuckle made her whole body tingle. "You are perfect, and I missed you, and I refuse to let you go to a convent, too."

Adaline smiled tentatively. "So I can stay here for a bit?"

"Did you not hear me? You can't leave. Well, unless you really want to. Then I suppose I'd let you, but please don't."

Adaline squealed and embraced Miria again, and Miria didn't bother trying to hold herself upright this time. Adaline was her rock, and Miria was not ashamed to want her support as much as Adaline needed hers. "I won't leave. I promise."

"You'll be miserable here," Miria warned her when she could breathe again. "No servants. No fancy dresses. No feasts or balls."

Adaline made a dismissive noise and held up a finger as she spoke. "I'm learning to cook and garden myself, and Tuli helps with chores." A second finger. "I can wear whatever I please, and Tuli is a wonderful sparring partner, and you promised to make me a magical cloak like yours this winter, which is more exciting than any normal dress." A third finger. "Balls are full of deadly social sparring and the need to dance with leering men. I have no use for them when I can sing to keep you entertained instead, and we can dance together anytime we want." She lowered her fingers and grasped Miria's hands. "But most importantly, I have you, and you'll have me as my wild, unladylike self. There's nothing else I could want." She paused. "I mean, except one thing."

"Which is?" Miria was already making a mental list of all the things she would need if Adaline (and Pearl) were to move in for good.

Adaline grinned. "To kiss you again and to never stop."

Chapter Thirty-Two

Ten Days After the Wedding

Adaline had not run to Miria empty-handed. She'd packed her saddlebags full of coins, jewelry, and whatever other small comforts from home she hadn't wanted to give up—some easy-to-carry clothes, a fine hairbrush, perfume, a beautiful mirror, two books filled with her favorite stories and another of poetry. And, of course, her sword. All the money wasn't necessary, but it couldn't hurt either, and Miria figured she'd find a way to use it, especially if it made Adaline feel like less of an imposition.

After a bath in the river (made more enjoyable by Adaline's company), Miria spent the remains of the day settling Adaline in and relaxing. Tuli was pleased to see her again, too, acting as jovial as a golem ever acted. He freaked out Pearl a bit, and that would take some adjustment, but they would make it work. Somehow.

She'd gone to sleep with her head full of plans.

Over fall and winter, she would expand the cottage again. When it had been only her and Yali, the cottage had never felt cramped, even before Yali had built Miria her own room. Whether two rooms or three, it had been cozy but comfortable. But although Adaline would never say so, Miria knew she was used to bigger, grander rooms, and certainly two women of their age could use more space than a nana and a little girl had required—particularly when one needed space for spell work and the other for sword practice. One day, Miria might even have her own apprentice, and she should be prepared. Besides, Tuli did not really fit in the cottage, and Miria wanted to change that.

Her first priority, however, would be to build a barn for Pearl. The horse needed somewhere warm for when winter came, and she and Adaline would need a place to store Pearl's feed. Once Pearl got used to Tuli, maybe they could build an extra tall room so Tuli could have a spot of his own there to do whatever he did when he was resting. (Another item on Miria's winter to-do list was learn more about her golem so she could care for him better.)

All of this was going to require a lot of effort on her part, but Miria was feeling optimistic. Every witch built or altered her own home, and it was time she stepped up and made the cottage hers.

Just like it was time to step up and make this territory hers, as well. Yali had been the best nana and teacher Miria could have wished for, but as the predicament with Rosmilda had shown, there were actions Miria could take to improve life in this part of Waere and Gawfrid Province. She finally felt ready to own that.

To that end, a week after Adaline had come to live with her, Miria set out for town. She'd had plenty of time to rest, and though Adaline continued to fuss over her, Miria knew she was well and truly recovered by the sense of restlessness that overtook her mind whenever she thought of her plans. She wanted to begin acting on the ones she could quickly. The chaos of the wedding was spreading new fear of the witch through the town, and fear was a stubborn weed. Eliminating it entirely was impossible (and, perhaps, not the best option anyway), but recent events fed it, sending the roots deeper, making it harder to rip them out. Miria couldn't let that happen.

Thanks to Sarel, she knew the names of the children whose blood Rosmilda had been using to draw her power, and through her own efforts, she'd learned where to find them. In time, the children should recover on their own, but Miria intended to both ensure that they did and speed along the process.

With Adaline at her side, Miria went from home to home, leaving gifts of healing magic for each child. They were simple charms of comfrey and sage and blackberry leaf wrapped in scraps of knotted linen and threaded through on string that could be tied around a neck or hung over a bed. After the recent magical spectacle (the tales of which had surely been embellished for those who weren't present to witness it), Miria considered the charms' plainness an advantage. It made them less frightening.

Still, not all the families were pleased to receive a gift from the witch. A couple slammed their doors in Miria's face. One family refused to open theirs at all. But most people were grateful, even if they were also suspicious. They took the charms with trembling hands, whispers of thanks, and plenty of assurance that these were gifts not meant to be repaid. Only a few asked questions.

"I'd heard Anida was feeling unwell," Miria said to those who would listen. Or sometimes it was Effi or Holger or Uwin. "Because I do not like children to suffer when I can help," was all she responded when asked why she'd come.

When Miria delivered the last charm, she felt lighter, though the charms themselves had weighed next to nothing.

"That went well?" Adaline sounded unsure as she looped an arm through Miria's own.

"I think so." Mostly, she feared it could have gone worse. It would take time to see how well it had been. But it was a first step on a long journey.

The sun was high as they headed toward the main road, and traffic in town was heavy as people would soon begin heading to lunch or the chapel, if they were so inclined. Miria was dressed in her best—and only—town clothes, but she'd done nothing to disguise her appearance otherwise. For once, she wanted people to see her face, though she could not shake how exposed that left her feeling. She was glad Adaline, with her noble features and all her social graces, had come along.

Scents of fresh bread and steaming fish emanated from the taverns and lunch carts, and Miria considered buying herself and Adaline a meal from one of the vendors rather than make them both wait until they returned to the cottage. Adaline was always hungry, so if Miria was feeling so too . . .

"Miri." Adaline squeezed her arm, pulling Miria from her thoughts of hand pies and doughy treats.

She turned in the direction where Adaline was looking and froze. Her brother was stopped on the other side of the road, Winda's and Katline's hands in each of his own.

Hans stared at her. Miria stared back.

Adaline waved at Miria's sisters, and they shyly returned the gesture, and that seemed to be the deciding factor. Hans led them across the cobblestone street.

Again, Miria was grateful for Adaline's company, as Adaline lowered herself to be closer to the girls' heights.

"Do you remember me?" she asked.

The taller of the two managed a nod and released Hans's hand long enough to curtsey. Seeing her sister's behavior, the younger girl followed suit.

"My lady," they both whispered.

"Oh, there's none of that anymore." Adaline grinned.

"You will always be deserving of the title, Lady Adaline," Hans said. He turned his head to Miria, "And you . . ."

Miria raised an eyebrow, unwilling to help him finish his thought. "Brother, I would like to be introduced to my sisters."

"Of course." Hans took a tentative step forward. The girls had already shown more bravery after being acknowledged by Adaline. "This is Winda and Katline. Girls, this is your sister. . . ."

He hesitated, and Miria filled in the gap, kneeling alongside Adaline. "I'm Miria. I'm so glad to finally meet you."

"Are you the witch?" Katline asked in a whisper.

"I am."

"You don't seem scary."

Miria smiled and glanced up at her brother. "A witch is only scary to those who have done horrible things and deserve to be scared."

Hans swallowed, but Katline nodded like this made perfect sense. "You don't have horns, either."

"No, witches don't have horns, but I do have quite pointy ears that stick up when I become an owl."

Katline gasped. "You can be an owl? I want to fly!"

"Kat!" Winda shook her head, then she turned back to Miria, and her lip trembled. "People are saying our mother is a witch, too."

"Your mother is very much *not* a witch."

"Do you know where she went?" Katline asked. "Hans said you might."

Miria could have smacked her brother for that, but she supposed it had seemed like a logical thing to tell the girls. "She went very far from here, because she did some very bad things. But . . ." Faced with the conflicted expressions the girls wore, Miria added, "But she was trying to be good to you. I hope you see her again one day."

That much, Miria believed was true. She was left without words after that, though, not knowing what her sisters knew or how they'd gotten along with their mother. Had they loved her? Feared her? Had they known she was hurting them? Miria had so many questions she needed answered before she could proceed.

Adaline came to her rescue, holding out her hands to Katline and Winda. "I'm famished, and the bread over there smells wonderful. Would you like some, too?" She led the girls down the street toward a vendor selling cheese-stuffed pastries, leaving Miria and Hans. Hans stared at his boots until Miria shifted.

"I have a lot of questions, but this is not an ideal spot for this conversation," she said. No one was paying them much attention, but town always felt crowded to her, regardless. For her comfort, never mind her safety, she'd rather confront Hans in the woods. Town was not her domain.

"I'm sorry."

Hans's words stopped her before she could suggest going elsewhere, and Miria held her breath, waiting. For what, she wasn't sure.

"I was a coward. I meant to protect us both, I swear. But when the time came to run, I . . . I panicked. I told myself you were right behind me, on my heels."

"You were a coward," Miria said, not feeling particularly moved. "And when you discovered I wasn't behind you? When you returned home to our father, alone? When you lied about what happened?"

Her brother stared at the dirt-dusted stones. "I was too shocked, too scared to do anything right away. You weren't the only one Father used to hurt, and I know that doesn't excuse anything, but I didn't know what to do. And Father seemed so—I don't know—pleased when I told him I escaped. It was like he was genuinely proud of me for the first time, so I kept embellishing the tale to make him happy. I thought, now that he was happy with me, I would find the courage to come back for you later, and he would be happy about that, too, but . . ." In the heavy pause, Miria realized Hans was fighting back tears. "I couldn't. I was terrified, and the guilt only made it worse. I was afraid if I went back for you, I'd learn I was too late."

"So you ensured that would be the case by doing nothing?" Miria crossed her arms.

Hans took a deep breath. "I wanted hope. As long as I didn't discover you were dead, I could hope you were alive. And when I realized how stupid that was—as you said—I just tried to put you out of my mind. To forget."

More than that—he'd tried to justify what he'd done. She couldn't forget the words he'd used at midsummer two years ago, and Miria shook her head, trying to decipher her feelings. She'd used up her anger, and the betrayal had faded. Mostly, surprisingly, she just felt sad.

It was true that their father had not always been good to Hans. He'd been treated better than she had, but Hans had endured his share of punishments, usually ones more violent than Miria had suffered. He had seemed so strong and brave to her at the time, but in retrospect, how much had been an act for her sake and his own?

The truth was, knowing that he'd played no part in Rosmilda and Garulf's schemes, she wanted to forgive him, and she told him so. "But not yet," Miria added. "I don't want to forgive you because it's easier than carrying around all this hurt. I need to believe you've become a better person, especially if Winda and Katline are your responsibility now. I need to know you won't repeat Garulf's mistakes, and that you will undo the damage you've done with your lies about the witch."

Hans was silent for a moment, his shoulders heaving. "That seems fair."

Miria thought it was more than fair, but she cut him a break for apologizing.

"When you're ready," Miria said. "bring the girls to the cottage. I think they'll like it."

She wasn't sure she wanted Hans there—yet. But if he came, if he was willing to confront his past, it would be another step toward earning her forgiveness. And if he did not, well, now that they'd been introduced, she could seek out her sisters on her own. She would not let Hans nor her father be the only one filling their heads with the stories of their mother and the witch. The girls deserved to write their own versions, and Miria would see to it that they knew they were loved in hers.

Chapter Thirty-Three

Three Weeks After the Wedding

One week after Miria ran into her brother by accident, she found her father in the chapel—on purpose. She'd watched him for several days first, observing the public bouts of piety that Adaline had told her about—this ruse of his to make someone else shoulder the responsibility for his actions, and the institution all too ready to allow it.

He came for the mid-day service, the most crowded one, the best one to attend if someone wanted to be observed attending, which he clearly did.

The priest always met him at the chapel door. They would converse about pleasantries, exchange a few token words to acknowledge what happened, and they always ended the conversation by carefully placing the full blame for the events on Rosmilda. After all, if the priest could have been duped, so could have Garulf. The priest wanted to believe he was not alone in his gullibility, and Garulf needed him to believe it so Adaline's family would not punish him further. It was a nice arrangement for them both.

Then the priest would conduct the service, and Garulf would stay a bit after everyone else had left, probably pretending to pray and making sure everyone noticed his penance.

The charade would repeat the next day.

But not today.

By this time, the crowd had left, including the priest, and no one else was in the chapel. Her observations had told Miria that her father would leave soon, as well—it was a small window she had if she preferred not to be seen.

Miria stepped inside, fighting the chill of the stone walls that always seemed to radiate cold, even at the height of summer. The rooms were filled with dozens of flickering candles that had been lit during the service to send a prayer. It was beautiful to behold, but all that light was not enough to convince Miria that the building was warm or inviting. Or maybe it was just the witch in her that disliked being confined in such a place.

Either way, she hurried her steps to the front of the chapel. The soles of her boots made no sound on the stones beneath them nor the hem of her skirts swaying about her ankles, and she kneeled next to Garulf as silent as a ghost. But he'd noticed her. She saw by the way he stiffened.

This close, he looked even older than Miria had thought before. It might have been the shadows or the events of the past few weeks. She rather hoped it was that.

"You." He narrowed his eyes. "You're still an unruly beast of a girl, aren't you? You didn't change at all."

"Neither did you, I see."

"If you want an apology, you won't get one. I had to protect us."

"By which you mean yourself and Hans. Not a little girl. Never little girls."

Garulf turned away. "You were the expendable one, and if you had a lick of sense in your head you would agree that I made a sensible decision. Every farmer knows that you have to cull the herd sometimes to protect its most valuable members. If your mother or grandmother had lived, you could have been their problem, and maybe the extra income could have kept you."

Miria didn't deign to respond to that.

Mistaking her silence for interest in what he had to say, her father continued. "If anything, you owe me an apology. You owe your brother. You took from him, too."

"By your logic, I should apologize for being born." Miria shook her head. "No, I'm not here to apologize, nor did I come to hear one from you."

"Then what do you want?"

Miria reached into her purse and pulled out a small red shard, barely larger than a speck of dust. In the chapel's dim light, it appeared nearly black except for when it caught the touch of one of the candle flames and burst into life. She cupped it in her palm.

"A wise woman once told me that to be a witch was to always be learning and to value education, for it's only through educating ourselves that we can become better people. So I'm here to teach you something, or try to." Then Miria placed her hand over his and drove the last remaining piece of her rage, the only piece that had been big enough to touch after she'd burned through the charm, into his hand.

She could have let it go, she supposed. She'd considered it, truly. She'd crushed her father's and Rosmilda's social climbing plans, denied him the title and power he'd worked so hard for at her expense. A better person might have accepted that and vowed to finally put his cruelty out of their head.

Miria wasn't sure if her inability to do so made her vicious or simply petty, but she did know she was tired of women bearing the brunt of the blame and punishment for actions that men never suffered for.

She would see that her father suffered. But like the witches had offered Rosmilda, she would give him the chance to atone.

Garulf cried out, but the pain could only have lasted a second. The charm slipped into his skin, and the wound healed over before he could climb to his feet.

"What did you do to me?" Anger colored his voice, but his face showed fear.

"I'm giving you the opportunity to learn empathy," Miria said, also standing. "From this moment on, anytime you see your family, you will have to feel the anguish you caused your first daughter. I hope that if you experience it enough, one day you'll become more kind, more pleasant, more deserving of those two sisters of mine. Or, you could choose to cut them out of your life so that you don't have to experience my pain at all. That's what I expect you'll do, but I am occasionally wrong."

She walked out of the chapel to the sound of him cursing her, and for once the noise didn't bother her at all.

Epilogue

Eight Months After the Wedding

The young witch leaned against the rowan tree at the edge of the cemetery. A sprinkling of snowflakes swirled in the crisp wind and settled against a ground that had already seen a few snows in the past couple of months. A layer of sparkling white covered the chapel and headstones like frosting on a wedding cake and brightened an otherwise overcast day.

The witch held out a gloved hand to catch a flake and watched it melt against the fur-lined leather. These were small ones, but their size was deceiving. Together, they would be formidable. By nightfall, the roads that had been cleared after the last storm would be covered again, and by morning, the path through her woods would be impassable and the trees dazzling in their winter glory.

"Will you make something with the snow again?" Adaline asked next to her. She rubbed the cloak Miria had made from the first snowfall between her fingers. It glittered a blinding white to Miria's eyes, and Adaline's as well, but it rendered her mostly invisible to others.

Miria wore one, too. Though cool to the touch, for the wearer, the cloaks were warmer than any fur coats and as soft as the finest leather.

"What will you make me if I do?" she asked.

Adaline pretended to think. "Very happy?" She laughed as Miria lightly poked her shoulder. "Another butter pie? With the caramel and the nuts and raisins?"

"I'll think about it," Miria said, although she could already taste the buttery crust and warm sugar.

The chapel door opened, and the hushed air suddenly filled with cheering as the bride and groom were ushered outside amid a swell of well-wishers. Hans looked happy, and his bride—the oldest daughter of a moderately successful shipwright—was radiant in a crown of tiny roses that bloomed in shades from the most luscious magenta to the palest shell pink.

No one had seen flowers quite like them before, and certainly not roses so far out of season, which was the point. They'd come from Miria's garden. Earlier in the day, Miria had left the headpiece as one of her wedding gifts, and everyone said that was a good omen. After Hans's last disastrous wedding, this time he had the witch's blessing.

The witch did small things like that every now and then—brought food to a family who was struggling, showed up with cures for illnesses without anyone asking, left surprises outside the doors of people who had shown some courageous act of kindness. Miria did not wish to meddle in the lives of those around her, but she could no longer accept inaction. She would not let another Rosmilda and Garulf rise to power, and though she could not stop the stories people told or the reasons why they told them, she was doing her best to push the direction the verses about her took.

In this case, no one knew why the witch had favored the marriage, but they all agreed it was a fortuitous sign.

Truthfully, the witch was just glad Adaline was not the bride, although she did hope the marriage would make everyone happy, including her sisters. Winda and Katline had been living with Hans these last several months, and they'd appeared to have made a full recovery from the effects of Rosmilda's magic. It had taken nearly a moon cycle, but Hans had eventually brought the girls to the woods several times, as well, and Miria and Adaline had visited them several times in return. Although winter made it harder to travel, the girls were no longer afraid of their strange sister. As for Adaline, Winda seemed to find her far odder than she did Miria, but Katline loved her sword lessons.

As if sensing Miria and Adaline's presence, the two girls turned their heads toward the rowan tree and smiled. Adaline waved, and Winda and Katline skipped on with the procession back into town.

"Could they see us?" Adaline asked.

"Possibly." With the magic in their blood, Miria couldn't rule it out.

When she'd told Hans of their gift, he'd made her promise that she would not raise either of them to be a witch, a promise Miria had no intention of breaking. Without Rosmilda's magic to hurt them, the girls lived happy lives and had a future full of possibilities. A witch rose to her power through bruises and blood and betrayal, not in the comfort of a soft bed each night and the arms of a loving family. While Miria was grateful for the family she'd been welcomed into and the legacy she'd been entrusted with, she was glad fate had offered her sisters another path.

"Are you sure you don't want to attend the reception?" Adaline asked.

Miria grabbed Adaline's hand, returning from her thoughts. "It's best if we don't. If we're seen as ourselves, it will distract from the celebration, and if I disguise us, people will want to know who the strangers in attendance are—also a distraction. Unless you're truly in need of eating my brother's food and dancing?"

There was also the possibility that Garulf might attend, but Miria did not speak of him since that day in the chapel, and Adaline had quietly picked up on this and never asked of him again.

Adaline pulled her closer, and they followed the revelers into town, keeping their distance. "How many times do I have to tell you? As long as I have you, I have all that I need."

"I don't know." Miria smiled "But I'm sure a few more times never hurt."

"Well, you did save me twice—three times? I've lost count, so I guess I can say it a few more."

"And how many times, and in how many ways, have you saved me? I think we're even, or at least we should stop counting."

"Not counting is fine with me. I've never liked numbers." Adaline swung their arms and turned her face into the snow. "From now on, we will simply continue to save each other, because that's what we do."

Snowflakes landed on Adaline's pink cheeks, making her skin glow, and Miria's heart beat with happiness. Despite the weather, she'd never been warmer, and despite it being the dead months, she'd never felt more alive. Adaline was right—that was what they did. Girls and women, witches and ladies. They built one small dam in the river at a time until they pushed the course of history in a better direction.

Now that she knew what they could accomplish together, Miria's story was just getting started.